"BITTER AND HILARIOUS . . .

"Domineering, authoritarian, selfish, arbitrary, even cruel, relegating all that is gentle or sensitive to the domain of women, [he] is a Marine pilot who runs his household with all the kindness and understanding of a drill instructor shaping up a bunch of raw recruits. . . . A fine, funny, brawling book."

The National Observer

"An impressive novel." San Francisco Examiner

"A tender, raucous and often hilarious story." Booklist

"Conroy has captured a different slice of America in this funny, dramatic novel." Richmond News-Leader

PAT CONROY

THE GREAT SANTINI

 AVON
PUBLISHERS OF BARD, CAMELOT AND DISCUS BOOKS

AVON BOOKS
A division of
The Hearst Corporation
959 Eighth Avenue
New York, New York 10019

First Avon Printing, June, 1977

AVON TRADEMARK REG. U.S. PAT. OFF. AND IN
OTHER COUNTRIES, MARCA REGISTRADA,
HECHO EN U.S.A.

Printed in the U.S.A.

This book is dedicated with love
and thanks to

Frances "Peggy" Conroy,
the grandest of mothers and teachers,

and to

Colonel Donald Conroy, U.S.M.C. Ret.,
the grandest of fathers and Marine aviators

1

IN THE CORDOVA HOTEL, near the docks of Barcelona, fourteen Marine Corps fighter pilots from the aircraft carrier *Forrestal* were throwing an obstreperously spirited going away party for Lieutenant Colonel Bull Meecham, the executive officer of their carrier based squadron. The pilots had been drinking most of the day and the party was taking a swift descent toward mayhem. It was a sign to Bull Meecham that he was about to have a fine and memorable turbulent time. The commanding officer of the squadron, Ty Mullinax, had passed out in the early part of the afternoon and was resting in a beatific position on the table in the center of the room, his hands folded across his chest and a bouquet of lilies carefully placed in his zipper, rising out of his groin.

The noise from the party had risen in geometrically spiraling quantities in irregular intervals since the affair had begun shortly after noon. In the beginning it had been a sensible, often moving affair, a coming together of soldiers and gentlemen to toast and praise a warrior departing their ranks. But slowly, the alcohol established its primacy over the last half of the party and as darkness approached and the outline of warships along the harbor became accented with light, the maitre d' of the Cordova Hotel walked into the room to put an end to the going away party that had begun to have the sound effects of a small war. He would like to have the Marines thrown out by calling the Guardia Civil but too much of his business depended on the American officers who had made his hotel and restaurant their headquarters whenever the fleet came to Barcelona. The guests in his restaurant had begun to complain vigorously about the noise and obscenity coming from the room that was directly off the restaurant. Even the music of a flamenco band did not overpower or even cancel out the clamor and tumult that spilled out of the room. The maitre d' was waiting for Captain Weber, a naval captain who commanded a cruiser attached to the fleet, to bring his lady in for dinner, but his reservation was not until 9 o'clock. He took a deep breath, opened the door, and walked toward the man who looked as if he was in charge.

"Hey, Pedro, what can I do for you?" Bull Meecham asked.

The maitre d' was a small, elegant man who looked up toward a massive, red-faced man who stood six feet four inches tall and weighed over two hundred and twenty pounds.

Before the maitre d' could speak he noticed the prone body of Colonel Mullinax lying on the long dining table in the center of the room.

"What is wrong with this man?" the maitre d' demanded.

"He's dead, Pedro," Bull answered.

"You joke with me, no."

"No, Pedro."

"He still breathe."

"Muscle spasms. Involuntary," Bull said as the other pilots whooped and laughed behind him. "He's dead all right and we got to leave him here, Pedro. The fleet's pulling out any time now and we won't have time for a funeral. But we'll be back to pick him up in about six months. And that's a promise. I just don't want you to move him from this table."

"No, señor," the maitre d' said, staring with rising discomfort at the unconscious aviator, "you joke with me. I no mind the joke. I come to ask you to keep down the noise and please not break up any more furniture or throw your glasses. Some naval officers have complained very much."

"Oh, dearie me," said Bull. "You mean the naval officers don't like to hear us throwing glasses?"

"No, señor."

2

Bull turned toward the far wall and, giving a signal to the other pilots in the room, all thirteen of them hurled their glasses into the fireplace already littered with bright shards of glass.

"It will be charged to your bill, señor," the maitre d' said.

"Beat it, Pedro," Bull said. "When I want a tortilla I'll give you a call."

"But, señor, I have other guests. Many of the officers in the Navy and their ladies. They ask me what the noise is. What am I to do?"

"I'll handle them, Pedro," Bull said. "You run along now and chew on a couple of tacos while the boys and I finish up here. We should be done partying about a week from now."

"No, señor. Please, señor. My other guests."

When the maitre d' closed the door behind him, Bull walked over and made himself another drink. The other pilots crowded around him and did likewise.

With a strong Texas accent, Major Sammy Funderburk said, "I did a little recon job early this here morning here. And I saw me some strange and willing nookie walking around the lobby of this here hotel here."

"You know me better than that," Bull said. "I'm saving my body for my wife."

"Since when, Colonel?" one of the young lieutenants shouted over the laughter.

"Since very early this morning," Bull replied.

"This here squadron here is the toughest bunch of Marine aviators ever assembled on this here God's green earth here," Sammy bellowed.

"Hear ye! Hear ye!" the others agreed.

"I'd like to offer a toast," Bull shouted above the din, and the room quieted. "I'd like to toast the greatest Marine fighter pilot that ever shit between two shoes." He lifted his drink high in the air and continued his toast as the other pilots elevated their glasses. "This man has lived without fear, has done things with an airplane that other men have never done, has spit in death's eye a thousand times, and despite all this has managed to retain his Christlike humility. Gentlemen, I ask you to

3

lift your glasses and join me in toasting Colonel Bull Meecham."

Amid the hisses and jeers that followed this toast, Captain Ronald Bookout whispered to Bull, "Sir, I think we might get into a little trouble if we don't hold it down a little. I just peeked out toward the restaurant and there are a lot of Navy types in there. I'd hate for you to get in trouble on your last night in Europe."

"Captain," Bull said loudly so the other Marines would hear his reply, "there's something you don't understand about the Navy. The Navy expects us to be wild. That's so they can feel superior to us. They think we're something out of the ice age and it is entirely fittin' that we maintain this image. They expect us to be primitive, son, and it is a sin, a mortal sin, for a Marine ever to let a goddam squid think we are related to them in any way. Hell, if I found out that Naval Academy grads liked to screw women, I'd give serious consideration to becoming a pansy. As a Marine, and especially as a Marine fighter pilot, you've got to constantly keep 'em on their toes. I can see them out there now mincing around like they've got icicles stuck up their butts. They think the Corps is some kind of anal fungus they got to put up with."

"Hell, I'd rather go to war against the Navy than the Russians," Ace Norbett declared.

"Ace, that's always been one of my dreams that the Navy and the Marine Corps go to war. I figure it would take at least fifteen minutes for Marine aviators to make Navy aviators an extinct form of animal life," Bull said.

"They'd have supremacy on the sea, though," Captain Bookout said.

"Let 'em have it. The thing I want to see is those swabbies storming a beach. I bet three Marines could secure a beach against the whole U.S. Navy. Hell, I could hold off half the Navy with just a slingshot and six pissed-off, well trained oysters on the half shell."

A long whoop and clamor with whistling and foot-stomping arose in the room. It took an extended moment for the room to fall silent when the maitre d' appeared in the doorway accompanied by an aroused Navy captain. The maitre d' smiled triumphantly as he watched the captain stare with majestic disapproval at the assembled Marines, some of whom had snapped to attention as soon as the Navy captain had materialized in the doorway. The power of rank to silence military men survived even into the pixilated frontiers and distant boundaries of drunkenness.

"Who is the senior officer in this group?" the captain snapped.

"He is, sir," Lieutenant Colonel Meecham said, pointing to Ty Mullinax.

"Identify yourself, Colonel."

"Lieutenant Colonel W.P. Meecham, sir," Bull answered.

"What's wrong with that man, Colonel?" the captain said, pointing to Colonel Mullinax.

"He's had the flu, sir. It's weakened him."

"Don't be smart with me, Colonel, unless you wish to subsist on major's pay the rest of your time in the military. Now I was trying to have a pleasant dinner tonight with my wife who flew over from Villa France to join me. There are at least ten other naval officers dining with their ladies and we would appreciate your cooperation in clearing out of this hotel and taking your ungentlemanly conduct elsewhere."

"Sir, this is a going away party for me, sir," Bull explained.

"Your departure should improve the image of the fleet considerably, Colonel. Now I strongly suggest you drink up and get back to the ship."

"Could we take one last drink at the bar, Captain? If we promise to behave like gentlemen."

"One. And then I don't want to see you anywhere near the area," the captain said as he left the room.

The maitre d' lingered after the captain departed. "Do you wish to have the bill now, señor?" he said to Bull. "It will include the broken glasses and damaged furniture."

"Sure, Pedro," Bull answered. "Better add a doctor bill that you'll have when I punch your taco-lovin' eyes out."

5

"You Marines are nothing but trouble," the maitre d' said, easing toward the door.

"I'd sure like to take me a dead maitre d' home from this here party here," Major Funderburk said.

"We'll be at the bar, Pedro," Bull called to the retreating maitre d'. Then he turned to the Texan and asked, "Hey, Sammy, did you bring that can of mushroom soup?"

"Got it right here, Colonel."

"You bring something to open it with?"

"Affirmative."

"Ace," Bull called across the room, "you got the spoons?"

"Aye, aye, sir."

"Now, young pilots," Bull said, gathering the whole squadron around him, "yes, young pilots, innocent as the wind driven snow, us old flyboys are going to show you how to take care of the pompous Navy types when the occasion arises. Now that used jock strap of a captain that was just in here thinks he just taught the caveman a lesson in etiquette and good breeding. He's bragging to his wife right now about how he had us trembling and scared shitless he was going to write us up. Now I want all of you to go to the bar, listen to the music, and act like perfect gentlemen. Then watch Bull, Ace, and Sammy, three of the wildest goddam fighter pilots, steal the floorshow from those cute little flamingo dancers."

The band was playing loudly when the Marines entered the restaurant and headed as decorously as their condition permitted for seats at the bar. Their appearance was greeted with hostile stares that shimmered almost visibly throughout the room. The captain's wife leaned over to say something to her husband, something that made both of them smile.

When the band took a break, Bull slipped the opened can of mushroom soup into his uniform shirt pocket. He winked at Ace and Sammy, drained his martini, then rose from his bar stool unsteadily and staggered toward the stage the band had just left. Out of the corner of his eye, he saw the captain and the other naval officers shaking their heads condescendingly. Their wives watched

6

Bull in fascination, expecting him to fall to the floor at any moment, enjoying the spectacle of a Marine wobbling toward some uncertain and humiliating rendezvous near the band platform more than they had the music itself. When Bull reached the lights of the stage, he fell to one knee, contorted his face in the pre-agony of nausea, then threw his head forward violently, pretending to vomit. The sound effects brought every fork in the restaurant down. As he retched, Bull spilled the mushroom soup out of the pocket, letting it roll off his chin and mouth before it dripped onto the stage. Bull heard Weber's wife say, "My Lord." She left the captain's table running but threw up before she passed three tables. Two other Navy wives passed her without so much as a glance as they sprinted toward the ladies' room. On stage, Bull was still retching and puking and burping, lost completely in the virtuosity of his performance. Bull rose up on shivery legs, and staggered back to the bar, his eyes uncomprehending and dulled with alcohol. Ace and Sammy, taking their cue, pulled out their spoons and in a desperate foot race with each other dove onto the stage as soon as Bull ceased to throw up. Their faces were twisted hideously as they grunted their way to the stage and began spooning the mushroom soup into their mouths. Ace and Sammy began to fight each other over the soup. Sammy jumped on Ace's back as Ace tried to spoon more of it into his mouth. Finally, Sammy pushed Ace off the platform and screamed at him, "Goddammit, it just ain't fair, Ace. You're gettin' all the meat."

The next morning Bull Meecham was ordered to report to the office of Colonel Luther Windham, the commanding officer of the Marine group attached to the *Forrestal*. Colonel Windham was hunched over a report when Bull peeked through the door and said, "Yes, sir, Luther?"

Luther Windham looked up with a stern, proconsular gaze that began to come apart around his eyes and mouth when he saw Bull's bright and guiltless smile. "As you may have guessed, Bull, this is a serious meeting. Captain Weber called me up last night, woke me up, and read me the riot act for fifteen minutes. He wants to write you up. He wants me to write you up. And he wants to get Congress to pass a law to make it a capital offense for you to cross the border of an American ally."

"Did he tell you his wife blew her lunch all over the Cordova?"

"Yes, Bull, and he still thinks that Ace and Sammy chowed down on your vomit. He said that he had never seen such a spectacle performed by officers and gentlemen in his entire life."

"Shit, Luth. Ace and Punchy were just a little hungry. God, I love having fun with those high ranked, tight-assed squids."

"That's good, Bull. But that tight-assed squid is going to have fun writing a conduct report on you that could end your career if I don't figure out a way to stop it."

"No sweat then, Luth. You're the best in the Corps at that sneaky, undercover kind of horseshit."

"Why did God put you in my group, Bull? I'm just an honest, hard-working man trying to make commandant."

"God just loves your ass, Luth, and he knows that no flyboy is ever gonna make commandant anyway."

"Do you know how many times I bailed you out of trouble since this Med cruise began, Bull? Do you know how many times I put my ass on the line for you?"

"Hey, Luth," Bull answered, "don't think I don't appreciate it either. And for all the things you've done for me, I'm going to do something nice for you."

"You're going to join the Air Force?"

Bull leaned down, his arms braced on Colonel Windham's desk, looked toward the door to make sure no one was listening, then whispered, "You been so good to me, Luth, that I'm gonna let you give me a blow job."

Bull's laugh caromed off the walls as Luther joined him with a laugh that was as much exasperation as mirth.

"What in the hell are you going to do without me, Luth?" Bull said.

"Prosper, relax, and enjoy your absence. Now, Bull,

8

here's how I think I'll handle Weber. I'll talk to Admiral Bagwell. He knows Larry Weber and he knows you. He outranks Weber and for some unknown reason he loves your ass."

"Baggie and I go back a long way together. He knows great leadership when he sees it. And Baggie ain't afraid to raise a little hell. I've seen him take a drink or two to feed that wild hair that grows up there where the sun don't shine."

"Bull, let Papa Luther give you a little advice."

Pulling up a chair, Bull sat down and said, "Shoot, Luth."

"This assignment in South Carolina is a big chance for you. Somebody thinks the last promotion board blew it and this is your chance to prove him right. Don't screw it up with your old Corps, stand-by-for-a-fighter-pilot shit. That Boyington shit is dead. Let the young lieutenants play at that. You've got to start acting like a senior officer because I'm not going to be there to cover for you when you pull some of your shenanigans."

"Luther," Bull said, suddenly serious, "I hope and pray I never start acting like a senior officer."

"Well, if you don't, Bull, you might have to learn how to act like a senior civilian. And it's up to you to choose which one you'd rather be. Now you're going to be C.O. of a strategically important squadron if this rift with Cuba heats up anymore. A lot of people will be watching you. Give it your best shot."

"May I have your blessing, father?" Bull said.

"I'm serious, Bull."

"You may not believe this, Luther, but I plan to have the best squadron in the history of the Marine Corps."

"I believe it, Bull. You can fly with the best of them. You can lead men. But you've got to become an administrator. A politician even."

"I know, Luther. I'll be good."

"When are you leaving, Bull?"

"Thirteen hundred."

"Your gear ready?"

"Affirmative."

"Will you give Susan a call when you get to Atlanta,

9

Bull? She's down in Dothan, Alabama, with her folks and she sounded a little depressed in her last couple of letters. You could always cheer her up."

"I can't do that, Luth. I don't want to break up your marriage. Susan's always been crazy about my body and I don't want to torture her by letting her hear my John Wayne voice over the phone. No kidding, Luth, I'll be glad to call her. Any other last minute directives?"

"Give Lillian a kiss for me."

"Roger."

"Same for Mary Anne and Karen. Tell Ben and Matt I can still whip both their tails with one hand tied behind my back."

"I wouldn't mess with Meecham kids. They'll find a way to beat you."

"O.K., Bull," Luther Windham said, rising to shake hands with Bull. "Keep your nose clean and fly right. And remember what I said."

"Did you say something, Luth? I must have been having a wet dream."

"You son of a bitch. You're living proof of the old saying, 'You can always tell a fighter pilot, but you can't tell him much.' "

"I'm gonna miss you, Luth," Bull said. "It's been great being stationed with you on this tub."

"Well, we started out in the Corps and we finally got back together after nineteen years."

"With you a colonel and me a light colonel. You're living proof of another old saying, Luth. 'The shit rises to the top.' "

"Have a good flight. What time are you due in?"

"Tuesday at 1530, Zulu time. I got a hop to Wiesbaden. Then one to Charleston Air Force Base."

"Give that squadron hell in South Carolina. I'll take care of the admiral for you."

"Come see me when you get Stateside, Luth."

"You ol' bastard."

"You cross-eyed turtle-fucker."

"Adios, amigo."

"Sayonara, Luth."

And the two fighter pilots embraced fiercely.

10

2

BEN WATCHED FOR the plane. His father was coming home. For much of his youth, Ben had strained to see black and silver fighter planes coming out of cloud banks or winging down like huge birds of prey from heights where an eye could not go unless it was extraordinarily keen or the day was very clear. He had lost count how many times he had waited beside landing strips scanning the sky for the approach of his father, his tall, jacketed father, to drop out of the sky, descending into the sight of his waiting family, a family who over the long years had developed patient eyes, sky-filled eyes, wing-blessed eyes. As a child, Ben had not understood why he had to stare so long and hard into a sky as vast as the sea to cull the mysterious appearance of the man who had fathered him, the man who could do what angels did in the proving grounds of gods, the man who had fought unseen wars five miles above the earth. But Ben's eye had sharpened with practice and age. By instinct now, it responded to the slanting wing, the dark, enlarging speck, growing each moment, lowering, and coming toward Ben and his family, whose very destinies were fastened to the humming frames of jets.

Now, as he watched, Ben wondered how much his father had changed in a year or how much his father could change in a year or a lifetime. He lowered his eyes and looked around at his mother, his brother, and two sisters. All of them were looking up toward the north where the transport plane would come; the plane bearing the father who had flown off an aircraft carrier in the Mediterranean for a year. A sense of excitement flowed through the family like a common blood. Ben's

11

mother stroked her hair with a nervous, raking motion of her hand. She caught Ben's eye and smiled.

"You look beautiful, Mama," Ben said, winking at her.

"Thank you, darling," his mother answered. "Get your shoulders back. You're slouching again. That's it. Now you're standing like a soldier. All right, children, let's say another Hail Mary that Dad's plane will have a safe flight."

"We've already said five Hail Mary's, Mom," Mary Anne Meecham said to her mother. "This is turning into a Novena fast."

Lillian Meecham disregarded her daughter's objection and in a clear, lyrical voice filled with the soft music of southern speech, prayed to the Virgin, "Hail Mary, full of grace, the Lord is with thee." The voices of her children joined her in an uneven chorus that lacked some of the fire and fervor of the first five prayers for their father's safe and punctual return.

A steady breeze came from the south. The family stood huddled outside the control tower of Smythe Field, a washed-out naval air station outside of Atlanta, Georgia. A windsock at the end of the field, swollen with moderate gusts, pointed like an absurd finger past the control tower and to the far runway. As lifetime students of windsocks and their essential reliable messages, the family knew from which direction the plane would be coming, knew that planes and pilots were bound by simple laws of physics, and would land according to the wind. The windsock reminded Ben of one of his father's sayings, "If you ever meet a man as truthful as a windsock, you have just met a hell of a man." Then he would add, "You've also met a real dumb ass."

Near the lone hangar, lethargic mechanics in grease-stained uniforms poked among the entrails of decrepit jets far removed from their vintage years. Three jets with their wings folded were parked like maimed insects awaiting rebirth among the tools and oils of the men who swarmed over the broken-open jet in the hangar. The hangar itself emitted a dark wet smell like a cave,

"C'mon, Mary Anne, let's take a walk up the runway while we're waiting for Dad."

"A splendid idea, Ben," Mrs. Meecham agreed.

"That's true form, perfect brother. The Great Peacemaker. You rack up brownie points with Mom and maintain the image of the perfect son."

Ben and Mary Anne began to walk slowly to the northern end of the runway beside the wire fence that paralleled the strip. The voices of their family dimmed with every step. As he walked Ben looked for the plane again and listened for the old buzzing sound, the old familiar anthem of an approaching plane to announce the descent of his father.

"Do you see anything yet?" Mary Anne asked.

"Yes, I do," Ben said, a smile inching along his face. "I sure do see something. If my eyes aren't playing tricks," he said rubbing his eyes with disbelief, "I see fourteen passenger pigeons, a squadron of Messerschmitts. Over there I see Jesus Christ rising from the dead. Mary being assumed into heaven. I see a horde of Mongols, Babe Ruth taking a shit, and a partridge in a pear tree."

"I mean, do you see anything interesting?" Mary Anne answered unemotionally. "By the way, Ben, how long have you been waiting for me to ask that question?"

"Oh, about eight months."

"I thought so," Mary Anne replied. "You have very limited powers of spontaneous thought. I knew you'd thought that up a long time ago. I maul you when it's just my mind against your mind."

"Baloney."

"You know it's true. I have a quicker mind and you just won't admit it."

"It might be a little quicker," Ben admitted, "but I want you to remember I can knock every tooth out of your head whenever I want to and there's nothing you can do about it."

"Big brave jock. Big, handsome, he-man jock. I admit you could do it. But I'd get you back."

"How?"

"I'd sneak into your bathroom and steal your tube of Clearasil. I figure that without Clearasil your pimples

15

would multiply so fast you'd be dead within forty-eight hours."

"Your cruelty knows no bounds."

"Of course not, I like to win arguments. In fact, I always win arguments. Back to the subject—have you noticed how bad your face has been breaking out lately?"

"It's not that bad, Mary Anne. When you talk about it, I start feeling like a goddam leper," Ben said, slightly irate.

"I've seen lepers who look a lot better than you do. You know, Ben, if Jesus were alive today, I'd go to him as he preached beside the Jordan, and throw myself at his feet. I'd intercede for you. I'd say, 'Master, you must cure my brother of his maggot face. His name is Benjamin and he likes to be perfect and kiss ass. If you think you're working miracles by curing these lepers, Jesus, my boy, I'll show you a face that will make leprosy look like kidstuff. This will be the greatest challenge of your ministry, Jesus, to cure Ben Meecham, the boy whose face is one big goob."

A sailor with a transistor radio blaring from his back hip pocket passed near Ben and Mary Anne. The long, pure notes of a clarinet spilled out into the Georgia sunshine as Mr. Acker Bilk played "Stranger on the Shore." The song ended, replaced immediately by Neil Sedaka's "Breaking Up Is Hard to Do." Both of them stopped talking until the music and the sailor faded out of earshot.

"Ah, yes," Ben sighed, philosophically, "breaking up *is* hard to do."

"How would you know? You've never gone with anybody."

"Neither have you."

"That's what you know. Boys are constantly lusting after my body."

"Oh yeah! I've seen your body cause other emotions. Like nausea. But never lust."

"Let's talk about your nose for a while."

"I surrender. God, with you talking about my skin and my nose, you're going to make me sensitive about my looks."

As they began the long walk back to their mother, the heavy languor of the afternoon soaking into them, Ben studied his mother.

Lillian Meecham was a stunningly beautiful woman of thirty-seven. Time had encircled her softly, enriched and deepened her beauty as the years tiptoed past her. Her hair was long, a dark luxuriant red, swept to one side of her head and half covering her right eye, a haughty, insouciant mane that added a touch of ingenuous naughtiness to a face that otherwise had the innocence of a Madonna.

Her face was a reflection of many things; a sum of many transfiguring, even violent events. Her smile was joyous, but the joy was fringed with grief. Her lips were full and passionate, her nose, mischievous and arrogant. In her face, hardening experiences were registered in soft places. Pain was exiled to the nearly invisible lines shooting out from the eyes. Grief radiated in tight stars from both sides of her mouth. These wrinkles were the only indications that the face had suffered and that time had left at least a few footprints in passage. It was a kind face; a face that sons could love, husbands worship, and daughters envy.

Her body was firm, ripe, and full. It had rich curves that invited the secret scholarship of men's eyes. She had borne four children and suffered three miscarriages, but her stomach was as hard and flat as her hand.

From a distance of a hundred yards, Ben saw her speaking to Karen and Matthew. She spoke with her hands, entertaining her two youngest children with fluid movements of such consummate grace that it seemed as though light music should be filtering from somewhere in the dizzying late afternoon heat. Her fingers could speak individual words. They were long and slender; each nail was richly translucent and sculpted into the small white eighth moons where her file had worked: she had more vanity about her hands and her stomach than any other parts of her body.

But Ben had watched his mother change as the day approached for his father to return from his year's journey overseas. It was a universal law in military families

17

that mothers could not maintain the strict discipline enforced by fathers to whom discipline was a religion and a way of life. When the military man left for a year, the whole family relaxed in a collective, yet unvoiced sigh. For a year, there was a looseness, a freedom from tension, a time when martial law was suspended. Though a manless house was an uncompleted home, and though the father was keenly missed, there was a laxity and fragile vigor that could not survive his homecoming.

Lillian Meecham was not a disciplinarian, but as the day of her husband's return neared, she knew instinctively that she had to harden into a vestigial imitation of her husband, so his arrival would not be too much of a shock to her children. His hand had traditionally been very heavy when he returned from overseas, so intent was he on re-establishing codes of discipline and ensuring that the children marched to his harsher cadences. For the last month she had been preparing them. She conducted unannounced inspections, yelled frequently, scolded often, and had even slapped Matthew when he argued about one of her directives. Tension flowed like a black-water creek through the family as the day of Colonel Meecham's arrival neared. The change of command ceremony took place the moment his plane arrived at Smythe Field. Lillian Meecham would hand the household over to her husband without a single word passing between them.

Mary Anne had a very different face from her mother's. Her face was wise, freckled, and touchingly vulnerable. Thick glasses diminished somewhat its natural prettiness. The gaudy frames of the glasses were cheap, drawing attention to features that needed no heavy emphasis. She was much shorter than her mother and seemed chunky and ungainly in comparison. Her breasts were large and full, but she dressed in loose-fitting tentlike clothes so as not to draw attention to herself. Because of the thick glasses, her eyes had a bloated appearance as though they were both trapped in a goldfish bowl. Her eyes were precisely the same blue as her mother's, but they nursed a wisdom and hurt strange to find in so young a girl. She opened a compact as she walked along and dabbed at several faded freckles. Never in her life had she liked the stories told by mirrors.

The wind picked up, died, and picked up again. It was a wind that offered no relief from the heat, but it caught Lillian's hair and pushed it softly back, an auburn shining pennant, a surrogate windsock, revealing a long, elegant neck.

"Mom looks beautiful today, doesn't she?" Ben said without looking at his sister.

Mary Anne frowned and said, "Yeah, Oedipus. She always looks beautiful. What else is new?"

"She must have spent a lot of time dolling up for Dad."

"About two weeks I'd say. She had her hair done, her nails done, her eyes done, and her clothes done. The only thing wrong is she couldn't have her children done."

"Do you think she's excited about Dad coming home?"

"Yes," Mary Anne answered. "She loves the creep. Like all of us, she's afraid of him. But also like all of us, she loves him. I read all of his letters to her. They're full of disgusting sexual references. It's very sicko-sexual."

"You read Dad's letters?" Ben said, amazed. "Mom would kill you if she knew that."

"It's my duty to keep informed. I will tell you one lewd, but fascinating piece of information. He refers to his penis as Mr. Cannon and her vagina as Miss Nancy. Isn't that lovely? It made me want to puke."

"I would advise you, dear sister, not to slip up and call Dad Mr. Cannon sometime. And I would never refer to Miss Nancy under any circumstances. But what the hell, I bet it's hard for a husband and wife to be separated for a whole year. I know it gets lonely for Mom, but God knows we need these breaks from Dad once in a while. I've got one year left with the big fellow before I'm home free."

"Dad is the most interesting person I've ever met," Mary Anne said thoughtfully.

"The fist prints on my jaw can attest to that."

"I don't mean that. He's hard to figure out. He loves his family, more than anything in the world except the

Marine Corps, yet none of us ever have a real conversation with him."

"Well, it's been a good year without him. I've loved being at Mamaw's."

"Anything would be a good year compared to the one before he left for Europe."

"It was definitely not a banner year. But that's over. Mom says he's changed a lot since he's been gone. He's evidently missed us a lot."

"I've missed him too, kind of."

"So have I," Ben said with difficulty. "Kind of." Then suddenly he said, "I hear a plane."

Far off, the quiet percussion of an approaching plane resonated over the field. Ben and Mary Anne sprinted the remaining distance to where their mother stood with Matthew and Karen. Ben ran backward trying to catch the first glimpse of the plane, watching for the sharp reflection of sunlight off a wing or cockpit window, but still he could not see it. The buzz of the plane seemed to fill the whole sky and came from no one source. It grew louder, more defined. When they finally reached Mrs. Meecham, she was smiling.

"I see it," she said simply.

"Where?" Ben cried. "I haven't seen it yet."

"It's at two o'clock just below that big cloud."

"I see it. I see it," Matt shouted.

"There's Daddy's plane," Karen squealed, jumping up and down in her new ruffled dress and patent leather shoes.

Mary Anne was staring blankly toward the noise. From long experience she knew that the plane was not in her range of vision, nor would it be for several minutes.

"I still don't see the goddam thing," Ben whispered to Mary Anne.

"Don't feel like the Lone Ranger," Mary Anne answered, "I won't be able to see it until I'm hit by one of the wings."

"Why don't you turn those glasses of yours around and use them as binoculars?"

"Very funny."

"Seriously, I tried that once with your glasses. For the

20

first time, I saw the rings of Saturn." Then he shouted suddenly, "There's the plane. I was looking right at the thing. I must be getting rusty."

Lillian Meecham gathered her children around her to choreograph the homecoming.

"Stand up straight, Ben and Matt. Shoulders back. Like Marines. Matthew, let me comb your hair. Girls check your makeup, we want to be beautiful for your father. When he gets off the plane, we'll all run to meet him. I'll go first, followed by the girls, then the boys. I'll give him a big juicy. Then the girls will give him big juicys. Boys, you shake his hand firmly. Very firmly, like men. Then say, 'Welcome home, Colonel.' "

"We better get a chair for the midget to stand on," Mary Anne teased, "Matt will end up shaking hands with Dad's bellybutton if we don't give him a lift."

"You heard her, Mama. You heard her call me a midget."

"Mary Anne," Mrs. Meecham called sternly.

"Yes, ma'am," Mary Anne answered.

"Be a lady."

The eyes of the air base turned in the direction of the fat-bodied transport plane that was bringing foodstuffs and airplane parts to Smythe Field, and Bull Meecham back to his family. It lowered steadily to the earth, flaps down, nose up, until the wheels screamed along the concrete and a black seam of rubber burned into the runway, marking the final leg on Colonel Meecham's journey home. As the plane taxied toward the operations tower where the family waited, a fuel truck sputtered into life by the hangar and rolled slowly toward the plane.

The door of the plane opened and steps were lowered. A man in uniform appeared in the doorway. He looked out, saw his family, and bellowed out to them with a large, exuberant smile, "Stand by for a fighter pilot."

Yes, as they ran to him, that echo from past memories rang in their brains, that password into the turbulent cellular structure of the past, the honeycomb of lost days, of laughter and fury, that told them as they ran to

21

his outstretched arms a simple message: Lt. Col. Bull Meecham, United States Marine Corps, was back from Europe. The father had landed. The Great Santini was home.

3

A MONTH LATER, on Rosebriar Road in Atlanta, an
alarm clock knifed into the darkness of two o'clock in
the morning. Bull Meecham was already awake and his
hand silenced the alarm almost as soon as it began. His
body was alive, vibrant, singing like an electric wire as
he dressed in preparation for the trip to Ravenel. He
cut on a lamp at a bedside table and shook his wife
gently.

He dressed in fatigue pants, a military issue T-shirt,
and combat boots. High on his left arm, a tattoo of a
red cobra, fanged, coiled, and ready to strike, stood in
stark relief to his pale, freckled skin. His hair was cut
short in a military burr. His neck was thick, powerful,
and cruelly muscled; his arms were long, athletic to the
point of being simian, threaded with veins, and covered
with reddish hair. Quickly, he did fifty pushups and
twenty situps. Then, he jumped up from the floor and
began to run in place. He pulled a rosary from the
pocket of his fatigues and began to say the first decade
of the rosary. The drumming of his feet on the floor
echoed throughout the darkened house. Lillian put a
pillow over her head and tried to cut out the noise and
light, tried to resume sleeping, although she knew it was
hopeless. Timing himself precisely, Bull quit running
after he had said three decades. He liked the idea of
caring for his body at the same time he cared for his
soul.

"C'mon, Lillian. Up and at 'em. No goldbricking this
morning. We've got two hundred and fifty miles of hard
traveling to get done. The movers are going to meet us
at the new house at 0900."

23

"Say one more rosary, darling. Then I'll be half alive."

"Get up, trooper. I'll get the kids. I want to be on the road in fifteen minutes."

He was sweating lightly as he moved to the girls' room. To wake Mary Anne and Karen, he flicked on the light switches and watched as they grabbed their eyes. It was the way D.I.'s awoke recruits when he was at Officers' Candidate School and it remained, to him, the most efficient way to rouse soldiers from their sacks.

"Let's move it, split-tails. South Carolina is five hours away."

Then he crossed the hall to the room where Ben and Matthew slept. He cut on the lights and walked quickly to Ben's bed. Before Ben's eyes could adjust to the light, Bull grabbed one of his legs and pulled him out of bed. Then he reached across and grabbed Matthew's leg and pulled him on top of Ben. Both brothers lashed out with their arms and legs, but Bull's weight had both of them pinned in ludicrous, humiliating positions.

"You Marines would never make it during a surprise attack."

"C'mon, Dad, get off us," Ben begged.

"C'mon, Dad, get off us," Bull imitated in a high-pitched whine. As he let the boys up, he ordered, "Be dressed and into the car in five minutes. We're breaking camp. The Japs are on the move again."

Bull went into the kitchen, listening for the sounds of the house springing to life. He heard his wife cough, water run in the girls' bathroom, a toilet flush, and Matthew yell something at Ben. He went into the kitchen of his mother-in-law's house, plugged in a pot of coffee, and studied a road map of Georgia. Silently, he read off the names of some Georgia towns. Moultrie, Ocilla, Dahlonega, Jesup, Waycross. The whole state depressed him, the blue lines representing highways that intersected towns whose names and destinies were mysteries to him. Southern towns choked with clay and grits. Black swamp towns who, like injured horses, ought to be shot and buried. South Carolina was no better, he thought; but at least it wasn't Georgia.

Alice Sole, sixty-three years old, struggled into the

kitchen where her son-in-law sat. She was wearing a blue houserobe sprinkled with roses and chrysanthemums. Her face had been hastily made up into a mask of almost clownish flamboyance.

Bull grinned when he saw her, and said, "Which whore house sold you that bathrobe, Alice?"

"The same one your mother worked for just before you were born," the woman growled back at him. "Now don't go messing with me at two in the morning, Bull. I'm in no mood. Why in the hell can't you drive during normal hours?"

"Amen," her daughter called from the bedroom.

"You make good time traveling at night," came the reply. "The kids can sleep, no cars on the road, it's cooler, and you don't waste a day getting there."

Alice sighed, unconvinced, "It must be the Yankee in you."

Soon Lillian was herding her children out of their bedrooms and toward the front door. The instincts of the military wife were beginning to assert themselves, the old efficiency of stealing away from temporary homes and entering the bloodstream of highways heading to new quarters. She led them out the front door and down the steep driveway and into the family station wagon. The car was already packed. A luggage carrier strapped to the roof was piled high with trunks, suitcases, and whatever cargo Bull deemed necessary for the first few hours in their new house. Ben and Matthew had flattened the back seats of the station wagon and inserted a double mattress so the children could sleep during the night journey through Georgia.

In the kitchen, waiting for his wife to give the ready sign, Bull poured himself a cup of coffee, drank it black, and felt the heat surge into his belly and flood through his body. The coffee burned into him, a dark transfusion that awakened him to his own desire to leave this house and set his eyes on long curves and highway signs.

"Mama, you're crying," Lillian said as her mother walked up to the car.

"I'm going to miss you, baby," Alice said embracing her daughter. "When you're my age you realize you have a finite number of good-byes to say in your life."

"Child," Lillian answered, "you are the healthiest human being on this earth. Don't you go talking nonsense."

"It is nonsense. But I'll cry if I goddam feel like crying."

"That's the spirit."

"Let me kiss my grandchildren."

She leaned through the window.

"Good-bye, Mamaw," Ben said to his grandmother as she kissed him on the mouth. "I love you."

"I love you too, Benjy," she said, crying softly. "You listen to your daddy, Ben. Just do what he says, and you won't get into trouble. All of you children do that. You hear Mamaw."

"Sure, Mamaw," Ben said. "If we don't listen to him, Dad has a good way of getting your attention. He knocks out a few of your teeth."

"Hush, boy. You talk like a fool," she snapped. "It's a child's job to adapt to a parent. You have a strict father and you have to adapt quickly."

"Or else you're not going to have a tooth left in your head," Mary Anne whispered to her brother.

The act of moving was in progress now, set in motion by an alarm clock, and the family that had moved four times in four years, traveling in summer nights, past bleached-out, sun-dried towns, moving along southern highways through the shrill, eternal symphonies of southern insects, humming old tunes and sleeping as the car rolled through the vast wildernesses and untransmissible nights: this family was tied to the image of the automobile; it was the signet of their private mythology. So often had they moved, shuffled on a chess board by colonels in the Pentagon, that it had become ritual; they moved through it all mindlessly, relying on spirit and experience, and with the knowledge that it was all the same, that the air bases were interchangeable, that mobility was the only necessary ingredient in the composition of a military family. The Meechams were middle class migrants, and all of them were a part of a profession whose most severe punishment was rootlessness and whose sweetest gift was a freedom granted by

26

highways and a vision of America where nothing was permanent and everything possible.

Colonel Meecham appeared on the front porch. He wore his flight jacket and gazed down the hill at the station wagon where his children jockeyed for position in the back seat. He felt good. Energy burned off him like a light. On the road, he was alive, vibrant, moving. It didn't afford the freedom of a jet plane flying through a clear sky, but a highway offered something almost as profound, an entry into the secret regions of the earth where towns with foreign, unrecallable names were violated once, then forgotten for all time. Yes, he felt good; everything was ready. The operation was proceeding flawlessly. In a loud voice that swept through the sleeping neighborhood, he called to his family, "Stand by for a fighter pilot." Then he strode to the car, his arms swinging like an untroubled monarch.

As the pilot neared them, Lillian turned to the children in the back seat for last minute instructions.

"Now remember what I told you. Don't do anything to upset your father. He's easily upset on trips," she said in a soft voice.

"I've already talked to them, Lillian," Mamaw said. "They'll be good."

Colonel Meecham entered the car. He arranged the things on the dashboard very carefully. On his far left, he stacked three road maps. Beside the maps was a box of Tampa Nugget cigars, blunt. On top of the cigars was a pair of aviator's sunglasses. Then, putting his hand into the pocket of his flight jacket, he pulled out a .22 pistol from it and laid the gun gingerly beside the cigar box. The appearance of the weapon caused a stir among his children behind him. It was the first time he had ever openly carried a weapon on a trip. The barrel of the pistol pointed at the squinting plastic statue of Jesus that was centered on the dashboard.

"Why are you carrying a gun, honey?" Lillian asked her husband.

"Is it loaded and ready to kill?" Matt asked breathlessly from the back.

"It's not loaded, sportsfans," the Colonel answered,

27

"but it's there. You never can tell what you might meet on the road these days."

"That's right, Popsy," Mary Anne called out. "They've been having quite a lot of trouble with stray dinosaurs and stuff in Georgia lately."

"Don't be flip with your father, young lady," her mother cautioned.

"This pistol," Colonel Meecham said authoritatively as if he were lecturing recruits, "is to be used only in case of emergencies." Then he glanced back at Mary Anne through the rearview mirror, smiled, and continued in a magisterial voice, "Such as dinosaurs. Indian attacks. Tartars sweeping out of the hills, surprise raids by the Japanese air force. But most of all because we are in the Deep South, and the times being what they are, you never know when I might have to give some wild nigger a new asshole."

A troubled silence invaded the back seat. The eyes of the children turned to Lillian awaiting a swift response. Lillian felt the silence and knew that the children were waiting for her to speak. She did not want to anger her husband, but she had no other options. Finally she said, "You know I don't allow that word to be used in this family, Bull. Only poor white trash use that word. So please don't use that word around our children."

"You're supposed to call them Negroes, Daddy," Karen said, highly offended by her father's vulgarity.

"Gee, thanks a lot, muffin. Negroes, you say," Bull teased.

"Yeah, and he said that other word too, because I heard it with my own two ears," Matt said.

"It's not sophisticated to use those words," Karen said.

"Oh goddam," Bull responded, starting up the engine of the car. "If it isn't sophisticated then I can't ever use them words again. Lordy me, to think ol' Bull Meecham let an unsophisticated word pass his lips. Why, it shames me even to think of it." Then his voice lowered an octave, and he spoke sharply to his wife, "What kind of happy horsecrap have you been feeding Karen since I've been gone?"

"For your information, I've been teaching Karen the art of being a lady. And I've taught your sons how to be gentlemen. Training they normally never receive at home."

"Oh, gentlemen. Excusem-wah," he said sarcastically. "There ain't nothing in this world that makes me puke faster than a southern gentleman."

"I'll remind you, Bull, that you are an officer and a gentleman."

"And I'll remind you that I'm not a pansy southern gentleman."

"True, you're not. There's not a place on earth you could qualify as a gentleman."

Ben and Mary Anne suppressed giggles into the pillows they were lying on, not daring to let their father hear them. Bull turned to his wife slowly, the engine running, and said, "You know, Lillian, I think after eighteen years of marriage, you're starting to develop a sense of humor. Now let's quit the yappin' and let's get down the road. I want to make some good time."

"Give me a kiss good-bye, fighter pilot," Mamaw said, an almost forgotten shadow standing by the side of the car. She leaned in and kissed her son-in-law on the lips. "Be good to the children on this trip, Bull. You hear me. They've been looking to your coming home. Don't spoil it. I mean it too. This is your lover girl speaking."

"Just so long as they do exactly what I say. They know that as well as you do."

"They're just kids, Bull."

"They're Marine kids, Alice, and that's what makes them different."

"Mother," Lillian said, her eyes shining, "thanks for everything. The year was wonderful."

"For me especially," Alice said reaching across Bull and grasping her daughter's hand. Alice looked very old under the street light. She was not good at farewells, especially when she was tired and her defenses down on the far side of two o'clock in the morning.

"All right, Alice," Bull growled impatiently, "we're all getting kind of weepy and you know there's nothing I hate worse than boo-hooing."

"You come see us, you hear, Mother," Lillian called.

"Yeah, you heah," Bull said, mocking his wife's southern accent. "Is that dumb dog in the car?"

"He's not dumb, Dad," Matt answered, offended, petting the sleeping head of a black mongrel dog in the back seat.

"All right, all right. Let's cut the yappin'," Bull said, picking up an imaginary microphone by his dashboard. "Control tower. Run me a check on the weather. Roger. Stand by for a fighter pilot. Over and out."

"Bye Mamaw," the children yelled.

The blue station wagon pulled away from the curb like a ship easing into the half black waters a stone's throw from the light of harbors. Soon the rhythm of shifted gears and the suppressed hum of an engine tuned for a long journey brought the car down Briarcliff Road to Ponce de Leon. At the light, Bull Meecham announced that it was time to sing.

"What should we sing first?" Mary Anne asked.

"What we always sing first, sportsfans," Bull answered. "Everybody ready?"

"Yeah," his children cried.

"Yeah?" the father asked.

"Yes, sir," they answered correctly.

"That's better. A-one and a-two and a-three."

Then together the family sang. The old words of the song burned into their collective memory. Images of other journeys flashed before them as they passed from light to darkness to light following the street lamps of Ponce de Leon into Decatur. It was the holy hymn taken from the bone and sinew of the family's life together, the anthem of both their discontent and strange belabored love for their way of life. With the singing of this song the trip began, tradition was paid its due homage, the rites of odyssey fulfilled. A lone car passed the Meechams' station wagon, and the stranger passing other strangers for the first and last time on earth heard the words coming toward him and leaving him quickly, unable to catch the tune. He caught only the word "battles."

"From the halls of Montezuma to the shores of
   Tripoli,
We will fight our country's battles on land, on air,
   on sea.
First to fight for right and freedom, and to keep
   our honor clean,
We are proud to claim the title of United States
   Marines."

It was the first song on all journeys the family took
together. Each of the children had heard it first in the
arms of their father; its rhythms had come to them
through their mother's milk. The song filled each child
with a bewitched, unnameable feeling; the same feeling
that drove men into battle. The Marine Corps hymn was
the family song, the song of a warrior's family, the song
of war, the Meecham song. "Families without songs
are unhappy families," Lillian Meecham would say. But
the song was theirs. They were traveling now, singing the
lead song, driving deep into an American night toward
a base where the great silver planes rested, waiting
for their pilots.

All during the summer, all across America, the highways filled up with the migrating families of the American military. They made crisp, mesmerized treks from
base to base where the men perfected the martial arts
and where families settled into counterfeit security for a
year or two. Movement, travel, impermanence, and
passing in the night were laws of the tribe. If the birds
of the North are born with a migratory instinct fused
into the albumen of eggs, then the military families of
America develop the same instinct out of necessity. They
pack, move, unpack, burrow in, and nervously await their
next orders. When summers come a moving fever hits
many of them, even when the orders command that they
stay where they are.

Orders usually came during the spring, filtered down
from the Pentagon, the long, spacious halls where un-
eyed, five-sided men fingered the destinies of millions
of men and their families, who set in motion the

marathon car trip, that took an Army family of eight from the Presidio of San Francisco across the continent, that sent a bachelor from Quantico thirty miles up the road to Arlington, and four naval families living side by side in Newport News to four different directions on the compass, that left an Air Force family of three in the same house on the same base for eleven years. Orders came to some men yearly; to others, rarely. But when they came, their obdurate, elliptical prose offered no choices. Orders simply informed men where they were to transport their families, the amount of time allowed for them to do it, and a description of their new assignment. Orders were a spare and skeletal literature.

"Now it's time for the Ol' dad to do a solo number," Bull announced.

"Oh, no. Not already," Lillian groaned.

"Stick your head out the window when you sing this, Dad, so the windshields don't crack," Ben said.

"Did your voice improve overseas, Dad?" Mary Anne asked. "Or does it still sound like an animal died in your throat?"

"You got the worst voice I ever heard in my life," Matt said.

"I like the way you sing, Daddy, don't listen," Karen said defensively.

"That's my girl, Karen. Defend your poor ol' father."

"Brown-noser," Mary Anne hissed at Karen. But her father had already begun singing the second traditional song of the trip.

"When they cut down the old pine tree,
    And they hauled it away to the mill,
    To make a coffin of pine
    For that sweetheart of mine
    When they cut down the ol' pine tree."

The dog, Okra, began to bark fiercely at Colonel Meecham. But Bull continued his crooning.

"Oh, she's not alone in her grave tonight
Alone, alone, she'll always be.
When they cut down the pine for that sweetheart
  of mine
When they cut down the ol' pine tree."

"I can't believe it," Mrs. Meecham said, "the worst voice in the world got worse in a year."

"I could bring tears to the eyes of millions with that recording," Bull retorted, his feelings ruffled somewhat.

"Even Okra thought you stunk, Dad," Matt said.

"Who cares what that worthless mutt thinks. I'd be doing the whole family a favor if I got the car up to ninety and threw Okra out the window."

"Yeah," Matt continued, "ol' Okra just hates your guts. I've never seen Okra hate anybody except you."

"That dog can't do one trick," Bull observed, lighting a cigar in the front seat.

"Okra has too much pride to do tricks for mere human beings," Mary Anne stated officiously. "His mind is on spiritual matters."

"Okra has one problem, sportsfans. The dog is stone dumb."

Lillian turned her head toward her husband and said, "He reminds me of a lot of Marines I've met."

"Touché," Mary Anne cried.

"O.K., enough yappin'. Let's sing the next song. What will be the next one?"

"You're going too fast, Bull. Slow down, please," Lillian cautioned.

"We got to make time. What's the next song?"

"You're going too fast. You're going over seventy."

"Christ, Lillian. I go five hundred knots in a jet practically every day of my life and you get nervous when I go seventy."

"This isn't a jet, Bull."

"What's the next song, sportsfans?"

"Let's sing 'Dixie,' " Karen trilled.

"Yes," the rest of the family agreed, except Bull.

"Naw," he said, "that's a loser's song. Nothing de-

33

presses me more than a loser's song. Let's sing something else."

"No, 'Dixie,' " the others insisted.

"O.K, you sing 'Dixie' and I'll sing 'The Battle Hymn of the Republic.' I'll sing a winner's song and you sing a loser's song."

So they sang rival songs at the same time. Soon it was evident to Bull that he couldn't match the fire power of his family's combined voices, so he quit singing and concentrated sullenly on his driving and his cigar.

"What a horseshit song," Bull mumbled when they were finished singing.

"Watch your language, Bull."

"Sing 'Dixie' if you want. But we all is heading out of Georgia, the armpit of Dixie. Of course we all is only going to South Carolina, the sphincter of America."

Mary Anne yelled from the back of the car, "You know what Chicago is, Popsy? It's the hemorrhoid of the planet earth."

The rest of the family applauded.

Mrs. Meecham said, "Good girl, Mary Anne. Defend the South."

"What's there to defend? The South ain't produced nothin' to defend. Except grits. Georgia ice cream or screwed-up Cream of Wheat."

"It produced every single one of your children," Lillian reminded him, "and your wife."

"Only because the Marine Corps puts its bases in these goddam southern swamps."

"With the taking of the Lord's name in vain, I suggest we now say a rosary for a safe trip," Lillian announced.

"Good idea. Then maybe everybody will quit yappin'."

Lillian opened the glove compartment and fumbled for her rosary beads.

"I know they're here somewhere," she declared. "They're those precious ivory beads your father bought me in Rome, Italy, blessed by Pope John the twenty-third."

"You haven't lost 'em already for godsakes," her husband grumbled.

"Of course not," she replied. "Certain things in automobiles never work longer than a month. Clocks for one. The lights of glove compartments for another. Here they are. Children, did you see this rosary? I don't believe I showed any of you. It is a treasure. Each bead is individually carved."

"Was it really blessed by the Pope, Daddy?" Karen asked.

"Yeah, I think the ol' pontiff blesses box cars full of rosaries for the tourists."

Lillian rebuked him angrily, "Bull, what a sacrilegious thing to say."

"What do you mean? Everyone's got a gimmick. Even Popes. I'm sure it's for a worthy cause like sending Maryknolls to Tanganyika to convert spearchuckers, but it's still a gimmick. I priced all the rosaries before I picked that one out for ya. I was going to get one blessed by the Pope and with a sliver of the real cross inside it, but I could have bought the Pietà for less money."

"How did they know it was the real cross, Dad?" Ben asked.

"Damned if I know, son. I think Jesus would have had to be strung up ten thousand times to supply enough wood for that rosary racket."

"I think we've had enough," Mrs. Meecham announced. "Let's say the rosary for the intention of a safe journey and the salvation of your father's endangered soul," she said to her children behind her.

Colonel Meecham laughed. "I'll buy that," he said. "Your poor ol' dad needs all the prayers he can get, sportsfans."

"Let's also pray for the conversion of Russia," Mrs. Meecham added.

"That's just small potatoes, Mama. Let's pray for something big," Mary Anne deadpanned.

"Don't be snip, young lady," her mother shot back.

"Yeah, Mary Anne, or your father's gonna take you dancing down at knuckle junction."

"That won't be necessary, Bull. I can handle the children without your help, thank you."

"I'm just trying to be supportive, dear," the colonel

said. His wife did not answer. Instead, she began a slow recitation of the Apostles' Creed to begin the rosary. "I believe in God, the Father, Almighty, Creator of Heaven and Earth."

In the back seat, brimming with hidden intentions, Ben drifted like a cloud into secret prayer leaning back on his pillow and silently turning his thoughts to God.

When he returned to the rosary Lillian was speaking the first part of the angels' greeting to Mary. Her enunciation was flawless as she spoke with such reverent clarity that it seemed like she was speaking the words for the first time. "Hail Mary, full of grace, the Lord is with thee, blessed art thou amongst women, and blessed is the fruit of thy womb, Jesus."

The whole family bowed their heads at the spoken name of the Lord. But their response was given in breathless haste: Holymarymotherofgod, prayforussinners-nowandatthehourofourdeathAmen. The words were packed together in an unintelligible lathered herd. As Lillian's fingers circumnavigated the beads, Ben's mind wandered and the prayers became thoughtless, untongued words whose meaning was bled out of them by repetition. Mary Anne kicked him with her bare foot and shot him the finger, making sure that the sign was too low to be intercepted by her father's omniscient eyes scanning the rearview mirror. The upraised finger almost caused Ben to laugh aloud, but sterner laws of self-preservation prevailed. Ben did remember the scurrilous version of the Hail Mary Mary Anne had written the year before that Lillian had overheard. "Hail, Benny, full of shit, a turd is on thee, blessed art thou among farters, and smelly is the corpse in the tomb. Cheeses." Lillian had not been amused and she restricted Mary Anne to the house for two weeks. Since Mary Anne never went anywhere, the punishment did not seem to compensate for the heinousness of the crime. Mary Anne enjoyed shocking Ben about religious matters. Several days before Colonel Meecham returned, Mary Anne claimed to have read that the Vatican was reconsidering its position on Mary's virginity. When Ben fell into the trap, Mary Anne explained with the casualness of a disinterested theologian

36

that St. Joseph had appeared to a shepherd near Padua and claimed that he had gotten it from the Virgin Mary at least twice before Christ was born. Because of these obscene forays into the realm of the supernatural, Ben was positive that his sister was not a favorite in the stern eyes of the Lord. He looked at her across the car, strangely saddened by the deep beauty of her smile. Glancing forward, he shot the finger back to her and smiled.

The car moved deeper into the Georgia countryside, prayer breaking out of the windows in wavering harmonics spilling into the ditches and moccasin strung creeks of the pine counties outside of Atlanta. A truck pulled suddenly behind the station wagon filling the car with light. St. Christopher, muscled like a weight lifter and crossing a stream of bronze, winked in the sudden light, giving fierce definition to an outsized staff and a Gerber baby Christ. Colonel Meecham disliked the intrusion of other vehicles in his post midnight dashes when he was moving his family to a new home. In the rearview mirror, Ben saw his father's eyes cast a glance of primal defiance at the lights that challenged their aloneness in this desolate stretch of road and at the very instant he heard his mother end a decade of the rosary and begin the first words of the Lord's Prayer, Ben felt the car respond as his father's foot pressed the accelerator. Lying on the mattress he felt as though he were part of the car's engine, that his father was stepping on some vital organ inside of him, that he was the cause for the sudden leap forward as the wind hissed through the back seat knocking some of the clothes and uniforms from the hangers. The truck fell behind them, the lights grew smaller, then disappeared forever in the middle of the third decade of the rosary. Night returned to the car and the foot relented gradually, then relaxed against the accelerator. The car sang with its solitude. Christopher and his enduring spine crossed the stream invisibly again. The wordless words of the rosary continued like the heartbeats of birds.

Finally, seventy miles outside the city, an hour and fifteen minutes into the heart of the journey, the rosary ended and Colonel Meecham asked rhetorically and unspecifically, "Who's on duty first?"

No voices answered him. Eyes strained almost audibly in the back seat as the brothers and sisters questioned each other wordlessly.

Finally, Lillian spoke, "You taught them never to volunteer for anything."

"Why don't you help your poor old husband stay awake, honey?"

"You taught me never to volunteer for anything too. Besides I'll perish if I don't get a little sleep. Tomorrow's a long day with the movers coming and everything."

"Ben," Bull cried out to his son in the darkness behind him. "Ben, don't pretend you're asleep already."

"I was asleep."

"Get up here. Right behind me. You've got guard duty first."

"Yes, sir," Ben said, moving lightly over Matthew, and pushing Okra to the back of the car. He rested his arms on the front seat and leaned forward so he could whisper to his father without disturbing the sleep of the others.

"We'll have a little man to man talk while the leathernecks get some sack time."

"Sure, Dad," Ben said hesitantly. "What do you want to talk about?"

"Let me ask you a question first, sentry. What are the responsibilities of a man on guard duty?"

"I don't know them all, Dad. I forgot some of them."

"Yeah, yeah. Your mother always slacks up on you when I go overseas. Give me the ones you know."

"To walk my post in a military manner, keep always alert, and observing everything that takes place within sight or hearing. To spread the alarm in case of fire or disorder."

"You skipped about a hundred of 'em. You ought to know those if you're going to be on duty. I'll give you a week to relearn 'em once we get to Ravenel."

"I haven't looked at them for a long time, Dad."

"Never make excuses."

"Yes, sir."

For the next ten miles the car was silent. Colonel

38

Meecham chewed gum belligerently and Ben watched the white lines until he was mesmerized by their repetitiveness. Both of them wanted to speak but could find no common ground to bridge the abyss that separated them as father and son.

"The Red Sox won," Bull said finally.

"How did Williams do?" Ben asked.

"Knocked three runs in with a double."

"Good."

"I flew with Ted Williams in Korea. You knew that didn't you?"

"Yes, sir. Dad?" Ben said, beginning a conversation he had fantasized when his father was flying from the carrier off the French coast. "Are you ever afraid when you fly?"

"That's a good question. Yeah. I'm always a little afraid when I fly. That's what makes me so damn good. I've seen pilots who weren't afraid of anything, who would forget about checking their instruments, who flew by instinct as though they were immortal. I've pissed on the graves of those poor bastards too. The pilot who isn't a little bit afraid always screws up and when you screw up bad in a jet, you get a corporal playing taps at the expense of the government."

"What are you most afraid of when you fly?"

"Most afraid of. Hmmm," Bull whispered, plucking at his left ear lobe. "Good question, sportsfans. When I'm flying a jet, the thing I'm most afraid of is birds."

"Birds?" Ben said letting a quick girlish giggle escape in his surprise.

"Yeah, birds," his father answered defensively. "You hit a bird going five hundred knots and it's like being hit with a bowling ball. Do you remember when Rip Tuscum was killed in a plane crash about five years ago?"

"Yes, sir."

"Well, he had his head taken off when he hit a buzzard."

"Birds, eh, Popsy," Ben intoned. "I can see the headlines now. Bull Meecham killed by a parakeet. War Hero Brought Down by a Deadly Sapsucker."

"Go ahead and laugh, jocko, but I break out into a cold sweat when I spot a flock of birds up yonder. The bad thing is that they're usually past you by the time you see 'em. I mean they are behind you before your brain registers that you've just passed a bird. You'll know what I mean some day."

"How, Dad?"

"When you're a Marine pilot flying your own plane."

Ben knew he was in familiar terrain now, old territory where the teasing had grooves and furrows of ground that had been plowed before.

"I think I'm going to be an Air Force pilot, Dad."

"If you want to fly with pussies it's O.K. with me," Bull flared, then remembered that his son had teased him about the Air Force many times before. "But if you want to fly with the best, you'll fly with the Corps, simple as that."

"What if I really decide not to go in the Marine Corps, Dad?"

"I want you to go in for a four-year hitch at least. If you decide not to make a career out of it, it's your decision. But I want to pin the wings of gold on you after flight training. You'll be a good pilot, son. You're athletic and have the quick reflexes. The coordination. The only problem I see is you have a little too much of your mother in you, but Quantico will ream that out of your system."

"I'll have plenty of time to decide whether to go into the Corps or not when I'm in college, Dad."

"That's negative," his father replied. "I've already made that decision. You'll decide whether to stay in after four years."

"That's not fair, Dad."

"Who said your ol' dad's ever been fair. Look, Ben, you'll thank me one day. Christ, the way the world's going now you may even luck out and get your wings when there's a war going on."

"That's lucking out?" Ben exclaimed.

"Shh, not so loud. If you're trained as a fighter pilot you'll never be happy until you test your skills against an enemy pilot. That, boy, is a law."

"What if I get killed?"

"Then you're a lousy pilot. Only lousy pilots get killed in combat. That's another law."

Ben thought for a moment, then said, "What about Uncle Dan. Your brother, the one killed in the Solomons. Was he a lousy pilot?"

The massive shoulders tensed beside him. Then slowly they relaxed, but the car lurched forward, moving faster and faster until Bull answered by saying, "Yes, Dan was a lousy pilot. But he was a brave one and he earned that K.I.A. on his tombstone. He earned it."

"Would you like to be killed in action, Dad?"

"If he has to go, every pilot would like to be killed in action. It's better than dying of the piles."

"But only lousy pilots are K.I.A., Dad. It's a law."

"That's right, sportsfans. Good thinking. That's why I'm telling you that I'm more afraid of birds than enemy pilots."

"It would have to be a great pilot who shot you down, wouldn't it, Dad?"

Bull turned toward his son and winked, "Inhuman, Ben. The bastard would have to be inhuman. Now go on and get some sleep. I'm wide awake now. I'll get Mary Anne or your mama up if I need company."

"Good night, Dad."

"Good night, sportsfans."

Alone now, the car voiceless, Bull strained to follow the white lines of the highway snaking through Georgia. Butterflies by the thousands fluttered maniacally before the headlights then exploded like tiny half-angels on the windshield leaving a scant yellow paint and the dust of broken wings as a final signature. The further into the journey Bull went, the harder it became for him to see through the windshield that was stained with the prints of so many inconsequential deaths.

Periodically, Bull would spot a turtle crossing the highway and with an imperceptible movement of his arm he would position the car expertly and snap the animal's shell, which made a scant pop like the breaking of an egg. It kept him from getting bored on the trip; it kept him alert. He always did it when his wife and children

41

were asleep. But when he pulled clear into the other lane to kill a turtle almost on the shoulder of the other side, Lillian awoke.

She whispered at him, her eyes still closed, but her lips tightened in a thin line, "It takes a mighty brave man to run over turtles."

"Who's running over turtles?" Bull asked innocently.

"I've been on enough trips to know when you're getting your jollies running over turtles. I think it's sick."

"Well, they shouldn't be on the road. They're a safety hazard."

"Sure they are, darlin'. You're always reading about car wrecks caused by marauding box turtles attacking defenseless Chevrolets."

"It's my only sport when I'm traveling. My one hobby."

"And you're such an All-American at it, darling. Maybe I should dress in a cheerleader's costume and shake a pompom every time you run over one of those dangerous turtles."

"Ah, Saint Lillian. Do you think I should drive real slow so I won't kill any butterflies?"

"I don't care what you do."

"Thanks, Saint Lillian. I'll be a good boy as soon as I pick off this next turtle. OOOOeeeee. He's a big mother." Then Bull laughed as the wheel made a short pop. "Yeah, we're in Georgia sure enough, sportsfans, I'm starting to see a lot of dead dogs on the highway. That ought to be the nickname of this horseshit state. The Dead Dog State. Now I'm gonna quit yappin' and start makin' some time."

"Making time." The phrase came back to Ben as he entered into an unsteady threshold of sleep, a sleep that wasn't quite, the groaning of a truck that passed them by in a vision of light, passed them in a momentary assault as the car ate its way through Georgia, consuming miles as Bull Meecham carried on imaginary conversations with phantoms only he could see. Ben saw his father stabbing the air with his fingers, saw his lips move, and his face grimace as someone responded to his interrogation improperly. Making time. Yes, as this inch of highway is past now, or then, as the sea draws nearer, smelling the sea, while sleep comes during the dying hours, the corpses of miles past, the pale memories of towns seen dimly—the pilot is moving, moving, moving toward a home they have never seen.

4

AN HOUR BEFORE DAWN, a long, timber-loaded train that smelled sweetly of pine resin stopped them at a country crossing. Colonel Meecham got out of the car and stood watching the train silently reciting the names of the railroad lines tattooed on the sides of the freight cars. Trains released strange lyrics in Colonel Meecham and though he could not articulate what he felt as he watched the great trains roll in passage along warm, silver rails, his children knew that whatever poetry might lurk in their large, often unreadable father, it surfaced whenever he heard a train whistle. The destiny of his family in Chicago was wedded to the movement of trains through the Midwest. If the potato was symbolic of the Meecham family's flight from Ireland, then the freight train was the lucky talisman of their redemption in the new world.

The children stirred slowly out of their sleep. Lillian groaned into awakeness with a loud, feline stretch. Bull walked back to the open door and said, "Pit stop. Head run. Get the dog out and let him lift his leg. Everybody out who needs to pee."

"Sugar," Lillian said, "I know this is an outrageous request, but the girls and I feel more comfortable powdering our noses and doing our business in a clean well-lighted bathroom."

"It's good for you to get a little night air. C'mon Mary Anne and Karen, you two go over there behind those trees."

"Don't you dare make a move, young ladies. We will keep our dignity."

"O.K., then let's get Matt awake. You too, Ben. Here,

44

Okra, I want you to pee on the track while the train's moving there."

"That's not funny, Dad. That's why Okra hates your guts," Karen retorted.

"I don't need to go," Matt said, only half awake and pulling his pillow tightly over his head to cut out the noise of the train.

"You better go now, son. You know your father doesn't stop often."

"He only stops for three reasons: trains, the death of someone in the car, or if he has to go to the bathroom," Ben said climbing out of the car over Matt.

As Ben walked toward his father, he was surprised to look up and see the universe shivering with starlight. Cotton grew in the field that bounded the railroad tracks and the air was laden with the opulent smells of greening crops and leafy forests. Approaching the sea the land had begun to slope gently, the hills were brushed downward, the earth was smoothing itself, and the rivers straightened for the final run to the sea.

Ben and the colonel were urinating in the ditch that paralleled the highway. Bull commented on each car that flickered past like a single frame on a long roll of film. His voice was excited. As always, Bull felt euphoric and princely in the company of trains. "There's the Illinois Central. The Southern Pacific. And right there goes the queen of them all, the Rock Island Line. That's the one that half your Chicago relatives work on, Ben. Watch where you're whizzin'. You almost hit my foot. Aim high and away. There's the Southern. Probably carryin' a box car full of grits to some southern pansy living in New York." Then in the regionless drawl of a conductor, the half-intelligible patois belonging to no country that Bull had learned by imitation as a child riding free on the Rock Island Line, he began to chant, "Davenport, Ioway. Next stop. Ioway City, yes Ioway, Ioway, Ioway City. Dee Moynes. Dee Moynes. Dee Moynes, Ioway. All off for Davenport." The voice of the conductor resided with great constancy just below the customary pose of the fighter pilot. "All aboooooard," he said, climbing back into the car as the caboose

45

flashed by and the thunder of the train diminished gradually into the darkness.

Bull barked out at Ben as the car moved across the tracks in first gear, "Did Okra whizz?"

"I think so, Dad," Ben answered.

"You're not paid to think, mister. I asked you a question."

"Yes, sir. He did," Ben said.

"You'd better be right. That was the last head stop before Ravenel. Ravenel. Rav-e-nel. Next stop, Rav-e-nel, South Caroli-na."

At dawn and according to the strict schedule Colonel Meecham had plotted in Atlanta, they had come within sixty-five miles of the Marine Corps air station at Ravenel. The sun filled the car and the children, sleeping in the back, began to stir heavily against the new day. Colonel Meecham reached for his aviator's sunglasses which rested among the other paraphernalia of the journey on the dashboard. "Best sunglasses in the world," he told his wife. "Civilian shades can't touch 'em."

"Isn't it a shame military doctors couldn't be as good as military sunglasses," Lillian said.

"Hey, not bad, sportsfans. That was a good line."

"Bull, there's nothing in this road, not even a pig. Are you sure we're going the right way?"

"Affirmative. The navigator has never made a mistake in his career."

"Oh, I don't know about that. I seem to remember a night when the navigator took a wrong turn and we ended up in eastern Tennessee instead of western North Carolina."

"Ah, the grits who put up road signs in the South never got past second grade."

"Just to change the subject, sugah, you haven't told me the gossip on the old squadron. Where are all the Cobras now and what are they doing?"

"Sam Pancoast and Ollie Oliver are stationed in Ravenel. Rocky Green's in El Toro. His wife left him six months ago to run away with a twenty-two-year-old corporal in his squadron. Rocky's got the kids."

"Poor kids."

The conversation centered around the Marine Corps, moving from one old friend to another, men and women they had been stationed with, whose destinies had crossed again and again. The fraternity of Marine fighter pilots was small, intimate, and exceedingly close. The year's absence from the military had put Lillian somewhat behind in following the lives of some of her friends. Transfers were constant among all of them and with both Lillian and Bull it was a peremptory requirement of their nomadism that they keep a vigilant eye on the travels of their peers. The two of them talked very little of politics, literature, or the arts. Most of their conversation was of the Corps or of their own family.

Ben shifted uncomfortably on the other side of the car. The sun was pouring in the car directly on his face. He heard his father say that they had been out of Georgia for a half hour. Out of Georgia, Ben thought. "Into South Carolina."

Georgia born, Ben felt a strong kinship to the blood red earth his father hated, loved the fragrant land he saw mostly in night passages, whose air was filled with country music and the virile smells of crops and farm machinery possessing the miles between towns. It was the one place he could hold to, fix upon, identify as belonging to him. He was rooted in Georgia because of the seal on his birth certificate. He lived there only when his father went overseas, but that made no difference to him. No matter how hard he tried, he never developed any imperishable allegiances to the washed-out, bloodless Marine bases where he had lived for most of his seventeen years. It was difficult to engender fealty for any geographical point when he had dwelt in four apartments, six houses, two trailers, and one quonset hut in his forced enlistment in the family of a Marine officer. Every house was a temporary watering place where warriors gathered for training and the perfection of their grim art before the tents were struck again. He longed for a sense of place, of belonging, and of permanence. He wanted to live in one house, grow old in one neighborhood, and wanted friends whose faces

47

did not change yearly. He renewed his tenuous claim on Georgia with every visit to his grandmother's house and with each dash through the countryside following the necklace of Marine bases strung through the swamplands of the Carolinas and Virginia.

Rising on one elbow, Ben addressed a question to the front seat, "When do ya'll think we'll get there?"

"Ya'll?" Bull roared. "Ya'll isn't a damn word. What's this 'ya'll' stuff? I go overseas for twelve months and I come back to my boys all talking like grits."

"Ya'll is perfect grammar, Ben darling," Lillian objected. "It's perfect and it's precise."

"Don't use that word when you're addressing me. You got to realize, Lillian, that a southern accent sounds dumb anywhere outside of the Mason-Dixon grit line."

"I think it sounds cultivated. Anyway, you've managed to make sure none of the children have a southern accent."

It was true. None of Bull Meecham's children had accents. Their speech was not flavored with the cadences of the South, the slurred rhythms of the region where they had spent their entire lives. Every time one of his children made a sound that was recognizably southern, Bull would expurgate that sound from his child's tongue on the spot. Though the Marine Corps put its bases in the South, he could never accustom himself to the sad fact that he was inevitably raising southern children. He could exorcise the language of the South but he could not purify his children of the experience that tied them forever to the South, to the strange separateness, the private identity of the land which nourished and enriched their childhoods.

"Let's see what else has gone to pot since the Big Dad has been gone," Bull announced. "What is the capital of Montana, Karen?"

"I just woke up, Daddy," Karen protested.

"I didn't ask you for a speech. I just asked a question."

"Bismarck," she answered after thinking for a moment.

"Wrong. You're supposed to know them all."

"Helena," Matt said.

"Right, Matt."

"Here's another one, Karen. This will be a chance to redeem yourself."

"It's too early in the morning, Daddy. I don't feel like playing 'Capitals.' "

"Too bad," he answered. "What's the capital of Idaho?"

"Just a minute. Don't tell me. Let me think about that one."

"You ought to know it right off the bat, girlsey," he said.

"Boise," she screamed.

"Yeah, but I gave you a hint."

"Mary Anne," Bull said, "what's the capital of Uruguay?"

"Montevideo."

"Ben, the capital of Afghanistan."

"Kabul."

"Good, good. I'll tell you kids something right now. You are lucky to be part of a Marine Corps family. There are no kids in America as well trained in geography as you. You've been to more places than civilian kids even know about. Travel is the best education in the world."

"Sugah," Lillian cooed, "the reason the children know all those capitals is because you threatened to kill them if they didn't learn them."

"It's called motivation, Lillian," Bull answered, grinning.

Ben sat back against his pillow thinking about what his father had just said. Then he said, "We sure have lived in some of the great cities of the world, Dad. Triangle, Virginia. Jacksonville, Havelock, and New Bern, North Carolina. Meridian, Pensacola, and now Ravenel, South Carolina. You can't get much luckier than that."

"I met some Air Force brats in Atlanta. Now they do some good traveling. They'd lived in London, Hamburg, Rome, all over Europe. They'd skied in the Alps. They'd seen the Leaning Tower of Pisa. One of the boys spoke three languages. All of them had been to operas and gone to symphonies. I wonder how the Ravenel symphony measures up to the London Philharmonic," Mary Anne said.

"I can tell you all you need to know about Europa," Bull said, "I just spent a whole year inspecting the continent."

"Did you go to the Louvre, Daddy?" Mary Anne asked.

"Sure, I went in to check out the Mona Lisa. You can stand anywhere in the room where that picture is and the Mona Lisa's eyes will follow you. Leonardo Da Vinci did a commendable job with that portrait."

"You really think so, Dad?" Ben said, winking at Mary Anne.

"The old Dad soaked up quite a bit of culture while he was sportin' around the capitals of Europe."

"You're just too modest to flaunt it, aren't you dear?" Lillian said softly.

"That's right. Modesty is one of my worse faults," Bull shouted, laughing, enjoying himself in the last fifty miles of his journey.

"Hey, Dad," Matt said, "why doesn't the Marine Corps send its families overseas sometimes?"

"They're probably afraid that Marine kids would whip up on Air Force kids."

"Could you imagine living in Gay Paree, speaking French like natives," Ben wondered aloud.

"I can say hello, good-bye, and kiss my fanny in eight languages," Bull boasted.

"Why, Bull," Lillian said, "I didn't know you were multi-lingual."

"I pick up languages real fast," he replied, missing the irony in her voice.

"If you'd only work a little harder on your native tongue," she said.

"Very funny."

Mary Anne spoke out brightly, extravagantly, "Let's talk some more about how lucky we are to be military brats."

"I'm so lucky that I get to go to four high schools instead of just one," Ben declared with feigned enthusiasm.

"And I, the lovely Mary Anne Meecham whose beauty

50

is celebrated in song and legend . . ." Mary Anne began.

"Boy is that a laugh," Matt said.

"Quiet, midget, before I feed you to a spider."

"Mom," Matt called.

"We just have a little ways to go, children. So try to get along."

"Or else I'm gonna have to butt a few heads," the colonel glowered through his sunglasses.

"Anyway," Mary Anne continued, "I'm lucky enough to be absolutely friendless through an entire school year until the month of May. Then I make lots of new friends. Then I'm lucky enough to have Daddy come home with a new set of orders. Then I'm lucky enough to move in the summer and lucky enough to be absolutely friendless when school starts back in the fall."

"I know you're kidding," Lillian said to Mary Anne. "And I know all of you are upset about leaving Atlanta."

"Tough toenails," Bull growled.

"But there are some wonderful parts about growing up in a Marine family. You learn how to meet people. You learn how to go up to people and make their acquaintance. You know how to act in public. You have excellent manners and it's easy for you to be charming. I've had many compliments about how polite my children are. This is the benefit of growing up in the military and the gift you take with you no matter where you live. You know how to act."

"But the main thing, hogs," Bull said, "you get to hang around me and all my good qualities will rub off on you."

His family groaned in chorus and the colonel threw back his head and bellowed with laughter.

"I can't wait to get out of this car," Karen said after a silent five-mile stretch.

Matthew added, "I've got to go number one. My teeth are floating."

"You should have gone when we stopped for the train," Bull said.

"I didn't have to go then," Matthew replied.

The car was silent as the Meecham family moved across the bridge that crossed the Combahassee River, toward their fourth home in four years. All hills had died in this last slant toward the sea. Stands of palmettos and live oaks met the car as the road ribboned out straight in its last sprint to the barrier islands. But the most remarkable feature of the land was the green stretches of marsh fringing the rivers and inlets that spilled and intersected through the whole landscape. These were vast, airy marshes, some of them thirty miles wide, as splendid as fields of ripened wheat, yet as desolate in some ways as the dark side of the moon. Every eye in the car filled up with marsh, moved by it, stirred, yet uncomprehending. It was an alien geography that thrust outreaching along the water's edge; a land of a thousand creeks, brown and turgid, but rich in the smell of the sea.

Lillian knew about marshes from girlhood summers spent on the Georgia coast.

The Chevrolet crossed a bridge that announced the entry into Ravenel County.

"Thirty more miles, hogs."

"Will you tell us about the new house, Bull? I'm perishing from curiosity," Lillian spoke.

"It's a surprise," Bull gloated.

"I gotta go number one real bad," Matthew said.

"Tough titty," Bull answered, his sunglasses eyelessly hunting for Matthew in the rearview mirror. "You should have gone when we stopped for the train."

"Cross your legs, darling," Lillian advised. "And offer it up for a good intention."

"Like the conversion of Russia," Ben suggested.

The air had a fetid, tropical feel to it as it passed through the car: the land was flat, lush and brilliantly green. On the road's grassy fringes, black men and women, sometimes alone but often in lethargic twos or silhouetted in triplicate, walked the long stretches between shacks and cabins where plumes of morning smoke trailed above rusty tin roofs and smells of breakfast spilled from open windows and entered the rush of air that caromed about the Meecham car.

"Bacon," Lillian moaned, as the car passed one small house. "I would rather eat bacon than a filet mignon."

Bull grunted, a monosyllable meaningless in any language, but an audible assent that he had heard and understood her. He was tiring now and his participation in conversation would diminish with each mile passed. The children were staring out the windows. As strangers, they entered Ravenel with sharpened, critical eyes assimilating every image that flashed by them, so that what they saw was the addendum of ten million impressions that registered briefly and almost tangentially in their minds like flags of undiscovered countries: each image a single frame of memory whose life span was light quick and heartbeat fast: each a mystery clamoring for preservation, for life, for admittance to the vaults of the brain where remembrance burns. Each child in the car hunted for the familiar; the sights that would relate Ravenel to the other towns that had served as temporary homes.

A jet passed overhead; the sound poured into the car like a liquid. Leaning his head out the window, Bull scanned the treeline for a glimpse of the plane. "That's the sound of freedom," he said. It was a sound familiar to all of them, its thunder rumbling across them as though they were long sheets of glass. It was a legitimate sound of home, one that would remind the Meecham children of their youth more strongly than the singing bells of ice cream trucks or the cadences of lullabies.

Moments later, Mary Anne began to cry. It was soundless weeping free from hysterics, unrelated even to grief. Her eyes glistened as the tears rolled down her face in clearly defined salt creeks.

"What's the boo-hooing about?" Colonel Meecham stormed at his rearview mirror, catching and holding the image of his weeping daughter. "You better get her to stop, Lil. I can't stand boo-hooing."

"Get a Kleenex to wipe your face, Mary Anne. There's nothing to cry about. You've got to give it a chance."

"I gave it a chance," Mary Anne replied miserably. "I hate this town too."

"You'll learn to love it. Give it time. If I were you, I'd say, 'I'm going to take this town by storm. I'm going to go out of my way to meet people and I'm going to be the most popular young lady in Ravenel by the time I leave here.' That's the spirit I'd take."

"Just get her to turn off the waterworks, Lillian. We don't need a speech."

"I'm trying, Bull. Just give me a chance. Mary Anne is just upset about moving. So are all the kids."

"Tell the hogs too bad from the Big Dad. I don't care if they're upset or not."

Mary Anne searched her purse for a Kleenex, but pulled out instead a teaspoon pirated from her mother's silver service. Crying gently, she held the spoon under her eyes, carefully catching each tear, preserving their sad silver in the hollow of the spoon. "I'm *real* depressed," she said finally. "I'm going to hate this town. I wish I were dead."

Bull replied, "You may get your wish if you don't cut the weepy scene."

When the tears filled the spoon to overflowing, when the edge of the spoon brimmed with the trembling residue of her grief, Mary Anne carefully flicked her wrist and the warm liquid flew the length of the car, only slightly dispersed, and splashed against Bull's head.

"I ain't believing somebody spit on me," Bull bellowed in disbelief, his hand feeling his hair. "Has someone gone nuts?"

"Excuse me, Daddy dear. The spoon slipped," Mary Anne protested innocently. Three more tears lit into the spoon. Aiming carefully, Mary Anne flicked them on her father's neck.

Lillian broke in, "Remember, darling, what I told you. If you have a lemon, make lemonade. You have to give a town a chance to grow on you. You have to open yourself up to a town. Be willing to take chances. You've been in the Corps long enough to know that."

"I am not in the Corps," Mary Anne said to her mother, tossing another sun-bright tear at her father's head; it missed, passing over his right ear and splashing down on his arm where it lay trapped on the dense red hairs of his arm.

"I ain't believing she's bombing me with tears, Lillian,

54

and you can't stop her," Bull said. "You want me to stop her?"

"Stop hitting your father this very instant, young lady," Lillian flared. But there was not much menace behind Lillian's attempts at discipline.

The next tear hit Matthew on the forehead.

"Weirdo just hit me with a tear, Mama."

"I'm gonna mix those tears with a little blood if she isn't careful," Bull said.

"I said stop, Mary Anne, and I mean it. Remember who you are."

"I'm a weirdo," Mary Anne answered.

"You are a lady," Lillian said imperiously. "And ladies don't catch their tears in spoons and hurl them at their families. A lady grieves in silence. She always has a smile on the outside. She waits until she is alone to express her sorrow."

"I like to do it in full public view. I'd like to draw huge crowds of people and weep all day. I'd flick tears at the crowd until each one of them was hit with a tear. I like people to share in my misery. I like them to feel it when I feel bad. God, I feel miserable."

"Don't take the Lord's name in vain," Lillian admonished her daughter. "Ladies . . ."

"I know, Mama. Ladies don't speak with vulgar tongues. How do ladies talk? I'd really like to know."

"A lady just knows how to talk. It's not something she is taught. It is something within her, something inherently gentle and refined. She says nothing that offends or upsets. A lady speaks softly, kindly, and the world spreads out before her and fights to do her favors. If a woman is not a lady at birth, no amount of money or education can make her one. A lady just *is*."

Mary Anne sang with false joy, "What a perfect description of me. Yes. That's how a dictionary would define me."

"Boy, what a joke that is, huh, Mom?" Matthew said.

"Was that a voice?" Mary Anne answered cupping her hand to her ear. "I thought I heard a tiny voice coming from a little insect body. It sounded almost human."

"Cut that out, Mary Anne. Quit teasing Matthew."

"Yeah, because you're gonna die real young if you tease me one more time, freckles," Matthew huffed.

Mary Anne retorted, "The only way you could kill me, little one, would be to enter my bloodstream."

"Let's cut it out," Ben said firmly.

"Ah," Mary Anne mocked, "the voice of sublime perfection. Was that the goodly one? The sainted brother? The perfect son?"

Before Ben could answer, Bull thundered out at all of them, "I'm gonna give you hogs about five seconds to cut the yappin' then I'm gonna pull this car over to the side of the road and I bet I can shut your yaps even if your mother can't."

"Hush," Lillian hissed at her children. "Not another sound." Her eyes cast a stern, desperate communiqué to her children.

But this time there was no need. Bull's tone had registered. Each child knew the exact danger signals in the meteorology of their father's temperament; they were adroit weathermen who charted the clouds, winds, and high pressure areas of his fiercely wavering moods, with skill created through long experience. His temper was quick fused and uncontrollable and once he passed a certain point, not even Lillian could calm him. He was tired now after driving through half the night. Behind his sunglasses, the veined eyes were thinned with fatigue and a most dangerous ice had formed over them. The threshing winds of his temper buffeted the car and deep, resonant warning signals were sent out among the children. Silence ruled them in an instant. They resumed watching the diminishing countryside on the outskirts of Ravenel. "Control," Lillian said soothingly. "Control is very important for all of us." She was looking at her husband.

5

"THIS IS IT, sportsfans. This is Ravenel," the colonel said, talking more to himself than to his family.

"And to think I mistook it for Paris, France," Mary Anne whispered to Ben in the rear of the station wagon.

They were riding down a street lined with sharply spined palmetto trees. To the right of the car, the last fingers of a tidal creek groped among the extreme frontier of marsh grass that edged up against the backs of gas stations and hamburger stands.

"Yes, it's a military town all right," Lillian said to her husband. "Half the town is liquor stores to keep the Marines happy. The other half is covered with mobile home salesmen to cheat the young enlisted men with families out of their pitiful salaries."

"This isn't the good part of town. So there's no sense yappin'," Bull muttered.

They came to a traffic light. To the right stood a decaying high school with a grassless campus. Behind the school was a garbage dump perched on the edge of a dying marsh. The school had an empty, dried-out look, like the shell of a June bug on the bark of a tree.

"If that's where we're goin' to school, you can forget it, Popsy," Mary Anne blurted out.

"That's the colored high school, Mary Anne."

"It looks terrible," Matthew said.

"That's where the spearchuckers learn to blow darts," the colonel laughed.

"Bull, you hush," Mrs. Meecham warned.

They turned the corner and soon were driving along a high, grassy bluff that sloped down to a glistening river that flowed through the main part of town. Live oak trees, festooned with cool scarves of Spanish moss, and gnarled by a century of storms, loomed over the street. On the left, large white houses with long columns and graceful verandas ruled the approach to the river with mute elegance. Each house was a massive tribute to days long past. In one of the houses drawling conspirators had planned the secession from the Union; in another, Sherman himself had slept after his long march to the sea.

On the other side of the town a drawbridge crossed the river, connecting Ravenel with the three sea islands that separated the town from the Atlantic Ocean. A yacht knifed through the early morning water in a long, green V. Sea gulls, balsa-light, hovered on invisible currents above the river. Three black fishermen fished from the bridge.

But Lillian Meecham was looking at the houses that bordered River Street.

"These are lovely, lovely houses, children. Bull, you didn't tell me Ravenel was such an incredibly charming town."

"I wanted to surprise you, sportsfans. But the big surprise is coming up later."

"You mean the house you rented, Dad?" Ben asked. "Affirmative."

"Why aren't we living in base housing? No one's told us that," Ben continued.

"Because all the quarters billeted for majors and above are filled up," Bull explained.

"That just means you're not high-ranked enough to get us a house, huh, Popsy," Mary Anne said.

"Of course that's not what it means," Lillian snapped. "Your father will be one of the highest ranking officers on this air base. It simply means that we'll have to wait for quarters to open up to move in."

"I guarantee you we won't move from these quarters I am about to show you," Bull said proudly.

"Tell me about the house, sugah. I'm still perishing from curiosity."

"Not until you see it."

"You know I'm not wild about two bedroom mobile homes, Dad," Ben said.

"Are you wild about having a fist slammed down your throat up to the elbow, wise guy?" Bull bellowed.

"Temper, temper," Lillian cooed. "Aren't these mansions lovely?"

"I gotta go to the bathroom," Matthew said.

"Cross your legs, Matt, and offer it up to the Lord," Lillian said.

"Look at that one, Mama," Karen said, pointing to a large two story mansion with ten columns on each level. It was encircled by a wild, untended garden fierce in its reckless blooming and accidental color.

"That is a true southern mansion," Mrs. Meecham said reverently. "It reminds me of Tara in *Gone With the Wind* except for its garden. Maybe it's hard to get help around here."

"I guess I kind of remind you of Rhett Butler in *Gone With the Wind,* huh, Lillian?" Bull asked.

"No, darling, you don't even vaguely remind me of Rhett Butler."

"You do remind me of somebody in the movies, Dad. I can't think of who it is. No, I got it. You remind me of Bambi," Ben said.

"Dad reminds me of Godzilla from the movie by the same name," Mary Anne suggested.

"Naw," Ben said, "I liked Godzilla."

"Ask a simple question, get a lot of yappin'," Bull growled. "Anyway, I remind myself of Rhett Butler. A real ol' stud horse."

"It's a desecration to compare yourself to Rhett, Bull. There's no comparison."

"Yeah, I guess not. Ol' Rhett just can't measure up to the Great Santini."

"That's not what I meant."

"Gone With the Wind was a real horsecrap movie."

"It is considered the best ever made."

"I still have to go to the bathroom," Matt whined.

"Put on the brakes, Matt. You should have gone when we stopped for the train."

"I told you I didn't have to go then, Dad."

"Offer it up, son," Lillian suggested for the third time.

"You got to learn, Matt," Ben said, "that Dad just

doesn't allow his children to excrete when he's on a trip. It's a family law."

"I didn't think men went to the bathroom when I was a little girl," Karen added, "because Dad never had to stop during a trip."

"We'll be there in a minute," Lillian said. "Think about something else and it will help."

"Think about how your kidneys are gonna blow up soon, if you don't take a whizz pretty soon," Ben said.

"Quit the yappin' back there."

Before them in two symmetrical files of stores stood the center of town. It was a three block area with stores facing the street, the river visible in fragments of green through the alleyways that cut through to unseen parking lots by the water. Some of the stores were old with graceful eaves and cornices; others had been modernized or sterilized with plate glass windows and neon; still others were new. In one alleyway, a large black man had parked his mule and wagon and was lifting off bunches of flowers to sell to the morning shoppers who were beginning to appear at both ends of the runny street. The hard fragrance of the salt river and the marshes filled the car. It was a smell that all of them would remember as their first smell in Ravenel.

"The river is beautiful, Bull," Lillian said after a moment. "Look, it runs right behind the stores."

"This town is hicksville," said Mary Anne.

"Give it a chance, honey. You're always too quick to judge."

"I've given it a chance," Mary Anne retorted, "and this town is definitely hicksville."

"You could find a turd in a scoop of ice cream, Mary Anne," Colonel Meecham said.

"Where's the main part of town, Daddy?" Karen asked.

"You're in it, sportsfans."

"We better find a priest," Ben said. "I don't think Matt's going to make it."

"Matt's turning yellow, Dad," Mary Anne said. "You know, Matt, I think you look good yellow."

"Yeah, and you're gonna look good bloody," Matt shot

back, though he was moaning in a rigidly held fetal position.

"Are we almost to the house, Bull?" Lillian asked.

"Almost," he answered. "Now I want all you hogs to look out the window and see if you can guess which house the Great Santini rented for his family."

"Since the Great Santini has the worst taste in the free world, this should be easy," his wife said pleasantly.

"Has the Great Santini ever let his family down?" shouted Colonel Meecham.

"Yes," the family shouted back, pleased by the spontaneous unanimity.

"You do not trust the Great Santini?" he asked with fake incredulity.

"No," the family screamed.

"Aha," he said, "then it is up to Santini to prove to his doubting Thomas family that he is the tops when it comes to choosing a house for his family."

"Watch out for a place that looks like a pentagon," Mary Anne said.

"Or an airplane hangar," Ben offered.

"Look for the one you think it is," said Bull, smiling under his sunglasses.

"I hope it's soon, sugah. Matt is undergoing rigor mortis," Lillian cautioned.

They had entered a neighborhood of splendid quiet, hushed gardens, and columned houses. The houses were not as spectacular as those that lined River Street, but many of them were older and more tastefully understated. The river had curved around to the boundary of this neighborhood. Four large houses sat at the farthest extremity of this point of land, each of them overlooking the water. Each house was almost hidden by huge oak trees that hovered over them. On the far right was a large house that looked straight to the most oblique curve in the river. It was a house that needed painting, one that seemed to cry out for habitation and laughter beneath its roof. The other homes along the river were vigorously tended. This one was vacant.

Bull Meecham pulled into the driveway of the house. Matt leaped from the car and sprinted to the other side of the house, the laughter of his family following him. Then for a moment, Lillian and her children sat quietly, stunned by the size and majesty of the house.

"Bull, the last time you chose a house for the family," Lillian said, "it was so small a family of fleas would have been cramped to distraction. But this . . ." She leaned over and kissed him on the neck, "It's beautiful, sugah."

"No," Bull said wistfully. "It's a southern mansion just like you always wanted to live in. It belongs to a man from Chicago who is gonna retire here in two years. He heard that the Chi-city kid needed a house and he cut fifteen big ones off the monthly rent. He knew I was class and would take good care of the house. I probably reminded him of Rhett Butler."

As Lillian wandered about the empty rooms of the house carefully making mental notes about furniture placement and room arrangement, Colonel Meecham herded his children to the front porch for a morale check. Mary Anne and Karen sat on the fourth step leading up to the front door; directly behind them sat Ben and Matthew. With his hands placed behind his back, Bull paced in front of them, clearing his throat, and gathering his thoughts for the traditional moving day speech. The sun was fully up now and the heat of the August day was beginning to assert itself with a blood-thickening power. Bull unzipped his flight jacket but did not take it off. In his right hand he carried a swagger stick which occasionally he slapped against his left palm, punctuation marks for the thoughts that crowded and strutted invisibly within him. Finally, he began to speak.

"At ease, hogs," he began. "I want you to listen and listen good. We have bivouacked all night and arrived at our destination, one Ravenel, South Carolina, at approximately 0800 hours, twenty minutes before your commanding officer had planned. Now I have listened to you hogs bellyache about moving to a new town ever since I arrived home from the Med cruise. This said bellyaching will end as of 0859 hours and will not affect the morale of this squadron henceforth. Do I make myself clear?"

His children nodded their agreement with expressionless eyes. The swagger stick slapped against Bull's hand in ten second intervals.

"Your C.O.'s philosophy has always been this: If a little shit comes into your life, pretend that it's milk chocolate. It just means that you have to bear down a little bit, reach way down there in that place where the guts reside, dig in, and say to yourselves, There's nothing that can keep me down. Nothing! If anyone gets in your way, you run him down. If anyone thinks they're better than you, you step all over him until he looks like the Graumann Chinese Theater. Now, I know it's rough to leave your friends and move every year. At least it would be rough for other kids. But you," he said, his eyes meeting the eyes of every child, "you are different. You are Marine kids and can chew nails while other kids are sucking on cotton candy. Marine kids are so far ahead of other kids that it's criminal. Why? Because of discipline. You've had discipline. You may resent it now, but one day you're going to look back at your ol' Dad and say I owe it all to him. If he had kicked my butt a few more times no telling how far I could have gone in life. You hogs have one more advantage that I have not mentioned, but I will mention at this time. It gives you the edge over even Marine kids and that advantage is this: you are Meechams. Now a Meecham has got more goin' for him than any other animal I know. A Meecham is a thoroughbred, a winner all the way. A Meecham gets the best grades, wins the most awards, excels in sports, is the most popular, and is always found near the top no matter what endeavor he undertakes. A Meecham never gives up, never surrenders, never sticks his tail between his legs, never gets weepy, never gets his nose out of joint, and never, never, never, under any circumstance, loses sight of the fact that it is the Meecham family that he represents, whose honor he is upholding. I want you hogs to let this burg know you're here. I want these crackers to wake up and wonder what in the hell just blew into town. Now just one more thing: just because a Meecham has more raw talent than anyone else, that doesn't prevent him from thinkin' about the Man Upstairs every once in a while. Yes, I think you know who I mean. Don't be too proud to ask for his help. I've got this feeling when it comes to favorites with the Man Upstairs, the Meechams rank as high as anyone. Even I myself get down and pray to the Lord Creator every night because I realize that without him I am nothing. The order of the day is to help your mother police up the house. When I return from the base I want to see you hogs sweating blood. By nightfall, this camp should be in A number one order. Inspection order. Do you read me loud and clear?" Bull roared.

"Yes, sir," his children answered.

"Sergeant," Bull said to Ben, "dismiss the troops."

Ben walked down to his father, saluted him sharply, about-faced and shouted, "Dis-missed."

From the veranda above them, Lillian called down to her husband, "When are you going to check in at the base, sugah?"

"Why don't I wait till Monday? I can help unpack boxes and supervise the hogs."

"Oh, no," said Mary Anne to herself, but her eyes blazed up to her mother in a silent entreaty.

"Our marriage can't survive your staying around here to help, Bull. No, you are banished from this house until late this afternoon. You remember what happened last time. Your fuse is too short on moving day. You check in and we'll take care of the movers."

Each child breathed easier when the colonel grunted his reluctant assent. It was always better when Colonel Meecham was exiled under edict from his harried wife and disappeared from the house on moving day, for long experience had taught them that the colonel's temper shortened considerably in the chaotic milieu of unopened boxes and pictureless walls. On the last three moves, Bull had swaggered among the movers shouting out commands as though they were laggard corporals in need of KP. He caused enough resentment on the last move to stir an eventual mutiny that led the head mover to ask him to leave the premises if he wanted his furniture anywhere other than on the front lawn. It is often difficult for military officers to grasp the fact that the civilian world does not hold them in shivering awe. Bull's family also remembered that Ben had been the victim of his father's frustration at the end of the three previous settling-in days, receiving backhands on two of those occasions, and a semi-strangling on the third. Wiser now, Ben had told his mother that he would disappear for the day if she did not devise a plan to keep the colonel out of the maelstrom of this ill-omened day. He was not offering his body as a human sacrifice again just because his father could not exist in the center of chaos.

"Let's face it, Mom," Ben had told her, "Dad ain't exactly priestlike when we move into a new place."

At nine o'clock, Bull pulled a clean uniform from a clothes bag that hung in the car. He took the uniform directly to Ben and told him to prepare it for use by the sharpest Marine officer in the Corps. Ben took the uniform from his father, smoothed it with his hand, spread a blanket on the lawn, then laid the uniform reverently on top of the blanket. Then he pinned the ribbons, insignia of rank, and appropriate decorations onto his father's blouse. It was a ritual he could perform in his sleep, one for which his father had trained him from childhood.

"Are you going to wear your inspection shoes or your work shoes, Dad?" Ben asked.

"Use your noggin, sportsfans," Bull snapped. "I'm not gonna be waltzing through a field of shit flowers this morning. This is a pretty important meeting. Do you get it?"

"Aye, aye, sir. Inspection shoes it is," Ben said. He walked to the front seat of the car and lifted a pair of shoes whose toes were covered by white sweat socks from under the seat. Gingerly, Ben removed the socks. He stared deeply into the gloss on the shoes.

"You scratched these shoes badly, Dad, the last time you wore them. You got to be more careful with these babies."

"I don't have to be careful as long as I have you around to shine 'em up," his father retorted, not gruffly, but as a statement of irrefutable fact.

"What did you do without me when you were sailing around on that aircraft carrier last year?"

65

"I got hold of a real ambitious corporal," he replied.

Under some road maps in the glove compartment, Ben retrieved a rusty can of cordovan polish and a thin silken handkerchief spotted with dried circles of polish. Out of the corner of his eye, Ben saw his father lift the uniform off the blanket, inspect the angle and position of the silver leaves, eyeing the placement of ribbons, then grunting approval without acknowledging his son. There are some things you can never forget, Ben thought. Finding a shady place on the veranda, he leaned up against a column and began to shine his father's shoes. Even though he resented the way his father took this duty for granted, he derived a guarded satisfaction from his custodianship of his father's shoes. With him rested the basic responsibility for his father's military appearance. The shoes were Ben's greatest challenge and most enduring joy. Bull was hard on shoes. Some Marines could make a good spit shine last for a week, but Bull's shoes would look as if they had been on a forced march after only several days' wear. Ben loosened the top of the can of Kiwi with a dime, wrapped the handkerchief tightly around his middle finger, put some water into the top of the polish can, dabbed a small amount of polish on the rag, then in a circular motion lightly applied the polish to the shoe. It delighted him always to find the mirror in the shoe's face, to rediscover the dark reflection released as the finger thinned the polish on the hard, good-smelling leather. Touch was the thing, lightness in the finger, the sparing use of water, never spit, the thinness of the rag, and a stingy use of polish. Once a shoe had a good base, it was a simple matter to restore its brilliance when the shine faded. As his finger moved, Ben watched his face appear as if he were standing over a clear pool; his eyes stared into his darker eyes, reflected in the black waters of cordovan. Looking up, he could see his mother through the large curtainless windows inspecting a fine old mantelpiece in the living room. He had never seen her happier with a new house.

For years she had dreamed of being the mistress of so splendid a house. She had been raised to appreciate anything that was old and to hold in mild contempt anything

66

new or showy. Here, standing on the living room's rift cut pine boards and studying the carved spandrel ornaments on the staircase, she seemed to have come to a place long destined for her. The disrepair of the house did not bother her at all, the crumbling plaster, the peeling wallpaper, the faded paint on the columns; none of it made any difference. She had been reared to inhabit a house as fine as this and only the accidental liaison with a man in love with the Marine Corps had interfered with this consummation.

"They don't build houses like they used to," she heard her husband say behind her. He was dressed in his uniform except for his shoes.

"You look absolutely Napoleonic in your uniform, Bull. Yes, you're right. People used to take pride in their work."

"This whole country's going to the weenie dogs. To build a house like this today would cost you an arm and a leg. I'd like to take this same house up to Chi-city, put her down by Lake Mich and sell her for about two hundred thousand big ones."

"No, sugah, this house belongs here. Nowhere else. It would be sacrilegious to move this house to the Midwest. By the way, Bull, I suggest you put on your little booties before you go saluting the brass."

"Ben's putting a spit shine on 'em for me."

"Ben's a fine Marine, isn't he?" Lillian purred sarcastically.

"Quantico will be a snap after he's been with me for twenty years," Bull boasted.

"Darling," Lillian said, "anything would be a snap after that."

"What's that supposed to mean?"

"Nothing at all. Now you run along and meet all the nice officers; the movers will be here soon and we have work to do."

"You sure you don't want me to supervise the hogs in putting away the ordnance?"

"Absolutely positive, Colonel."

Bull paused at the front door and asked Lillian, "How should I handle Varney, Lil?"

"I've been waiting for you to ask me that question."

"Maybe I'll wait till Monday. That'll give me some time to plan a little strategy."

"Get it over with today. Then you won't be thinking about it and brooding over it tonight. You're professionals. You can work it out just by being mature."

"No, we can't. It goes too deep."

"Well, you better try, Bull. He outranks you."

"Can you believe all the goddam luck. Of all the group commanders in the world, I get cornholed with that pussy son of a bitch."

"Watch your language, please. Little ears might be listening. What I would do if I were you is to walk in there bold as can be as though he were my best friend. You never believe me but more flies are caught with honey . . ."

"Than with horseshit," Bull finished.

"Shame on you. Now go so we can start to work. And Bull. This house. You outdid yourself."

The colonel's face lit up with pride. He looked around the house unable to contain his euphoria over his selection of a dwelling. He saluted his wife smartly. Then he shouted to his invisible children scattered about the grounds, "You help your mother today and no yappin'." As an aside to his wife, he said, "If any of the troops give you any lip, there will be a summary court-martial when the Great Santini gets home."

"I've been handling the troops without you for a whole year, Santini, and I've done a darn good job of it."

"They're a little ragged, but I'll whip 'em into shape."

"That's what I'm afraid of."

"You don't think I can handle 'em, Lil?" he asked darkly.

"No, I think you can, Bull. That's what I'm afraid of. How you'll handle them."

Colonel Meecham pulled the station wagon out of the driveway. It was caked with the night dirt of Georgia and South Carolina. His family watched him leave, then fanning out in well-drilled squads they set about assaulting the long-standing dust from the recesses and corners of the massive house. Armed with sponges, soap, brooms, and mops, they sweated together in the climbing August sun, working hurriedly before the movers arrived. Mrs. Meecham wanted her furniture placed in a clean house.

The movers arrived at eleven that morning, powerfully muscled, red-faced men who grunted officiously over the dead weight of refrigerators and air conditioners. In alternating currents of laughter and profanity, they journeyed time after time from the inside of the truck to the interior of the house, authentic beasts of burden accustomed to inflamed muscles and sugar-voiced housewives like Mrs. Meecham who thought a mover's only goal in life was the destruction of irreplaceable heirlooms and fragile glassware. Ben would catch snatches of his mother's lamentations to the movers and smile every time he heard them answer in a peremptory "Yas'm."

"Be careful, sugah," he heard her say to the largest of the men. "My best china is in that box, darling, and I declare you are throwing it around like a shot putt."

To another, Mary Anne heard Lillian plead, "Sweetie pie, a man of your Gargantuan proportions can wreak untold destruction if you're not careful. The treasures of my heart are in that box. Pretend you're carrying eggs. They ought to hire tiny little men to move the fragile objects and have ya'll giants move pianos and things."

In the middle of the move she whispered to Ben, "You have to watch movers very closely, son. They are brutes like your father. They are destroyers of beautiful things."

By three o'clock, the movers had laid out carpets, positioned furniture, hooked up the washing machine and dryer, and filled each room with the stencil-marked boxes that the Meechams would have to unpack. When the ordeal was over, when Lillian Meecham half believed that her personal riches were not reduced to dust from mishandling, and when the movers drove off griping about incipient hernias, the gears of the truck grinding against the humidity of the afternoon, the family was left with the task of getting the house into inspection order for the critical gaze of Colonel Meecham. For them, the day was beginning in earnest.

"All right, darlings," Lillian called to her children, slapping her hands together, "here's the battle plan. We'll concentrate on the downstairs. Let's unpack all the downstairs boxes and get them out of sight. We will hang the pictures, try to make things look natural, and hope that your father does not realize that the house is a long way from being in tiptop shape. Then you each will be responsible for unpacking the boxes in your own room. But you can do that tomorrow morning. As for now, let's get to the business of the living room."

"God, it's hot, Mama," Mary Anne said. "I feel like Dante."

"It must be a hundred in the shade," Matt added.

"Just think about being in a cool place. That always helps. Let's pretend this is our new home in Norway. There's a fjord outside and snow on the mountains."

"That just makes me all the hotter, Mama," Karen said. "Let's go for a swim at the base pool and do this later."

"Can't do it, little sister," Ben said. "Godzilla will be back at six."

"Ben," his mother warned.

They began to unpack the boxes that contained the accoutrements of the living room. Ben emptied one box that held ashtrays from Japan, four statues of Buddha in various postures and degrees of corpulence, six oriental silk screens, and two camel seats from Morocco. The room was already studded with five sets of brass candlesticks from Taiwan. On one wall was a large painting of a Seine river scene which Bull had bought while drunk in Paris. Soon the room was piled with goatskin rugs from Lebanon, richly embroidered blankets from Arabia, Libyan tapestries, and swords from Toledo crossed over a coat of arms. In the center of the room, fronting a large, overstuffed sofa, was a large brass table with mahogany legs and a single oriental letter embossed in its center.

"What does that Chink letter mean, Mama?" Matthew asked.

"It means that this table is a piece of crap in Chinese," Mary Anne answered.

"I don't know, Matt," his mother answered. "Your father picked it up when he was overseas one time."

"Ol' Wespac housing," Mary Anne sniffed. "Nothing is

70

so tacky as this junk Marines pick up when they're overseas."

"Some Marines know what to buy. Your father has some difficulty in telling the difference between treasure and garbage."

"No, that's not fair, Mama. Dad is an expert when it comes to garbage."

"Hey, Mama," Ben said, "half this house looks like the Teahouse of the August Moon and the other half looks like A Thousand and One Nights."

"We don't have anything from America," Karen said, as though she were seeing her family's possessions for the first time.

"Dad's taste is so terrible," Mary Anne announced.

"Yes," her mother replied, "but he thinks the things he buys are beautiful and we don't want to hurt his feelings."

"I don't mind hurting his feelings," Mary Anne said. "Besides, we've got enough stuff from China to make me think I've got slanty eyes, Mama. We ought to get something to remind the little children of this family that we are American. A couple of Coke bottles or something. Maybe a box of Hershey bars."

"I've told kids that I spoke Chinese before I spoke English and they believed me after I showed them the house," Ben said.

"Did they ask you to prove it?" Lillian asked while cutting some masking tape from a box.

"Sure," he answered. "I just recited a few prayers at the foot of the altar. Introibo and Altare Dei. Poor ol' Protestants don't know any better."

"Ben, do you remember that time I told Jamie Polk you only spoke Latin and that was the only language Catholic boys were allowed to speak. Every time he would ask Ben a question, Ben would hit him with a line from the Confiteor."

"Shame on you both. It's not something I would be proud of."

They emptied the boxes with the expertness of four straight years' experience. Everything had a place, Mrs. Meecham kept reminding her children, everything belonged somewhere. Linens were placed on closet shelves.

71

China was dusted and neatly stacked in a glass-fronted cabinet; the silverware was filed away in the kitchen drawers nearest the sink. The kitchen began to rattle with implements. Matt and Karen hung pots and pans on nails in the pantry. Slowly the boxes downstairs began to empty and Ben piled them in the backyard where they lay like the discarded shells of reptiles.

Order was drawn from chaos by cunningly applied laws tested on previous moving days. Some boxes were stacked in closets, others were hidden in the attic. The downstairs began to shape up at about the same time that Lillian sensed her children could take no more.

Lillian walked to a box in the front hall stenciled "shrine." Always, in every move, she unpacked this box. She did not allow her children to touch it. In the box, carefully wrapped, was a crucifix, a slender graceful icon of the Virgin Mary, a smaller statue of Michael the Archangel standing astride a fallen angel whose face was swollen with fear, two small candlesticks, a box of milk white candles, a small font for holy water, and rosary beads her husband had given her when she converted to Catholicism. Finally, she removed a plastic model of an F–8 Crusader, paused to fix a misplaced decal with a small application of spit, then set it down in a window ledge.

She had chosen the location of her shrine the moment she entered the door of her new home. It was in the vestibule underneath the stairway, to the left of the front door. She set up a card table which she covered with a filigree lace tablecloth from Florence. The crucifix she hung from the wall, fascinated, as she always was, by the realism of the tiny nails lodged in the crockery feet of Jesus. Next, she twisted the candles into the small brass holders, filled the font with stale holy water, put a small oriental rug in front of the altar, and positioned Michael strategically to the far left. Finally, she placed Mary directly below her crucified son. At her feet, she placed the airplane Bull Meecham flew.

Behind her, the children gathered, watching each ritualistic step in the installation of the shrine.

Mary Anne whispered to Ben, "Oh, Jesus. Here we

have the Lady of the Fighter Pilot again. Why don't you tell Mom that it's a bit much?"

"Why don't you tell her, big balls?" Ben whispered back.

Before Mary Anne could answer, Lillian motioned for her children to come to the vestibule. "Let's say a prayer, thanking the Blessed Mother for a safe trip."

The children knelt while Lillian lit the candles. Then she began to pray aloud and Ben, her son, had an image of her prayers floating light as pollen into the ear of God.

6

OLEANDER BUSHES FLANKED the road leading up to the main gate of the Ravenel Marine Air Station. Colonel Meecham watched as an F-8 lifted off an unseen airway, cleared the treeline, thundered eastward, accelerating and rising in a clean parabola. As Bull's eyes followed the plane, he had an old feeling come over him and he knew he wanted to climb into a jet very soon. He heard the afterburner of the jet kick off, the plane bank to the right and fade like a sliver of light into a blue sky. The feeling was a thirst, a thirst borne of time, of memory, of blood; an almost diabetic thirst that afflicted him whenever he passed a long period of time without flying. He had not flown in the month he had been home and he felt this abstinence in his mouth and bones.

Pulling up to the gate, Bull studied the young PFC who stared at the unfamiliar bumper sticker on the front of the car. The dust from the trip and the dried butterfly parts made it difficult to decipher. Finally, the guard looked into the car and spied the silver leaves on Bull's collar. Gracelessly, the PFC pumped a salute. Instead of returning the salute, Bull stopped the car completely and stared with visible truculence at the guard who held his salute as rigidly as some umpires who call strikes on batters with exaggerated formality. Bull spoke to the boy in a frozen, humorless voice.

"You call that a salute, mister?"

"Yes, sir."

"I call that an abortion. I call that a disgrace. I call that an insult to a Marine Corps officer. I call that a court-martial offense. Now straighten that arm, get that elbow up, and don't bend your neck to the right. You salute like you have no pride, son. Now salute me again. Make it snap. That's it. Old Marines should have arthritic elbows from snapping salutes. Good. That's outstanding. Now if I ever see you give me one of those spaghetti salutes again I'm going to have your arm amputated up to the shoulder. Carry on, Marine, and tell your buddies at the barracks that Colonel Bull Meecham has just reported in and that he will be making his presence known soon."

"Yes, sir."

Bull drove straight to the Operations Building. Like all bases where he had worked the buildings he was passing were bleached-out structures of white and gray as though the architect had applied special leeches in the heart of each foundation to bleed off color should it ever appear. The architecture had a spareness and an economy of line that were pragmatic to the point of absurdity.

He drove into the parking lot of the Operations Building. Two Marines saluted him as they left the building. Bull returned the salute and grunted "good morning."

Bull walked down the long polished hall with a bouncing gait that was distinctively unmilitary. Old friends could pick him out of a dismissed battalion, so singular was his walk, so indelibly a part of him, and he could change it no more than he could change his blood type.

He opened the door of the operations officer and entered a sparsely furnished anteroom where a hairless sergeant with a mechanical bearing so stiff that he seemed to be composed of metal parts looked up from the typewriter and said, "May I help you sir?"

"Where is Colonel Hedgepath, Sergeant? Colonel Meecham is here to see him."

"He's indisposed at this moment, sir."

"Oh, he's indisposed," Bull mocked. "I surely would hate to bother anyone who was indisposed." Then, his voice changing, he said, "I asked you where he was, Sergeant, I didn't ask for you to practice your mastery of the English language."

"He's in the latrine down the hall, sir."

"Is he taking a shit?"

"The sergeant doesn't know, sir."

"Did he take a magazine with him?"

"Sir?"

"Did he take a magazine with him when he went to the latrine?"

"The sergeant believes he did, sir."

"Then he must be taking a shit. I think I'll go make sure he wipes himself good. Does the sergeant know," Bull said bending down conspiratorially, "that Colonel Hedgepath never wipes himself after he takes a shit? He says that animals don't have toilet paper and he personally thinks it's unnatural. What is your opinion of that, Sergeant?"

"The sergeant has no opinion, sir."

"You don't believe in toilet paper either?"

"The sergeant does, sir. The sergeant certainly does."

"Then that's an opinion, Sergeant. You are taking a stand for toilet paper. You are on the side of clean assholes and I, for one, commend you on your vigorous defense of good hygiene. Now I think I'll mosey on down to check on Colonel Hedgepath."

There were two stalls in the latrine. A pair of cordovan shoes gleamed in the stall nearest the door. Bull entered the one next to the wall. He sat on the toilet without taking down his pants although he made noises like undoing his belt and unfastening his zipper. He wanted the sound effects to be natural so the colonel in the next stall would suspect nothing. He bent down and looked at the shoes underneath the partition. Bull thought to himself that Virgil Hedgepath was one of the best groomed officers in the Marine Corps even when his pants were down below his knees. The shoes were impeccably shined; the pants had a fresh crease.

Finally, the man wiped himself, flushed the toilet, and stood up. Before he could pull his pants up, Bull reached under the partition and tackled the man by grabbing his pants and jerking them into his stall. Bull heard the man scream and a splash as the man's arm sank into the toilet as he crashed down. Bull, taking advantage of the surprise, yanked the man by the ankles and pulled him into his booth, holding him upside down by the feet. Then with considerable effort, Bull climbed atop the toilet, battling the flailing arms and legs of the desperate, upended officer, and was about to dip the colonel head-first into the toilet when profanity filled the latrine and for the first time Bull realized that the man he held suspended so inelegantly was not Virgil Hedgepath. Skinny arms struck inconsequential blows at Bull's legs. On one of the arms below him, Bull glimpsed the bent wings of a corporal's chevrons.

Bull opened the door to the stall, dragged the corporal out, laid him gently on the men's room floor, then crossed his arms as the corporal pulled up his pants. The corporal clenched his fists and was ready to swing at Bull's face when he noticed for the first time that his attacker held the rank of lieutenant colonel. A moment of indecision passed while the two men stared at each other. Bull finally spoke: "Corporal," he said seriously, "do you love the Marine Corps?"

"What?" the corporal half screamed, breath and spit.

"Corporal," Bull roared at the top of his voice, "Corporal, if you ever address me again without using the word 'sir,' I'll make your life in the Corps a fucking nightmare. Now pop to attention when I talk to you, mister.

"That's better," Bull smiled as the man before him drew rigid. "Now, Corporal, you are probably wondering why I attacked you like that. Am I correct?"

"Yes, sir," the man answered.

"Think about it, Corporal. It should be clear to you."

"I don't know, sir."

"What's your name, son?"

"Atchley, sir."

"The attack was prompted by threefold considerations. First, I wanted to test your readiness in the face of a surprise attack. Do you realize, Corporal, that several Marines were killed by the Japanese while they were taking shits at Pearl Harbor? Now that is not exactly a noble way to die, is it, Atchley? A fighting man can never relax. He must be vigilant to attack no matter where he is. Our nation's survival is dependent on the readiness of Marines all over the world. Where are you from, Atchley?"

"Green Bay, Wisconsin."

"Are you a Packer fan, Atchley?"

77

"Yes, sir."

"I hate the Packers, Atchley. And I hate Packer fans. That's the second reason I attacked you. Nothing I hate worse than taking a shit next to a Packer fan. Now for the third reason, Atchley, and here we come to the crux of the matter. You stink up a latrine worse than anybody it's been my pleasure to sit next to. You also, and I know I'm getting a bit personal, Atchley, but I'm trying to make you a better Marine, you also only wiped your ass twice. I suggest that two times is insufficient. Do you realize the number of germs and the kind of germs that can breed in a human asshole, Atchley?"

"No, sir," the corporal answered.

"Right now, this very moment, Atchley, germs with names you can't even pronounce are preparing to launch a devastating attack against your asshole that will render you helpless as a Marine and useless in the defense of your country. I'm gonna let it go this time, Atchley, but if I ever find you neglecting that portion of your anatomy again I'm gonna have you up before a disciplinary board so fast it will make your eyes swim. Now get out of here, Atchley, and if you ever attack a senior officer again I'm gonna jack it up that filthy ass of yours."

"But, sir, you attacked me."

Bull shook his head in patient exasperation. "That's why you're not going to make it, Atchley. You've obviously peaked out as a corporal. Countermanding a statement by a superior officer. Now I want you to forget what happened in here today. Do you read me?"

"Yes, sir."

"Good man, Atchley. I also want you to remember my name. It's Jones, Colonel John J. Jones. I'm only at Ravenel for the day. I fly around the country testing the readiness of troops for combat and what just happened here is part of my duties. I want to impress upon you, Corporal, that this was strictly a confidential test of combat readiness classified Top Secret. Tell no one, Atchley, because I may be trying this test on your direct superior. Now, you are dismissed, Corporal, and good luck in your career. Be proud, Atchley, proud of yourself and proud of the Corps."

When Atchley retreated from the latrine, Bull straightened his uniform, winked at the mirror, and spoke again to his reflection, "You silver-tongued bastard. Shame on you." Then he walked swiftly back to Colonel Hedgepath's office. The sergeant was typing a report with two thumblike fingers.

"For your information, Sarge, Colonel Hedgepath is not in the latrine."

"He's in his office now, sir. If you'll have a seat I'll see if he can receive you."

"Relax, Jocko, I want this to be a surprise visit. We have this affectionate way of saying hello," Bull said putting a finger to his lips. He tiptoed to the door that led to the inner office and leaned against it heavily, listening for sounds of movement in the room. The door opened suddenly, and Bull, caught off balance, stumbled forward into the room. A hand caught him by the neck and a foot tripped him. He fell sprawling onto a thin carpet that did little to cushion his precipitous fall to the floor. Colonel Hedgepath was on Bull's back applying a half-nelson and laughing in victory before Bull was ever aware there was a fight.

Virgil solidified his hold and said coolly, "Repeat after me, Colonel. 'Bull Meecham has menstrual cramps.'"

"Kiss me where the skin turns pink," Bull bellowed.

Virgil applied more pressure and said, "Why is it, Bull, that I'm always about five steps ahead of you?"

"Yeah," Bull retorted, his face pressed against the rug. "What kind of pussy is it that jumps a man from behind? You should have been a Jap, Hedgepath."

"What kind of man is it that pulls a corporal underneath a latrine stall and assaults him with his pants down?" the colonel answered in a voice remarkable for its softness.

"You heard that?"

"I didn't hear a word of it, Colonel John J. Jones."

"You worthless son of a bitch," Bull said, then broke up laughing. The colonel released his grip and rolled over on his back giggling like a schoolboy. Colonel Hedgepath laughed so hard that he loosened his belt and lay spread-eagled on the carpet. He did not see Bull leap at him.

Before Virgil could renew his combativeness, Bull had flipped on his stomach and bent the colonel's leg back to his buttocks where he applied pressure to the colonel's foot. It was Bull's favorite hold in the wrestling matches that breached a twenty-year friendship in the Marine Corps.

"Who's the best goddam fighter pilot in the Marine Corps?" Bull crowed.

"You're holding his foot, you chicken shit bastard."

Bull bent the foot forward toward the spine. "I'm not a harsh man, Virgil," Bull said apologetically, "so I'm gonna give you one more chance to answer that simple question before I stick this big ol' gun boat of yours into your left ear. Now who's the best goddam pilot in the Marine Corps?"

"Colonel John J. Jones," Virgil answered, snickering.

Releasing the colonel's foot from the hold, Bull stood up and waited until Virgil finished massaging his foot and also rose. They faced each other. Then Bull rushed toward Virgil and grabbed him in a violent but amicable bearhug and walked around the office with him. Bull set him down and they pretended to box each other, weaving and feinting with exaggerated aggressiveness, cuffing each other on the head and punching each other on the shoulders.

"Welcome aboard, Bull," Virgil said at last.

"Just tell me one thing, sportsfans. How did you know I was coming out here today?"

"I heard the movers were moving you into that big house in Ravenel today and I knew that Lillian would figure out a way to get you out of the house."

"How's Paige?"

"Fine, she's looking forward to seeing Lillian and the kids."

"Hey, Virge, how do you like flying this large mahogany desk? Do you get much flight time in?"

"I fly the L.M.D. a hell of a lot more than I do an F-8. But I like it, to tell you the truth. I'm a little different from you in that respect. I don't get a hard on every time I get into a cockpit. Hey, you're looking good, Bull. It looks like that Med cruise agreed with you."

80

"A lot of good flying. After going off that carrier for a year, I figure I could land on a match box in case of an emergency."

"I guess I ought to congratulate you on getting a squadron. I know that's a dream come true."

"You said it, sportsfans. Of course you know what's worrying me, Virgil."

"Varney."

"Please be so kind as to inform me what son of a bitch in the Pentagon put me in Varney's group and then tell me why Varney agreed to take me."

Virgil Hedgepath walked around his desk and sat down. With this wordless gesture, Bull thought, Virgil is suddenly a full colonel again.

"Here's the way I understand it, Bull. The squadron's had trouble. It used to be one of the best, as you know, but the past two C.O.'s have let morale slip. The guy there now, Bill Curry, had family problems and it wasn't really his fault but the guy before him, Bear Woods, Jesus, he was bad. You add up all his good qualities and you still come up with absolutely nothing. Now Varney's got a good chance for a star but he's smart enough to know that if he's going to make general, he's going to have to shape up 367. It's that simple."

"He hates my guts, Virgil."

"At least he has *one* saving grace. I thought he was a complete asshole."

"No kidding, Virge. Do you think he'll leave me alone to do my job?"

"Affirmative. He wants you to do good so he'll look good. Varney's no fool and he knows you can handle men. Even though Varney doesn't like you, he's smart enough to know that you're just what the doctor ordered. There are some crackerjack pilots in 367 and they just need leadership."

"Varney and I were in WW Two together and that's when the bad blood began."

"I've heard rumors."

"I need a good fitness report out of Varney. You heard about my getting passed over, Virge."

"Somebody fouled up, Bull. That's all. They obviously

think they made a mistake or they wouldn't be giving you a squadron. Just keep your nose clean and don't go terrorizing corporals in the latrine."

"You're coming up for a star soon, aren't you?"

"Yeah."

"You're a cinch. They love promoting scum bags like you."

"No, that's not true. They rarely promote anyone with my erudition, aristocracy, and style."

"Shit, you and Varney were cut from the same after-birth. You like literature and art while ol' Varney sits on his duff yappin' about wine."

"There's nothing inherently wrong with liking wine, Bull."

"Let me tell you something, Virge. The world is divided up into two parts, beer drinkers and wine sippers. In other words, the world is divided into beer drinkers and assholes. Now I don't mind you putting on a few airs cause we go back a long way and you've always sort of been limpwristed, but that Varney: Do you know that guy is starting to have an English accent and the nearest he was ever stationed to England was Arlington, Virginia."

"Varney's not bad, Bull, and you've got no choice. You have to get along with him. He outranks you."

Bull stood up and began pacing the room and hitting his open palm with his left fist. "That's what I find hard to believe. Here I am one of the best fucking leaders in the Marine Corps. One of the best, Virge, and you know it. You could give me a platoon of Marines and I could make Harlem safe for white people in three days. Give me a squadron and I could turn Havana into a parking lot in a few hours. I'm good and I know I'm good and here I am a goddam light colonel while you and Varney are bird colonels. Now I'm not saying you shouldn't be a bird, Virge, but you know what I'm saying."

"I think you've had trouble in the Corps, Bull, because you are just too modest about your abilities. You lack self-confidence and motivation. If you weren't such a quiet, timid guy, Bull, I think you would do well when the promotion boards meet."

Virgil Hedgepath threw his head back and laughed. He

was thinking that he and Bull Meecham were as different as two men could be, yet there was no one in the Corps that Virgil Hedgepath loved more. The love was based on solid ground, for Virgil believed that it was a very easy thing to love a man who had saved your life. They also had complementary personalities. Bull ruled the men under his command by his physical size and the power of his voice. Bull never understood how Virgil accomplished the same results; he could not fathom the mystery that Virgil speaking quietly but firmly could inspire a quality of fear that men who yelled could never approach. Beneath Virgil's placid surface was a terrible ice. With Bull, volume was the thing, but Virgil could achieve the same results by letting the interior ice harden his eyes or freeze the edges of his voice. Bull, pacing in front of Virgil's desk, brought a restlessness and a fever to command, a yeoman's rigidity, and a genius for inspiration, whereas Virgil had the natural instincts of a general. When both were second lieutenants, Bull had the makings of a good drill instructor while Virgil had the stuff to command many divisions of Marines. As he watched his best friend pace, Virgil thought to himself that Bull still was the best D.I. he had ever met.

"You're right about one thing, Virge. I've got to get Varney on my side. I've got to kiss his ass a little bit or whatever it takes because I need a good fitness report out of him."

"You're both professionals, Bull. Remember that. The only advice I'll give you is to play it low-keyed around Varney. You have one problem with him as I see it from here. Have you ever read Saint Crispin's Day speech by Shakespeare, Bull? It's in *Henry V*."

"Oh, yes, indeed. Of course, Virgil. I think I read that the other night after I had finished translating Homer from the original Greek. Shit, no, I ain't ever read Willie except for one J. Caesar when I was a sophomore in high school."

"Well, you ought to look at that speech. Ask Mary Anne or Ben. I read it to them one time. One of your problems, Bull, is that your whole life is one long Crispin's Day speech. You never let up. There're never any peaks and valleys for you. Only peaks, and they're always Himalayan or Alpine. Varney is a measured man. That does not mean he is a bad Marine. He's thorough, cautious, and extremely capable. Granted, he is also full of shit. But you are going to have to find a way to fit into his style of command. He's like the president of a civilian corporation, not the old type Marine aviator who would drink all night, puke all morning, and fly all afternoon. You'll have to adapt."

"You're right, Virge. Maybe I'll even start drinking a little vino. I'll drop by the liquor store and take him a little Manischewitz as a bribe. You know, start out on the right foot."

"That's not a bribe, Bull. That's cruel and unusual punishment. No, don't take any wine."

"You think I should just drop below the desk and give him a real low-keyed blow job?" Bull grinned.

"Goddam," Virgil said quietly. "Changing you, Bull, is not even in the sphere of possibility. Let's get together for a drink after you see Varney. How about the "O" Club at 1700?"

"It's good to see you, Virge."

"Welcome aboard, Bull."

Bull Meecham strode into Colonel Varney's office, snapped to attention when he stood directly in front of the colonel's desk, clicked his heels cleanly, and waited for Joe Varney to welcome him into his air group. Instead of looking up, Varney perused some papers on his desk as though some imminent life or death decision was upon him and he could not spare a single moment's intrusion on his time. Bull stood at attention a full thirty seconds before Colonel Varney even looked up. When he did, he grunted at Bull that he would be with him in a moment. Another sixty seconds passed, and Varney still studied the papers with unhurried concentration. "The little pimp," Colonel Meecham thought. "You'd think he was getting ready to sign the fucking Declaration of Independence."

"What are you thinking, Colonel?" Varney asked suddenly, looking up at the man who stood before him.

Varney had narrow, undemonstrative eyes, gray eyes, as though they were issued by the Marine Corps.

"Nothing, sir," Bull answered.

"Yes, you are, Wilbur," Varney said using a given name known by very few Marines. "You are thinking, 'Why doesn't that little son of a bitch quit reading those goddam papers and welcome me aboard this base?' Isn't that what you were thinking?"

"Yes, sir," Colonel Meecham answered, "that's exactly what I was thinking, sir."

"Don't get smart with me, Wilbur. You can't afford to. Have a seat. I want to have a long talk with you."

As Bull sat down, he spotted a picture on the wall behind Varney's desk of a squadron lined up in two rows in front of a Corsair. In the back row, he and Joe Varney stood beside each other, their arms draped around each other's shoulders. In the photograph, they both wore sunglasses and neither of them smiled. Fighter pilots rarely smiled in group pictures.

"Wilbur," Varney said, emphasizing the name that Bull despised being called, "you and I entered the Marine Corps at about the same time. We have been stationed together on two previous occasions and we have had bad blood between us on two previous occasions. Is that not correct?"

"Affirmative, sir," Bull agreed, aware of a stickiness under his arms and behind his knees.

"We have had professional and personal difficulties that have made it almost impossible for us to meet and talk civilly under any circumstances. Therefore, we are faced with a grave problem. Since you are about to assume command of a squadron under my jurisdiction and since I am determined to be the finest group commander in the Marine Corps, it is essential that we forget the past and carry on as though there were nothing between us. Do you agree, Wilbur?"

"Yes, sir."

"Well, it's very hard for me to forget some things. I personally find you a bit nauseating. So I want to tell you why I agreed to let you take over the command of 367. There are other pilots that I think can do a far superior job, but none of them were available. So I agreed to take you because you were the best of the dregs. You are being assigned to this particular squadron because the present commander of the squadron is a poor leader, a mediocre pilot, an inept administrator, an alcoholic, and a disgrace to the Marine Corps. I say this confidentially, of course, Wilbur. Now in your case, you are very close to being an alcoholic, you are a disgrace to the Marine Corps, but you are a fair leader and a crackerjack pilot. I've always admired the way you handled an airplane."

"Thank you, sir."

"I didn't ask for your thanks, Wilbur. You just sit there and listen," Colonel Varney snapped. "Things are beginning to happen in this world that make it necessary, Wilbur, for you to shape this squadron up pronto. Cuba is hot, very hot as you know, and if something happens there we will be right in the middle of it. So I want you to shape this squadron up, Colonel. I want you to walk into that squadron and give those pilots one of your Cro Magnon, Guadalcanal pep talks that is the Pablum of young minds. You have inherited a serious morale problem, Wilbur, and even though I need you to improve that squadron, I'm hoping you can't do it. I'm going to be watching over you night and day praying that you make a mistake so I can have your ass in the palm of my hand and end your career with a poor fitness report."

Here, Colonel Varney pushed himself away from his desk and eyeballed Bull Meecham, who stared at him with cold blue eyes that registered nothing. He studied the silver leaves that shone dully on Bull's hard shoulders. Joe Varney saw clearly that the body before him proclaimed an easy confidence and that Bull still retained the violent frame of his youth. Bull was thicker around the waist and buttocks but it seemed to have increased his formidability instead of diminished it. But Varney also perceived something else: the silver eagles on his collar rendered all the muscles of all the light colonels in the Marine Corps impotent.

As Colonel Varney studied him contemptuously, Bull caught secret glimpses of the man he would serve under for the next year. "He hasn't changed much," Bull thought. "The same bantam rooster. The same adder eyes." Yet he had to admit that Joe Varney was an impressive looking Marine. His short, powerful body took to a uniform well. Varney used his head and nose when he spoke, slashing the air with his sharp aquiline face as though it were an ax chopping at some invisible woodpile just below his eyes.

But it was not his appearance that grated against Bull Meecham's sensibilities, rather it was his aristocratic posturing: the clipped, slightly British pronunciation of words, the carefully manicured nails, the bloodless smile, the natural condescension, the refined air of the aristocrat. To Bull, it was as if Varney were an exiled prince slumming it among the foot soldiers of the world. "Varney is a goddam snob and he always will be," Bull thought. They would work together under siege, enemies bound by treaties, and a professional ethic.

"Another thing, Wilbur, and I know I don't have to say this, but I really want to. Lieutenant colonels do not hit colonels without being court-martialed. Nor do light colonels frown at colonels or talk back to colonels or even think bad thoughts about colonels. To put this parlance directly on your level, light colonels ain't shit. Especially when they've been passed over once by the promotion board." Varney said this smiling, but he was driving in nails now, attacking deep and hard, sensing that the man in front of him could not even blink an eye in rebuttal. "But lieutenants sometimes hit other lieutenants. Is that affirmative, Wilbur?" Varney asked.

Colonel Meecham did not answer.

"I asked you a question, Wilbur. Lieutenants sometimes hit other lieutenants. Isn't that right? Answer me. That's an order."

"Yes, sir. Will that be all, sir?"

"No, that's not all. I don't want anyone on this base to hear about our previous run-ins, Wilbur. That's between you and me. I don't ever want to hear any rumors about it or so help me God, I'll run you straight out of the Corps." He paused, then looked closely at the hands of the man who sat before him, and said, "Clean

87

your fingernails, Colonel. They look like they belong to an enlisted man. That's all."

Colonel Meecham rose and turned to leave. Varney halted him before he reached the door. "Incidentally, Wilbur," he grinned, "welcome aboard."

It was the angle of the light or something in the way the face spread out with the smile, but Bull caught a glimpse of a crooked nose. He had forgotten that the nose was awry because he had once broken it.

7

A JET PASSED OVER the river near the Meecham house, its thunder shivering every pane of glass. Bull awoke and tried to identify the plane by listening to its pitch. The plane sang in a deep tenor and Bull decided that it was an F-8 in the morning sky, though he was not certain. He turned his wrist to the sun coming through the blue curtains into his room. It was seven o'clock. He would give his family fifteen more minutes of sack time, he thought, before he would wake them up. There was still a lot of policing up to be done around the yard and house. It would be a good day for the work detail. He reached into his night table drawer and pulled a fresh cigar from it. He lit the cigar and blew a long pennant of smoke to the ceiling. It hit the ceiling, broke up, and fell disembodied back into the room.

Lillian stirred in a half sleep, caught the smell of cigar smoke, and smiled.

The smoke filled the room, commingling with the warm scent of the river that spilled into the marsh seventy yards from their window.

Colonel Meecham appreciated the eminence of ritual in relationship to the morale of troops in peace and war. He also understood its essential importance in giving his family a feeling of place and belonging in a new town. A family without ritual and order was a rootless tribe subject to boredom and anarchy, lowered heads, pouting mouths, and sorrowing memories of friends left behind. At the center of the dilemma, it was a family whose leader had failed to provide the requisite guidance. He did not tolerate sadness or regret over a move in any member of his family, just as he did not tolerate poor morale among Marines in his squadron.

He shaved and showered quickly, then put on his most faded and beloved fatigues, pulled his swagger stick from a top drawer, laced up his combat boots, and strode toward Ben's room.

"Ta-*ta*-ta-ta-ta-, ta-*ta*-ta-ta-ta-," he played on an imaginary bugle. "It's time to get up, it's time to get up. It's time to get up in the morning. Rise and shine, soldier. Hit the deck with your boots on and head for the goddam trenches. The Japs are overrunnin' the camp."

"What?" Ben said, coming out of a heavy sleep. Then he remembered the game and rolled off his bed fingering a machine gun. By this time his father had stolen into Matt's room, crawling on all fours. He shouted at Matt, "We got to get these soldiers moving before the Jap artillery finds out where we're camped." He snatched the pillow from beneath Matt's head and rolled him to the floor. Matt was sleeping in the nude.

"The little homo's sleeping naked," Bull roared. "Get your skivvies on and hit the battle stations on the double."

Bull sprinted for the girls' room where he shook Karen and Mary Anne, yelling, "The women will be raped by the slimy yellow bastards if they don't man the trenches; follow me to the ridge in the living room," he cried, plunging out the door and down the stairs in melodramatically elephantine steps.

"I've always wanted to be raped by a slimy yellow bastard," Mary Anne called after him. "I wouldn't mind a slimy yellow bastard or a slimy black bastard either." She turned over to go back to sleep.

"You'd better come on," Karen said.

"I never cared for his childish games," Mary Anne replied.

Karen followed her father out the door and down the steps. She met Matt coming out of his room, holding a broom on his shoulder.

"What's that, Matt?" she asked.

"A bazooka," he answered.

In the living room, Colonel Meecham had overturned

the coffee table, his eyes scanning the dining room for troop movement.

"Do you see anything, Sergeant?" the colonel cried to his son, Ben, dug in behind the flowered sofa where Okra slept.

"Yes, sir," Ben yelled, sighting Matt and Karen tiptoeing down the stairs, "here come three hundred crack troops from the emperor's own regiment."

"Don't fire," his father ordered, "until you see the yellow of their skins and the slant of their Buddha lovin' eyes."

The Marines fired in delirium, cutting down the first advancing wave of Japanese infantry. Death cries of Bonzai, Kamikaze, and Minolta hovered over the battlefield and the carnage of battle stained the beachhead a terrible crimson as the two Marines, employing the courage and wisdom of the Occident, prevailed in the first deadly moments of the assault.

"Kill those yellow son's a bitches, Sergeant," the colonel screamed above the din of battle.

"These ain't Mother's Day cards I'm sending 'em," Ben replied toughly while sliding a clip into his automatic.

"Goddammit, Sarge, here they come again. Hundreds of them."

"It looks like curtains for us, Colonel."

"Sarge, I just want to say I've never fought with a braver man."

"Thank you, sir," Ben answered. "And I ain't ever fought with a bigger chicken shit in my whole life."

Before Bull could answer, Matt and Karen charged from the hall. "Here they come," Bull bellowed. "A goddam yellow horde. It looks like it's gonna be that proverbial hand to hand combat. Fix bayonets, Sergeant."

The horde burst into their perimeter. Matt was shouting "Simba Barracuda, Simba Barracuda" as he ran.

Matt lunged at Ben's throat but was disemboweled by a quick thrust of a brass candlestick by Bull Meecham. Karen lingered in the hallway.

"You're dead, Matt-Jap," Colonel Meecham declared.

"No, I'm not," Matt retorted, "you only wounded me. Simba Barracuda. M. Meecham lives." He then lay the

91

broomstick on his shoulder and began pumping bazooka shells into Bull's midriff.

"Wounded, my ass," Bull said. "I cut your goddam yellow guts out."

"I guess the big bazooka isn't doing any damage to your beer gut either. Yeah, sure. That's close."

As the argument raged between the two enemies, Colonel Meecham, ignoring a classic principle of warfare, left his flank exposed to the sprinting figure of Karen who exploded from the hallway bearing a bathroom plunger in her hands. As Bull debated the state of Matt's ability to continue in the holocaust, Karen stabbed the plunger into the dead center of her father's buttocks.

"I killed Daddy. I stuck him in the butt," Karen crowed in triumph.

"You only wounded me," the colonel countered angrily.

"Then you only wounded me," said Matt.

"You are dead, Matt-Jap," the colonel answered. "I am wounded. A good Marine can be brought down only when his heart stops beating."

"My heart's still beating."

Ben was doubled up on the sofa giggling. "Karen stuck the Great Santini in the butt with a plumber's friend." He was easy prey for Karen, who ran him through with no resistance.

"Shut up and fight, Jocko," Colonel Meecham shouted at Ben.

"Simba Barracuda," Matt shouted, thrusting his broomstick at his father.

The battle raged on until Mrs. Meecham descended the stairs on her way to the kitchen.

"It's a regiment of Marines come to relieve us," the colonel cheered.

"America's finest coming in the nick of time," Ben shouted as his father hummed the Marine Corps hymn.

"Why do we always have to play the Japs?" Matt whined.

"Yeah, we never get to play the Marines," Karen added.

"That's because you're a bunch of stinking Japs," Ben said grinning and poking Karen with the candlestick.

"If I'm a Jap then you're a Jap too. Cause you're my brother," Matt said.

"None of you are Japs," Colonel Meecham said, entering the argument. "We're just conducting war games. In war games somebody has to be designated as the enemy. When you get older, you'll get to be Marines. You've just got to prove yourself worthy first."

"Simba Barracuda," Matt said, as a form of agreement.

"What's this 'Simba Barracuda' crap?" the colonel asked.

"Matt picked that up when you were gone, Pops," Ben said. "He thinks it strikes fear into the hearts of men."

"Any time I'm about to fight someone I yell 'Simba Barracuda' real tough like. It works every time."

"You could yell 'Simba Barracuda' at me until your butt fell off and it wouldn't bother me," Bull said.

"Then I'd have to use my other approach. I don't use this one unless it looks like curtains."

"What's that, sportsfans?"

"I say real cool and tough, 'Hey man, you mess with me and you'll have to answer to Angelo Delucci.' "

"Who's he?"

"Nobody, Dad. But people get scared when Big Matt talks about Angelo Delucci."

"I don't get it, Big Matt," Bull said. "What's so scary about an Eye-talian?"

"Eye-talians have been known to do a little rubbin' out, Pops. You haven't been watching 'The Untouchables' overseas."

"What a bunch of horsecrap. Ha. Ha. Angelo Delucci."

"Simba Barracuda."

At this moment, her face a portrait of scorn, Mary Anne walked through the middle of the war game and said, "Is the war over, creeps?"

"Uh-oh," her father teased, "here comes Miss Hang Crepe, morose as ever."

"Who was killed this morning?" she continued, as though she had not heard her father. "The Japs or the Creeps?"

93

"Here she comes, Miss America," Colonel Meecham sang.

"Dad," Mary Anne said, "I'm writing a book about you."

"Good," Colonel Meecham answered, following her toward the kitchen. "You couldn't find a more fascinating subject."

"Here's the first line: 'I was born to the beast on December 12, 1946.'"

"I like it. It captures my unique personality."

"Nothing could capture your personality. The English language is too limited."

"You're right, Mary Anne, I'm an enigma, like a Chink. But a great subject for literature. No doubt about it. You can be my Boswell."

"What a surprise, Dad," Mary Anne said, pulling out a chair by the kitchen table. "How'd you know about Boswell?"

"The ol' Dad knows all kinds of things."

"Why, Bull," said Lillian sweetly, "you keep it so well hidden."

"Bring me the chow," Bull said. Then pounding on his chest he shouted, "It is I, Santini. The Great Santini. Soldier of Fortune. Beast of Ravenel. Minister of Death. And the best damn pilot in the Marine Corps."

"How much sugar does the Beast of Ravenel want in his coffee?"

"No sugar. I don't want nothing to make me sweet."

8

"This is the day," Colonel Meecham announced to his family, the second Saturday in Ravenel. "There's been a lot of pootin' around but very little maximum effort on the part of this outfit. It has become apparent to me that this outfit is operating behind the power curve."

"This is not an outfit, sugah. This is a family."

It was over a week before the change of command ceremony would take place that would give Bull his first fighter squadron. In the interim he was intoxicated with an overabundance of free time and his whole frame trembled and fidgeted with impatience. He had awakened on this morning with a hungering need to bark out orders and have them carried out with speed and efficiency. Since they had moved to Ravenel, Lillian had charted his moods like a cartographer, and her instinct for defusing his temper before it erupted told her this was a day for caution. Early that morning she whispered to her children in a voice accustomed to conspiracy, "Keep busy, keep quiet, and keep out of your father's way."

Bull was incapable of relaxation. He was one of those men whose blood seems to flow too fast, whose brain seems to glow in the dark, whose eyes can never be still, and whose body is in motion even when sitting on a chair or sleeping. Only in his work could he find redemption; only in the Corps was this manic quality channeled into a useful function. He was a man without hobbies except on those occasions when he would challenge his son Ben in some sport. He did not work in the yard, help in the house, wash cars, shine shoes, or anything. His only duty in the household was to issue orders and to marshal the

95

energies of his wife and children to tasks that he would assign with a sense of exigence.

"Listen up, hogs," he said to his children. They placed their forks on their plates, folded their hands in their laps, and listened with eyes that betrayed nothing. The Meecham children had mastered the art of staring at their father with eyes that were dazzlingly bland.

"At promptly 1100 hours, your commanding officer will conduct the first Saturday Morning Inspection of the quarters. You will be at strict attention by your doors as soon as you hear the Marine Corps hymn played on the commandant's lawn. You *will* clean up your rooms. You *will* police up the bathroom. You *will* help your mother in all matters. You *will* salute the colors. You *will* report to me when you are finished. You *will* work cheerfully until your detail is completed to my satisfaction. You *will* report to me any goldbricking on the part of any brother or sister who tries to take advantage of my kind nature and tries to shirk his or her responsibility. Now do you hogs have any questions?" he asked.

They held their blank stares. They asked no questions, their mother's warning still fresh in their ears.

"Would my executive officer like to address the hogs?" Bull said, turning deferentially to Lillian.

Lillian untied her apron and walked over to the table, hit it with her fist, and began to imitate her husband, "I want to tell you hogs a few things. First of all, you *will*. Secondly, you *will*. Thirdly, you *will*. Then after that task is completed you *will*, you *will*, you *will*."

Karen giggled, like a handful of coins tossed in the air. Then everyone laughed, Bull with less relish than the others, but he quickly recovered his lost momentum.

"O.K., now that the exec has sounded off and you hogs have had the big laugh, get upstairs and police up your rooms. Square the barracks away on the double and prepare for Santini's inspection at 1100 hours. After that you will come downstairs and help your mother."

"What are you gonna do, Dad?" Matt asked.

"I'm the head honcho, mister. I don't have to tell you what I'm gonna do."

"I bet you're gonna do nothin'," Matt blurted out, not perceiving the warning signals given off by Lillian.

"No," Bull answered, "that's not quite true. I may do something that might be of some small interest to you, Matt. If you don't get upstairs on the double, I just may stomp your face in."

"I haven't finished my toast," Karen complained.

"Finish it later. The inspection team is due in soon and we *will* shine when the general troops the line."

When the children had faded silently out of the kitchen, Lillian spoke to her husband in a mollifying, supplicating tone. "Bull, you're getting on edge. I can see it coming like I was reading a map. You're getting nervous and fidgety as a treeful of crows about this squadron and I just don't want you to take it out on the kids. You've been good since you've been home and I've been proud of the way you've controlled your temper and your drinking."

"I'm not nervous," he said.

"Sugah, you have the personality of a jack hammer. You can make inanimate objects nervous. Please relax."

"I'm relaxed. I'm relaxed. What do I got to do, write a book?" Bull said, lunging at a piece of bacon.

He ate breakfast as he always did, by the number. A second piece of bacon was mutilated and consumed in two carnivorous gulps. Next he drank a whole cup of coffee before he even looked at his fried eggs. When he finally turned his attention to the eggs, he trimmed the egg white up to the yolk. Then he slid a spoon under the fragile, trembling sac of yolk, and popped one, then the other into his mouth. As was customary, in their nineteen years of marriage, he left the grits on his plate untouched, an unexpressed but articulate declaration, rooted in geography, that the society he married into had not assimilated him. All the totems of Bull's disenchantment with the South could be carved from pillars of congealed grits. Since they had married, it was a point of honor between them that Lillian serve grits and Bull refuse to eat them. What had begun as a joke between them had become a resolute ceremony fraught with competition and

97

even with something deeper, something almost mythological that separated them.

"I'm going to bury you with a box of grits," she had once told him, laughing at the thought.

"Then don't bury me alive," he had answered.

"You're such a Yankee, Bull. Living in the South so many years, and you still haven't been touched by the South. The gentility, the courtliness, none of it."

"I've only heard of one way to fix grits so I like them," Bull told her. "And he was a good southerner."

"How's that?"

"Well, you start boiling grits in a pot. Then you go down by the highway and get some horse turds or as you civilized southerners call them 'road apples.' Well, you take the road apples and dump them into the grits. You boil the combination for fifteen minutes. No more. No less. When you're done, you pour the grits down the drain and eat the road apples."

After he swallowed the egg yolks whole, Bull spread a gluttonous helping of Crosse and Blackwell orange marmalade on two pieces of toast and consumed them with as much noise as relish.

"Darling," Lillian said, "have I ever told you that you eat like a pig?"

Bull looked up at her and answered with orange teeth, "Yeah, you've yapped about that maybe ten thousand times."

"You still chew with your mouth open. If you hope to make general, you'll have to learn the table manners of a gentleman."

"That's one good reason not to make general."

"I'd sure like to be a general's wife."

"Well, it don't look like you'll ever be one."

"Nothing's impossible."

"Me makin' general is."

"Close your mouth," she ordered. "I can become physically ill watching you eat."

Bull pulled back from the table and belched, a low sour note from an old tuba. When Lillian failed to correct him, he screwed up his face again, worked his throat muscles and summoned an even louder burp, this one an octave higher, more musical, more evocative of the meal just completed. He saw her wince. When Lillian winced her whole body was affected. She looked up from washing dishes and saw the river full of small sailboats leaning toward the far shore and knifing toward the bridge which was not in her view. The day was bright, the water green, and the wind full as Lillian saw her whole kitchen window fill up with the September regatta, as though she were watching a painting that changed as she watched it.

"The sailboats are so beautiful. It looks like the river is full of white butterflies, Bull. They're having a race."

Bull walked to the window and looked.

"You mean those boats are racing?" he asked.

"Yes, of course they're racing. I used to sail down at Sea Island when I was in high school. Or rather my boy friends used to take me sailing."

"Hey," Bull said, "now there's a sport you can get enthused about. Sailboat racing. Man, look at 'em go. My blood is boiling with excitement. I'm a veritable bundle of nerves awaiting the outcome of this race."

"You're such a peasant," Lillian said, going back to her dishes.

"Yeah! yeah! yeah!" Bull said, walking toward the living room with the morning paper. "Finish the dishes."

Whenever Bull left a room it was a natural reflex for him to leave an order behind him. It was efficacious for an officer to keep the troops busy, he thought, and when he exited a place, he left a trail of assignments in his wake no matter where he was. He sat in his favorite chair and began to read the Charleston *News and Courier*. Already, he had heard the locals refer to it as the Newsless Courier, and he had immediately adapted the bastardized version as his own. Each day, Bull poured torrents of contumely on his morning paper. Lillian could hear him in the kitchen. The children could hear him upstairs.

"Hey, newspaper, give me the scores, would ya? Oh, here they are in the goddam women's section. C'mon, White Sox, get me some hits. Die, Landis, die, so the Sox can buy a decent center fielder. Hey, Mantle makes every catch look easy while Mays makes a routine pop fly look like his Vic Wertz catch in the Series. Ted, hit another one. Attaboy, Thumper, tell 'em you flew with Bull Meecham, too. Killebrew's picking his nose again. He's got two knuckles stuck up his nostrils looking for a lamb's tail."

After he finished the sports section, having checked the progress of the White Sox, memorized the rankings of the teams in the majors and the statistical leaders in the race for the three most important batting titles, he turned with reluctance and ire to the front page. He could not control the news, and the front page was a source of continuous aggravation to a man who wanted life to be cut into symmetrical quadrants and accessible frontiers. With a bellicose finger, he jabbed at a picture of Fidel Castro. "You bearded fag. I'd like to fly an F–8 to Havana, chase you down main street, and blow smoke rings up your ass. Oh, and McNamara. Cutting fat off the Pentagon budget requests. I can't believe my man, Kennedy, put McNamara in charge of Defense. Russia will attack us with everything she's got and we'll be throwing rocks because McNamara cut the fat. De Gaulle. De Gaulle," he said as if the word caused him physical pain. "Lord, why did you put so many jerks in the world at the same time?"

"Amen," he heard Lillian call from the kitchen.

"Amen," he heard Mary Anne echo upstairs.

"Get to work, Mary Anne," he yelled upstairs.

Bull got up to answer a timid knock at the door. Before him was a blue-haired, aristocratic woman, very small, elegant, and old. On first appearance she looked to be composed of various shades of blue and white. In one thin arm, threaded with veins in a kind of senescent bas-relief, was a basket. In the other was a brown paper bag.

"Good morning, sir," the woman chirped in a voice that reminded Bull of a small, extinct bird. "I live two houses down from you on the Lawn in the old Hall Mansion. I've been unforgivably derelict for not having paid a social call before now, but my doctor thought I was going to die last week."

"That's no excuse," Bull said.

"I know it, and I might perish from sheer embarrassment. But no mind, I brought you a little gift to repair the damage," she said, handing him the paper bag.

Bull peered into the bag unconfidently, paused for a moment, then said, "Ma'am there's nothing I like better than zucchini."

"Sir, I'm delighted to hear it, and on my next social visit, I promise to bring you some. That's okra."

Bull threw his head back, laughed, then invited the woman inside. "C'mon in, and set a spell, honey," he said in an exaggerated southern accent.

"I thought you'd never ask. I'm perishing in this heat. My name is Earline Grantham, sir. Who are you?"

"They call me Bull Meecham, ma'am. I'm a colonel out at the air station."

"I heard you were a military family. Word travels around fast in this neighborhood. So you, Mr. Bull, are a Marine officer."

"A fighter pilot, ma'am. Best one in the Corps. What was your name again, ma'am? I didn't catch it the first time."

"Mrs. Earline Grantham."

"Earline, eh," Bull grinned. "It always tickles me, these names you southerners come up with. Earline, eh. It sounds like something you put in your crankshaft."

Mrs. Grantham had pulled some knitting from her basket and the click of needles, like the rubbing of the smallest of bones, entered the conversation. "Earline was my grandmother's name, sir," the woman answered. "Is Bull a family name?"

"Ha, ha, Earline, buddy, you're O.K. Hey, Lillian," he called to the kitchen, "c'mon out here and meet my new buddy."

"Just a sec, sugah. Let me dry my hands and I'll be right out."

"My grandfather was a military officer, Colonel. A major. He died for the Gray at Antietam."

"No kidding. My great-grandfather might have killed him."

"Then your great-grandfather fought for the Union, I surmise."

"He fought for the winners. I surmise that your grandpa was picked off while fighting for the losers."

"My grandfather died nobly for a cause in which he deeply believed."

"My ol' granddoodle got drafted."

"Where are you from, Colonel?"

"Windy City, U.S.A. The Hog Killer of the World. Shycago, Illinois."

Mrs. Grantham nodded her head, "I find that easy to believe."

"Let me get my wife out here, Early. I married a grit during the war and her great-grandfather got his behind shot off fighting for the losers too. You would have a lot to talk over."

But Lillian was already entering the room, closing the door to the dining room lightly as she came. She swept past her husband and with elaborate gestures that seemed natural on her, she grasped Mrs. Grantham's hand and introduced herself, "Hello, I'm Lillian Meecham. So very happy to meet you."

"You are such a beauty, child. You remind me of myself when I was younger."

"Did you hear that, sugah?" she said turning toward Bull. "Did you ever meet a sweeter thing in your life? But I'm not pretty at all. I just have my mother's strong features and I'm good with makeup."

"Honey, I know women who are artists with makeup and still are ugly as homemade sin."

"You're so sweet to say that."

"My name's Earline Grantham, Lillian. I was telling your husband, here, the strange man with the given name of an animal, that I live in the old Hall Mansion two houses down, the one by Peterkin Landing. I would have come sooner to visit, but I've been feeling under the weather. I brought you this present," she said handing Lillian the bag of okra.

"Well, bless your heart. Okra. There is nothing that the colonel and I love more than okra. Fried, boiled, baked, or raw. We could eat okra and nothing else."

"I thought it was squash," Bull said.

"Honey, isn't it time for you to inspect the children's rooms? Why don't you go on up and Earline and I will chitchat about women's things."

"Sure. Well, Early, it was good meeting you."

"A pleasure to meet you too, sir."

"C'mon back to the old Meecham Mansion any time you want to," he said, ascending the stairs with an ursine heaviness, his footsteps an intentional warning to his children.

In his bedroom, the colonel dressed in his fatigues, laced up his field boots, pulled a pair of clean white gloves out of his top drawer, aligned his belt, then found his swagger stick on his closet shelf. Before he left his room, he turned on the small phonograph wedged beneath his night table and laid the needle down on the only record in sight. "Ten-hup," he bellowed to his children as the first cataclysmic strains of the Marine Corps hymn reverberated through the upstairs rooms. "All troops report to their stations immediately. That is an order. I repeat. All troops report to their stations immediately."

Ben grabbed a pile of clothes and stuffed them under the mattress of his bed, smoothing the mattress with his hand to ensure that no lumps were visible. Then he repaired the envelope corners of the bedspread, pulling it tightly, until it stretched across the bed like a drumskin. He surveyed his room once more, then flung his door open, stood at attention, and awaited the coming of his father. When the choir of two-fisted tenors on the record were "proud to bear the title" Colonel Meecham entered the room slapping the swagger stick in a steady, tautological rhythm that seemed ominous, even predatory.

He analyzed his son's posture with slouch-hating, dust-loathing eyes. When he held inspections, the colonel's business was posture and cleanliness.

"Shoulders back," he barked. "Stomach in. Eyes straight ahead. Don't look at me, boy, unless you're going to ask me for a date. Get your back straight. Head back. Goddam, you've forgotten a lot in a year."

Turning away from Ben, his expression pained, condescending, as if he were performing an odious task among a doomed genus of animal, Colonel Meecham walked over to Ben's desk and rubbed it with a gloved forefinger. Then he examined the glove to see if any dust had soiled it; none had.

Next, he removed a glove and fished a quarter from the pocket of his fatigues. A new, shiny quarter selected from the pile of change on his dresser, the coin was designated to test the tightness of the sheets and blankets, to test how well the troops made up their beds. Ben had never seen his father use a dull coin for this ceremony. Bull flipped the coin above his head and watched it drop on the bed. It made an anemic, soulless bounce.

"You call this bed made, gyrene?"

"Yes, sir," Ben answered.

"You do?" Bull roared.

"No, sir."

"You don't?" Bull roared again.

"I mean yes, sir."

"You mean nothing, hog. The next time I inspect this room, I want that quarter to bounce up and put my eye out."

"Yes, sir."

Bull turned his attention toward the closet, inspecting the arrangement of shoes, the hanging clothes, and the shelves.

"Your coat belongs on the far left, followed by the shirts and pants. Not vice versa," he said as he opened the drawers of Ben's bureau. "Your underwear and socks are just thrown in this drawer. No order here at all, troops," he said flinging the socks and underwear on the floor.

"Let's check your military knowledge," Bull said, walking up to Ben. "Name all the planes I have flown in the Marine Corps."

"I don't think I remember them all, sir."

"I didn't ask you to think. I just asked you a question, sportsfans."

Ben remained at fixed attention, his eyes not moving from a crucifix that hung on the wall opposite him. Then, in an unsteady voice, he began naming aircraft, not thinking of the individual plane, just letting rote memory do its work, these forgotten phantom aircraft wing out of his brain on their own accord.

"You missed two of them, but they were both trainers so it's not that important," Bull said turning away from Ben. Bull examined the crucifix. "Two demerits here. Jesus has got toe cheese." The colonel's laugh boomed through the house. Walking to Ben's desk, Bull pointed at one of the books with his swagger stick.

"Look over here, hog. Is this a skin book?"

"Pardon me, sir," Ben asked, blushing deeply.

"Is this a skin book? Is this a book you read to pound your talleywhacker?"

"No, sir. That's *Anna Karenina*. Mom gave that to me and Mary Anne to read. That's a Russian novel."

"Of course it's Russian. I was just testo-testing you to keep you sharp. Take your eyes off me, mister. Do you want to get in my pants?"

"No, sir."

"Good. Now these novels, to return to the subject, which your mother has you read, are a total waste of time. They're not real. They have no relationship to anything tangible. They don't help you accomplish anything. Do you know, son, strange as it may seem, what is the best book I've ever read?"

"No, sir."

His father paused, and looked around as if he was unwilling to let this priceless shard of information fall into the wrong hands. Finally, he said, *"The Baltimore Catechism*. It has all the answers. It's clean, concise, and it doesn't make your little earthworm hard. These novels you and Mary Anne read all the time are just so much bullshit. You ought to concentrate on the classics like *The Baltimore Catechism."*

His father did a right face, walked briskly to the doorway, and ran his finger along the doorjamb. His finger was black with dirt.

"He's probably going to wipe my behind to make sure there's no dust up my rectum," Ben thought, again wishing he had the guts to think aloud but knowing that an elaborately structured sense of self-preservation controlled whatever demonic persona within him dreamed up these things to say, heavy with both wit and the seeds of fatality.

Colonel Meecham stood before Ben with a look of incredulity spreading across his face, as if this dirt, this soil of the doorjamb, was somehow a sign that all systems had failed, that some fatal flaw lay hidden in the soul of the entire army. Bull held his disbelieving grimace for a full ten seconds, staring at his finger as though a stigma had formed on his dust-violated digit.

"I'm not believing this, hog, I simply am not believing this. Tell me this is not dirt, hog," he said, putting his finger up between Ben's eyes. "Go ahead and tell me it's not dirt."

"It's not dirt, sir," Ben answered.

"Well, what is it, gyrene?"

"It's blood, sir."

"Blood?" his father said, his frame tightening, attuned to disrespect. "You better not be screwin' with me, troops."

"Sir, a Navy pilot was in the room yesterday and I heard him say, 'Colonel Bull Meecham of the United States Marine Corps is the biggest son of a bitch in the armed forces.' "

His father stared at him, his demeanor blinked on and off, between disbelief and outrage. "And what did you say to him, hog?"

"I didn't say anything, sir. I just beat the hell out of him."

"Well, good man. Good man. You pass inspection with flying colors."

After Colonel Meecham had conducted the inspections of the other rooms, Mary Anne walked into Ben's room holding her stomach with melodramatic hyperbole. "You don't mind if I puke all over the room, do you?" she said.

"Look, Mary Anne," Ben answered, "my one goal this year is to survive without him mopping the floor with me. I'll play his little games as long as his fists don't bounce off my head every night. It looks to me like you're going to have to learn the same thing after this morning's exhibition."

106

"He just yelled. He didn't hit. I just happen to think his games are jejune."

"What does 'jejune' mean?" Ben asked.

"Poor dope. Poor jock of a brother. You've been practicing basketball for so long, your brain has atrophied. I'm getting more and more brilliant, while you're getting a better hook shot. When I'm giving my Nobel Prize speech in Stockholm, Benny-Poo, I'll let you stand behind me to throw up a couple of hook shots."

"Just tell me what 'jejune' means."

"You should know. Karen was born at Camp Jejeune."

"Very funny."

"You look it up. I learned it by reading and preparing myself for the production of great literature. So you do the same."

"No, I am going to learn it the easy way," Ben said tackling Mary Anne and pinning her to the bed. "You are going to tell me or I'm going to sit on your head all day."

Ben pinned Mary Anne's arms with his knees and removed her glasses very gently. "Those spectacles have more glass in them than the telescope at Mount Palomar."

"I'm going to spit in your face if you don't let me up."

"Just tell your favorite brother what the word 'jejune' means."

"I'll use it in a sentence, bully. 'Ben, Pimple-face Meecham, often acts jejune when he forces his charming sister to tell him the meaning of words.'"

"That's not good enough, charming sister."

Mary Anne looked toward the open door, smiled at her brother, then yelled, "Hey, Mom, Ben's trying to screw me."

Ben clapped his hand over her mouth and listened for the drumming of avenging feet on the stairs. When he turned back to Mary Anne, she was laughing through his hand.

"Are you trying to get me killed, Mary Anne?"

"Well, it is a little sicko-sexual for you to be sitting on top of me like this. I feel like puking."

"Why, just because I'm sitting on you?"

"No, Ben, I just remembered the words of a great man.

'I didn't say anything, sir, I just beat the hell out of him.' "

"I'm playing the game. You notice that I came out of that one with no broken bones."

"He'll get you. He always gets you," his sister said.

When Bull descended the stairs, Lillian was on the front porch saying good-bye to Earline Grantham. Earline was making a graceful exit and one got the feeling from watching her leave that there would always be grace and symmetry to her departures.

Lillian was talking, "If you can send that girl on Monday I would sure appreciate it, Earline."

"She's wonderful. Hard-working, doesn't drink, and is honest as the day is long."

"And you're sure she'll come?"

"She'll be here. Good-bye, Colonel. The pleasure was mine."

"Ya'll come back, you heah?" Bull mocked, but a glance from Lillian stopped his mimicry cold.

"I've hired a maid," Lillian said. "A squadron commander's wife needs one."

But Bull was not listening. He had walked to the end of the veranda and was staring at the dilapidated garage beside the house. Though the manic edge had lifted since the inspection, still the juggernaut of Saturday moved over him, the nothingness implicit in a day of rest, when his world lay fallow, and he suffered all his demons running within him, sprinters in a bottle. He called to Lillian to come look. "That lazy kid of yours hasn't put the basketball goal up yet. Tell him to get on it before I bat him in the head."

Lillian, who had her strategies and moved from one to another with instinct her only guide, ignored her husband's grievance. She said, "A squadron commander's wife needs a maid."

9

AN HOUR PAST DAWN on the following Monday, a thick, grandly muscled woman arrived on the back steps of the Meecham house and waited for the sleeping house to stir. Though she was barely an inch over five feet tall, her arms were massive with thick, knotted biceps and her forearms were threaded with protruding veins and hard sinew. She had the appearance of a displaced and bespectacled Sumo wrestler. Her flesh was dark in the deep ebony of a lowcountry black. As she waited, she sat perfectly still watching the river. Her expression was tranquil, indecipherable. The lines in her face were in those regions where sorrow had tracked its passage.

The woman was sitting on the back steps when Bull Meecham hurried out the back door. He was on his way to the air station for additional briefings on the squadron he would soon command. Before he reached the first step, he stopped and regarded the dark Buddha blocking his passage. If there was a single group in America that Bull had difficulty with over the simplest forms of address, a group as mysterious to him as children, it was southern blacks. He had nothing at all to say to them so he generally retreated into his self-aggrandized mythology.

"Stand by for a fighter pilot," Bull boomed at the woman.

"What you say, Cap'n?" the woman answered, turning around to look at Colonel Meecham.

"I am the Great Santini," Bull said, beating one fist against his chest and smiling without confidence. He knew he was making a complete ass out of himself but had no idea how to organize a retreat at this juncture of the conversation.

"I never work for no Eye-talian family before."

"Do I look Eye-talian, madame?"

The woman appraised him with deepset charcoal eyes. "I reckon," she said finally.

"Pure Irish, ma'am. Not a trace of anything lower flows through my veins."

"I guess I'm 'bout near pure as you, Cap'n," the woman said, causing Bull to throw his head back and holler with laughter. The woman stood up and faced the colonel.

"Now you are a solid-looking woman, ma'am. And I mean that as a compliment. You look solid all over."

"I can punch hard as a man, at least that what my dead husband used to tell the other boys that work the shrimp boat with him."

"Well, I'd stick with punchin' women, ma'am. You'd be no match for the men I hang around. I'm in the Corps, but I guess you could tell that from my uniform."

"You want to punch my shoulder?" the woman asked.

"Pardon me, ma'am?"

"You want to punch my shoulder? I used to win money when mans try to trade punches with me."

"No, ma'am. I might hurt you and cause internal bleeding or something."

"Shoot, man. Who you talking to about bleeding. You go on now and hit Arrabelle's shoulder first," the woman said, climbing up to the back porch where she and the Marine could be on the same level. Bull saw immediately that he had activated competitive juices within this prodigiously constructed woman. Making a fist, Bull punched lightly against the woman's shoulder.

"Hey, you're solid as a rock," Bull said with true admiration.

"Now, my turn," the woman said, eyes gleaming.

"You want to hit me?" Bull said. "All right, ma'am, but you be careful you don't hurt yourself."

"Move on down a stair," she directed as Bull followed her orders and descended one stair.

The woman spit on her right fist and rubbed it in with her left hand. It was an effort for Bull to keep from bellowing with laughter. With her fist cocked beneath her chin, she backed up against the porch railing, then, hopping like a shot putter, she flew across the porch, left her feet at the precisely strategic moment, and landed a punch on Bull's shoulder bone at the exact juncture where it met his arm. If he had not been holding onto the railing, Bull was positive he would have been airborne at the moment of impact. As it was, his shoulder was paralyzed by a shockwave of pain that traveled the length of his arm. He fought for breath.

"I fought with lots of mans in my life," she said in explanation. "I beat a few of 'em, too."

"You call that punching?" Bull said, regaining his poise under fire. "I thought you were really going to show me something."

"Let me do it again."

"Naw, I'm worried about your hand. If you get hurt then the law's gonna come and say I have to pay all the doctor bills."

"Watch out for internal bleeding, Dad," Ben said, laughing from an upstairs window.

"Get out of here, jocko," Bull roared, then turning to the black woman he said, "You looking for a little money, ma'am?"

"You givin' it away?" the woman asked.

"I'll always help the needy and infirm, ma'am. Here's a dollar. That'll buy a couple of watermelons and keep you going for a couple of days."

"Thank you, Cap'n."

"Well, you can go now. I guess you kind of make a circuit of this neighborhood getting handouts. It looks like pretty good hunting grounds to me. I'd be doin' the same thing if I thought I could make a living at it."

"This is might fine hunting grounds right here on this step," the woman said. "I just made me a dollar bill sittin' and waitin' for Mrs. Meecham to come down and unlatch the door. I be Arrabelle Smalls, your new maid, Cap'n. You be seein' a lot of Arrabelle 'cause she's a hard-workin' so and so and you can ask anybody white or colored and they tell you the same thing."

"Shoot," Bull sneered, "I talked to some folks already and they told me that Arrabelle Smalls was the laziest,

111

most worthless, most good-for-nothing so and so that ever spit between two lips."

"Don't you put no mouth on me, Cap'n. You didn't talk to no one 'cept maybe some crazy man walkin' around with a fool rattlin' around in his head if you hear that about Arrabelle."

"Well, everyone I talked to agreed that you were real nice," Bull said, rubbing his shoulder. "It's just that they seemed to think you were lazy as hell."

"Who puttin' that kind of trash mouth on me?"

"Everybody I've talked to in this town."

Lillian Meecham opened the back door and said, stretching out her hand in greeting, "Good morning. You must be the woman that Mrs. Grantham said she was going to send. I'm Lillian Meecham. And this gentleman who is now teasing you is Lieutenant Colonel Bull Meecham, my husband and captain of this sinking ship."

"I've got to hit the road, sportsfans. Nice meeting you, ma'am. By the way, Earline Grantham told me you spent a few years in jail for stealing silver out of nice houses."

"Miss Earline didn't say nothin' about no stealin'," Arrabelle answered.

"You'll get used to his teasing, Arrabelle. Or else you won't. But it'll be there one way or the other."

"That's a teasin' fool of a man," Arrabelle said, a broad grin breaking across her face. From the smile, Lillian could tell that Arrabelle thoroughly enjoyed her initial encounter with Bull Meecham.

"What's your full name, darling?" Lillian asked.

"I be Arrabelle Smalls. I be married to Moultrie Smalls till he drown when his shrimp boat break up in a storm off St. Catherine's Island three year ago."

"I'm dreadfully sorry about your husband."

"We all got to die of somethin'."

"Sit down while I get us some coffee," Lillian said, gesturing toward the kitchen table.

"I stand," Arrabelle said.

"Please sit down, Arrabelle. We're going to get to be too good of friends for me to be sitting and you to be standing while we're having coffee each morning. Now tell me. Where have you worked before?"

"There ain't much of a place where I ain't done some work in my years. I been shuckin' the oyster for five year but Mr. Peeples done gone and buy himself an Iron Man and put over thirty girls out of work, some of which been with that sorry man for over twenty years. Before that I headed shrimps when Moultrie Smalls's boat comes in. I do some headin' now. You can't even follow my hand I move 'em so fast. For that I works for many famblies as a maid and raise up lots of white children for their mamas. Lord, I raise some white childrens that love me so much. Even right now. Hobie downtown at the restaurant one of my babies. The preacherman at the Baptist Church a baby of mine. So his wife is. When I be younger, I pick the tomato, the cucumber, the bean, the cotton. Anything that need pickin', I pick it. In the Hoover years when I was very young, I do anything to get by. My man, Moultrie, catch the mink, the coon, and the otter those years and sell the hide to any mans what got a nickel to his pocket. That was tough in those coon and possum Hoover years. For white folks, too."

"I can vouch for those white folk in Alabama, Arrabelle. What do you take in your coffee?"

"A lots of cream and sugar up the spoon just a little bit."

"Do you have any children?"

"I got me a fine boy that you can see up on the store street selling flower to the folk that come downtown."

"With the mule? Selling flowers from the back of the wagon?" Lillian asked.

"That the one. That's my son. Toomer, the flower boy. For eighteen years he be right there in that alley makin' a nice livin' from his flower, his herb, and his honey. My whole family ain't never been afraid of no hard work."

"I can tell that by looking at your hands, Arrabelle," Lillian said, glancing down at lined, leathery hands as distinctive as gloves. "And this house is going to be hard work. In fact it's going to be hard work for both of us. This is an old house in need of repair and we aren't going to be repairing anything. We're just going to apply makeup in the right places when the old girl starts to show her spots and wrinkles."

113

"It smell faintish in these old houses," Arrabelle said, working her nose away from the coffee.

"There's a lot of dampness trapped because the sun can't work its way beneath these balconies. Do you cook?"

"Lord, honey, if it moves Arrabelle can cook it. And if it don't move, she can always throw it in the pot with some greens and hamhock."

"Then you're my kind of cook. We might have to send Bull out for T.V. dinners a couple of nights a week but he may even get to like southern cooking before he's toothless, hairless, and being measured for a pine box."

"When the shrimpin' mens bring me the shrimps and the fishes, I'll fix 'em up for you and your fambly. Nothin' so good in the world as mull shrimp with lots of onion and brown gravy."

"When can you start work?"

She lifted her left foot above the chair for Lillian's observation. "These shoes I got on my foots are the workin' shoes. I told my boy Toomer to drive his wagon by at about five."

"Do you live far from here?"

"Not far. I live down in Paradise behind the jail. You know where almost all the colored folk live who not out on the island. My boy just like to come pick his mama up if he can. You can meet my nice boy when he come."

That afternoon Ben set up his mother's dining room and kitchen chairs in a straight line, at intervals of three feet, from the back of the paved driveway to the front. He was dribbling a basketball through the chairs, weaving skillfully through the inanimate defenders, the fantasy of crowd-choked arenas lighting up his mind's eye and his ear filled with the applause of phantom thousands. Perspiring heavily, he looked up when he heard Okra barking at a mule-drawn wagon that pulled around the corner of Eliot Street and was coming toward the Meecham house at an unperturbed pace. Ben had seen the flower boy each time he had ventured downtown on River Street. He had heard the high-pitched stuttering song the flower boy lofted into the fierce August sunlight. But Ben had never studied the features of the black man who was simply a part of the landscape, of no more interest to him than a storefront or a balustrade. Now, with the addition of Arrabelle to the household, the flower boy had a name, Toomer Smalls. As the wagon neared the house, he began to have a face.

He was a short man like his mother, extraordinarily dark with a fine high-cheekbone structure to his face that gave his whole demeanor a darkly brooding nobility. On his left foot he wore a corrective shoe and he walked with a slight limp. He leaned far over on his knees and held the reins lightly as he pulled up beside Ben. His eyes were amused and curious.

"That's just about the ugliest c-c-cat I ever did see, white boy," he said to Ben, pointing a stubby finger at Okra.

"Well, that's just about the ugliest cow pulling that wagon that I ever saw, too," Ben replied.

"This ain't no cow. This h-h-here is Man-O-War, winner of the Ken-tucky Derby."

"It sure looks like a cow to me," Ben said noticing the man had not smiled yet. "But this ain't no cat. This here noble beast is Rin-Tin-Tin, star of stage, screen, and T.V. set."

"I ain't never seen no white boy b-b-bounce no basketball through no sittin' chairs. And I seen me lots of crazy white boys."

"You've never seen a white boy that can dribble half as good as I can. Your name's Toomer, isn't it?" Ben asked.

"That's what my mama called me."

"My name's Ben Meecham, Toomer. I live here at the house. I met your mama this morning and she seems like a real nice lady."

"She sure raise a fine boy," Toomer said, breaking out finally in a huge smile.

Reaching in the back of the wagon, Toomer chose a bunch of wilted flowers wrapped in Spanish moss and said, "Give these flowers to your mama when she gets home."

"Mom usually likes flowers a lot better when they're alive."

"Sassy ol' white boy, ain't you. Just put these things in a little water and they'll come back g-g-g-good as when I pick 'em fresh this morning."

Arrabelle and Lillian walked out of the front door. Lillian was dressed in a white summer dress and sandals. Her fine, tanned skin looked coolly fresh even during the hottest days of summer. The bridge to the islands was opening for a two-masted schooner that was maneuvering down the inland waterway. "I wonder who s-s-stole my boat," Toomer said, winking at Ben.

"Miss Meecham," Arrabelle said, "this here is my boy, Toomer Smalls."

"The pleasure is all mine, Toomer. I've seen you downtown many times and I always planned to stop and chat but something always interfered."

"How you, ma'am," Toomer replied, averting his eyes from Lillian.

"Toomer wanted me to give you these flowers, Mom," Ben said, handing her the wilted bouquet.

"Why, Toomer, you sweet thing. I can't take these. Let me pay you for them."

"No, ma'am. I was gonna toss them over the bridge when I w-w-went home, anyhow. You just put 'em in s-s-some water."

"Well, they are lovely as they can be, Toomer. Bless your heart," Lillian said.

"They almost look real, don't they, Mom," Ben said.

"Hush, Ben, don't be silly. Anyway you need to be getting my good chairs back in the house. What if it starts to rain?"

"Toomer grows most all his flowers right at his own place on the other side of the bridge," Arrabelle said. "It so pretty where those flowers be. But I so shame for anyone to see where Toomer lay his head. That boy won't build himself no decent house to live in. I not even tell you what he live in, it make me feel so bad."

"Toomer, tell me some way I can repay you for the flowers. Let me fix you up an apple pie over the weekend."

"Here, Mrs. M-m-meecham, you go on and take another bunch," he said, reaching back and lifting another moss-wrapped bunch from the back of the wagon.

"Why do you wrap them in Spanish moss?" Ben asked Toomer.

"Hold in the moisture better than any ol' thing," Toomer replied.

"What you doin' this weekend, son?" Arrabelle asked.

"I'm goin' up the river to catch some shrimps and crabs. Might even do a little fishin'."

"You bring me back some nice flounder I can fix up for this fambly. And a couple pound of shrimps," she said, then turning to Ben she said, "You ever been fishin' much, Ben?"

"Not in salt water."

"Toomer," Lillian said, suddenly. "Could Ben go along with you and just watch? It might save my dining room chairs and he doesn't know anybody in town yet. It would get him out of the house. His daddy's a Yankee and never encouraged him to participate in any outdoor sports like hunting and fishing. The men in my family when I was growing up would rather spend their time in the woods than anywhere else. Ben doesn't know what it means to be a southern man."

"You want to go, dribblin' man?" Toomer asked.

"Sure," Ben said, spinning the basketball on his finger, holding the spin for thirty seconds, showing off to the three observers who fixed their eyes on the ball and waited for it to drop or for Ben to lose control.

"You can look at Toomer's ol' nasty boots and know that boy's been way back up in the woods," Arrabelle said.

"I'll show you somethin' come Saturday n-n-night you'll never forget. Saturday the full moon time, ain't that right, Mama?"

"That better be right, son, or the world be done ending fast."

"I saw a fallin' star last night, Mama. It look like it was gonna hit right on top of my head. It scare me so bad."

117

"I feel so hurt up inside when I see one of those thing," Arrabelle lamented.

"Why, Arrabelle?" Lillian asked. "Falling stars are beautiful."

"That ain't no star really, chile. That's tear of Infant Jesus falling on account of a sinful, hateful world."

The black woman climbed up on the wagon and took a seat beside her son.

"You gettin' awful old, Mama," Toomer teased.

Arrabelle answered by balling up her fist and punching him in the shoulder.

"This is the hittin'est woman in this country," her son said, shaking the reins. The mule moved out slowly, the joints of the wagon whining and rattling as it moved across the Meecham lawn and went over a curb to reach the small lane that led to Eliot Street.

"You see that, son?" Lillian said, watching the slow departure of the wagon. "We've been living on bases and in cities for so long that I forgot what the South really is."

"What is it?"

"You're looking right at it," she said, "but as for you, mister, these chairs better be in the house before your father gets home."

On Saturday afternoon Ben rounded the corner of River Street and heard Toomer's voice calling out in a wailing summer canticle to the last shoppers of the day. In a way, Ben thought, Toomer sounded like a priest chanting during a Mass for the dead. "O be the wildflower, O come the wildflower, come the rose, come the sweet daffodil, come the good honey, come the ripe berry, come the wildflower. Come the flower, come the herb and the light of molasses." Ben noticed that while Toomer sang he never once stuttered.

He crossed the street and began to help Toomer load the back of the wagon with the potted herbs, plants, and jars of honey he had not sold. Only two bunches of flowers were left that day. In a cardboard box, a half dozen deviled crabs shifted as Ben placed the box in the wagon. "I didn't know you sold crab, Toomer."

118

"I sell anything these folk want to buy, dribblin' man."

Soon the mule was pulling the wagon down River Street toward the bridge, keeping close to the parked cars on the right so the regular traffic had room to pass. At Granville Street, the mule paused, then turned to the right and started toward the bridge. A boy with bright red hair sat on a Coca-Cola box near the gas pump outside of Fogle's General Store and shouted at Toomer. "Hey, T-t-t-t-toomer. H-h-how you doing? Wh-wh-where you g-g-going?"

Toomer just waved, shook the reins, and urged the mule on faster. Soon they had mounted the causeway and were staring at the flowing bronze river below them.

"Who was that, Toomer?"

"That boy. He ain't nobody. He name Red Pettus and he and his family l-l-live not far from me over on the island. Pettus family like chickens. They h-h-h-hatch out all over this country. Red tease me about my s-s-stutter. That burn me up but R-r-red usually don't bother too much with me. When he was just a little boy, he used to come round and mess with me some. I taught him how to throw a cast net right. Red and his family hate a black m-m-man just for being black and just laugh when I tell 'em that J-j-jesus don't cotton much to hatin' white or black and that the world's a hatin' place and that there are t-t-too many hatin' white man and hatin' colored man runnin' around loose anyhow. B-b-but Red leave me be most of the time. He m-m-mean cause that's all he ever know. He used to come up and feed my dogs when I be up the river fishin' f-f-for a couple of days."

"He still do that sometime?"

"No, man. Y-you don't leave the chicken to watch the feed. He stole some stuff from m-m-me. A shotgun my daddy gave me. I w-w-went down to talk to his daddy but his daddy just run me off."

"Why?"

"He say a n-n-nigger ain't got nothin' his boy would want and he would 'preciate it to the highest if I would h-h-hustle my black ass down the same road I come up which I did as fast as this no-count mule would take me."

Toomer reached back and grabbed both bunches of

119

leftover flowers. He asked Ben to hold the reins for a moment as he stood up and hollered up to the bridge-tender's house. "Yooo, Mr. Harper," Toomer yelled. A thin man in khaki work clothes came out of a diminutive octagonal aerie and leaned over a steel gangplank. Before the wagon passed beneath him, Toomer tossed the flowers up to the man, who caught them in a burst of falling petals.

"How did it go today, Toomer?" Mr. Harper called down.

"Made me a million dollars today. How 'bout you?"

"I bought me the Southern Railroad. See you Monday."

The wagon crossed the bridge and took the first paved road to the right, a road that cut through a thick forest until it emerged into the clearings of vast stretches of tomato fields that appeared even in the wildest, most inaccessible reaches of the island. A mile down this road the mule veered off toward the river, shuffling down a heavily tracked dirt road that ran parallel to a large, plowed-under tomato field. Soon they entered an archway of low-hanging oaks, the bottommost branches consumed by soft stalactites of moss. Both Ben and Toomer had to duck to avoid the moss. When Ben looked up, the wagon was passing between a dozen beehives, six on either side of the road. Then the wagon was surrounded by dogs of every possible size and description. More were baying at them from the woods. Two of the more agile dogs leaped into the back of the wagon and joined Toomer and Ben on the seat, licking their faces until Toomer pushed both of them off.

"How many dogs you got, Toomer?" Ben asked. He saw collies, boxers, terriers, Labradors and combinations thereof.

"Twenty—s-s-s-six last time I checked," Toomer said.

"Where do you get them? Why do you have them?"

"Most of 'em I just pick up off the road. Marines leave 'em behind a lot when they move out from this country. Some of these dogs half dead when I find 'em."

"It must cost a lot of money to feed them."

"You tellin' Toomer somethin' he don't know? That's

120

a fifty-pound bag of food under that blanket back there. These are some eatin' dogs."

"They ever bother the bees in the hives?"

"If they do, it only be for one time," Toomer laughed. "B-b-bees teach 'em fast."

"Where's your house, Toomer?"

"You lookin' right at it," Toomer said.

The house was a discarded school bus stripped of its wheels. Its axles were set on piles of cinder blocks and the formerly yellow vehicle was painted a rather haphazard eggshell white. The logo of the State of South Carolina could be read through the whitewash. To the left were three fenced-in acres of flowers. The air was rich with the combined perfume of the garden and the river which was visible through a clearing fifty yards behind the school bus.

For the next hour, Ben helped Toomer feed the dogs, put the mule to pasture, and unload the wagon. Ben carried a basket into the school bus that was very heavy although he could not see the cargo since it was covered with a layer of Spanish moss. When he set it on the small wooden table near the wood-burning stove in the back of the bus, Toomer discarded the moss through an open window and revealed a bushel of single oysters.

"I traded some honey for Mr. Oyster t-t-today," he said. "You ever eat an oyster?"

"Raw?" Ben asked.

"That's the only way to eat an oyster. I-i-i-if you cook 'em up he becomes something d-d-different from what he really is."

"I don't think I want to try it but you go on and eat as many as you want. I don't mind at all."

"Let me open you up one. M-m-m-man, when you eat an oyster, you taste the ocean and the river and the marsh and shrimp b-b-boats. Man, you bite into a livin' piece of the lowcountry." He inserted a pocket knife into the joint of the shell and twisted his wrist to the right. The shell popped open. The oyster glistened in a translucent liquor that spilled onto Toomer's hand. With a certain dramatic grandiloquence, he slurped the oyster into his mouth. "Now that's fine. That's f-f-fine, white boy. When

I pop me open Mr. Oyster, I think about growin' up and my papa and Captain Bimbo, the first shrimp boat I e-e-ever work on. Let me pop one of these sweet things for y-y-you."

"Why did you quit working on a shrimp boat, Toomer?"

"This g-g-gimp foot. I caught it in the winch and it took a few t-t-toes."

"That must have hurt bad."

"You'da thought so. The way I screamed and such. Here, open wide and let it slide," he said tilting a half shell into Ben's mouth. The oyster hit Ben's mouth. It felt warm, salty, and had the consistency of loose phlegm. For a moment, Ben thought he was going to vomit. Somehow, he got the animal down his throat.

"Wasn't that g-g-good?" Toomer said, opening another one. "You got to keep eating them. One oyster w-w-wouldn't keep a sand flea alive."

This time Ben swallowed faster as though he were ingesting his own saliva. Speed, he thought, was the secret behind the enigma of why men would torture themselves by placing these raw quivering bivalves on their tongues. He couldn't rid his mind of the image that he was eating shelled snot. But after the second oyster, he noticed a pleasant after-taste in his mouth similar to the one he experienced as a child when he was driving home with his family after a day at the beach. There was the tang of salt, of sun, of weakened brine, and grit dissolved in the breakers. Still, he was delighted to see Toomer fold his pocket knife and motion him to come outside the school bus.

"You gotta make friends with the Gray," Toomer said.

"Who's the Gray?"

"Come on out here and you'll see 'im. I got to get you to make friends or the Gray's gonna eat you up when I ain't lookin'. There he is. Get on out here, dog. I see you."

At the edge of the forest, a huge lean dog fixed a cold, green eye on Ben. His lips were curled back over his teeth and Ben thought the dog was probably a combination of Great Dane and German police. But one look at the animal cleared up any doubts Ben might have had about the acknowledged monarch of the pack.

"What's he mad about?"

"He don't like white folk too much."

"That's funny. Okra hates colored people worse than poison."

"Yeh, but that little ol' ugly dog of yours can't do much but a little bit of barkin'. The Gray there would be all over you if you didn't come up that road with me and the mule."

"I bet all the dogs would."

"No. Most of these is g-g-good dogs. All except the Gray. I got s-s-some more that'll jump you if they catch fire. I try to keep 'em stayin' right around here. Folks have shot a few of my d-d-dogs."

Slowly, the gray dog left the woods, walking with its head cocked to one side, sidling toward Toomer with one eye riveted on Ben. The other dogs cleared a path for the entrance of the Gray to the fraternity that surged through the yard. When he reached Toomer, he reared back on his hind legs and lifted his head to be scratched by the black man. But one eye stayed with Ben.

"Here, man, f-f-feed him this biscuit."

Ben held out the biscuit, but he did not offer the gift audaciously. The biscuit was held between his index finger and his thumb, and Ben's entire weight was shifted to his back foot in case the dog was more inclined to sup on his forearm than on a piece of bread.

"You're a-a-afraid of the little dog."

"Damn right I am."

The dog, detaching its forepaws from Toomer's shoulders, moved toward Ben, menacing, suspicious. With strange delicacy, the dog removed the biscuit without touching Ben's flesh.

"You ack like you feedin' an a-a-alligator, boy," Toomer laughed.

"This is the meanest looking dog I ever seen."

"Naw, what you talkin' about, m-m-man?" Toomer said, the dog licking his face. "He's not mean. He's just prejudiced."

Behind him, beneath the giant oaks arched over water,

123

the sun had dipped below the western line and Ben saw over Toomer's shoulder a deep and chilling gold cutting across the river and lighting in small pools of water across the marsh. A blue heron panned for small fish and a sail blazed against the shimmering green of the marsh. Toomer's dogs swirled around them, nipping at each other, and keeping their distance from the Gray.

That night, Toomer put Ben in the front of a wooden bateau and steered him through small creeks, a river, and a vast sound before landing on the backside of one of the most remote barrier islands. With a Coleman lantern to lead him, Toomer secured the boat and then plunged through the woods until he came to a row of dunes covered with sea oats. The crash of breakers against sand and the distance of the journey alerted Ben while he was trailing Toomer through the forest that whatever surprise Toomer was planning had a strong relationship to the Atlantic Ocean.

No matter what ploy Ben tried, Toomer would not explain their presence on this wild and seething stretch of beach. But Toomer's eyes never wavered from the waves. The full moon hung low, a fresh coin that threw its silver grandly on the water in a ribbon that dazzled for a thousand miles.

Finally, at eleven o'clock Toomer pointed toward the breakers. Ben looked and saw nothing. Then his eye focused on the enormous shape of a sea turtle struggling out of the sea and ponderously making its way up the sand. Holding Ben's arm, Toomer put his fingers to his lips for silence. They watched as the turtle selected her spot and positioned herself for the night's excavation. With her back flippers, she began digging the hole that would become the womb of her offspring. It was not until she began laying her eggs into the hole that Toomer rose, and with his strangely graceful limp, made his way down to the turtle.

"This is the biggest thing I've ever seen, Toomer," Ben screamed. "Why didn't we come right down?"

" 'Cause mama would-a gone back h-h-home," Toomer answered, stooping down behind the turtle and catching four of the eggs as they dropped into the hole. "We'll keep these four to eat and let mama have the r-rest. Don't get near mama's m-m-mouth, Ben. She can do an arm some powerful hurt."

"She's crying."

"You ever see a w-w-woman have a baby? It hurt."

"I'd like to see my father run over this turtle with his car. This hunk would blow him right off the road."

"This mama don't go on no trips 'cept this one right here. She b-b-born right here on this beach and like it so well she come back and have her kids."

Unpacking his knapsack, Toomer soon started a fire on the beach. He made coffee, grits, bacon, and fried the turtle eggs as he and the white boy watched the turtle cover her eggs, camouflage her tracks, and plunge back into the sea. Opening up four oysters he had also carried with him, Toomer passed two of them to Ben who ate them with greater ease in the glow of firelight and with the coffee to wash them down.

"This is the best time I've had since I've come to this smelly town, Toomer."

"That's good. On our way back we'll gig us a few f-f-flounder at a sandbar near here. Tomorrow morning, if Gray don't get you d-d-during the night, I'll show you how to get honey out of them hives."

"I ain't going near no bees," Ben said.

"Mr. Bee is a gentlemans. He don't bother no one that don't bother him. Ain't this a fine night, white boy?" Toomer said lying on his back and staring straight up into the stars.

Ben lay back too and thought about his mother and how right she could be about some things. He knew that her sending him out with Toomer had a lot to do with his father and things he was and was not learning as the son of a fighter pilot. Here in the night he thought that somehow the secret of this marsh-haunted land resided in the quivering flesh of oysters, the rich-flavored meat of crabs, the limp of the flower boy, and the eggs of the great turtles that navigated toward their birthing sands through waters bright with the moon.

10

BEFORE THE CHANGE of command ceremony, the weeks seemed composed of six Saturdays to the Meecham children. Their father, as Mary Anne would say, was too much with them. One Tuesday afternoon, the heat of August lying on the town like a corpse, Colonel Meecham ordered Ben and Matthew into the car for a trip to the base.

"Why are we going to the base?" Matthew asked.

"Because I said we're going to the base," his father answered.

"No special reason, Dad?" Ben asked cautiously.

"Yeah, sportsfans. I got a special reason. I'm gonna blow apples off your head with hand grenades. Now get in the car," his father replied.

On the way to the base Colonel Meecham announced to his sons in a calm, didactic voice that they were both in critical need of a haircut.

"You're starting to look a little scruffy. Your mother let you grow too much hair on your noggins while I was overseas. You got to remember the old Marine sayin', 'Hair is the glory of a woman, but the shame of a soldier.' "

"We aren't soldiers," Matt said.

"You ain't women either," Bull answered.

"We just got one two weeks ago, Dad," Ben whined.

"Well, we're startin' back with the old regime now. The Old Corps. From now on it's gonna be a haircut every week by a qualified Marine barber. If you don't like it, you can stick it up your butts 'cause I ain't asking you if you like it or not. I'm telling you." Then with an arch, almost imperial toss of his head, he said, "The Great Santini has spoken."

126

Argument was fruitless once the name of Santini was invoked, both boys knew that, and both knew that if they continued to milk the issue they were merely inviting calamity. Of all the strategic fields on which to wage war against Bull Meecham, the automobile was the most precipitate. It was an enclosed arena with limited avenues of escape. The doors, of course, but their value decreased as the speed of the car increased. Also missing in the necessary props for a showdown was the presence of Lillian Meecham. Ben had instructed Matt and his sisters never to confront, challenge, or anger Bull unless their mother was in shouting distance. Over the years Ben had formulated fire-tested strategies. The other children looked to him as their strategist, their Clausewitz, and Matthew said nothing as they drove up to the main gate of the Ravenel Air Station.

As they walked into the PX, Bull asked his sons, "Do both of you have your I.D. cards?"

"Yes, sir," Ben said.

"Let me check 'em to be sure they haven't expired," Bull said.

"They don't expire for two years," Matt offered.

"Give them here."

Bull studied the two cards and began to laugh.

"Those are mighty fine pictures of you two boys."

"Yeah, Dad, the Marine Corps spares no expense on those I.D. photographs. It must cost them at least a nickel for every million dependents they take pictures of," Ben said.

"They're just for identification," Bull said.

"Dad, there's not a person in the world who could identify me from that photograph."

When they entered the barbershop, Ben remembered how much he hated Marine Corps barbers. They were interchangeable from base to base, like returnable bottles. Always, their ranks were made up of humorless civilians culled from the lowest species of southerner that could plug in an electric clipper. Somehow, the barbers always became self-important, thinking of themselves as tough, no-nonsense guys because they cut the hair of tough, no-nonsense guys every day. Of course, Ben had to admit that

127

the Marine Corps did not require artists for the job; the Corps wanted butchers, haters of hair, and surgeons who kept platoons harmoniously mutilated in the form of old masters. In the Corps barbershops, the heads of the entire base were handcrafted for the edification of visiting generals and inspection teams.

The old enmity came back to Ben as he sat down in the chair farthest away from the entrance of the shop. For a whole year he had gone to civilian barbers in Atlanta, had come to love the virile smells of tonic and powders, the laughter of old men gossiping above the drone of clippers, and all the joking and the storytelling, and the sound of the bootblack's rag popping. It had been the first time in his life when he could describe to a barber how he wanted his hair to look, then lean back, stare into a mirror that reflected his image in a dance toward infinity, and wait while the barber did his bidding, shaved his neck with hot foam, and spun him around like a king to see if the job was properly done.

Now, he felt rough hands grabbing at his throat. The man who glowered before him conformed to the classic stereotype of Marine barber Ben had envisioned in his mind: the face was saturnine, pock-marked, and the mouth was grim. The man's hands trembled. He also had a nervous habit, which Ben noticed while being garroted with the barber sheet, of blowing tiny spit bubbles that were scarcely noticeable unless his face happened to be a foot away from your own. The bubbles were small, inconspicuous, and held a strange, unpalatable beauty when shafts of light pierced them and brightened his mouth with a briefly degraded spectrum of color. "I'm going to be sick," Ben thought, as he offered his head up for sacrifice.

Colonel Meecham, after delivering precise instructions to Matt's barber on the far side of the room, came up to Ben's barber, and said, without looking at his son, "I want you to cut the sides as short as they go, mister. Cut those sideburns all the way off. Leave a little bit on the top to comb, but on the sides, whitewalls all the way. I'll be in the pool hall, Ben."

"Why don't you have him shave my head, Dad?" Ben said, but his father was out of earshot.

When his father left the shop, Ben said to his barber in what he hoped would pass for a voice of substance and command, "Just trim the sides, mister. Very lightly."

"Your father said whitewalls, sonny," the man answered sourly.

"Yes, I heard him," Ben said, then in a sterner voice, "but the guy who is getting the haircut—namely me—and the guy who is paying for the haircut—me again—said trim the sides."

"Your old man's a colonel, sonny. You get whitewalls."

"What if he had told you to cut my nose and ears off?" Ben said. "I guess you'd just whack 'em off right before you brushed the hair off my neck, huh?"

"At ease, dependent," the barber replied, his shears cutting deep swaths into Ben's hair. He was pressing hard with the clippers.

Ben relaxed once the point of no return was reached. Then he spoke again, looking at the barber in the skinny mirror in front of them which Ben recognized as Marine Corps issue. "Do you know what I like about military barbers? You guys are such high class people. I mean it. Sincerely, I do. The absolute cream of military personnel. Handsome, aristocratic, urbane, without being affected."

"What are you talking about, dependent?" the man said between spit bubbles.

Ben continued, warming to his topic, "Scientists conducted a study last year, fine sir. Would you like to hear the results?"

"You're a real wiseass, dependent."

"Yeah, but you're a little afraid of me because my daddy's a colonel, right, fine sir? Now let me tell you about this scientific study. The scientists did a study of all Americans. The average white man had an I.Q. of one hundred. The average Negro had an I.Q. of ninety. The average Mongoloid idiot had an I.Q. of thirty. Now—and this is the interesting part, the truly fascinating part to me—Marine Corps barbers had an average I.Q. of twenty-one. They say the Mongoloid idiots are in an uproar that you guys came so close."

"You officers' kids think you're hot shit," the man

hissed, the pressure of his clippers harder against Ben's scalp now.

"There's an opening downtown at the morgue for a man to shave the pubic hair off the balls of male cadavers. With your talent and personality, you'd be a shoo-in."

"You've got wax in your ears, dependent," the barber said. "Don't you ever clean 'em?"

A moment later the barber spun the chair around to face the mirror. Ben's hair was now as short as his father's.

"Why didn't you just give me a trim, fella? Huh? What's such a big deal about a trim?"

"The colonel said whitewalls."

"You know I'm one of those weird guys who likes a few tiny filaments to be left on top of his head after he has a haircut. It wouldn't have hurt you to ease up a bit."

"Just pay up, dependent," the man said, a bubble of saliva darting out of his mouth.

Matthew had also fared badly. His hair was cut shorter than Ben's. A prickly tuft of hair ran down the middle of his head, bisecting it.

"You look like the Last of the Mohicans, Matt, my boy," Ben said, grinning at his brother.

"I wish Dad would go on another Med cruise."

They walked out of the barbershop toward the pool hall. As they passed a jeweler in a cubicle hunched over a watch, Ben told his brother, "Today you are going to witness a beautiful sight, Matt. You are going to get a chance to watch me whip Dad one on one in basketball. And seeing Dad lose in a sport is a sight beautiful to behold. He's the worst loser in the world. Of course, he's the worst winner in the world too."

"He'll kill you," Matt said. "There isn't a sport in the world he can't whip you in."

"Look, I've been playing basketball almost every day of my life for the past three years. I'll be eighteen soon. He's getting older. It's time I started whipping him."

"Yeah, yeah, yeah," Matt protested. "I've heard you talk for years how you were going to beat him. You might start winning, but then he'll start talking to you. You'll choke like you always do."

"Nope. I've been preparing for this grudge match for a

130

whole year. He's good at psyching me. But not this time," Ben said.

"It's too hot to play basketball."

"Why do you think I chose this particular day, little brother? He'll melt like a Popsicle out there."

"Don't call me little."

"O.K., mohawk."

"Don't call me anything."

The challenge match was set for five o'clock that afternoon. Ben swept off the cement court that spread from the back porch of the house to the garage. While Bull dressed upstairs, the rest of the family gathered by the side of the court to cheer Ben while he warmed up. Matt fed Ben passes out beyond the foul line, and Ben, dribbling twice, would fake a drive toward the basket, then go up with a quick awkward jump shot that was adequate even though it lacked artistry and the essential purity of flow always found in good jump shooters. Then he began to drive all the way to the basket, dribbling slowly, then exploding toward the basket, changing hands in midair and letting the ball roll off his fingertips and into the basket.

Lillian coached him from a wicker chair by the porch. "You can't listen to him, Ben. Once you listen to him, he has you beaten. Keep your mind on the game. Your game. And don't worry about him. If you start beating him, he'll start to cheat. You just concentrate on your game."

Bull appeared on the back porch wearing a sweat suit with "United States Marine Corps" stenciled on it. Standing on the porch, he raised his clasped hands over his head and pranced like a boxer going into the ring.

"Boo, booo," his wife and children jeered.

"You ready to go one on one, Dad?" Ben called from under the basket.

"With you?" Bull said, skipping lightly down the stairs. "You ain't man enough to go one on one against the Great Santini."

"Let me play too, Dad," Matt pleaded.

"Naw, you get out of here, Matt. Go sit under a toadstool or something," Bull said. Matt ran into the house. Only Mary Anne saw that he was crying and she followed him. Ben threw a pass to his father. Dribbling three times

131

with both his right and left hand, Bull went into a strangely graceful crouch and threw up an arcing two-hand set shot that swished through the net. Bull crowed with delight, a self-indulgent but euphoric eruption that silenced his wife's catcalls for the moment. Looking toward Lillian, he said, "The old boy's still got it, huh, Petunia."

"That shot went down with the Titanic, Dad," Ben teased.

"It still counts two points, does it not, jocko?" Bull snapped back, shooting another arcing set that hit the back of the rim and bounced back to him without ever touching the court. Mary Anne slipped out of the back door without Matt and sat down again by her mother. Bull shot another time and once more the ball swished through the net.

"What was it like, Dad," Ben said, throwing him the ball, "shooting at a peach basket?"

"You're gonna find out what it was like having a fist stuck up your left nostril if you don't quit your yappin'."

Mary Anne squealed from the sidelines, "You could stick two fists and a leg up Ben's left nostril with that schnozz of his."

"Ha, ha, very funny," Ben sneered at his sister.

"I'm surprised Mommy let her sweet little boy play any nasty sports at all when the Big Dad was overseas," Bull taunted.

"Don't listen to him, Ben. He's starting on you now. Just think about the game," Lillian called out.

"There's a reason I'm going to beat you, Dad."

"Do tell, sportsfans."

"It's because," and here Ben paused, ensuring that everyone was listening, "it's because you're getting fat."

"What'd you say?" Bull had picked the ball up and was holding it in the crook of his left arm.

Lillian doubled up with laughter in the white wicker chair.

"Not real fat. Just kind of chunky. You look kind of slow now, Dad."

"We'll see who's slow. I told you never to mess with greased lightning, son."

"Greased lightning don't weigh no two hundred twenty pounds."

"I could eat you for breakfast, sportsfans."

"You been eating somethin' real big for breakfast, that's for sure."

Bull threw up another set shot. It was good. Then he looked toward Ben with hard eyes. "Your mouth has improved since I left, but you're still a mama's boy. You still haven't developed the killer instinct. I could psych you out even if I was a hundred years old. If I was paralyzed from the neck down I could still beat you in a spitting contest. And there's one thing we both know. I'm a hell of a lot better athlete than you."

That was true, Ben thought. The sons of Bull Meecham lived with the awareness that they would never match the excellence of their father in athletics. In all sports, they lacked his inextinguishable fierceness, his hunger for games. It was not that they were not competitive; they were, compulsively so. It was that this sense of competition was not elevated to a higher level. In Bull Meecham, the will to win transformed all games into a furious art form. The game was a framework in which there was a winner and a loser. Bull Meecham was always the winner. He played cow bingo with the same fervor as he played his last college basketball game at Saint Luke's. He played Old Maid with Karen and Matt with the same competitiveness as when he battled Japanese pilots in the Pacific. The stakes could be higher in some games than others, but Bull played them all to win. Ben had inherited his father's speed afoot, his good eyes, and much of the competitiveness, but he had not received his father's genius for games, the raw nerve ends and synapses that brought a game up from a region of sport into a faith based on excellence, a creed toughened by fire. But on this hot August day in Ravenel, South Carolina, under the blaze of a terrible sun, Ben thought that he had a great equalizer working for him, called youth.

Ben was five feet ten inches tall and weighed 165 pounds; his father was six feet four inches tall and weighed two hundred twenty pounds. But Ben had been correct when he observed that Bull had thickened over the last years. He had become heavy in the thighs, stomach, and buttocks. The fast places had eroded. Rolls of fat encircled

133

him and he wore the sweat suit to keep his new ballast un-
exposed. He was planning to lose weight anyway. There
was nothing Bull Meecham hated worse than a fat Marine.

It took a long time for Bull to warm up and it gave Ben
a chance to study his moves. Lillian called from the sidelines for Bull to "quit stalling." But Bull remained unhurried, gliding around the court with the definitive moves of
the natural. Though his speed was gone, his quickness was
not. His hands were still very fast. He could handle a basketball with remarkable dexterity for one who had abandoned the court so long ago. He was heavy yet he was still
a dancer and the easy moves of the old predator came
back to him effortlessly as he went from spot to spot testing
his eye.

"Let's get the game going," Lillian said, clapping her
hands.

But Bull would not be hurried. He was seriously practicing his two-hand set shot. The hands that could make jets
perform exotic gymnastics in the sky had a softness of
touch and an inborn surety that made him an excellent
outside shooter. The pilot with the good eyes for spotting
enemy troop movements, for columns of tanks, and for
artillery positions could also use those eyes for looking up,
and for judging the distance between the basket and his
hands, for that silent worship of rims. He shot his two-
hand set in a soft, spinning arc, that when true, snapped
through the net in a swishing voice that is the purest music
of the game. Even when he missed, the spin on the ball
made it die on the rim and it would often bounce once or
twice between the rim and the backboard before falling in.
As Ben fed him passes from under the basket, Bull made
eight out of twelve set shots, moving in a semicircle outside the scratched-out foul line. Time after time, Bull
brought the ball to eye level, almost resting it on his nose.
He sighted the rim, bent his knees, and in a rhythm that
never changed launched his body, his arms, and the ball
upward toward the basket, his fingers spreading out like
fans with the two index fingers pointing toward the center
of the rim. Like all good shooters, the pattern of Bull's
shooting did not deviate; in fact it was unconscious, buried
in instinct, and rooted in long hours of boyhood practice.

He did the same thing each time the ball left his fingers to hunt the chords. Over, and over, monotonous, without change, until finally he said to his son, "Let's play ball."

"You sure you don't want to warm up for a little longer?" Lillian said. "You've only taken about an hour."

"Do any of you creeps realize that this is not exactly a world-important event?" Mary Anne said.

"Uh, oh," Bull answered, "Miss Funeral Shroud has come to spread joy."

"Don't give him a clear shot, Ben," Lillian coached. "Keep him away from the basket and don't let him take his set."

"Someone ought to cheer for Daddy," Karen said.

"You cheer for him," her mother answered.

"Yeah, Karen, give your Big Dad a few cheers. All the raspberries are coming his way."

"You take it out first, Dad," Ben said, bouncing the ball to his father. "Play to ten baskets by one. You have to win by two."

"Two? Why not one? First guy to ten," Bull protested. "Of course, it's not gonna be that close, sportsfans."

"You have to take it behind the foul line after each shot, Dad."

"Don't stand under the basket, jocko. You might get killed by one of my shots crashing through the basket."

"If you get a shot off."

Ben moved in close to guard his father, who began dribbling toward the basket with deliberate caution. He turned his butt toward Ben and backed toward the basket, dribbling first to the right, then to the left. When Ben tried to reach around to swat at the ball, Bull prevented this by holding him off with his free arm. He took Ben almost underneath the basket, then in a quick, fluid move, he pivoted for a hook shot that caromed lightly off the backboard.

"One to goose egg, sportsfans," Bull shouted at his booing family.

Taking the ball behind the foul line, Ben saw that his father was not coming out to play defense on him. He made a move for the basket, went up for a jump shot. His father, off balance, poked him in the stomach as he went up, but the ball went in.

"He's starting to cheat," Lillian cried out.

"One to one," Ben said.

Bull did not even dribble this time. He set himself immediately and before Ben could recover had launched a high two-hander toward the rim that missed. Rebounding the ball quickly, Ben brought it past the foul line, changed the direction of his dribble twice, gave his father a head fake, a stutter step, then drove toward the basket as recklessly as he knew how. To his surprise, he had broken completely free and laid the ball in effortlessly. "Two to one," he called to his father.

The game became rough. Sweat poured down Bull's face and Ben caught an elbow under the left eye when he tried to block one of Bull's hook shots. Each time Bull received the ball he would take his time, dribbling cautiously, moving backward, taking his smaller son under the basket. Ben, for his part, kept driving past his father, changing speeds, and sweeping past him as Bull lunged heavily after a son who had fooled him, betrayed him with speed.

Ben kept saying to himself, "I'll make him work on defense. I'll get his legs tired trying to stop me. When his legs go, his shooting will go. He's out of shape. If I can't get him tired, I'll get him mad. If I can get him mad, I'll beat him."

The game remained close, both combatants missing shots they should have made and sinking baskets that defied all principles of the game. Finally the score was tied nine to nine, and the family on the sidelines readied themselves for a denouement. Bull had the ball.

Ben pressed in close to him with left hand waving in front of his father's eyes. He wanted to be sure to prevent the two-handed set. During the game, over and over again, he had proven that Bull was no longer fast enough to drive around him. Bull was breathing as though steam engines were working his lungs, his lips were flecked with dried saliva, and sweat was pouring off his body. He made two half-hearted feints toward the basket hoping to catch Ben off balance and get an unchallenged set shot. But Ben stayed close to him, his chest almost against his father's belly, their sweat commingling and their breaths crossing like two alien winds.

"Have you ever read *Moby Dick,* Dad?" Ben asked.

"Shit, no," Bull murmured, pivoting around and beginning a low, cautious dribble, inching his way toward the basket with Ben fastened to his rump. "Why do you ask, sportsfans?"

"Because you kind of remind me of the great big, fat, white whale."

"Touché, touché," Lillian screamed.

"This looks like the last shot of the game, jocko."

"If you make it," Ben said, leaning with all his weight against his father's rear, trying to slow the inevitable move toward the basket for the easy hook shot.

"Does a maggot live in dead meat?" Bull said.

"God, Dad is disgusting," said Mary Anne.

"He's just low born," said Lillian. Then she began shouting, "Kill him, Ben. Keep your hands up."

At that moment Bull glanced over at Lillian, irritation spliced on the corners of his mouth. When Ben saw his eye depart from the center of action, he stepped backward, like a caboose uncoupling from another car. In that single instant, Ben was unseen and unfelt by his father. He slapped Bull on the left buttock, then swept low around his father's right side. Feeling Ben's release and the hand hitting his left side, Bull reflexively looked to his left and switched the ball to his right hand. As he did so, he realized his mistake and tried to recover, but by this time Ben had flicked the ball away from him and retrieved it near the porch.

The family of spectators broke into applause when they sensed that Ben had a chance to win the game. At the far edge of cement, almost touching the porch, Ben stood motioning for his father to come out to play defense.

"Whip his fanny, Ben," Matt's voice cried out from behind the screen door in the kitchen.

"It is I, the Great Bentini," Ben mimicked as he began to dribble the ball between his legs trying to shame his father into open court where he knew he could drive around him.

"Let's play ball," Bull rumbled, his face blood red from anger. His eyes had narrowed into starpoints of cold, the killing edge of a personal fury that marked a crossing of the line which Lillian recognized immediately.

"Why don't we just call it a tie, and call both of you winners?" she said.

"I said let's play ball," Bull growled in a lower, more frightening octave.

"Why don't you just come out here and get it, Great Santini?" Ben teased, unaware of the changes that were taking place in his opponent.

"I'd quit now, Ben," Mary Anne advised. "He's getting that same look on his face that he gets when he runs over turtles on trips."

Dribbling slowly, Ben started toward his father, changing hands with each dribble, hoping to catch Bull with his weight shifted in the wrong direction. "Do you know, Dad, that not one of us here has ever beaten you in a single game? Not checkers, not dominoes, not softball, nothing."

"C'mon, mama's boy," Bull whispered. "Bring little mama's boy up to Daddy Bull." Right hand, left hand, right hand, left hand, the ball drummed against the cement as Ben waited for his father to move out against him and Bull held back, fearing the drive to the basket. At the foul line, Ben left his feet for the jump shot, eyed the basket at the top of his leap, let it go softly, the wrist snapping, the fingers pointing at the rim and the ball spinning away from him as Bull lunged forward and drove his shoulder into Ben's stomach, knocking him to the ground. Though he did not see the ball go in, he heard the shouts of his mother and sisters; he saw Matthew leaping up and down on the porch. He felt his father rise off him slowly, coming up beaten by a son for the first time in his life. Screaming with joy, Ben jumped up and was immediately flooded by his family, who hugged, slapped, pummeled, and kissed him.

Lillian and Matt tried to pick Ben up, but he was too heavy and all three of them fell into the grass laughing, forgetting the lone figure of the father standing under the basket, sweating, red-faced, and mute, watching the celebration of his wife and children with the inchoate, resurrected anger of a man who never quit in his life. Mary Anne saw him standing alone and went over to say something comforting.

"You played a good game, Dad," she said.

"Get out of here."

"You didn't lose by much," Mary Anne continued, ignoring the vital signs.

"Get out of here before I start knocking every freckle off your face."

Mary Anne put her hands to her face, removed her glasses, and looked at her father with eyes that were filling with tears. "That was mean, Daddy. You had no call to say that," she said, running toward the front yard.

Then Bull shouted at Ben, "Hey, jocko, you gotta win by two baskets."

The backyard became quiet again. Ben looked at his father and said, "You said by one."

"I changed my mind; let's go," Bull said, picking up the basketball.

"Oh, no, Bull," Lillian said, marching toward her husband. "You're not going to cheat the boy out of his victory."

"Who in the hell asked you anything?" Bull said, glaring at his wife.

"I don't care if anybody asked me or not. He beat you fair and square and I'm not going to let you take that away from him."

"Get over here, mama's boy," Bull said, motioning to Ben, "and let's you and me finish this game."

Ben moved forward until he heard his mother shout at him, "You stay right there, Ben Meecham. Don't you dare move."

"Why don't you go hide under your mother's skirts, mama's boy?" Bull said.

He was gaining control of the situation again and was entering a phase of malevolent calm that Lillian was having difficulty translating.

"Mama, I'm gonna play him," Ben said.

"No you're not," his mother answered harshly, with finality, then speaking to her husband, she said, "He beat you, Big Marine. He beat the Big Marine where everybody could see it, right out in the open, and it was beautiful. Big Marine can't take it that his baby boy just beat him to death on the basketball court."

"Get in the house, Lillian, before I kick you into the house."

"Don't threaten me, Big Tough Marine. Does Big Tough Marine have to pick on his family the day his son becomes the better man?"

Bull pushed Lillian toward the house, spinning her away from him, and kicked her in the buttocks with a swift vicious kick.

"Stop that, Dad," Ben shouted. "You stop that."

"Quit kicking Mama," Karen screamed.

He kicked her again. Each kick was directing her toward the stairs. Finally, Lillian started to run for the kitchen. Bull would have kicked her another time but Ben got between him and his mother. The screen door slammed as Lillian disappeared from view. Bull's face was hideously contorted as he stood face to face with Ben, who was trembling involuntarily.

"You sort of like winning, don't you, Dad?" Ben said, trying to sound unconcerned and in control, but fear lay heavy on his voice.

Bull went up to Ben until they were almost nose to nose, as Ben had seen Drill Instructors do to recruits. With his forefinger, he began poking Ben's chin. "You get smart with me, jocko, and I'll kick you upstairs with your mother so you pussies can bawl together. Now guard me. You gotta win by two."

"I'm not gonna guard you, Dad. I won," Ben said, his voice almost breaking. He could feel himself about to cry.

Bull saw it too. "That's it, mama's boy. Start to cry. I want to see you cry," Bull roared, his voice at full volume, a voice of drill fields, a voice to be heard above the thunder of jet engines, a voice to be heard above the din of battle. Bull took the basketball and threw it into Ben's forehead. Ben turned to walk into the house, but Bull followed him, matching his steps and throwing the basketball against his son's head at intervals of three steps. Bull kept chanting, "Cry, cry, cry," each time the ball ricocheted off his son's skull. Through the kitchen Ben marched, through the dining room, never putting his hands behind his head to protect himself, never trying to dodge the ball. Ben just walked and with all his powers of concentration rising to

140

the surface of consciousness, of being alive, and of being son, Ben tried not to cry. That was all he wanted to derive from the experience, the knowledge that he had not cried. He wanted to show his father something of his courage and dignity. All the way up the stairs, the ball was hurled against his head. The hair short and bristly from the morning haircut, the head this moment vulnerable, helpless, and loathed. Ben knew that once he made it to his room the ordeal would end, and he would have the night to consider all the symbols of this long march: the heads of sons, the pride of fathers, victors, losers, the faces of kicked wives, the fear of families, the Saturdays in the reign of Santini—but now, now, through this hallway and up these final stairs, I must not cry, I must not cry. Until he saw his room. Breaking into a run, he felt Bull release him, free him, his head throbbing, dizzy; and the son of the fighter pilot fell onto his bed face downward, afraid that tears would come if he did not stem their flow in the cool whiteness of his pillow. His father stood in the doorway and Ben heard him say so that the whole family could hear, "You're my favorite daughter, Ben. I swear to God you're my sweetest little girl."

Then turning toward the door, blinded by water and light, Ben spit back, "Yeah, Dad, and this little girl just whipped you good."

The door slammed.

11

THAT NIGHT Ben heard a basketball thumping on the court. Lifting the curtain by his bed, he saw his father shooting baskets beneath the night light. He was practicing sets and hooks, dribbling and pivots. It was ten o'clock and the house was silent, as it had been since the game. Bull had left the house and not returned until suppertime. Not a word passed between Bull and his family at supper and at times the noise of the silverware clinking on plates seemed deafening. Ben did not appear at supper, sending word to his mother that he was sick. During the entire meal Bull read the newspaper. He did not try to begin conversation, for he knew through long experience that whenever these sudden choreographies of violence erupted, he had to endure an exile of silence with his wife and children for an indeterminate period. After dinner, the children drifted off to their rooms with their poker faces congealed and their imposed vow of silence unbroken. Had their father asked them a question, they would have answered, "yes sir" or "no sir," or given a brief unembroidered reply, with voices bled of all emotion, uninhabited voices related more to silence than to communication. The house brooded into the night. The Meecham children were gifted in the fine art of brooding. The energy of brooding affected their father like no other weapon they could turn against him. Ben was lying on his bed studying the cracked geometry of falling plaster that hung above him. Dreams and imaginary dramas were projected on the ceiling as Ben's brain danced with dazzled portraits of his father and him locked in duels to the death. At these times, alone, Ben consciously extended his frontiers of hatred and longed for a reprieve from his father and the freedom of not being a son. Then he heard his father shooting baskets under the light with the river invisible and boatless beyond the house and only the braided string of lights of houses across the river to mark the far shore. Everyone in the house heard the ball thumping against the concrete and its hard ring as it bounced off the rim. Ben studied his father's hook shot from the window. The easy sweeping grace fascinated him on so large a man. He did not hear Lillian come into the room behind him.

"How are you feeling, sugah?" she said.

"I'm O.K., Mama," Ben answered, still watching his father. "How are you feeling?"

"My posterior's a little sore, but I'll live through the night, at least," she said.

"You've got fabulous taste in men, Mama, no kidding."

"Don't get smart with me, mister. It's been plenty hard on me today without your getting smart. Remember, I'm the one that's in the middle. I'm the one that catches it from both sides. It's me that's got to walk the tightrope."

Ben sat on his desk, put his gym shoes on his chair, unlaced them, then tied them tighter. He tied and untied his gym shoes as thoughtlessly as he blinked his eyes. It was one of Ben's many nervous mannerisms that worried Lillian.

"If he ever does that to you again, Ben, I'll leave him. So help me God, I'll leave him."

"Sure, Mama," Ben said. "That's what you said the last time. That's what you say every time. You've been leaving him ever since I was born."

"I'm serious this time."

"You were serious last time and the time before that and time before that. I don't care anymore, Mom. I'm getting out of this family this year. I just gotta make it before he tears me apart."

Lillian was sitting on the foot of Ben's bed. With almost inappropriate grace, she pulled a cigarette from a package of Lucky Strikes. She handed the matches to Ben and waited as Ben clumsily lit a match and held the flame in front of her. Lightly, she touched his hand and inhaled deeply.

"He's working on his temper, darling. He knows he's got to work on it. We've got to help him work on it."

"I don't have to help him. I hate his guts. I don't even want to help him."

"If you don't, then it's going to be bad for Matt and the girls," she said, then added, "and for me, of course."

"Let me tell you what I was just thinking, Mama. I was just sitting here praying that we would go to war."

"Shame on you, Ben. That's a terrible thing to say."

"No, let me finish. I was praying for a special type of war. One that required only Marine pilots and I didn't care who we fought against. I thought about Cuba, Russia, and China, of course. But then I decided if it got Dad out of here, that I'd be satisfied with France, Monaco, Vatican City, Florida. It doesn't make any difference. I just want somebody to declare war against this country, so King Kong out there can fight against someone besides me."

"You act like he hits you all the time. Today was the first time he's touched you since he's been home. He's been excellent until today and even you have to admit that."

"Oh, he's been a peach. See, Mom, I know he doesn't hit me every day. But do you know I wake up every day with the possibility of him hitting me? I mean if he gets mad, he goes for me. You got in his way today, so he kicked you a few times. But I'm his primary target. He hones in on me when he's angry."

"He expects a lot from his oldest son."

"That's the funny part to me, Mom. It's not like I was a juvenile delinquent and went around slashing tires and smoking cigarettes. When we lived on base I never got in trouble with the M.P.'s. I wasn't like Bill Poindexter or Larry Kinston; I didn't string a rope across the road and almost strangle that M.P. who was chasing them that night on a motorcycle. I've seen a thousand Marine kids and you and I both know that they're the most screwed up bunch of kids that ever lived. And I'm not like them. I don't do anything and yet I get knocked all over the place."

"Now, Ben," his mother said soothingly, "you know he's improved over what he used to be. He's mellowing in his old age. His temper used to be a lot worse when you were younger. You've got to give him credit for that."

"It's a miracle that I've lived to grow pimples."

"Don't be flip with your mother. I'm speaking seriously. I've worked with him on controlling his temper. We've even prayed together about it. He's improved. That's the point."

"I used to keep count of the times he hit me and the reason. I did it for about two years. It makes funny reading now. In October of 1958, I was slapped by Dad for not moving fast enough across the room when I was bringing him a beer. The next year he punched me for striking out three times in a baseball game. Another time he got me by the throat and slammed my head against the wall over and over again until you stopped him. That time, I had woke him up after he had been on a cross-country night flight."

"You're exaggerating again. I don't remember those times."

"Yeah, Mom, you always defend him. I always exaggerate. I always make things up. Look at this scar on my lip. I got that when I ran real fast and threw myself into Dad's fist just for kicks."

"Don't 'yeah' me, mister. It's 'yes ma'am.' And don't be sarcastic. You're a very unattractive person when you're sarcastic."

"Sorry, Mama. I'm upset. What he did was bad."

"I want to talk to you now, Ben, as a boy who is almost a man. You've got to realize that your father's always been under a great deal of pressure in his job. All day long he is under pressure from superiors and both of us know he flies off the handle very easily when things don't go his way or when a colonel gets mad at him."

"Why doesn't he punch the colonel?" Ben said, untying his shoes again.

"Now you're talking nonsense."

"No, I'm not," Ben said, looking up from his shoes. "Why do I get hit when some jerk colonel gets on Dad's back? Dad screws up an assignment in Cherry Point, and I get slapped when he flies back to Ravenel. He receives a reprimand in a memo from Washington and then he gets pissed off at me for breathing too hard when he gets home that night. Well, the kid is out of it come June first. Then Mary Anne will be the prime beef."

"Light me another cigarette, darling." As the flame came to her she said, looking into her son's eyes, who quickly dropped his, "Your father has many good points."

"Sure, Mom. They're the knuckles on his left hand."

"Don't try to be so clever, sugah. You and Mary Anne always have to verbally joust with the rest of the world and it's not very becoming to either one of you. And one thing you're not keeping in mind, Ben. One thing that is very important. Your father loves you very much."

"Ha!" Ben laughed. "He's got a fabulous way of showing it." Then a mellowness entered his voice, an exhausted gentleness. "Mama, we've had this talk a million times. It starts out with you leaving him. Then it ends with you telling me all his good points. How much he wants the best for his children. How much he loves us all and sacrifices for us all. Do you know something that I know, Mama? He loves the Marine Corps more than he loves us."

"He's supposed to, son. That's his duty. His job. All men are like that."

"No," Ben said harshly. "It's different. Do you think Dupree Johnson's daddy loved his gas station more than his family? Or Robbie Chambers' daddy loved his doughnut shop more than his wife or kids?"

"Well, you're just talking now. You don't really know what your daddy thinks, but I do."

"No one knows Dad, Mama. No one knows him. He's an actor. He acts out being a Marine. He acts out being a husband. He acts out being a father. In fact, Dad is the only person in the world who has to act out being a human being."

"You're wrong there, son," Lillian said, staring into the bluish plume of smoke she exhaled toward the opposite wall. "There's a lot of people like that."

"But the real secret of Dad is, it's all the same act. It's the same thing. It's all that fighter pilot crap. I bet when you're alone with him, he's still humping right along with his same old act."

"If it weren't for you children and our differences over

discipline, we would have the happiest marriage possible. All of our fights are over the children."

Ben untied his shoelaces again and began lacing them up, tighter than before.

"You're going to cut off all the circulation in your feet," Lillian said, but Ben kept on pulling at the laces.

"Do you love Dad, Mama?" Ben asked and Lillian saw that he was blushing.

"Of course I love your father. He's my husband."

"I don't mean that. I mean do you really love him in such a way that you wouldn't want to live with anybody else?"

"What God hath joined together, let no man put asunder. I'm very satisfied. Your father is a good provider and he is kind to me."

"I think he treats you crappy."

"He blows his stack at me sometimes, but I let it roll off like water on a duck's back. Harsh words were never fatal to anyone."

"What about harsh fists, Mama? What about when he hits you?"

Lillian said nothing for a few moments. She paused to give her son time to light another cigarette.

"You're smoking these too fast, Mama."

"What ever gave you the idea that your father hits me? He never hits me," Lillian said, looking directly at Ben.

"Gee, Mom, ol' crazy me thought he kicked you today."

"That wasn't much. But I'd leave a man who hit me."

"I've seen him hit you," Ben said, looking into his mother's eyes, and holding his gaze steady.

"You're upset, Ben," Lillian said. "You're starting to imagine things. Your father has never hit me during our entire married life."

"I have seen him hit you at least three times."

"You're exaggerating again, Ben," Lillian answered, laughing to break the tension. "I swear your imagination plays funny tricks on you sometimes."

Ben walked to his bureau drawer and fumbled through several layers of clothes in the bottom drawer. He retrieved a T-shirt, military issue, covered with dried blood. "When Dad hit you two years ago, Mom, I held you in my

147

arms and you were crying. It was on a Friday after happy hour and he came home singing 'Silent Night,' which was strange because it was in March. You met him at the door and started fighting with him because he'd been drinking gin, and you said gin made him wild because it did something to his system. He started hitting you in the face. I ran in and grabbed his legs. He started punching me in the head. Mary Anne came in, and started screaming. He left the house. Your nose was bleeding, and that's how I ruined this T-shirt. I've kept it, Mama, because I wanted it as proof. This is your blood, Mama. Your blood."

"He never hit me," Lillian insisted.

Ben threw up his hands in exasperation, almost despair. "Then I'm a liar."

"I didn't say that."

"Yes you did. I say that he's hit you. You say that he hasn't. So I'm a liar, and I'm going to stay a liar."

"You exaggerate, son."

"No, I lie. I love to lie. Lying makes me feel good. I'm addicted to it."

"You're upset."

"No, Mama, not me. I just happen to be one of those fun-loving people who enjoy getting a basketball bounced off their heads twenty or thirty times. I like it even better when it's a bowling ball."

"I'm warning you, mister, don't get smart with me. I don't like that, Ben. I simply don't like it."

"I'm sorry, Mama."

"I'm in here because I'm on your side, and I wanted you to let off a little steam. But you've got to understand how hard it is to try and keep peace between your father and you children. All I want is for peace to rule my house. Peace and quiet and good feelings. It's so much easier to have good feelings than discord. I abhor discord."

"We didn't have discord last year, Mama. When Dad was overseas. It was the best year of my life. Why don't you just leave him?"

Lillian reflected a moment, then said, "Because of you children."

"Would you repeat that please. I am near hysteria, but I want to be sure of what you said."

"I won't leave your father because of you children. I know what it's like to grow up in a broken home. I know how terrible a broken home can be. I made a vow that my children would never have to go through what I went through."

"Well, I have also made a vow," Ben said, in slow deliberate words. "My children are never going to have to go through what I have gone through."

"Well, if I were you, mister," Lillian shot back, "I'd count my blessings. Other children haven't had your advantages. Some children don't have enough food to eat, others are sickly, others don't have a roof over their heads, others have parents who hate them."

"And some children have diabetes," Ben said, "and some have leprosy, some get eaten by tigers, some are born without arms, some get struck by lightning, and some use leaves for toilet paper."

Lillian laughed to herself. "You're like him in so many ways."

"Like who?"

"Like your father."

"Don't say that," Ben said, as if in pain.

"I can see him in your face. In your inflection. The way you walk. The way you gesture with your hands. He's everywhere in you."

"That's it, Mom. Drive me to suicide."

"Mark my words, what happened today won't make any difference in five years. You'll look back in later years and understand your father a lot better. He does what he does because he loves you, and wants you to be the best."

Ben began to dance around the room, saying, "I love you, Ben. Punch. I want you to be the best, Ben. Kick. I think you're great, Ben. Throw downstairs. I want you to be tops, Ben. Slug with brass knuckles. I love you too much for words, Ben. Stomp on kidney."

"You can have your fun, but there's one other thing that's important for you to know. Your father can't live without me. He loves me very much. He worships me."

"You could get other men to worship you. Other men do."

"Your father's my husband."

She took Ben's hands in hers and tried to look into his eyes, but Ben turned his head away from her. The basketball still sounded on the backyard court. Bull was practicing his two-hand set shot from long range. Standing Ben up, she led him to one side of the window, and they both watched Bull shooting and retrieving the ball on the driveway below them. A minute passed without either of them speaking. Finally, Lillian spoke. "Have you ever heard your father apologize to anyone for anything?"

Ben shook his head. "I've never heard him say 'I'm sorry' to anyone."

"He never has," Lillian said. "But I know him better than you do, better than you will ever know him. Do you know why he's down there practicing his shooting tonight?"

"No, ma'am."

"He's admitting to you that the gap is closing. That he has to practice if he's going to beat you from now on. He's admitting some hard things. He's admitting that he's getting older."

"That doesn't change anything."

"I'm sure it doesn't, son. Because you're angry," Lillian said, walking toward the door, "but the real reason he's down on the court tonight is that he knows you'll hear him. You've got a strange father, Ben, but in his own way, that's him down there saying, 'I'm sorry, Ben. I was wrong.'"

150

12

COLONEL MEECHAM sat behind the desk, savoring the richness of his first moments as the commanding officer of squadron 367. He was alone for the first time since the change of command ceremony and the forceful chords of the Marine Corps hymn and the proud rhythms of men marching in cadence still sang in his brain: the memory of guidons fluttering and heads snapping to the right to pay homage to the new commander filled him with profound gratification; the pomp of flags and the joy of watching a mass of men on the march because he had shouldered the lonely accoutrements of command caused him a moment of fear, awed by the long files of men who marched to fulfill the demands of ceremony, the long grip of tradition.

His family had stood with him on the reviewing stand. His sons and daughters lined up like a squad, shiny as new dimes, performed their minor functions well. Lillian Meecham had been radiant, a dazzling partner who added charm to a family so drilled and weighted down with the responsibility of obedience that they seemed to function and move together like a machine. It had gone well. The command had passed to him. Yet now that the command was his, the fulfillment of an old and troubled dream, he suffered a hollowness of spirit that had the unmistakable dimension of anticlimax. He had wanted this for so long, scratched his way along the belly of the beast for so many years, fighting off mediocre fitness reports and the rumors that he was too unstable, too volatile to lead a squadron, that the being there seemed less real than the struggle and long ascent to get there. It was a paradox, and Bull Meecham could take anything with more equanimity than paradox. He was, at this very moment, behind this desk, the commander of a fighter squadron, and by some fraudulence or legerdemain of time, all the sweetness had gone out of it, the honey of triumph left his lips dry and his greatest moment with only the memory of what he thought it would taste like to sustain him.

Then he thought, "I'm a Marine, not a fucking philosopher."

He rang for Sergeant Latito. A dark, grizzled man with a face that looked as though a war might have been fought over its craggy terrain stood at his desk a moment later.

"Yes, sir," the sergeant said.

"Did all the pilots get the word about the briefing today, Sergeant?" the C.O. asked.

"Yes, sir, all pilots and officers will meet in the briefing room at 1230 hours."

"Good man, Sergeant. Where are you from, by the way?"

"Brooklyn, sir," the man replied.

"You're a Jewish boy, aren't you?" the colonel asked, without smiling, but his eyes shined with a mirth the sergeant did not see.

"No, sir, I'm an Italian. My father came from the Old Country."

"Your Daddy's from Israel, eh? It's no crime to be Jewish, Latito. Don't be ashamed of it."

"I beg the colonel's pardon, sir. But I swear that I'm Italian."

"Look, Sergeant," the colonel, said, his voice lowering now, the brightness fading from his eyes, fading into a stone and hardness, "if I want to think you're Jewish, then you are gonna be Jewish. If I want you to eat matzo balls instead of pizza, then you'll do it. I like men under my command to jump at everything I say. Especially my top sergeant."

"Sir," the sergeant sputtered, "I'm proud of being an Italian."

"Sarge, you can learn to be proud of being a Jewboy just as easy. That will be all, Latito."

"Yes, sir," the sergeant saluted.

As the sergeant turned to leave, Colonel Meecham

called to him, "Does your wife make good lasagna, Latito?"

The sergeant stopped and without turning around, but coming to stiff attention, said, "The best, sir. At least in this part of the country."

"I'd sure like to get a little lasagna the next time she fixes a batch."

"You will, sir," Latito said, smiling. "You will."

At precisely 1230 hours, Colonel Bull Meecham strode into the briefing room to meet the officers of his squadron for the first time. He had known several of them in previous assignments and other bases and he had met almost all of them in the days preceding his inauguration as their commander. This would be the first time he addressed them as a group.

He had rehearsed this speech for twelve years. By studying the strengths and weaknesses of commanders he had served under, he had collected shards and fragments of the speech he would one day deliver to men who looked upon him as their commander. He had descanted his theories about leadership and command, his love for the oldest traditions of the Corps, his definition of duty so often and in the tumult of so many crises that he had practically assured himself that whatever came out when he spoke on that appointed day would be the effluent of hard experience, the natural residue of his years in the Marine Corps, and his philosophy of the officer.

He began to speak, aware that he had come to the barricade, that he was mounting it, that this time would never come again—the commander spoke, without notes, but from deep in the hardest, holiest place of him.

"You men," he began, "now have the privilege of serving under the meanest, toughest, screamingest squadron commander in the Marine Corps." He paused, eyed each man in the room, then finished, "Me," he growled. "You also have the privilege of serving the best squadron commander," he said, and paused, then said, "Me again.

"Now I am in a very special and very fortunate position. I am the commander of a squadron that has the best goddam pilots ever to put their asses on the seats of a jet air-

153

craft. If you are not the best pilots in the Marine Corps, if you are not the best pilots in the armed forces, if you are not the best pilots in the world, then you will be after spending six months with me as your commander. In the next couple of months you are going to fly like you have never flown before, do things with jet planes you never thought possible, become proficient in phases of aviation you never dreamed of. In the next couple of months you have a tough steak to chew, men, but you are going to get so goddam good at flying a jet, you are going to forget you have wives and children at home and that the White Sox are going to win the American League Pennant.

"Now I don't want you to look at me like I was just your Commanding Officer. I want you to look at me kind of like I was a god. If I say something, you pretend it's coming from the burning bush. If I sneeze, you sneeze. If I catch leprosy, I want to see some noses dropping off. If I wipe my ass, I want to see the hand of every pilot reaching down to clean up his rectum. We are Marines. We are members of the proudest, most elite group of fighting men in the history of the world. There is not a force on earth that can stand up to us, that can defeat us in battle, that can prevent us from performing our duty, that can deny Marine Corps fighting men. Marine Corps fighter pilots. us victory, that can interrupt our destiny. We are Marines. Marine Corps warriors. Marine Corps killers. We will wear our uniforms with pride. We will honor the traditions of the Corps in all things we do as a squadron. As the commanding officer of this squadron, I am going to tell you that this squadron is going to become a legend in the Marine Corps within thirty days, because I am going to lead the toughest, flyingest sons of bitches in the world, or I am going to kick some ass all over this base." He shouted, his face red, and his eyes affixed on the essential rectitude of his goal. The men of his squadron sat transfixed. There was no shifting, no clearing of throats, no coughing, and no restlessness. They were not bored.

"Now. I want obedience and devotion to duty. But there is one kind of Marine I hate," he said, as all ears in the room waited for the word. "I don't want nobody sniffin' my farts. Fart sniffers become generals unless they happen to get under my command. If you want to suck on some balls, I suggest you buy a pack of marbles because I hate a nut suckin', ball swingin', fart sniffin' bastard worse than I hate all the Russians in the Kremlin." He roared, looking about the room, rolling now, caught up in the rhythms of his own oratory, the fever and righteousness of his message. "You men are under Bull Meecham now and you're gonna look back at all this as the finest days you spent in the Marine Corps. If a pilot of mine fucks up, then I'll take a pound of his ass, but if anyone outside this squadron tries to nail 'em they will have to nail Bull Meecham too. We are in this together, men. We are members of the Werewolf Squadron 367 and we are going to make history. I would like to welcome you, gentlemen, to the best squadron ever assembled.

"Now," he said, the rhythm broken, the major portion of his address over, "I'd like to ask a few general questions. Did anyone in this squadron attend an Ivy League school?"

One pilot raised his hand in the back of the room, raised it hesitantly, like a banner of surrender. "Where did you go, Lieutenant?" Colonel Meecham asked.

"Cornell, sir," the lieutenant answered.

"Cornell," the colonel thundered.

"Yes, sir, Cornell," the lieutenant answered, less sure of himself.

"You proud of it, son?" the colonel asked.

"Yes, sir."

All eyes turned to Colonel Meecham who was leaning forward on the balls of his feet, glowering with unconcealed menace at the Ivy Leaguer. "Sheeeee-iiitt," the colonel hissed, "that's what I think of the whole Ivy League. The Ivy League is what's wrong with this country today. Cornell! Cornell! Cornell is a pansy school. Lieutenant, I want you to make me forget you went there by becoming the flying tiger of this outfit. Do I make myself clear, Lieutenant?

"Yes, sir," the lieutenant shouted.

"Now," the colonel said, "is there anybody from the Naval Academy?"

155

Once again, a single hand went up from the gathering of pilots.

"What class were you in, mister?" the colonel asked.

"Class of 'fifty-seven, sir," the young captain, who rose to attention, answered.

"That's nice, Captain. That's very nice. That's a gentleman's school, sure enough. Why didn't you fly with the pelicans like the rest of your classmates?"

"I wanted to be with the best, sir."

"Good man. But you have to be careful. Pelicans from the Naval Academy have this way of wearing their rings in their noses. Think they're blueblooded. Think their shit smells like Chanel Number 5. They usually don't do very well in the Marine Corps. You know that, don't you, Marine?"

"I've heard that, sir."

"I consider the Navy the cheese between the Marine Corps' toes. The only time we are on the same side is when we're at war and when Army plays Navy. Otherwise, I want the pelicans to water their lilies away from me. Now, men, this is the beginning of this squadron. You're flying with Bull Meecham in the eye of the storm. Three-sixty-seven is born this day. We are going to make it the best and we are going to do it together. If you have a problem, come to me, and we'll kick the shit out of that son of a bitch together. Dismissed."

The pilots filed out. By their lightness of foot and jauntiness of exit, Bull Meecham knew that part of the morale problem in 367 was over. He was new blood and a strong shot of the Old Corps. He was, he thought, just what the doctor ordered.

There was a knock on the door. A diminutive captain cutting an unstalwart figure in his flight suit, walked to the colonel's desk and saluted.

"Captain Johnson reporting as directed, sir," the captain said, his voice as high pitched as a castrato's.

Colonel Meecham looked hard into the little man's eyes before he spoke. The captain's eyes did not waver.

"There's two questions I want to ask you, Captain," the colonel said. "The first is this: How did you ever make it out of Quantico with a voice like that? The D.I.'s must have given you hell."

"They did, sir. When I graduated with my platoon, one of them told me he had never heard a voice like mine in boot camp."

"I thought your wife might be a ventriloquist hiding out in the hall."

"No, sir. This is my voice."

"The next question, Captain. How tall are you?"

"Five feet five inches tall," the man replied.

"Bullshit, Captain, a man five feet five would look like a giant next to you."

"I'm small boned, Colonel."

"You must have the bones of a canary bird. Let me tell you my theory of small men, Captain, then let me hear what you think," the colonel said, leaning back and eyeing the man who stood before him with a bemused admiration. "At ease, Johnson. Have a seat."

When Captain Johnson sat down on the chair in front of Bull Meecham's desk, his head seemed barely to peer over the C.O.'s desk.

"Give me a guy less than five feet eight, Johnson, and I'll give you a real bastard nine times out of ten. It has been my experience that short men get a chip on their shoulders as big as an aircraft carrier. They're pissed off at life and God and everybody else just because they're midgets. They come into the Marine Corps just so they can be proud and tough once in their lives. They like to strut around in their uniforms, flashing their wings around and pretending their dicks are as long as anyone else's. I'm a blunt man, Johnson, and I'll tell you that I always keep my eye out for a little guy because I know he's down there low with his hands around my nuts waiting for a chance to give me the big squeeze. What do you have to say about my theory?"

The small man puckered his lips and narrowed his eyes for a moment. He did not answer immediately. He is not taking the theory lightly, the colonel thought.

"In my case," the captain answered, his high-pitched voice somehow coming up out of his flight jacket like a sacrilege, "your theory is generally correct. I came into

157

the Marine Corps to prove to myself that I could take everything the Marine Corps could dish out. I was always too small to excel in sports and my voice has always been too high pitched to take seriously. That's why I've worked so hard to become the best pilot in the Marine Corps."

The colonel smiled and said, "That's why I called you in here. The former C.O. and the exec both told me you were the best young pilot in the squadron. I didn't know you were, Johnson, and if I'd had to take a pick, you'd have been my last choice."

"Yes, sir," the captain replied, "I understand that and that's what makes me even more determined to be the best."

"You're going to have to wait a while before you're the best, Captain," Colonel Meecham said harshly.

"I beg your pardon, sir."

"You're the second best pilot in the squadron, Johnson. You are talking to the best."

"No, sir," the captain answered, without a change of expression. "I'm still the best."

"Did you hear what I said, Johnson? I said I was the best."

"You are second best, Colonel," the captain said again.

"Ha, ha!" the colonel roared, "you cocky, squealy voiced little bastard. You and me are gonna get along, son. I like somebody that don't take no shit. Of course, we're gonna have to fly together someday, so I can find out what you can do."

"Be glad to, sir. I've heard you're good."

"That is affirmative, Captain. That is affirmative. We'll go up at the beginning of next week to see if you're as good with a jet as you are with your mouth."

"I'll be looking forward to it, sir," the captain said, coming to attention.

Still smiling, Colonel Meecham said, "I enjoyed talking to you, Johnson. I like your attitude. It's a good attitude. It's a real good attitude to find in such a measly body. Good afternoon."

"Good afternoon, sir."

After Johnson left, Colonel Meecham walked to his window and peeked through the venetian blinds at the jet planes, their wings folded, sitting just outside the hangar. He was thinking about Captain Johnson, a crackerjack pilot, a dedicated Marine who would never go far in the Marine Corps because of his voice. A voice like that cannot sway men, Colonel Meecham thought, a voice like that cannot stir the roots of a man's soul and send him into the fire of combat, a voice like that cannot cause a man to want to die, nor order him to a place where he will have to die. Gary Johnson might be a good pilot, but he would never be a good Marine. Men were needed for that.

He snapped the blind shut and returned to his desk, shouting for Latito in a strong, sure voice, "Get in here, Latito, before I call the rabbi on you."

13

No MATTER HOW SEDULOUSLY Ben and Mary Anne prepared for the nightmare, nothing could ameliorate their discomfort at entering a new high school for their annual pilgrimage among strangers. They had speculated that growing up in the American military could affect the personality of an individual in one of two ways. One could either brim with hidden reservoirs of counterfeit personality, walk up to mobs of inbred teen-agers, say the proper things, smile the winning smile, or enter into the mainstream of high school life without experiencing the painful days of walking the school hallways like unearthed troglodytes. Invariably, it took Ben and Mary Anne months before they could overcome their native diffidence, which actually was an obstinate refusal to make themselves vulnerable. They were afraid of being laughed at, of being the object of derision, of isolating themselves further because of a strategic error that caused them to insinuate themselves too soon into that hostile, unforgiving world where adolescents practice the small atrocities and petty cruelties of adults. It took at least three months before they quit hating to wake up in the morning for school.

Each year before the first day of school, Lillian would deliver a buoyant address that was always a variation on a theme. "I think y'all are among the luckiest children in America. You're always traveling, gaining new insights, learning how different people think and act, and learning how to meet people by putting your best foot forward. If I were you on that first day of school, I'd just pick out somebody that I wanted to meet, walk up to them with my head held high and tell them I was new in town and would appreciate a friend. Now that's how I'd do it. Of course,

I'm not you, but instead of moping around with your eyes down, I'd just say to myself that it's a new day and I'm going to make friends with everybody in sight."

"I like moping around with my eyes down," Mary Anne would say.

"Me too," Ben agreed.

Both of them knew how the cycle of friendlessness would end. Eventually someone very ugly or very unhappy would spot a new kid walking around and in tentative, irresolute gestures would offer friendship to you with no ulterior motives except to end their own intolerable loneliness. For a while you would have an ugly, unpopular kid for a friend. Through him you would meet someone else you liked a lot better and gradually your friendship with the first person would erode, then vanish into aggrieved memory. In a new school one had to build a set of friends on the abandoned carcasses of unhappy boys and girls who befriended you during the days when you had no choice. In the middle of the year the new kid would have reached the middle ground. He would begin to unfold, come out, like the moon in half phase. When he regained his equilibrium and began to experiment with the persons he had kept at bay, terrified that someone might steal a peek at the human he actually was, when at best he relaxed and was awash with the beneficent realization that he was a stranger no longer, that he belonged almost as much as anyone else, it was then that the Marine would come home with orders and announce that the family would move again that June.

John C. Calhoun High School was a red brick, two story structure with a statue of the South Carolina statesman pointing a bony twelve-inch finger at the river that curved at a ninety degree angle in front of the school. The school had a colonial facade with a graceful cupola on its roof. Two wings had been added to accommodate the yearly accretions of Marine children who came into town as Ravenel Air Base expanded. A long covered breezeway paralleled the main structure and connected the two wings. In the rectangle created between the wings, the old school, and the breezeway, flowers bloomed beside a stone fountain which did not work. The gymnasium was contiguous to the east wing of the school, and a grassless football field with cracked baked mud harrowed by cleats formed the far boundary of the campus to the north. Both the statue of Calhoun and the front door of the high school looked downriver and by sitting on the front steps one could watch the heavy traffic of yachts and barges work its way past the sandbars and oyster banks of the inland waterway.

Ben and Mary Anne paced the halls of Calhoun High together, deriving strength and comfort from each other's desolation. Both felt that it was a period of high visibility, that their faults and blemishes were sinking into obscurity in an inversely proportional matter. Paranoia was always the first malady to contend with when entering a new school. Ben and Mary Anne felt all eyes were upon them when in actuality no one noticed them at all.

For homeroom, Ben had a large bovine woman named Mrs. Troutman who had an errie sadness about her face even though she smiled all the time. It was as though tragedy lingered discreetly around her. She had a large pleasant nose that sniffed the air at irregular intervals like a heifer catching the scent of blood in the stockyard. She was also Ben's American Civilization teacher during the last period and read from the textbook word for word, pausing to render editorial commentary whenever a particularly salient point was raised by the author of the text. It was obvious to Ben that she was a lot more interested in the politics of homeroom than the muddled breastworks of state and local government.

On the first day of school Mrs. Troutman had risen in the front of the room for her opening address to the homeroom. "I am Mrs. Troutman," she began imperially. "I would like to welcome all of you to the hallowed halls of John C. Calhoun High School. For those of you who are new at our school, and from my records I see that two or three of you are indeed new, I would like to tell you about some of the traditions we hold sacred. In the front hall, embedded in the floor, you will find a block 'C' generously bestowed by the Class of 1960 to instill pride in our athletic squads and our academic endeavors. No one is allowed to walk on the block 'C.' Try to remember that because if one of our big football players catches you, then there may be the devil to pay. Also, as seniors, you have the privilege of cutting in front of the lunchline. Now I will be passing out a school handbook which has most of this information. If you have any questions, I will always be available to my boys and girls from homeroom 4B."

She paused, cleared her throat, her tone taking on an ever deeper seriousness. "The first order of business is to elect homeroom officers. Now I have a reputation of having homerooms that are the envy of the school. Four-B has always been the best. Four-B is the best. And 4B always will be the best. Therefore it is very important to elect the best people to homeroom office. Now I would like a moment of silence for all of you in here to think about who would make the best leader for 4B. It's not always the most popular person you know. Sometimes the quietest person in the room makes the best leader. Everyone sit still now and think about whom you personally think will serve the interests of 4B best. It's not an easy decision, I know. The qualities of a good homeroom president are these, in my opinion." Her voice was getting lower and lower. But she continued to whisper her message, "Courage, Prudence, Aggressiveness, Loyalty to 4B, Charity, Faith, an ability to overcome adversity, and Hope."

"No," Ben disagreed silently, "no homeroom president has ever had a single good quality." The other students fidgeted and looked around at each other, searching each other's eyes for indisputable signs and glimmers of leadership.

Finally Mrs. Troutman began to speak again. "Now I've checked the records and I've found to my shock and disappointment that only one boy in the class has the grades to be eligible for homeroom office."

"Oh, gad," Ben groaned, expecting the worst.

"A 'C' average is required and Benjamin Meecham is the only boy in class that has the grades."

"Benjamin!" Ben heard a boy toward the rear of the class laugh.

"Now I am not going to interfere with the elections at all. But I feel that at least one boy should be nominated for

163

each office, otherwise we'll have all girls as homeroom officers. Could Benjamin Meecham stand up and let everyone in the class get a good look at him? Oh there you are. Welcome to Calhoun High, Benjamin. Now there he is. Take a good look at him."

Ben could feel a blush begin at the cuticles of his toes, rush through his entire body, and assault the very roots of his hair. The other students stared at him as though he were a urine sample.

"I am going to put Benjamin's name in nomination for president of 4B. Are there any other nominations?"

Ben later told Mary Anne it had been a banner day in his history as a high school student. In rapid succession he had been defeated for homeroom president, vice president, secretary, treasurer, sergeant at arms, homeroom representative to the Student Council, and homeroom alternate. The most humiliating aspect of his successive defeats was that he had not garnered a single vote. Not even the new kids had voted for him.

"Who wants a zit-face for homeroom president," Mary Anne had said.

"It wasn't that, sister. They just didn't feel I had any leadership qualities."

On the Thursday of their second week in school, after a lunch of Sloppy Joes, blackeyed peas, apple sauce, coleslaw, and milk, Ben and Mary Anne turned the corner of the breezeway near the shop and were drawn by a surge of bodies toward a central, unseen drama that had an ozone smell of violence about it. A tall freckled boy with carrot-hued hair slicked back was holding a smaller dark haired boy in a headlock as the rest of the crowd laughed at the smaller boy's efforts to free himself.

"Let me go, Red," the smaller boy pleaded.

"Sammy. Now you and me are good buddies, ain't that right?" Red said.

"That's right, Red. So why don't you let me go."

"I want to let you go, Sammy. But you've got to say what I told you to say."

"I won't say that," Sammy answered.

"Then I'm goin' to keep on squeezing your scrawny little

164

Jewboy neck," Red said, tightening his hold. "Now say it, Sammy. Say it before I start gettin' pissed."

"Heil Hitler," the boy said quietly.

"Louder, Jewboy," the other boy commanded. "I want everybody to hear how much you love ol' Adolf."

"Heil Hitler," the boy said louder.

"That ain't loud enough, Sammy," Red said, winking and smiling at the crowd.

Mary Anne turned to Ben and whispered harshly, "Help that boy, Ben."

"Hell no, Mary Anne. Let's get out of here. He'll let him go in a minute."

"If you don't then I will," she said, starting to weave through the crowd.

"Goddammit, Mary Anne, stop," Ben pleaded. "Let's just walk down the hall and mind our own business."

"They're humiliating that boy," Mary Anne said, pressing forward. "He's crying."

Sobs erupted from beneath the jacket of the red-headed boy and Ben knew he had a quick decision to make. Mary Anne would try to scratch Red's eyes out if she reached him and Ben would have a dilemma explaining to his father how he had sided with discretion and prudence while his sister defended the principles of honor and courage by fistfighting a bully at the noon break. Mary Anne was much braver than Ben but he reasoned it was because she had never been punched in the mouth and had no conception of how it hurt.

Ben caught Mary Anne by the arm and said as he went by her, "I ought to punch you, turd."

"Heil Hitler," Sammy said again.

"Any teachers comin', Lee?" Red asked one of his friends.

"Naw, I'm watchin'," Lee answered.

"Now then, Sammy. One more thing and I'll let you go. I love Jesus Christ."

"Leave him alone," a voice said.

Red looked up and saw Ben glaring at him. Several of Red's friends shifted toward Ben, keeping to the edges of the crowd. Ben noticed that Red was a good two inches taller than he was, but he also was certain that he outweighed Red by twenty pounds. Of course, Ben thought, Red has ten or twenty of his buddies surrounding him which gives the battle of poundage back to Red by several thousand pounds.

"Who in the fuck are you, buddy?" Red snarled.

"Just let the guy go and try someone your own size."

"And just what if I don't let go, bubba," Red said, aware that he was losing part of the crowd to this newcomer.

"If you don't let my good friend Sammy go, Red, I'm going to make you say how much you love Martin Luther King," Ben said, and much of the crowd laughed.

"You think you could, bubba. What's the matter with you? Are you a Jewboy too?"

"Yeah, Red. I'm a Jewboy too. And I don't like seeing other Jewboys being picked on by red-headed punks."

"He's a Marine brat," someone shouted to Red. "He ain't no Jew."

"Twinkie, you a Marine brat?" Red asked.

"Yeah."

"I hate Marine brats, Twinkie."

"You're gonna hate 'em a lot worse in a minute," Ben fired back.

"How would you like a fist where your mouth used to be?" Red asked.

"He's a goody goody, Red. Stomp his butt," a voice said from behind Ben. Ben was becoming aware of the voices of satellite greasers moving in and around the perimeter of the fight.

"Hit 'em, Ben," Mary Anne cried out. She was directly behind Ben.

"Who's your fat friend, Twinkie?"

"That's my sister, you red-headed fart, and you say anything about her they're gonna have to clean you up off this breezeway."

"Whip his ass, Red," someone called. By this time, Red had released Sammy and turned to concentrate his full attention on Ben. Sammy slipped out of Red's grip and disappeared, leaving Ben to face the menacing crowd alone. Red and his friends began to close in on Ben. Mary Anne was pushed back deeper into the group of spectators. Someone pushed Ben from behind. He turned and pushed

166

his assailant back. When he did, Red reached into his dungarees and pulled a switchblade from his back pocket. When Ben turned around, the blade of the knife was up against his throat.

Lillian had provided Ben with an inestimable theory that leapt to his brain as soon as he felt the knife point near his larynx. "If a southern boy ever pulls a knife on you, Ben, it is because he knows how to use it." "Red," Ben said. "Red, ol' buddy, you have just won this fight." Adrenaline burned through his stomach like two tributaries pouring into a river. Someone had grabbed him from behind, pinning his arms.

"No, I've just started to win it, Twinkie. You've pissed me off real bad and you're gonna spend a long time paying for it. Now, I want you to say real loud, "I got a fat, ugly sister."

"No!" Ben said.

Then a voice in the crowd began to scream, "Teacher, Teacher." It was Mary Anne's voice. The knife disappeared in an instant. Ben's arms were freed. Ben whirled and sprinted through the crowd.

"There ain't no teacher," a voice behind Ben called.

Red, realizing he had been duped, started through the crowd, which now was milling about in an agitated state with some people pressing forward toward the action and others fleeing away from it. Ben reached Mary Anne who was waiting for him, in the grassy quadrangle off the breezeway. "You've got to beat him up, Ben. Dad will kill you if he finds out someone pulled a knife on you and you didn't do anything."

"Yeah, I know, Mary Anne. And the next time you get me into anything like this . . ."

"He's coming," Mary Anne shouted. Ben grabbed for a history book Mary Anne was taking to her first afternoon class. As Ben turned to face his opponent, he saw Red ominously reaching for his knife again. Without hesitation and with a quickness that caught Red off guard, he slammed the history book against the boy's head with a stunning shot that echoed the length of the breezeway. A tall, thick-lipped boy who had trailed Red in pursuit of Ben caught the history book full in the face, his nose splitting

167

like an overripe piece of fruit, blood spouting down his face. A fist hit Ben on the side of his face just below the ear. Ben staggered against a steel post that supported the overhang to the breezeway. The boy who had hit him was charging forward but was tackled from behind by a screaming Sammy, who mounted the boy's back and was punching him in the back of the head. Mary Anne scratched Red's face as he tried to rise and re-enter the fray, but Red shoved her down as he rose to his knees, stunned and uncomprehending. Ben saw his sister fall into a hedge that bordered the classroom window. He came straight down on Red's skull from a high, splendid angle and this second blow sent Red's face crashing into the cement walk. It was Red's last violent moment of the morning. Though Mary Anne rushed up to kick· Red in the ribcage before Ben could calm her, no one else sallied forth to take up Red's gauntlet.

Suddenly, the breezeway thronged with teachers who began moving groups of kids in different directions, getting the flow of bodies aimed again in the natural pattern of traffic. When Mrs. Troutman spied Ben he heard her wail, "Oh no, not one of my 4B boys." A pair of formidable arms grabbed Ben from behind. Male teachers whose faces were unfamiliar to Ben helped Red up from the cement. One pulled Sammy from the back of the boy who had connected with Ben's face.

Finally, a voice behind him asked Ben, "Who are you, son?"

"My name's Ben Meecham, sir. I'm new here."

"That's nice, Mr. Meecham. I'm your principal," the voice whispered in his ear.

The principal's office was a cramped, achromatic cubicle separated from the library door by a glass trophy case that overflowed with the gilded booty of athletics earned over the past thirty years. Its walls were painted with a postwar bureaucratic gray. The wall behind the principal's desk was covered with photographs of a tall slender man with fluid, long muscles and sandy hair frozen into graceful poses while participating in a variety of sports. In one, he was throwing a football. In another, he was shooting a one-hand set shot. But in most of the photographs, he peered out from behind two sixteen-ounce boxing gloves, crouched low in a boxer's stance, his arms poised and coiled like snakes. Ben was sitting on a chair facing the principal's desk. It was the first time in his life he had been summoned to a principal's office for disciplinary reasons and he did not find the circumstances prepossessing in any way. Running through his mind were lies or excuses he could offer his father for his involvement in the fight. Bull would not mind that there was a fight, only that Ben had lacked the stealth not to get caught. Ben cheered his spirits somewhat by dreaming of strangling Mary Anne with barbed wire or cutting her heart out like an Aztec and eating it before her eyes in her last moments of consciousness.

These images of revenge vanished when the principal, John Dacus, walked through the door and sat down at his desk. The principal had a blond natural grace that made him look younger than he actually was. His voice had a soothing gravity and his smile was disarmingly gentle. He was an older, more formidable version of the man in the photographs. A quiet strength and subterranean power exuded from his body with understated insistence. It was readily apparent to Ben that Dacus was a man of awesome strength. He was looking over Ben's transcript, which a short, bloodless woman had brought from Guidance.

"You're an athlete, Mr. Meecham," Mr. Dacus said, studying the transcript.

"Yes, sir," Ben answered.

The telephone rang. Mr. Dacus picked it up, grunted monosyllables of assent and negation, then hung up.

"That was the doctor, Mr. Meecham. You gave Lee Wicks a broken nose. Doc thinks Red will be O.K. but he has to wait for some X-rays to come through before he can tell for sure. Now we don't like and we don't allow fighting in this school. You just tangled with some upriver boys and they're about the roughest group of white boys in the county. They've given me a hard time ever since they were in the ninth grade. You swing a mighty mean history book, son. Now one important question. Red told me you picked the fight with him. Is that true?"

"Not exactly, sir."

"I started it, Mr. Dacus," a voice called from outside the door. Mary Anne stepped into the room. "I made Ben jump in and help that boy."

"Who are you, young lady?" the principal asked, amused by the intrusion.

"Mary Anne Meecham, sir. I'm Ben's sister and if anyone should be punished for what happened it should be me because I told Ben if he didn't help that poor boy I was going to help him and Ben knew Dad would kill him if he ever heard that I got into a fight to help someone and Ben chickened out. But if you ask me, neither one of us should get in trouble because those tacky, nasty boys deserved everything they got. But it was me that started it. I made Ben do it."

"Oh," the principal said. "You mean it's that simple."

Leaning back in his chair, propping his feet up on the desk, Mr. Dacus picked up the telephone, dialed a single digit, and when a voice answered, said, "Mrs. Whitlock, send me the transcript of Mary Anne Meecham, please." He held his hand over the receiver and asked, "What grade are you in, Miss Meecham?"

"Eleventh, sir."

"She's in the eleventh grade, Mrs. Whitlock. Thank you for your trouble," he said, replacing the phone on the receiver. "It appears to me that the Meechams are an extraordinary family . . ."

Before he could finish there was a determined knock on the door. It was Sammy. "Sammy, what can I do for you, my friend?" the principal said.

"Mr. Dacus, I came to tell you that this boy fought Red because of me. Red was pulling the ol' Hitler routine again and this boy stopped him. Now, of course, you and I know, Mr. Dacus, that if I had gone wild, which I was about to do, I would have torn Red and his pals apart."

"Red was sure lucky you didn't go wild, Sammy. By the way, you ought to convert to Christianity. No religion's worth all the crap you take," Mr. Dacus joked.

Sammy smiled and said, "Yeah, my name sounds real

Christian. Sammy Wertzberger. I'd fool a lot of goys like that."

Mr. Dacus turned his gaze back on Ben. "Where did you learn to fight with a history book, Mr. Meecham? Do you have something against fists?"

"I'd have used my fists, sir, but he pulled a knife."

"Are you sure?" the principal asked, displaying anger for the first time.

"Yes, sir. He stuck it up to my throat."

"You're lucky he didn't use it on you too. Red Pettus is as mean as anybody in this school," Sammy said to Ben.

"That sorry damn pissant," Mr. Dacus said. "I warned him not to pull a knife on anybody at my school again. Were there any other knives pulled or was that the only one? Did Wicks pull one?"

"No, sir," Ben answered. "Just Red."

"Well, that does it for him. He's out for the year."

"No sir, don't do that," Ben pleaded. "He was just showing off. I don't think he'd have cut me."

"You don't," the principal said. "Well ol' Red cut a boy's face real bad at this school two years ago. He was in a reformatory for six months. The one thing you've got to learn in this town, Mr. Meecham, is to avoid fighting with anybody named Pettus. The Pettus family is the meanest upriver family of all. I feel sorry for any child stuck with that name because that means he's gone through the sorriest kind of upbringing possible, but I can't let him go around cutting up the other students. No, that's the end of the line for Mr. Red Pettus."

"It's dangerous to mess with a Pettus," Sammy said to Ben and Mary Anne. "But it's even more dangerous to mess with Fightin' Sammy Wertzberger. Did you see me on top of that Heisley jerk, pounding his head without mercy, the crowd cheering me on, 'amazed at my strength'?"

Everyone in the room laughed. It was the first time Ben had truly relaxed since he came in the door. He was beginning to feel confident in Mr. Dacus's intrinsic sense of justice and fair play; his fine, relaxed humor prescribed the mood in the room.

Then the principal said, "You are suspended, Mr.

171

Meecham. And so are you, Miss Meecham. And so are you, Mr. Wertzberger."

The three of them formed an astonished trinity as they stared at Mr. Dacus with disbelief. The image of his father flashed in Ben's mind.

"Sir," Ben said. "Could you think of another punishment for my sister and me?"

"Like throwing us into a pool of piranhas or ripping our fingernails out?" Mary Anne suggested.

"It's only going to be for one day. I want a chance to talk to Red's little gang before you come back to school. I don't want them jumping you tomorrow. And I want all of you to be careful after school today. I know how those boys think," Mr. Dacus said seriously.

"How do you know how they think, Mr. Dacus?" Mary Anne asked.

"Because, honey," Mr. Dacus answered, "my mother was a Pettus. Ol' Red is a distant cousin of mine."

Ben said, "We're worried about our father, sir. If he finds out we're suspended I could tell him I had a fistfight with Judas Iscariot and it wouldn't make any difference."

"I'll call your father and explain. He'll understand after I tell him the whole story. Leave him to me. Y'all just be careful after school. Now get on to class and don't worry about your father. I'll tell him about the knife."

"I'll name my first child after you, Mr. Dacus," Mary Anne said.

"I'm naming my first child after Judas Iscariot," Sammy said.

"Thanks, Mr. Dacus," said Ben, rising to leave.

"Welcome to Calhoun High School, brother and sister Meecham," the principal said, getting up, and punching Ben on the shoulder in an amicable gesture. Ben's shoulder hurt until the bell rang at three o'clock releasing the students like a pistol at the starting blocks. From two-thirty to three, at Calhoun High School, and every school he had attended, Ben's mind wandered far away from the teacher's voice and concentrated on the energy of escape that poured out of each student like light, then became something tangible, almost nuclear, something to be reckoned with in the half-hour before reprieve.

172

They took their time going home that day, reliving the fight again and again, proud now of their participation and of their decision to help Sammy. Walking down River Street, they stopped at every window and planned exorbitant purchases when they made their first million dollars.

"I want a diamond to put in my navel," Mary Anne said in front of Liebman's Jewelers.

"It'd have to be the size of a volleyball. Your navel is huge. I saw Okra walk across your stomach one time and disappear from sight when he hit your bellybutton."

"Very funny, feces face."

Past the Palmetto Theater where they studied the stills of coming attractions, past Sarah Poston's dress shop, past the bookstore which contained almost no books, and the barbershop which was really a pool hall, and the bank, which was an old refurbished mansion, they walked toward home. When they reached "The Lawn," a large greensward that lent its name to their neighborhood, with its columned white houses arranged around it, Ben was the first one to hear the car doors slam behind them. As he looked around he saw four boys spilling out of a 1955 Ford. One of them was Red Pettus.

"Run, Mary Anne," Ben said, looking toward his house and seeing his father's car in the driveway. "Get Dad, quick."

Mary Anne dropped her books and ran with surprising speed for their house which was situated at the far corner of the rectangle formed by the Lawn. Dropping his books, Ben turned to face the four antagonists who now bore down on him.

"Don't drop those books, Twinkie. 'Cause that's the only way you can fight." Red snarled, "I thought you were gonna stop me with a speller this afternoon."

"Red, I don't have any bone to pick with you."

"Is this the one, little brother?" a heavy, narrow-eyed boy said, appraising Ben carefully and moving around to his left with an impatient caution. He was in his early twenties and his hands were calloused and hard from labor. He also had red hair, but of a deeper, less offensive color than Red's.

"Yeah, Mac. This is the Twinkie, O.K. I guess you don't

173

have any bone to pick with me. I sure got a big one to pick with you," Red said, going for his knife again. "You got me kicked out of school for a whole year, Twinkie."

"Put that knife up, Red. Use your fists or nothin' at all," his brother warned. Red slipped the knife into his back pocket and advanced toward Ben. The other two boys, who had remained silent, moved behind Ben and waited for Red or his brother to make the first move.

"You need three guys to whip me, Red. You chicken shit," Ben said.

"I could tear you in half, Twinkie."

"Why don't you prove it, you carrot-topped bastard. Your hair is sure ugly. It looks like someone shit on the top of your head."

"Let's get him fast, boys, and get the hell out of here," Red's brother said. "That girl's probably got the cops coming already."

A fist burned into Ben's kidney from behind, dropping him down on his knees. Another blow caught him flush on the cheekbone. He dove at Red's legs and succeeded in bringing him to the ground. Ben began to swing and kick at everything until he himself was kicked in the solar plexus and he lay gasping for breath, tears rolling down his cheeks.

The station wagon backed out of the Meecham driveway, came down Eliot Street at an unobtrusive pace, then accelerated across the Lawn at fifty miles an hour, stopping between the combatants and the '55 Ford parked in the road. Two men wearing flight jackets jumped from the car, removing their jackets as they did so and slinging them behind them as they advanced forward toward Ben who had quit fighting and had rolled into a defensive crouch to minimize the damage inflicted by the fists and kicks.

Ben heard his father say, "Which two do you want, Virgil?"

"Shit, Bull, let me kill all four of them by myself. You go back to the house and fix a couple of drinks. I might even break out into a sweat."

"No, Virge, that wouldn't be fair. I don't want you to have all the fun. I want to kill at least one of them."

The four boys were looking for possible routes of escape

174

when Red's brother decided that in arbitration lay his salvation from this swiftly retrograding dilemma. He proffered his hand to Bull and with a sincere but uncertain smile he said, "I've no quarrel with the Marine Corps. No sir. I've always admired and respected the Marine Corps."

"That's mighty nice of you, sir," Bull said, taking the boy's hand. "And I've got a real feeling your respect for the Corps is going to sky-rocket in just a few minutes." Bull began to squeeze the boy's hand in a pincerlike grip until the boy attempted to pull away. Soon Bull began to work the bones of the boy's right hand against each other, applying more and more pressure, until the boy began to scream for his friends to pull Bull off. Then, without haste, Bull waited for the right opening and hit him with a left cross that jerked the boy backward as though he had been shot. He would have fallen but Bull had not released his hand.

His breath coming back to him, each new lungful of air a gift of infinite price, Ben rose to one knee and watched the fight with eyes that were clouded with pain. He saw Colonel Hedgepath crouched in a boxing stance weaving toward the two boys who had attacked Ben from behind. One of them began to swing wildly at the colonel, who stepped back, and aimed a kick that landed solidly in the boy's scrotum. Then, with careful deliberation and without a wasted movement, he punched the other boy to the ground with two punches to the stomach and two to the face.

Red circled behind Bull, coming at his back carefully. Reaching for his knife but thinking better of it, he threw himself against the colonel's legs. Bull stumbled but did not hit the ground. Instead, he lifted his legs and brought his shoe down hard on Red's wrist. By this time Ben was up and game again, his sore places numb and his temper deepening into a white heat manifested by a low, animal whine emitted as he charged the prone figure of Red. He left his feet and came down on Red's back with his knees, the air rushing out of his lungs as though he were a beach toy. All four of Ben's assailants were stretched out in the grass in various postures of defeat and pain. Dancing like schoolboys, Bull and Virgil went from one boy to the other as though touching bases, pleading with them to rise and fight again. Then Bull, seeing their car parked on the road behind his, sprinted toward it and mounted the front of the car with a single leap. He began to leap up and down on the car's hood, caving it in to the loud accompaniment of crumpling steel and Virgil's hurrahs. Then, he danced on the Ford's roof, leaving footprints of steel in his truculent clog across the top of the car. As a final signature, he leaped from the roof to the trunk and finally back to the ground, then, still seized with a demonic energy released by the fight, began pulling Red and his friends off the ground and kicked them toward the car.

"If you punks ever mess with my boy again," Bull screamed, "they'll find pieces of you all over town."

That night after dinner Ben came downstairs with Mary Anne to say good night to the adults.

"How's my godson?" Virgil Hedgepath said.

"He's sore, Colonel," Ben answered.

"I'll tell you one thing, Virgil. I didn't know Mary Anne could move so fast," Bull said. "She ran that hundred yards from Ben to the house in just under three minutes."

"You will notice, Poopsy, that I am not even vaguely amused by your juvenile sense of humor. I look on myself as the heroine of the entire episode. You were the minutemen. I was Paul Revere."

"Well, Mary Anne, I have you to thank then for one of the most enjoyable afternoons I have spent in many a year. That reminded me, Bull, of the first time we got liberty when our carrier docked in San Francisco after the war," Virgil said.

"We must have fought with half the Pacific fleet during that week and a half," Bull said.

"It looks like my godson, old Marine Junior here, can use his fists when it's necessary."

"I got a phone call from your principal, Mr. Dacus today, Ben. He told me about the Jew you and Mary Anne helped out. I was right proud of both of you. I bet the reputation is going to spread around that school real fast that screwing with Meechams is like playing with fire."

Lillian and Paige Hedgepath joined their husbands in the

den. Lillian served coffee to Bull and Virgil, putting a shot of Irish whiskey in each cup.

"I was just trying to talk Paige into coming to the tea I'm going to give for the senior officers' wives in December, Virge. You work on her at home and I'll make a novena once a month."

"Honey," Paige said, "it would take a lot more than God and Virgil Hedgepath to get me to one of those godawful boring teas where those dumb wives sit around counting each other's wrinkles."

"Behind every successful Marine officer stands his loyal and uncomplaining wife," Virgil joked.

"My tea will be stimulating, Paige. That's why I want you to be there so much."

"I've always admired you for not going to those silly things, Mrs. Hedgepath," Mary Anne said.

"You may wish everyone good night, sugah," Lillian said coldly to her daughter. "You too, Ben, my pugilist son whom I have failed to raise as a gentleman."

"C'mon, Mama. I was a victim of circumstance. I've explained the whole thing to you."

"Yes, you've explained it. You've explained that you behaved like a beast all day picking one fight after another. I thought I was doing a better job than that of making you into something a bit more civilized than a chimpanzee."

"Hell," Bull said to Virgil, "I'd hate to be that civilized."

"You obviously have more of your father in you than I thought," Lillian said. "Now good night, you two. It's been a long day."

Mary Anne kissed Colonel Hedgepath on the lips. "Good night, demon lover," she said. "Good night, Godzilla," she said to her father. "Good night, Paige. Don't you think I'm old enough to call you Paige? We're both mature women."

"Hell no," Bull shouted.

"That's disrespectful," Lillian said disapprovingly.

"Call me Paige when they're not around, Mary Anne. That goes for you too, Ben. Give me a kiss, Ben."

"O.K., Mrs. Hedgepath."

"That's it golden boy. Get in a few brownies before you go to bed," Mary Anne said. "Good night, Paige."

"What've I gotta do. Write you a book? It's Mrs. Hedgepath to you," Bull said.

"Hush, Bull," Paige snapped back. "Good night, you two. Ben, when are you and I going to run off and get married?"

"Soon. Very soon," Ben said, smiling. His whole body ached and there was a sudden pain when he smiled through split lips.

"Those are two fine kids," Virgil said after Ben and Mary Anne had left the room.

"They still need to be whipped into shape," Bull said.

"Horseshit, Bull," Paige flared. "Appreciate what you have and be goddam glad that you have it."

"You know our children look on you as their second parents, Paige," Lillian said softly. "That must mean something."

"It does," Paige Hedgepath said, close to tears. "It means everything."

14

IN BULL'S MIND, a rational structure that underwent analysis, change, decay, transfusions, and bright injections of insulin whenever he found a flaw undermining the whole system, he plotted out the course of how he would be the best squadron commander in the history of the Marine Corps. In his bones he could feel war with Cuba an inevitability and he constantly exhorted the young pilots to hone their skills because he felt that their day of fire was very near. He knew the mechanics of being a good commander: the tricks, procedures, requirements, and occasional gymnastics one had to employ to keep morale high and the higher echelons pleased. Much of it was natural to him; the rest he would pick up as he went along. Three weeks after he took command, he had talked to every man in his squadron and knew something personal about each one. He had a limitless capacity for being everywhere, for appearing on the flight line when he was supposed to be signing weekend passes. His methodology was simple. While he had inherited problems in 367, he was determined to purify it of difficulties, procedural or spiritual, within a short period of time. If he could not, he told his Exec, "the squadron will bleed."

Part of this command superstructure that had accumulated over an entire career was not completely fleshed out but still had impact on the colonel's persona as a commander. One intuitive feeling he had that he could not trace to anyone or anything, except perhaps to some footnote in the *Marine Corps Officers' Guide,* was that a Marine commander should establish a good rapport with the civilian population of the local town. He had noticed that none of the other squadron commanders ever mentioned this secondary responsibility, but once Bull thought about it, he hunted about for a satisfactory solution. It was this extra attention to detail, a supernumerary zeal to approach perfection that led him to spend part of each weekday morning at Hobie's Grill.

Hobie Rawls was the mayor of Ravenel and was the size of a tight end gone to seed. His grill was the gathering place for the men of the town who liked to monitor the traffic on River Street or who wanted to hear gossip when it was still lean and stringy, before it developed the corpulence of passing between too many lips. Bull knew that every town had its Hobie's, a rallying place for both the withered and the bright pharisees who had a passion for assembly and a genuine need to keep a tab on the why's and wherefore's of their town.

It was no easy task for a stranger to become a regular at Hobie's. The men who peopled the grill in the early hours of morning were not just regulars to the restaurant, they were regulars to the town and their family names were on street signs and monuments. It was a closed and grandly intolerant brotherhood. But Bull had broken into the inner circle just by appearing at the restaurant one morning at 0715 hours. Routine was a powerful icebreaker with the boys who drank their morning coffee with Hobie.

He had liked the restaurant immediately. It was unpretentious, masculine, decorated with a nautical motif, and had a constant smell of fried bacon about it. Photographs of shrimp boats and fishermen with their splendid catches of blues and whitings lined the walls from top to bottom. One wall was lined with high-backed leather booths opposite a long counter with twelve stools. A huge beveled mirror gave a man sitting on the stool a view of the whole grill. Bull had chosen a stool in the middle of the counter on the day he first became part of the crowd.

Several men had turned to look and nod at him when he walked through the door. He perused the menu perfunctorily and listened to a conversation resume that he had interrupted when he walked through the door. He marveled at the slowness of their speech; words seemed to crawl from their mouths and drop like stones to the floor.

"Did you see that movie playin' at the Palmetto?" Cleve

180

Goins, the auto parts man asked without directing the question to anyone in particular. No one answered, but Cleve continued anyway, "What's this damn world comin' to anyhow? Will someone tell me? There was bare titty all over the screen. My wife made me cover her eyes. I told Wyatt Gosnell that I wasn't gonna set a toe in his motion picture house until he could start showin' some family entertainment."

"Yeah, it must have been bad all right," Ed Mills, the postman said. "Wyatt told me you stayed through that movie twice."

"He didn't say any such a thing, Ed."

"You wouldn't a missed that pitcher show if it'd been playin' in Red China," Johnnie Voight hissed into his coffee.

"I heard they had to pull ol' Cleve away from that screen four or five times 'cause he kept runnin' up there to get a closer look," another man said.

"Liar. A doctor of medicine lyin' like a field nigger," Cleve shot back. "I was just tryin' to tell you all that someone ought to do something about that trash that's being shown in this town. There was one scene, sure enough, when I thought the hero was gonna slap it to her right before my eyes. He was a rubbin' and a underlatin' and a pantin' like an old boar tryin' to get hisself a little."

"God bless us all," the doctor whined. "Can't somebody go over to Cleve's store and buy a carburetor or something so we can escape this ungodly chatter."

"I just thought you boys might be interested," Cleve said, his feelings hurt.

"What time does that movie start?" Ed asked. Everyone in the grill laughed except for Cleve, who assumed a posture of righteous disgruntlement.

Hobie Rawls, his ample frame encased in a white apron, approached Colonel Meecham and asked if he was ready to order.

"Yes, sir, I am," Colonel Meecham answered. "I'll take two eggs over light, bacon, a cup of coffee, and hash browns."

"Sorry, Colonel. We only serve grits. It's kind of a custom down here."

"No hash browns, eh? That's a shame," Colonel Meecham said.

"Where are you from?" the doctor asked, sitting two stools down to Bull's right.

Bull glanced up and answered the doctor's reflection in the mirror, "Chicago, Doc."

"You just get stationed here?" Hobie asked.

"I've been here for a while. I'm C.O. of 367 over at the air station."

Ed Mills said, "It seems to me that a man who flies jets ought to be able to eat a few grits."

"I wouldn't mind eating grits if there's ever a famine," the colonel answered.

Ed studied the colonel's features. "Do you live in the old Huger place over on the Lawn?" he asked.

"Yep, at least I guess it's the old Huger place. It doesn't have a nametag."

"Your name's Meecham. I've been delivering mail to your house for a couple of weeks now."

"That's one thing about this town, Colonel. A man can't fart in this town without it sounding like a thunderclap. I'm Zell Posey. If you ever need any legal work done, I'm at your service." Posey was a starkly thin man with vulnerable eyes and a leg brace. These were the first words he had spoken to anyone.

"Thank you, sir. I'm Bull Meecham and if anything comes up, I'll remember you. By the way, Ed," he said to the postman, who occupied the first stool by the door, "how long have you been delivering mail?"

"He's been messin' up people's mail for thirty years now," a man with a florid, hawk-nosed face said from a far booth.

"Just like you been messin' up people's hair, Pride," Ed retorted.

"Kilgo can plain mess up a man's head of hair," Cleve agreed.

"Well, with you, Cleve, I ain't got a great deal to work with," Kilgo said.

"Ol' Lady Medusa won't go to nobody 'cept Pride Kilgo," the doctor added.

"Don't listen to them, Colonel. I'm a master of my

trade. An artist," Kilgo said. "Which is more than I can say for the Doc. I knew a man that went to Doc Ratteree with a hangnail one time and ended up getting his arm sawed off to the elbow. And I swear on a Bible, it was the wrong damn arm."

"God bless the dimwit," the doctor exhaled.

"There's been many a man who walked into ol' Doc's office healthy as a roach and come out with a sheet over his face," Cleve said.

"Damn you, Cleve. You weren't talking so big when your wife had pneumonia last year."

"It's O.K., Doc," Ed Mills rasped. "I can say for a fact that you've saved one or two people from certain death in your career. And if I stay here all day I can probably even come up with their names."

"He saved Hoyt Simms's life for sure, by insurin' his wife didn't live through that operation."

From behind the counter, Hobie called out, "Any of you gentlemen want any coffee, raise your paws."

"Yeah, I don't think Hoyt could have lived another day with that woman."

"Why did Doc operate on Mrs. Simms?"

"He didn't operate," Ed Mills said. "He was giving her a blood test and she bled to death."

"God bless 'em to hell."

"He made Stinky Sanders, the mortician, the richest man in town, Colonel," Hobie Rawls said while pouring coffee into Bull's cup from a steaming glass globe.

"Stinky gives the sonbitch ten percent on every stiff he delivers to get drained," Cleve said, jubilant that the heat was off him.

"That's a goddam lie," Ed Mills objected in his acidulated voice, "and I'll fight any man who says that about the Doc. He gets twenty percent on a stiff if he gets a nickel."

"Hobie," a man from a back booth cried out, invisible to Bull, "something's wrong with my eggs. They taste good."

"Well, send it back to the kitchen. Don't let Hobie get away with somethin' as serious as that."

"Colonel, I think I better warn ya," Ed Mills said from his position on the first stool, "Jimbo Punt used to eat an

183

egg a day on that same stool where you're sittin'. He dropped dead of blood poisoning less than a year ago and the boy was only twelve years old."

"He drowned in the river, and he was eighteen, Colonel," Hobie corrected.

The cluster of bells thong-tied to the upper hinges of the entrance door jingled and a short, thin woman with a cigarette hanging straight downward from her mouth walked in. The laws of gravity were about to apply to a long ash that clung to the cigarette. In her face, Bull read a history of too much caffeine and nicotine and too much of something else, but whatever it was, it was much worse. The lines in her face looked earned; they were not decorations casually bestowed. She chose the stool by Ed Mills and barked to Hobie for a cup of coffee. Though she was the only woman in the grill, she did not seem to notice, nor did her entry diminish the feeling of fraternity that enriched the early morning banter.

"If it ain't Bertha Grimmitt—you ain't been in here in a coon's age," Cleve Goins shouted.

"Shut up, Cleve," Bertha answered in a strong, slow voice with a brassy resonance that could hang in a room for a long time. "I've always hated you."

Bull thought, "That'll shut ol' Cleve up, I bet."

"Wa-hoooo," Cleve yelped instead.

"Where'd you park your broom, Bertha?" a voice asked from a middle booth.

"You boys leave Miss Bertha alone," Hobie said.

"Don't worry about me, Hobie," Bertha said, "these boys don't worry me."

"Truer words were never spoken."

After taking two deep swallows of coffee she announced to all the men in the grill, and Bull took note that the boys at Hobie's took their cues from Bertha, that "It's great to be here among the Dead Pecker Club again, listening to all the dead peckers mouth off like they still had a little vinegar left in them."

"Ah, the flower of southern womanhood," the crippled man at the kitchen end of the counter sighed. It was the lawyer, Zell Posey, and by his tone Bull knew that bad blood moved between him and Bertha.

"I hope I didn't offend his royal highness by including him in the Dead Pecker Club."

"Offend me, Madame?" Posey replied with regal disdain. "I barely even admit to myself that you're alive." Zell Posey spoke with a voice that was a cry of pain. His face was noble; a face sculpted from an aggrieved aristocracy that was bleeding out through weak tributaries in the long delta of the twentieth century. His eyes contained a fire that could not ignite the other frontiers of his body.

"That's because you've got that nose of yours stuck so far in the air that you never get to look down to see us common nits on the ground."

"Oh, c'mon, Bertha," a voice said. "Zell's got blue blood. That's why his nose is stuck up in the air."

"Yeah, I know," Bertha said. "He's gotta have his nose up in the air so he can sniff that angel shit." Then she turned her eyes down the counter and saw Colonel Meecham stirring the grits that Hobie had insisted on heaping on his plate. He enjoyed eavesdropping on verbal swordplay that had edge, and even wickedness. Bull heard Bertha speaking to him. "The Dead Pecker Club has a new member, I see. Colonel, my name is Bertha Grimmitt. I'm your friendly neighborhood florist."

"Bull Meecham, ma'am," he answered saluting her in the mirror.

"Got any kids?" she asked.

"Four, ma'am," he answered.

"A real live pecker here at Hobie's. That's as rare as a good joke on these stools," she laughed.

Hobie asked, "Ya got any kids that'll be going to the high school?"

"Yep. Two of them, Hobie. And one of them is going to be your star basketball player."

"Is that right?" Hobie answered. "My girl's gonna be a senior."

"You Marines breed like mink. I know one sergeant over on the island what had eleven children. Most of 'em boys," Cleve said.

"You'll have to excuse these Philistines, Colonel," Zell spoke up. "I assure you that the trash you heard in Hobie's this morning is not indicative of the citizens of Ravenel.

There are many gentlemen and ladies [he said bowing hostilely toward Bertha] of genuine distinction and cultural awareness."

"Thus speaketh the deadest pecker in the family of man. A fossil imprinted with ferns and the skeletons of fish," Bertha said through a cigarette.

"There is no culture or refinement here. That's what I detest about this restaurant," Zell said.

"Why do you think we come here, Zell?" Ed Burns answered from the opposite stool.

Colonel Meecham rose to pay his check. He looked down at his grits and said, "That's the worst Cream of Wheat I've ever tasted."

"That's Georgia ice cream," Doc Ratteree said.

"Every time I eat grits, it becomes perfectly clear to me why the South lost the war."

"We gonna see you again, Colonel?" Hobie asked.

"You boys are gonna have a hard time getting rid of me," Bull answered. "Enjoyed it."

"Give them Russians hell, today, Colonel," Bertha called as he left the restaurant.

He walked out into the smoky brightness of River Street which was beginning to shake off the inertia of the dawn. It was a moist, hot September day and the air was heavy enough to exact a toll from anyone consuming it. Before the colonel could get to his car, a voice hailed him from behind. He turned around and watched Zell Posey limping toward him.

"Colonel," Zell said, when he reached him, "I just wanted to tell you how much I admire the courage and professionalism of the Marine Corps."

"Thanks very much, Mr. Posey."

"I tried to join the Marines during the Second World War, but they didn't seem to have room for one-legged men. I really wanted to fight with the Corps. I really did," he said, looking past the colonel toward the curving road. "I lost the leg in a boating accident when I was a child. But I wanted you to know that."

Bull was fidgeting as he always did when someone stripped away an outer layer of himself and revealed something intensely personal. Not even a metatarsal of any family skeleton interested Bull Meecham if the family was not his own. But Zell continued to open up until Bull, renouncing his role of confessor, insisted that he had to get to work.

"Of course," Zell said. "But just one other thing, Colonel. Don't take seriously what Bertha says. She doesn't mean a thing by it."

"I know she doesn't," Bull said. "That's some broad."

"She was once my wife," Zell said, turning to walk to his office.

15

THREE WEEKS after the beginning of school, Bull arrived home from the squadron at the precise instant that Lillian was setting dinner on the table. In her career as a Marine wife she had failed in her efforts to train her husband to call when he would be working late or not returning home at all. Bull washed his hands at the kitchen sink, dried them on one of Lillian's aprons, and joined the family for grace. As the pilot said grace, he rubbed his hands together in anticipation of the evening meal and spoke the words of the prayer so rapidly that it would take a most patient deity to find gratitude in the stream of rhetoric offered at the Meecham table. Then Bull, in an expansive mood, shouted, "Chow down, troops," lifting a piece of roast from the platter and biting into it before the meat even touched his plate.

"Bull, sugah," Lillian said, "they've invented these weird new instruments. They're called forks."

"Yeh, that's right," Bull acknowledged, still fingering the roast. "They've also got these weird old instruments called hands. They work better."

"I don't think you should eat like that in front of the children," she said.

"Get off my back, will you!" Bull shouted. "I've had a tough day at the office making the world safe for democracy. I'm hungry."

"I'm thinking about having a trough built at your end of the table so you can just stick your whole head into a pile of slop."

"Mama thinks you eat like a pig, Daddy. She's just trying to help you develop good table manners," Karen said.

"I've heard that pigs get sick to their stomachs while eating at the same table with Dad," Mary Anne said.

"O.K., O.K.," Bull sighed, placing his meat on his plate and lifting up a fork with mock delicacy. "Will someone please pass the Coquille Saint Jack."

"I'm trying to set a good example for the children."

"They have great table manners."

"That's because their mother happens to be a woman of some refinement."

"Who married a damn prince among men," Bull grinned. "If one of the hogs doesn't do something right, let me know and I'll deck 'em."

"That's not the point."

"Lillian, I'm in a good mood. No kidding, honey. And we all know how rare that is."

"Amen," Ben said quietly.

"Hey. I got a great surprise for you, sportsfans," he said to Ben.

"Why am I suddenly finding it difficult to swallow my food?" Ben said rolling his eyes at Mary Anne. "What is it, Dad?"

"I talked to Lieutenant Colonel Matthews at the club this afternoon."

"You never thought to call and tell me you were going to be late."

"You remember his daughter, Ansley, from New River, don't you?"

"Yes, sir," Ben answered.

"Well, she's been going steady for two years with this football player at the high school, Jim Don Cooper. Well, Colonel and Mrs. Matthews are trying to put a stop to this little relationship by making Ansley date other people. The long and the short of it is, you've got a date with Ansley Matthews this Saturday night."

For ten seconds, the only sound in the dining room was the clink of silver on china.

"Tell him I'm not going, Mama," Ben finally said.

"You might enjoy it, Ben. Ansley is a sweet girl."

"A team of internationally known scientists did a study on Ansley Matthews last year and came to the unanimous conclusion that she is an idiot," Mary Anne said.

189

"Well, you're going," Bull said, his voice chilling into ultimatum.

"Dad," Ben said looking at his father, "you can beat me or torture me or kill me or do anything you want to me. Just don't make me go on that date Saturday night. Tell Colonel Matthews I have leukemia or terminal hemorrhoids. Anything. I just can't go on that date."

"Hey, you never date at all, jocko. You're almost eighteen and you've never had a date. I'm beginning to think you're some kind of homo."

"Bull, shame on you for saying that to your own son," Lillian flared.

"When I was your age," Bull declared, "they couldn't keep me away from the girls with a stick."

"He's been sicko all his life," Mary Anne explained to Ben.

"I just haven't seen anybody I want to date in this town," Ben said.

"Ben dated quite frequently when you were overseas last year," Lillian lied.

"Baloney, he's never touched a girl in his life," Bull said.

"I think you're right, Dad," Mary Anne said, sipping from her iced tea. "I think Ben's a homo. I see him looking at you real funny sometimes."

"I am not going out with Ansley," Ben said.

"Wait a minute, hog. I ain't asking you whether you are going out with Ansley or not. I'm telling you that you are. The date is set. It is this Saturday evening at 1900 hours and you will pick her up and you will be on time and you will have yourself a blast or I will personally ruin your whole day."

"I think the Matthews just want Ansley to date some nice, wholesome boys for a change, Ben," Lillian said.

"Parents love Ben. Girls don't, but parents do. It's like sending their daughters out on a date with young Jesu, the carpenter," Mary Anne said.

"This is just like that time you took me to that church dance up in Arlington, Dad," Ben said, "when you bought me that ugly shirt and the ugliest tie ever made and forced me to go to that sock hop where I didn't know one single human being."

"You ended up having a ball at that dance."

"No, I didn't. I walked in through the front door and right straight out the back door. Then I walked two miles to a library, read for a couple of hours, then walked back to the church, went in the back door and out the front where you were still sitting waiting for me. Then I told you I danced every dance. Of course in telling you this story, Dad, I do it with the firm belief that you won't belt me for something I did two years ago."

"I don't mind belting you for something you did two years ago."

"Hush up, Bull," Lillian scolded, "and try not to act like you're losing your mind. Ben, think of it this way. We've known the Matthews for a long time and you'll just be doing the family a big favor. Eileen is very worried about this boy Ansley is dating."

"She ought to be. Jim Don has a striking resemblance to the Java Man," Mary Anne said. "But that's not really fair. He looks more like a combination of the Java Man and Dad."

"Could you imagine if I said that?" Ben asked his parents. "I'd be airborne, flying toward Mars right now. The girls in this family can say anything."

"Mary Anne, what do I have to do to make you have a more deferential attitude toward your parents?" Lillian asked, as though pained to the point of numbness just to have to ask the question.

"A punch to the mouth would do it," Bull stated.

"Apologize to your father, young lady."

"I'm sorry I noticed the resemblance between you and the Java Man, Dad."

"Go straight to your room, young lady, until you can learn the meaning of the word 'respect,'" Lillian demanded.

"Let me just punch her," Bull said smiling. "You underestimate the power of the fist, Lillian."

"Gentlemen do not punch ladies, sugah. Beasts punch ladies," Lillian stated.

Mary Anne rose from her chair and walked over to her

father. "Mom's right, Dad. When you hit me, just try to knock out a couple of back molars so it won't mess up my Ipana smile."

Bull rocked with laughter, picked up his roast with his fingers and resumed eating.

On Saturday night, Ben eased his father's squadron car up to the main gate of Freedom Bay, the Capehart housing section that sheltered the Marines stationed at Ravenel Air Station. The car was a 1951 Plymouth that had passed down to five consecutive C.O.'s of 367. Two large circular decals featuring the grotesquely salivating Werewolf emblem that symbolized the historical ferocity of the squadron adhered to the sides of the car. The decals glowed with a truculent orange in the dark. Lillian refused to drive the car, declaring that she felt like a moving advertisement for a Lon Chaney movie. Though Ben had pleaded for the station wagon, Bull had insisted that the Plymouth was a conversation piece and would help break the ice on Ben's first date.

The corporal on duty at the sentry box braced to attention when he saw the officer's sticker on the front bumper of the car. Lowering the visor and sitting up as high in the seat as he could, Ben nodded at the guard with grandly exaggerated condescension and, mimicking his father, said, "Good evening, son." Ben took a young lieutenant's joy in being saluted.

Turning left on Iwo Jima Boulevard, Ben smiled as he always did when he found himself navigating through the hall of mirrors known as military housing. Freedom Bay was a collection of one thousand brick homes designed by an architect with a passion for duplication. The Meecham family had lived in these houses, all of them, at different times in Bull Meecham's career. In the Corps, there was a uniformity of dress, of ideology, of conduct, and of housing. Twice in his life, Ben had walked into his own house only to find startled strangers eyeing him with both fear and outrage until the mystery was clarified and he was directed toward his father's house by laughing captains' wives who claimed they frequently made the same mistake after nightfall. The Capehart housing of Freedom Bay, Ben thought, as he curved down Iwo Jima

Boulevard, had all the architectural complexity and stylistic flamboyance of an oyster bed. A small, minnowless creek formed the one demarcation line of significance in the entire housing project. The creek itself was viscous as phlegm, but its indentation marked the beginning of the brass curtain that separated the officers and their families from the enlisted men and their families. Once he crossed the creek, Ben was in officers' country, his native land.

He picked up Ansley Matthews at her house on Command Circle, charming her parents with a pleasant volubility that marked him as a blood member of the tribe. The child of the Marine officer was a prodigy of the first impression. The old courtesies poured out of him at the approach of an adult. So often had Ben been drilled in the proper manner in which to greet Marines and their wives that his act was no longer an act but an intrinsic manifestation of his personality. Obsequiousness came easy to him. In fact, he enjoyed the worm's-eye view that servility offered to him. Sitting in the living room, Ben had shone brightly in the companionship of Colonel and Mrs. Matthews, overpowering them with the heavy artillery fire of impeccable manners. He wished he could sit in that living room decorated heavily with the dreck of Okinawa, and hold forth with the adults all night, but Ansley entered the room with a look on her face that articulated a strong desire to leave the house immediately.

As he saw her, two thoughts occurred to Ben. One was that Ansley was far too pretty for him to date or to consider dating, especially on his first excursion. He felt toadish beneath her gaze. The second was that Ansley had wanted to go on this date even less than he did. Her face was flushed with anger and resignation. She did not speak to either of her parents as they left the house, Ben filling in for her hostile silences by exuberantly bidding the Matthews farewell again and again.

Standing before the glowing decal of 367 and staring with horror at the dripping fangs of the Werewolf mascot, Ansley put her hands on her hips and shrieked, "I'm not going anywhere with this silly, horrid thing on the side of the car. Do you want to make me the laughingstock of

Calhoun? It's going to be embarrassing enough for me tonight without riding around in this disgusting car."

Ben opened the door to the car, his knees so weak that he seemed likely to collapse in the driveway. "This is the only car I could get tonight, Ansley," he said.

She shook her head, clicking her teeth, and slid into the car. Rounding the car, Ben was trembling so hard he wondered if he would be able to drive.

For five minutes, Ansley refused to speak, ignoring every question he asked. Finally, Ben said, "Look, Ansley. I can take you back home if you want. My father and your father set this date up, you know."

"My father forced me to go," Ansley said. "I have a steady boy friend."

"I know you have a boy friend. My father made me go tonight, too. Do you have any particular place you want to go?"

"I don't want to go anywhere in this car. I'd rather die."

"Do you like being a cheerleader?" Ben said, changing the subject and grateful that at least she had begun answering his questions.

"I'd rather cheer than anything in the world," she said, then looking at Ben asked, "Why don't you play football? You're big enough."

"I don't like football."

"You're nothing at this school if you don't play football."

"You don't play football."

"I guess that's supposed to be funny."

"I play basketball."

"Basketball's nothing. An absolute zero. Jim Don plays basketball and that's the only reason I even like to cheer at the games. He's captain of the football team, you know. I never saw you at any of the football games. Where'd you normally sit?"

"I never went to any games."

"Boy, you sure are eaten up with school spirit, aren't you, Ben? My daddy's trying to break me and Jim Don up. But he'll never be able to do it. I just hope Jim Don doesn't see us tonight. He beat up one boy that dated me."

"Oh, that's great," Ben said, instinctively checking the rearview mirror.

"He's insanely jealous. But he's so sweet. I just hope he doesn't see us tonight. He told me he'd be out cruising looking for us."

"We won't go anywhere where he can see us."

"Oh we have to. We just have to. We have to make the scene at the Shack. My daddy told me to show you where all the gang hangs out. Jim Don has a new Impala. He packed tomatoes last summer and made enough money for a big down payment. Are those Weejuns you're wearing?" she asked Ben.

"What?" Ben asked.

"Weejuns. Loafers. Everyone at the school wears Weejuns."

"No, they're just loafers. I don't know what kind they are."

"That's a Gant shirt, isn't it?"

"It might be. Mom bought it at the PX yesterday."

"No, it's not Gant," she said impatiently. "The PX doesn't sell them and there's no loop at the back."

"It's Ivy League, though," Ben offered. "It's got buttons on the collar."

"That's no big deal."

"I've never been to the Shack," Ben said.

"It's real close to the colored high school. The cutest colored boys in the whole universe work there. They'll just die if they see me with you."

Ansley turned the dial until she heard the Ape bellow from WAPE in Jackonsville. "Every car in the Shack will be tuned to the Big APE," she said, singing along with the music.

Ben turned into the parking lot of the Shack as Ansley slid down in the front seat until her head was not visible to anyone looking in through the driver's side of the car. To his mortification, Ben could see people laughing as they spotted the squadron decals on the side of the car. Choosing the loneliest, most desolate spot he could find, he backed under an overhanging tree in the far corner of the lot. Only then did Ansley's eyes rise to window level and make a peremptory examination of the other cars.

"You don't mind if I say 'hi' to a few of my friends, Ben. I see some cheerleaders and their boy friends parked over there under the light. Order me a cheeseburger without onions, a Coca-Cola, medium, and a large order of fries if Lewis comes while I'm gone," she said, blowing him a kiss through the window. She seemed shamelessly gratified to be escaping Ben's presence.

Ben rolled down the window and leaned his elbow on the door. He tried to tighten up his face into a mask of insouciance, worldliness, and control. His stomach, though, felt like a ship breaking up on invisible shoals. As Ansley went from car to car, Ben watched her secretly, watching her leaning her breasts into other boys' arms, flirting with a self-indulgent expertise that seemed vilely calculating from Ben's observation post. Her perfume lingered in the car and attacked him in the soft places of his boyhood. He saw her point his car out to a crowd of faces he half recognized, then he heard her high-pitched giggle and the laughter of her companions; he turned the radio up louder. He stole another look and saw how achingly pretty she was, this curving, mindless nymphet who had perfected the insensate cruelties and the small meannesses of adolescence and sent them marching in snickering battalions toward Ben. Sitting there in the half-darkness, Ben felt cheapened, irreparably damaged by this girl he had known most of his life. But he was not surprised. He knew intuitively that girls like Ansley would elude him always, dance away from him, mocking him, whispering about him in those savagely thoughtless clusters of children living in the pure oxygen of their ordained season. Ansley was part of an aristocracy that brooked no intrusion, at least not now, Ben thought.

Ben ordered two cheeseburgers without onions, two medium Coca-Colas, and two large orders of fries when Lewis, a tall, expressionless black came to take his order. He was grateful to Lewis just for coming to his car. When the cheeseburgers came, Ben glanced toward Ansley to see if she would return to the car when the order arrived. But she remained where she was in the middle of several football players. Her fingers were traveling secretly to their necks, running along their collars.

Then he saw Jim Don Cooper's car pull up beside her. He watched as Ansley entered the car, rushed across the seat, and kissed him long and passionately on the lips. They talked, made out some more, then talked again. He saw Jim Don turn completely around in his seat and stare belligerently at Ben. "Oh great," Ben thought, "now he comes over and beats the shit out of me while I'm sitting in the Werewolf Squadron car." But Jim Don did not leave his car; Ansley did. With her girlish, provocative gait, she ran over to Ben's side of the car and began eating french fries as she whispered to Ben.

"Ben, I want you to be the sweetest boy in the world and let me spend the rest of the night with my steady. We're going to a party one of the cheerleaders is giving out at the beach. You don't mind, do you?"

"No, Ansley, I don't mind at all," Ben said.

"You're so sweet. I told Jim Don you'd be glad to help us out. Now you won't mention this to your parents, will you, Ben?"

"No. I won't say a word."

"O.K. Bye-bye. And I really had a great time with you tonight. I mean that seriously. You have a wonderful personality. And thanks tons for being so understanding," she said, leaving the car.

"Do you want your cheeseburger?" Ben asked.

"No, you eat mine too. Jim Don just ordered me one," she said, turning and running back toward the Impala.

No one seemed to notice the car after its abandonment by Ansley Matthews; no one seemed to notice the modest solitaire of Ben in his fall from the grandeur of courting cheerleaders. He was skewered by the eyes of strangers no longer. Thank God for the Big APE radio in Jacksonsville that sang to Ben with the same dispassion it sang to every other car in the Shack. Ben ate his cheeseburger slowly, thinking about what he could do for the rest of the evening, knowing he could not return home early to face the interrogation of his parents or the teasing of Mary Anne.

He started up the car, his eyes burning. Good-bye, my cheerleader, my first date. Good-bye my colonel's daughter, my dark-lashed duchess, my beauty, my brown-eyed queen. Good-bye my one-hour bride, my sixty-minute love, my red-lipped empress, my Weejun-shod inamorata. Why do I love you and girls like you? Ben thought. Why do I love you in secret? Then, coldly, as he looked at her again, one final time, as he drove his car past her boy friend's Impala, as he saw her laugh at the decal and point, it was then that he knew her for the first time and he had an urge to lean out of his window and cavalierly shout au revoir to his enemy.

In a fury, he turned from the Shack and drove toward town. He didn't see the car pull out behind him and follow him. He heard a car blowing its horn at him as he pulled in front of the National Cemetery on Granville Street. Pulling over to the curb, Ben peered into the interior of a red and black Rambler American that pulled alongside of him. Ben turned out his lights and waited for the driver of the Rambler to identify himself. The Rambler pulled in front of him and a small-boned boy leaped out of the car and walked back toward Ben with a ludicrously exaggerated swagger.

"You're probably saying to yourself, Ben, that a true stud like Sammy Wertzberger always has a date with some gorgeous honey on a Saturday night. But it just so happens that I'm resting my body from a drive-in movie last night where I was attacked again and again by a lovely nymphomaniac."

"Sammy. I've never been so glad to see anybody in my whole life."

"I just heard about what Ansley the asshole did to you. I thought you'd already left when I saw you pull out."

"I've known her for a long time. She used to be pretty nice."

"Why don't you ride shotgun up there in the Jewish

198

submarine and I'll show you the town. Maybe then we can catch the late movie at the Breeze Theater."

"That sounds great to me."

"Let's make like horseshit and hit the trail."

"Thanks for following me, Sammy."

"The night is young," Sammy said to Ben. "And there are thousands of women waiting to get their hands on the both of us."

16

RAVENEL HAD a single Catholic priest and his name was Thomas Aquinas Pinckney, a thin tubercular man who stood six feet seven inches tall and was rumored to drink too much of the blood of Christ at the Consecration. When Father Pinckney opened his rectory door, bending down to duck his head beneath the doorway, the first thing the new colonel said to him was, "My name is Colonel Bull Meecham, Father. I think it's a disgrace that this burg doesn't have a Catholic school. And since you're the C.O., I hold you personally responsible."

"Boston?" the priest asked.

"No, Father, Chicago," Bull answered.

"Come in, Colonel, and we'll drink something sinful while we discuss this important spiritual matter."

Bull had mostly listened that first day as this stricken, energetic man paced the sitting room of his rectory speaking with a mellifluous basso profundo voice that demanded and received unwavering attention. His gestures were theatrical and wild, generated by an animal impatience that possessed his body. "Colonel," he shouted, "do you realize that Red China has more Roman Catholics than the state of South Carolina. And do you realize that the good Sisters of Mercy are strained to the very limits of endurance to send us one good sister to labor in the vineyards of Ravenel. And Colonel, do you, in your wisdom, understand that numbers dictate the Bishop's decision over whether to build a Catholic school in Ravenel. We are growing, yes, but as for a Catholic school, we are many years from such a prodigious undertaking."

"Begging your Father's pardon," Bull said, "but baloney."

"Colonel, why does the Lord send two or three Marines a year to torment me on this subject? Why does he punish me?"

"He wants you to build a Catholic school."

"And I want to build you another drink," Father Pinckney said, taking Bull's glass to the bar. "In my early day dreams, Colonel, in those high fantasies one deludes himself with in the first days of priesthood, I imagined myself a prince of the Church, a robed and venerated Cardinal, perhaps, enshrined in Gothic cathedrals and worshiped by flocks of sinful parishioners. I never thought I would be fighting verbal banana wars with Marines and their wives over bingo games and Catholic schools in this gnat of a town. I am a priest whose inclination is toward the great cities of the world but whose destiny was to degenerate in this sad village."

That day Bull had signed Ben and Matthew up to serve the 11:15 Sunday Mass for the entire school year. He also enrolled Ben and Mary Anne in the Wednesday-night catechism class sponsored by the Confraternity of Christian Doctrine. He reminded his children that it was his duty as a Catholic father to ensure that their souls did not rust during their year away from Catholic schools. Nor did Ben's argument that eleven years of Catholic school were eleven more than Jesus Christ himself received dissuade his father from sending his two oldest children to the night classes held at St. Philomena's Hall, a resurrected Victorian house purchased and refurbished as a classroom for young Catholics in a hostilely Protestant world. The first class was held the last Wednesday in September with Sister Loretta Marie presiding.

The nun's face was blanched out like Lenten candlewax. Its whiteness contrasted starkly with the black veil that framed her head like a shroud. Her voice was a disapproving monotone. Whether discussing Herod slaughtering infants or Christ rising from the dead, her voice registered the same faint level of disapproval. When she walked, her long rosary clicked with a most repressed, arrhythmic music. Ben had watched her at church and her pinched bloodless face and the stiffness of her bearing, as though her joints lacked oil, made him grant her a wide and respectful berth. Both expert at translating the character of nuns, Ben and Mary Anne divided them into two distinct and irreconcilable categories: the Smiles and the Vampires. The Smiles were joyous women who took pleasure in life's smallest, most inconsequential gifts, who loved children and the act of teaching, and who loved God with a simplicity and ingenuousness that made one believe in the efficacy of a nun's vocation. The Vampires were terrible, desiccated women who entered the convent because they hated themselves and thought that by surrendering their lives to their redeemer, this self-hatred would turn to something good and palliative. But it never happened that way. The convent never solved their problems, only magnified them a hundredfold. When they taught, they were at best bloodless and inoffensive; at their worst, they could ruin a child's life. Two Vampires had ruled Ben in their reign of terror. One, Sister Mary Patricia, had put clothespins on his ears and nose for an entire afternoon when he failed to turn in his math homework. Another, Sister Mary Bernadette, wrapped her wool shawl around his head and made him walk with her for a thirty-minute recess period, his head in darkness burrowed into her breasts which were full, forbidden, and untouched. So when he appraised Sister Loretta Marie it was with eyes that had spent a lifetime studying the habits and peccadilloes of nuns. When he asked Mary Anne what she thought about the new nun in their lives, Mary Anne did not answer; she put up her two hands and covered her throat.

The nun began the class with the Lord's Prayer and the Pledge of Allegiance. In her hand was a small clicker or cricket which she snapped when she wanted the class to stand up or sit down. She had a passion for the simultaneous. For a full minute, the class practiced rising and sitting in unison as she pressed the lever of her cricket and appraised the harmony of ebb and augmentation of her new charges. Finally, she was satisfied and gave a last deliciously full click that had the sound if finality about it.

At the very rear of the room, Ben and Mary Anne wrote each other notes while Sister Loretta Marie intoned about the dangers to the soul represented by dancing cheek to cheek and rock and roll music. Mary Anne wrote to Ben in her scrawling penmanship that even her long apprenticeship in Catholic schools did not correct, "You have a huge pimple at the end of your nose and everybody is looking at you and laughing at you. It's real ugly."

Ben replied, "Some people think freckles are cute. I don't. It looks to me like millions of ants pooped on your face."

"Now, class, everyone listen up. You two back there," Sister Loretta said, talking to Ben and Mary Anne. "You're not required to take notes tonight. I want everybody's strict attention as I discuss a matter of utmost importance. You are all young adults; therefore, I feel as though I can speak to you as young adults. I've been watching several members of this class as they walk back from receiving the Eucharist at Sunday Mass. What I have seen frankly disturbs me very much. It might behoove this class for me to remind them that the body and blood of Our Lord Jesus Christ is on our tongues when the priest gives us the host."

Mary Anne scribbled something on the paper and Ben read, "Jesus Christ tastes a lot like bread."

"You're going to hell for all eternity," he wrote back, underlining the word "all."

"What has shocked me," Sister Loretta continued, shaking her head in repugnance, "and I mean literally shocked me, was when I saw certain members of this class, and I am not going to mention any names, actually chewing the host like it was a Hershey bar or something. Let me ask all of you one question. Would you like someone chewing on you?"

"No, Sister," the class answered.

"Of course you wouldn't. Neither does Jesus. The host is supposed to dissolve on the tongue. It should melt slowly and you should think about the Lord being present on your tongue. You want Him to stay present on your tongue as long as you can. You do not want to hurry Him along by crudely chewing Him up and sending Him quickly to your stomach."

"I bet He likes the stomach better than where He goes next," Mary Anne wrote and Ben put his hand over his eyes.

"For those of you who are chewing up the Lord instead of letting Him melt slowly on your tongue, I can say very little except that I am sure the Lord finds it most unpleasant to be chewed up quickly by the hasty molars of young Catholic boys and girls who do not treasure the sanctity of His company. Frankly, it has been all that I could do to keep from yanking those individuals by the ear when I see them walk by like cattle chewing their cud. The proper way to receive communion is to let your mouth fill up with saliva and let the saliva slowly and beautifully melt the body of the Lord and then let Him repose in your soul, in the temple of the Holy Ghost."

"Help, I'm drowning in spit," Mary Anne wrote. "Signed, Jesu." But Ben refused to even read what she had written; flirtations with sacrilege bothered him deeply.

"Sister, Sister." A boy raised his hand in the front of the room. Sister Loretta clicked and he rose to his feet.

"You're slouching, P.K. That's better. Now what is your question?" the nun asked.

"A lot of times, Sister, the host gets stuck on the roof of my mouth. I mean it sticks up there like flypaper and it even makes it hard to breathe. Does the Lord get mad if I take my tongue and lick it off the roof of my mouth, because to tell you the truth, it gets mighty uncomfortable up there."

The class giggled. P.K. turned around and smiled, proud that he had asked a question that aroused laughter from his peers behind him. Giggling was a form of mutiny to the nun and she quelled it with a wintery narrowing of her eyes.

"That's a very good question, P.K., and one that requires serious deliberation. Does anyone have any ideas about that particular theological consideration? How about you, Miss Carters Marie Simon?"

"Brown-noser," Mary Anne wrote.

A pretty girl who was in several of Mary Anne's classes at the high school stood up and answered, "I don't think a body should remove the host from the top of the mouth. When it happens to me, I let the host alone and suffer, offering it up to the poor souls in purgatory. I think my suffering is the least I can do since the Lord Jesus suffered so for me."

"Oh, puke," Mary Anne whispered in Ben's ear, abandoning her pen and paper since Ben was adamant about refusing to read what she had written.

"I think that is a wonderful answer, Carters. That is exactly the answer I expected from this class. It seems crude and ill-bred to peel the host off the roof of your mouth simply because it is uncomfortable. Christ, too, was uncomfortable on the cross. Yes, He was very uncomfortable with the nails tearing His hands and feet, the crown of thorns splitting His head." She turned toward the crucifix that hung above the blackboard; all eyes in the class followed her lead. "For three agonizing hours He hung on the cross, suffering for us. For Carters, for P.K., for Andy, for Father Pinckney, for Sister Loretta Marie—for all the Catholics who would ever live, so that we might sit on His right hand in the golden kingdom of God. Yes, Jesus suffered and this is one reason why we should never complain about the insignificant pains and frustrations we have in our lives. The next time you have a headache, think about having a nail driven through your foot."

Sister Loretta was still staring balefully at the crucified redeemer. Cupping her hand, Mary Anne whispered to Ben, "The next time you pick your nose, think about having a nail driven through your nostril."

Ben laughed and the whole class turned around, as if obedient to one of Sister Loretta's clicks, to witness the removal of a malignancy from the class.

"Perhaps, Mr. Meecham, you could enlighten the class as to what is so humorous about a crucifixion."

"Nothing, Sister," Ben said. "I just thought of something funny that happened a few days ago."

"Please share it with the class," the nun demanded.

"I've forgotten it already, Sister," Ben stammered, and the class laughed.

"Indeed," the nun hissed. "Since Mr. Meecham is not interested in the lesson, I think I will use him for a little experiment I thought up to illustrate the suffering of Christ on the cross. I was going to save this for another class, but this might prove to Mr. Meecham that I take these C.C.D. classes very seriously. Come to the front of the room by the blackboard, Mr. Meecham."

Casting a single murderous glance at Mary Anne, Ben walked to the front of the room and stood before Sister Loretta's podium.

"You are a big, strong boy, Mr. Meecham. Let us see how really strong you are. Go to the blackboard, turn, and face the class. Now put out your arms. All the way out, Mr. Meecham," the nun said with sudden fierceness, "as if you were stretching them out to be nailed to a cross. That is it. That is fine. Now there are only forty-five minutes left in this class. I want you to hold your arms out until the class is over. No fair bending your arms at the elbows. Just like that for forty-five minutes. Before long, class, Mr. Meecham's arms will feel like lead. Somebody watch and tell me if Mr. Meecham cheats by bending his arms."

"I will, Sister," Mary Anne said cheerfully.

"Thank you, Miss Meecham. It would behoove us to remember that Christ was not able to bend his arms on the cross. Is that not right, children?"

"Yes, Sister," they chanted.

Ben was not taking his symbolic crucifixion with any excess humor. He was not one who enjoyed public exposure or ridicule. The arm muscles would begin to hurt, but it was the personal denuding he experienced under the many-eyed gaze of the class that was the prime cause of his discomfiture and embarrassment.

Sister Loretta continued her monotone: "But the subject tonight was the Eucharist and I was reminded of a true story about the Eucharist that I heard firsthand from a Benedictine father who conducted a retreat at my Mother House in Philadelphia last summer. This true story took place in France and I think it would behoove us to think of P.K.'s question as I relate this story to you."

"Mr. Meecham is bending his elbows," Mary Anne said, raising her hand sweetly.

"Thank you, Miss Meecham. I know your brother does not wish for me to have a conference with your father. Therefore, I am sure we will not have to interrupt class again to admonish him," she said, turning toward Ben as though he were an anthropomorphic representation of a genuine sin.

Ben shot Mary Anne the finger with both of his invisibly nailed hands.

"There was a bad little French boy by the name of Pierre who went to Communion at his tiny parish church in the South of France. At the time, Pierre was in a state of mortal sin as he had eaten a full breakfast only minutes before he came to church. When it came time for Communion, Pierre went to the altar and received the Blessed Eucharist. Instead of going back to his pew, he went out the back of the church and into the graveyard across the street. There, he took the sacred host out of his mouth . . ."

Here, Carters Marie Simon gasped in horror and put her head down on the desk.

"And held the host in his nasty, grubby, unwashed little hands. He wanted to see if he could find a sign that this was indeed the body and blood of our Savior. He laid the host on a tombstone and took a knife from his pocket. Then he cut into the host with his knife. Can anyone in the room tell me what happened?"

A moment of anesthetized silence filled the room until P.K., raising his hand, rising, and ejecting out of his seat, shouted, "God killed the little booger."

"Of course not, P.K.," the nun sneered. "But something almost as terrible happened. The host began to bleed. At first it was a small flow as though a tiny vein had been cut. Pierre tried to stop it with his handkerchief, his filthy, snot-ridden handkerchief. But that only increased the amount of blood spurting from the host. Soon it was as though an artery had been cut. It burst out of the host and covered the whole tombstone. Pierre tried to stop it by covering it with his hands, by lying on it with his whole body. But nothing would stop the blood. Before he knew it the blood was gushing from the center of the host like a river, spilling onto the holy ground of the cemetery and flowing toward the church. Pierre ran to the church, racing the river of Christ-blood. He flung the church door open and cried out to the priest who was saying the prayers at the foot of the altar. The whole congregation turned and saw Pierre, covered with blood, his eyes frenzied with the sin he had committed. The priest ran toward Pierre, who led the priest to the cemetery, telling him what he had done as they ran. The priest went to the host, to the source of the blood, and touched it with his hands. The blood instantly stopped. The priest looked at Pierre and, trembling with anger, he told the bad little French boy, 'You did wrong, Pierre.' Later that morning, Pierre went to confession. He is now a Catholic priest presiding over the very same parish where he had once desecrated the host." Sister Loretta paused and took a deep breath. "So I hope that will be a lesson to all of you."

"That's the most beautiful story I've ever heard, Sister," Carters sighed, fulfilled.

Is that what happens when you chew the host with your teeth, Sister?" P.K. asked.

"I wouldn't say it happens every time, P.K., but I am saying it could happen at any time. The Lord works in mysterious ways."

After the class Ben and Mary Anne walked home, following the curve of the street which followed the curve of the river, past lovely lit-up houses with chandeliers glittering in empty dining rooms, past a gloomy arcade of live oaks, past King Tut's used car lot with its multi-colored pennants fluttering from an overhead wire like trapped butterflies, past the dentist's office built on reclaimed marsh, past the old elementary school, past a vast marsh that was a dark and pungent gold in the salt-sweet rush of wind that filled their nostrils with smells born far out at sea; they walked slowly and felt good in each other's company.

"I thought Sister Loretta might bury you for three days after we cut you down from the cross," Mary Anne said as she watched Ben massaging his triceps and shoulder muscles.

"Let me just ask you one question, Mary Anne," Ben said calmly. "Do you want me to mangle your face or do you want me just to work you over with a rubber hose so all the damage will be internal?"

"Dad would kill you if you laid a single digit on his adored Mary Anne."

"Baloney," Ben answered, "he wouldn't notice if I ripped your nose off your head."

"You're probably right. Dad doesn't pay attention to anything that doesn't wear a uniform or have a jump shot. Of course, I think I would be doing you a big favor if I did help surgically remove your nose. Have you looked at that thing in the mirror lately? Seriously, Ben, is your nose infected?"

"What do you mean infected?" he asked.

"Your nose is so red and runny looking. At least my nose isn't red. I've heard people say you could get a job leading reindeer," Mary Anne said.

"Let's quit," Ben said turning his head toward the river. "I'm tired of the game."

"That means I won," Mary Anne exulted. "Why did you give it all to me, God? Beauty, brains, poise, charm, and devastating wit."

"And a million freckles," Ben added.

"Look who's talking. The old Clearasil kid."

"Pimples don't last forever; freckles do."

"I bet you have pimples when you're seventy years old. You're never going to be able to eat a potato chip," Mary Anne said.

"Let's talk about something serious," Ben said.

"All right, King Solomon. Talk serious."

"What do you think it will be like later on? What do you think we'll be doing?"

"I'll be very famous. Some great men will throw themselves on subway tracks because I refuse their hand in marriage. I'll write several best-selling novels that will be banned by the Catholic Church and my mansion will be a watering place for the great literary and social figures of the late twentieth century. You will still be a zit-faced golden boy throwing up jump shots."

They turned down Eliot Street where the smell of deepset gardens and the bark of aroused dogs followed them past old brick walls covered with lichen and ivy. The moss was thick on the overhanging trees and the light of every star was extinguished in the leafy chapel through which Ben and Mary Anne walked home.

"Be serious, Mary Anne. What do you think will really happen?"

"You'll be a Marine pilot. I'll be married to some creep, having children and wishing I was dead."

"Why? Why does it have to be like that?"

"Because it's written all over both of us."

"I'm not going to be a Marine, Mary Anne. I swear I'm not," Ben said bitterly.

"Yes you will. You'll go to some two-bit southern college and then go into the Marine Corps after you graduate. Dad will swear you in and Mom will be lovely and beautiful and proud. Slowly, all that's good about you will dissolve over the years and you'll begin believing all the stuff Dad believes and acting like Dad acts. You're a golden boy and a fair-haired child. You've got to have people love you and fuss over you. You've got to have them approve. That's where you and I are different. I've never had anybody's approval, so I've learned to live without it. That's why I'm going to be a better person than you before it's all over."

"Do you think either one of us will ever write, Mary Anne?" Ben asked.

Mary Anne thought for a minute, then said, "No. We won't write any books. Writing books is something you talk about when you're very young and continue to talk about all your life until you die. You'll write fitness reports on young Marines and I'll write witty notes to my kid's teacher."

"I'm not going to be a Marine! I'm not! I'm not! I'm not!" Ben said.

"Oh, yes you are," Mary Anne said. "Yes you are! Yes you are!" as they crossed the open field of the Lawn. "You are because the Lord, to quote a great woman, works in mysterious ways."

17

ON OCTOBER the eleventh, in the darkest, coolest part of the morning, Bull shook Ben awake. The clock on the nightstand beside Ben said that it was four o'clock. Bull ordered his son to dress on the double, to meet him at a muster formation in the kitchen, or be put on report.

"Why are you getting me up now, Dad?" Ben asked as he swung his feet to the floor and groped for his bluejeans.

"Who dares question the Great Santini? Anyway it's classified top secret until you get downstairs."

Bull was in a grand, exuberant mood. His father was one of the few people Ben had ever met who could wake from a deep sleep fully refreshed. Bull needed no period of adjustment, no time for the luxurious stretching and lolling that Ben thought was the most exquisite pleasure of morning. As he heard Bull's footsteps on the stair, Ben staggered toward the bathroom. Splashing cold water on his face, the tonnage of missed sleep stacked on his brain lightened only slightly. The bathroom light blinded him as though he were a bat flushed from his cave at noon. Going downstairs, he smelled the pot of coffee perking in the kitchen. His father, in full uniform, sat at the kitchen table, sipping from a steaming cup. On the table was a large gift-wrapped package.

"Happy Birthday, boy," Bull said, averting his eyes from Ben's.

"Hey thanks, Dad," Ben said, rushing for the package. "Of course, I can't believe you woke me up at four in the morning to give me the present."

"This is just the beginning of the morning. The head honcho has some big plans for your birthday. But I wanted you and me to be alone when you opened this present."

"What is it?" Ben asked, lifting the package and measuring its satisfying heaviness.

"It's a training bra," Bull said, grinning into his coffee. "Open it, boy. I've been saving this for your eighteenth birthday for a long time."

Ben ripped the paper off the package, then lifted the cover off the box. Inside Ben stared at an old leather flight jacket with a warm fur collar and the patch of the Red Cobra Squadron on the sleeve. He removed the flight jacket and held it up for a moment, the odor of leather mingling with the coffee smells.

"What do I do with it, Dad?"

"Put it on. It's yours. That was my first flight jacket. The one I wore when I flew in WW Two with the Cobras," Bull said as Ben slipped the jacket on.

"It's really nice."

"They don't make 'em like that anymore. That's part of the Old Corps. That jacket shows me a lot of class."

"This is a wonderful gift, Dad. Thanks a lot," Ben said looking at his father, feeling somehow transfigured and invulnerable as he zipped up the jacket that was much too large for him.

"Just remember that there are some Marines who would cut your balls off if they saw you wearing this around town. It's not a damn letter jacket. I don't want you to wear it to school or anything. It's something between us. You can wear it around the house or at night."

"I'll be careful."

"Good soldier. Christ, Ben, you're eighteen. I was just sitting here thinking about when you were born. I was on a hop when you were born. All I heard when I landed was that your mother was in the hospital. I went crazy. I hit a hundred miles an hour getting to that hospital. Three M.P. trucks were chasing me as I ran through the front door and up the three flights of stairs to the maternity ward. Then all of a sudden there's this weird skinny Navy doctor telling me I had a fine healthy son and I was nearly thrown out of that hospital I was

213

whooping so loud. I ran down to that window as fast as I could go, knocking nurses out of the way, running over small children, and crashing into patients on their way to the operating room. I'll never forget you screaming your head off while I tapped at the window and bragged to everyone who passed by that the toughest little fighter pilot in the world had been born. Then I ran down to see your mother, expecting her to look like horseshit from hell after punching you out of her system. Well, she was sitting up in that hospital bed looking prettier than I'd ever seen her. Your mother's the only woman in the world that looks like a million bucks ten hours after she's delivered a child. That was eighteen years ago. Eighteen years ago today. I was twenty-three then, just five years older than you are right now," he said, studying Ben with new interest.

"I've got to register for the draft within ten days," Ben said, adjusting the fur collar.

"I'll get off early from the squadron one day next week and take you. But I got something big planned for this morning," Bull said, looking down at his watch. "Let me pour you a cup of coffee, then we have to hit the road. What do you take in yours?"

"Mama doesn't let me drink coffee."

"I ain't Mama. You'll take it black," Bull said, pouring out a cup. "You won't like the taste at first but you'll get used to it fast. I've never trusted a man who put cream or sugar in his coffee. Just like I never really trusted a man who put Coca-Cola in his bourbon. You can drink this in the car," Bull said, handing it to Ben.

"Where are we going?"

"Are you a detective?" Bull answered, then remembering it was his son's birthday, he said, "This is all part of the surprise I have in store for you. So let's double time out to the car. I told Sergeant Hicks we'd be outside of B barracks at 0500 hours."

As they drove toward Biddle Island Marine Corps Training Depot, Ben downed the hot, acrid coffee as though he were enjoying it. Bull drove through the dark streets of Paradise past the peeling warped shacks and dog-ruled groceries with their glowing Coca-Cola signs.

Bull was talking and smoking one Camel after another. It was during these night rides with his father that the feeling of what it was like to be an adult often possessed Ben. A swift prescience with the strength of adrenaline flowed through him and heralded a day when he would speak to Bull Meecham man to man, as a friend and equal. Only at brief moments had Bull given his sons glimpses of what it would be like to be accepted in that fraternity of men that Bull felt comfortable around. Now, sitting behind the headlights, Bull speaking easily and unselfconsciously, Ben in a sudden blaze of perception realized that Bull had forgotten, at least for the moment, that he was addressing a son.

"I've known Sarge Hicks since Korea. If you want to see a Marine's Marine then this guy's the one, Ben. He's a small little turd, but he's built like a fireplug, low, squat, and he's got the face of a man who likes to hit cripples. He looks like he should have a job killing snakes. I called him the other day and asked him when he was getting in a new bunch of recruits. It happened to fall on your birthday so I asked him if I could bring you out to see him whip his boys into shape. I told him he could trust you not to say anything to anybody about what you see. These boys you'll see this morning have been here a couple of days already. They got haircuts and uniforms but this will be the first day they'll really know what it's like to be in the Corps. He can eat recruits from what I've heard. I asked him if he still broke recruits in like he did in 'fifty-eight. He told me he'd think about it. That's Hicksie's way of saying O.K. We just can't go mouthing off about what we see here this morning. It's classified. Roger?"

"Roger," Ben answered.

The car moved through the darkness at a rapid speed, turned left at the Sanctified Church of the Crucified Jesus, and took the Biddle Creek Road which followed the river toward the training depot. Ben grew aware of the flight jacket again. The gift had substantiality and an indefinable quality of endurance. The leather flight jacket was an anachronism in 1962. It had been replaced by a nylon, light-weight flight jacket that was bled of glamour or romance. The leather jacket belonged to the days of the Corsair when men dueled in the skies for possession of Pacific atolls and for airspace above the gray, endangered fleets. But many pilots kept the leather jackets, not only for the sake of tradition but for a more aesthetic reason: the leather jacket looked better than the nylon pretender and made the pilot who wore it look better. Pilots who gathered together wearing the old style flight jacket looked like a well-bred motorcycle gang.

Ben folded his arms and felt the cracked, lined leather between his fingers. The jacket felt good all over. He could not have felt more changed if he had put on the silks of Father Pinckney, prayed over a piece of un-leavened bread, and felt it quiver with the life and light of God. The jacket he wore was a part of his father's history, a fragment of Bull's biography that occurred before Ben's birth. Ben put his nose into the leather sleeve and breathed in rich memories of his own life. He could remember burrowing his head into his father's jacket when he was a child, in the days when he was allowed to hug and caress his father, in the days before his father declared it inappropriate. The sons of Marines all come to a day when their fathers moved away from their embrace. The men of the flight jacket. The strong fathers. Ben could see them all, coming through the door of his home, his score of homes, the men who played such a large role in his life. He could see them in their leather flight jackets, their dark mantles, having just come down from doing things that smaller, punier men could never do, doing things that only gods could do. All during his growing up, boys would brag to Ben about their fathers. "My father works for the second largest real estate company in eastern North Carolina," or "My father is the most important lawyer in this town." And Ben would only smile and tell them with the maddening condescension of a child who knows he has won a contest that his father and all his father's best friends could fly faster than any birds, set an army on fire, or reduce a city of a million people to dust and memory. And it was dust and memory that had Ben now as they rode past the gate at the entryway of Biddle Island Training Depot,

216

the guard saluting them in the sudden light of the sentry box, his form revealed in surreal and unclear lines, as they pushed down the main road that turned into a causeway crossing a vast marsh. The marsh stretched for miles on either side of the road with an ominous symmetry. A man escaping from Biddle Island would do better to try his luck with the river, the tides, and the sharks, than to test the quiet susurrant heart of the marsh. Though the marsh had a look of lush maternity, Toomer had taught Ben that the marsh was a monster. The tall grasses were green razors that could section a man's flesh into an infinite number of fine, almost invisible slices. The oyster beds that lay hidden in the marsh could cut like axes. But worst of all, a man could get lost in the marsh, lose all sense of direction and wander aimlessly in circles, being sucked in by the mud, and maddened by the sameness of the earth, no matter which way he turned. Ben wondered how many young boys from New England or the Midwest had escaped from their barracks in a fever of desperation and tried to cross the marsh on foot. Or how many had come to the river's edge, seen the lights of Ravenel blinking across the river, and had begun the long swim, until too late they realized that no swimmer could fight the power of the moon, this recall of water by oceans, and had let the water take them toward the black, roiled whitecaps along the lips of Prince Ashley Island where they died soundlessly, far from the eyes of Drill Instructors, safe from the mayhem of barracks. He did not know. He felt the jacket again and knew that he wore a part of his father.

They parked in the shadows beneath a live oak directly in front of B barracks. Beside them, a parade ground stretched for two miles until it stopped at a cluster of buildings that Ben could barely identify as the PX and commissary. Bull extinguished his lights, lit a cigarette, passed it to Ben, lit one for himself, and began to smoke in silence.

"I don't smoke, Dad," Ben said.

"Shhh! Not too loud. We aren't even supposed to be

here, sportsfans. Go ahead and try it. You've probably been sneaking smokes on your mother for years."

"No, I really haven't. I thought you'd kill me if you ever caught me smoking."

"That's affirmative," Bull said, grinning at his son who fingered the cigarette without a trace of expertise. "I'd have had to ruin your whole day. Take a few heavy drags. Wait a minute. Put it out. Here comes Hicks and the boys."

Shouts and obscenities poured out of the windows of B barracks, a two story shingled building that had the unmistakable appearance of military architecture circa 1945. More shouts and more curses cut out the windows and traveled across the parade ground, dying out somewhere across the dark pavement.

"That sounds like our house when you get home," Ben said.

"Quiet," Bull growled, but he broke into a half-suppressed giggle.

By now, frantic shadows were running out the front door of B barracks. A voice of overbred brutality roared from an invisible source within the building.

"That's Hicks," Bull whispered. "He's one of the last of the great cannibals. They've cracked down so hard on the D.I.'s in the past couple of years that it's like they're running Aunt Fanny's Finishing School for Young Girls."

The drumming of feet down wooden stairs continued unbroken as recruits with their shaved heads, vulnerable necks, combat boots, fatigue hats and pants, and new white military issue T-shirts, spilled out into the night and lined up without skill or finesse at the edge of the parade, not fifteen yards away from the Meecham car.

A Drill Instructor appeared in the doorway, his distinctive, somewhat ludicrous hat pulled low over his eyes. He was carrying a swagger stick and had a revolver strapped to his hip. The man wore malevolence and formidability as though they were part of the uniform of the day. There was something so incarnately evil in the man's expression that Ben looked toward his father for assurance that they were indeed supposed to be there.

Sergeant Hicks seemed to be laid out in squares as though he were constructed out of cinder blocks. There was a hardness to his body that made his uniform appear to be little more than a paint job. He walked as if each step he took was driving a hated enemy toward a precipice.

In the car, Ben removed the flight jacket and folded it on the seat beside him.

"Can you hear me, turds?" Sergeant Hicks said in a malefic whisper that seemed to hiss out of his bowels.

"Yes, Sergeant," the recruits screamed as one.

"That's good, turds. Because I want you to hear me real good this morning."

"There he is!" Bull whispered to Ben in the car and pointed toward someone in the platoon of rigid, faceless men.

"Who?" Ben asked.

"Sergeant Blakeley," Bull answered.

"Who's Blakeley?"

"Another D.I. Look in the fourth row. Third one back. You can't see his face very good but I saw him waving at us."

"What's he doing there?"

"You'll see."

"Why's he dressed like a recruit?"

"Just watch and quit your yappin'."

The voice of Sergeant Hicks silenced Ben instantly as the D.I. screamed, "Look at me, turds. Look at me because I want you to stare at me when I talk to you this morning. Now it makes me sick to my stomach that shit-eating maggots like you can pollute an elite group of fighting men like the United States Marine Corps. So I look upon it as my sacred duty to run as many of you fart blossoms out of the Marine Corps as I can. Because when I look over you bunch of turds and when I think about you wearing the uniform of the Corps, I want to walk up and down each rank and strangle the guts out of every fucking one of you abortions." Hicks paused to catch his breath, then walked up to a small, rotund recruit who stood in the front of the second squad.

"What do you think the sergeant had for dinner last night, fat maggot?"

"The recruit doesn't know, Sergeant," the boy answered.

"Would the recruit believe it if the sergeant informed the recruit that he dined on shit sandwiches."

"No, Sergeant."

"Are you calling me a liar, turd?"

"No, Sergeant."

"I told you I ate shit sandwiches, turd, and you're standing there calling me a liar in front of my turds."

"No, Sergeant."

"Then what did I eat last night, turd?"

"You ate shit sandwiches, Sergeant."

"Why you fat maggot. You disgusting piece of blubber shit. If you ever tell me I eat shit again, I'm going to run this swagger stick so far up your ass, they're gonna find my wedding ring in your small intestine. I'm gonna remember you, fat maggot, and if you make it through this camp alive then I'm gonna turn in my uniform."

Then Sergeant Hicks began to address the entire platoon again. To Ben, his father's voice was the most fearsome he had ever heard, could inspire the most panic per decibel. But Bull's voice, at its worst, was reassuring and soothing compared to the D.I.'s. And Hicks's whisper was, if anything, worse than his scream, for the whisper carried with it a quality of institutional menace, even fiendishness, that the scream lost in its projection across the parade ground and through the ranks of bald men.

"You turds probably heard about the Pennant Creek incident before you joined the Corps," the D.I. barked. "That was the event in which an overanxious D.I. drowned a couple of turds in a force march. They ran that D.I. out of the Corps but I just want to let you maggots know that I personally feel they should have given that sergeant the Congressional Medal of Honor. Any D.I. who drowns a couple of turds who would further fuck up the U.S. Marine Corps is a man who deserves the highest honor this country can bestow. Do you maggots agree with me?"

"Yes, Sergeant."

"That's good, turds. Because I'm gonna take you for a hike across that same creek. Only, I'm gonna make you tie anvils and boulders to your feet right before we cross. I'm gonna sink every goddam one of you turds, because this sergeant ain't gonna leave no witnesses. Do I make myself clear, turds?"

"Yes, Sergeant."

Suddenly, Sergeant Hicks broke toward the first rank and began screaming at a large, well built recruit who took a step backward in surprise, so sudden was the attack. "You think you can whip my ass don't you, maggot. You're sitting there thinking to yourself, 'If that little fucking fag sergeant gives me any lip I'll tear him apart limb by limb,' isn't that what you're thinking, you overgrown piece of shit?"

"No, Sergeant."

"Don't lie to me, you brainless sack of Kotex. You told your bunkmate last night that I was the biggest asshole you've ever seen. Isn't that right, turd?"

"No, Sergeant."

"You don't think I'm an asshole, turd?" Sergeant Hicks said, his voice forming into a whisper again.

"No, Sergeant."

"Well what am I? Do you think I'm a ballerina? Or a violinist? Or a goddam Army general? I'll tell you one thing, turd. It's my job to be an asshole. I'm paid by the U.S. Marine Corps to be the biggest asshole in the world for twenty-four hours a day, seven days a week, fifty-two weeks a year for the rest of my goddam life. Now, turd, I want you to tell me and the rest of these maggots what the sergeant is."

"The Sergeant is an asshole," the boy said, his voice breaking on the final word.

The howl that Sergeant Hicks emitted was demonic enough to startle Ben, who watched from his anonymous vantage point in the car.

"You scum sucking son of pig shit. If you ever call me an asshole again I'll make sure they send you home to your maggot mother in no fewer than a hundred boxes. You and fat maggot are going to be my special project these next couple of weeks. I'm gonna be all . . ."

Someone in the platoon coughed loudly. Stopping in midsentence, Sergeant Hicks stepped back, his face contorted with disbelief and fury. He began to slap the swagger stick into the open palm of his left hand again and again. It was the only sound Ben could hear. The platoon was motionless, soundless. They waited for the D.I.'s wrath to descend upon them collectively, in a truculent visitation as though the whole platoon had sneezed together. "Which one of you turds coughed?" Hicks asked in a baleful whisper. "I want to know which one of you worthless nits had the brass balls to cough when I was talking. I will tell you this, turds. No one in this goddam platoon coughs, farts, shits, pisses, or beats off without my permission. Is that clear, turds?"

"Yes, Sergeant."

Then the cough came again. Ben heard it and froze. He looked to his father for some sign of affirmation. But Bull was smiling, leaning back, and enjoying the performance.

"I see you, maggot," Hicks screamed. "I see you, maggot. Beat feet it up here, scumbag. You. Yes. You, scumbag. You beat feet it up here before I tear your fucking legs from your putrid body."

The third man in the fourth rank ran to the front of the platoon and stood trembling at attention before Sergeant Hicks. Circling the man, Hicks began muttering and shaking his head, saying, "What am I gonna do, turds? I try to be fair. I try to do my best to produce the best goddam Marines in the Corps. But I got to prove to you turds that I mean what I say. I don't want you maggots to draw a breath without asking my permission. I am pissed off, turds. I am really pissed off. And when I get pissed off, really pissed off, I become a goddam homicidal maniac." His voice was rising again. "I want to kill this piece of shit. I want to kill this piece of shit because he's hurting the Marine Corps. I want to take this swagger stick and poke his eyes out, to mutilate him. I told you not to cough, turd. I warned you. I told you not to cough. And I don't waste my time with any turd more than once."

Very slowly, Sergeant Hicks transferred the swagger stick to his left hand, unsnapped his holster, and slowly drew his pistol. "I hate to do this to you, turd. But you pissed me off bad." Hicks began shooting bullets into the chest of the recruit, firing in a calm synchronized salvo that had a violent harmony to it. Bull was convulsed on the driver's side of the car. "It's Blakeley," he whispered to Ben.

Blakeley lay writhing at the edge of the parade ground, his agony sounding out of him in excruciating groans. Replacing his pistol with extraordinary calm, Hicks screamed out, "Fat Maggot, you and that other turd beat feet it out here on the double!"

The two recruits departed their ranks with terrific haste and stood before Hicks, both of them visibly shaking. "Take this dead maggot," Hicks said, pointing to Blakeley whose chest was now soaked in blood. "Take him over there and throw his ass into that Dempster-Dumpster."

The recruits lifted Blakeley by the arms and legs and carried him rapidly to the Dempster-Dumpster which sat behind B barracks. As they passed the car in which he sat, Ben could hear Blakeley moaning to the recruits who bore him toward the garbage, "Help me. Please help me. I'm only wounded." But his pallbearers did not lose a step as they hustled to the Dempster-Dumpster, opened the steel door, and hurled the man toward the fetid dark interior where cans rattled and a bottle broke. The pleas of the grievously wounded man reverberated through the steel walls enclosing him, but the fat recruit closed the door quickly and both recruits sprinted back to their place in line.

"Good work, maggots. Now Sergeant Taylor will march you off to breakfast. I got to stay here and finish this turd off with my bayonet. It wouldn't be humane to let the poor bastard suffer."

Another D.I. materialized from behind the barracks, issued some sharp, resonant orders and soon the platoon was moving toward the mess hall. Not a single head turned in the entire platoon. Not one man looked back.

Sergeant Hicks walked over to the car, a broad smile on his face. The smile was an incongruity on such a formidable man. Bull Meecham got out of the car and both men shook hands warmly. Then they fell against the hood of the car laughing. Ben ran to the Dempster-Dumpster and unhooked the latch. Climbing out, Sergeant Blakeley immediately peeled off his stained T-shirt. He hurled the T-shirt back into the interior of the dumpster. He saluted Colonel Meecham, blew Sergeant Hicks a kiss, then walked toward the barracks to take a shower.

"Catsup is stickier than blood, son," Sergeant Blakeley said to Ben as he passed him.

Sergeant Hicks walked up to Ben and said, "Happy Birthday, Ben."

"Thank you, sir."

"You're old enough to be part of this platoon now. You want to sign up today? I'll see what I can do about gettin' you in."

"No, sir. I think I'll wait."

"I saw your jacket in the car. Your dad told me he gave it to you as a present. You'll have to be a hell of a man to come up to the Marine that first wore it."

"That'll be a piece of cake," Ben, said, grinning at his father.

"You don't remember this, Ben, but I first saw you on the flight line in Cherry Point when you used to come down there with your dad. He used to ride you around on his shoulders on top of that same flight jacket. That was a long time ago, wasn't it, Colonel?"

"It doesn't seem like that long ago. You still got that same ugly puss that would scare God, Hicksie."

"Well, I scared some boys this morning, sure enough. Now, Ben, you know that this little exhibition today is just between us girls. They'd hang me up by my thumbs if they heard about this little training technique. I've already been busted once for having a little fun and games with my turds."

"Do you ever have any trouble from your troops after one of these performances?" Bull asked.

"Colonel, that platoon you just saw will win almost every award for excellence when they graduate from this island as full-fledged Marines; they'll also be tough enough to hold off half the Russian army. What they learned this morning was just play-acting. Right now, they think they're in the clutches of a wildass killer. It makes my job a lot easier."

"I won't say anything, Sergeant," Ben said.

"Good. That's fine. That's real fine," Sergeant Hicks said, stepping back to salute Bull Meecham. "Excuse me, sir. I've got to get back to my turds and kind of detraumatize them. Happy Birthday again, Ben."

"Thank you, Sergeant."

As they drove back toward Ravenel, the sky was beginning to loosen up in the east, fingers of pink and mauve light touched the rim of the earth, enlarging imperceptibly with each moment passed. Bull asked his son what he had extracted from the morning exercises.

"I'm glad I'm not a recruit on Biddle Island."

"Here's what I want you to take away from this morning," Bull said. "I want you to know that the Marine Corps could get along without its officers just fine. A lot of officers are a bunch of dingle berries going along for the ride. But the NCO's. Those guys are the cream de the cream. You get rid of the sergeants and there is no Marine Corps. There's just a bunch of guys walking around wearing funny green suits."

"Then why aren't you a sergeant, Dad?" Ben asked.

"I am," Bull said. "That's my secret; I am."

Bull dropped Ben off near the kitchen door. Before Ben could reach the step, Bull called to him, "Don't forget, jocko, I want you to meet me at the club at 1700 hours. Tell your mama we'll be home at about 1830 for a little dinner and cake cutting."

"See you at five, Dad," Ben said. "Thanks again for the jacket."

"Just don't wear it to costume parties. You could get your sweet ol' Dad into all kinds of hot water if the wrong guy sees you walking around in it."

"I'll just wear it around the house. Can I show it to Toomer?"

"Yeah. Toomer don't know shit from Shinola anyway. See you at the club, sportsfans. Wear a coat and tie."

"Yes, sir."

Bull drove downtown for his morning coffee at Hobie's Bar and Grill. Since he had begun to show up regularly at Hobie's, he had found a minor addiction to the small talk among the regulars who drifted in after the grill opened after seven in the morning. Already he knew that Ed Mills would be working on his first cup of coffee, occupying the stool nearest the door and casting dark, scowling salutations at all who entered after him. It was a matter of intense pride to Bull that the regulars had accepted him after a brief period of trial and initiation.

Lillian had risen and was sitting at the kitchen table reading the Charleston *News and Courier* and finishing her first cup of coffee. Walking softly, Ben entered the kitchen.

"How does it feel to be eighteen, sweetheart?" Lillian said, rising and going over to kiss her son on the cheek.

"It feels good. I can now get married without my parents' permission, buy liquor in South Carolina, and die in any war that comes up. Dad told me this morning that he thought I'd win some air medals in either Cuba, the Middle East, or Southeast Asia."

"I was just nineteen when you were born. I was eighteen when I married your father."

"I hope you were eighteen when you married him."

"Hush, sugah."

"It's hard to believe, Mama, that you were my age almost exactly when you married Dad. I can't imagine myself married right now. I guess you got to date a little before you decide to get married."

"I was a child when I got married," Lillian said, returning to her coffee. "My mother should have known better but she grew up in a generation where girls married the first man who could provide real security. You know, of course, that some of the boys who proposed to me in Atlanta are some of the richest, most prominent men in the South right now. But the war was going on and the future was so uncertain. Then your father showed up. The handsomest thing you have ever seen in your life in that uniform of his. And all those medals. He was also the most charming talker I had ever run across. I had always thought that southern boys could outtalk any race of living creatures until I met your father. Mother was a little worried about his being a Yankee and she almost

226

died when she found out he was Catholic, but he charmed her faster than he had me. Your daddy's tongue was all honey and cotton candy when he went courtin'. If I hadn't married Bull, I think mother would have disowned me. Your father can still do no wrong in your grandmother's eyes. When I complain about Bull, she tells me that I don't know what a mean man is and to thank my lucky stars I don't have to live with one."

"Dad puts on the biggest act I've ever seen around Mamaw," Ben said.

"Your father is one of the great actors of the world, Ben, but he is a child actor and his role hasn't changed or developed since I've known him. I sometimes wonder what would have happened to your father if he had left the Marine Corps and become an insurance salesman or a used car dealer. I wonder what that would have done to his self-image. I see the need for a fighter pilot to maintain an enormous ego because without it his life might be endangered."

"I don't believe that, Mama," Ben said with sudden seriousness.

"It's true, Ben. Every time your father goes up in a plane, there's a chance he won't come back. There's a chance that something will go wrong with the plane or some horrible accident will occur. I think your father brags and struts and pretends he's the greatest pilot in the world because he's covering up something. He's covering up his fear."

Ben walked to the stove and poured himself a cup of coffee. "What do you think you're doing, mister?" his mother asked. "You're not old enough to drink coffee."

"Dad let me drink some this morning," Ben answered. "I drank it black."

"If you want to drink it when you get away from my house, then drink it. But in my house you won't touch it. The caffeine's bad for you."

"The reason I don't believe that fighter pilot stuff, Mom," Ben said, pouring the coffee back into the pot, "is that I remember Major Finch."

"You barely even knew Lamar. He was a prince of a man."

"I went to school with his son and I used to play pick-up basketball games with Marines who worked on his plane. Do you know what was different about him?"

"There was a lot different about Lamar Finch."

"I heard over and over again that he was the best pilot in the Marine Corps. And he never said a single word to anybody. He was quiet and polite and just a nice guy. Billy Lamar told me that his father didn't drink, cuss, smoke, or brag, or anything. That's what everybody said. But the story I loved the best was that Major Finch whipped Dad's fanny when they hassled together on maneuvers. So if Major Finch didn't have to drink and brag and kick his kids around, why do Dad and some of his other Marine buddies have to?"

"Major Finch was the exception. He was not seduced by the myth of the Marine Corps."

"What do you mean?" Ben asked.

"Your father has taken the whole mythology of the Corps, or what he interprets as the mythology, and entwined it with his own personality. Sometimes your father acts like a living, breathing recruitment poster. I don't know if he was like that when I married him because I don't really know what I was like when I married him. I just think the ego is bloated into something monstrous when a man decides to make the Marine Corps a career. Had your father become something in the civilian world, our lives would have been very different. Major Finch didn't need the Marine Corps. He had the quiet confidence of a man who believes in himself and who doesn't need a structure to reinforce that belief."

"No. With Dad it doesn't make any difference, Mama," Ben said. "He could be an insurance salesman and still be the same type of guy. I can see him coming home from work, kicking a door down, and shouting, 'Stand by for an insurance salesman!' He's the way he is because he can't be anything else."

"You're wrong, Ben. The Marine Corps is a stronger force than you know. It can take a stupid, spineless man and make him feel like he could face the armies of God and stand a fifty-fifty chance of winning. If the Corps gets a strong man in the beginning, then it can make him feel that the armies of God are kamikazes for having the nerve to challenge him in the first place. The Marine Corps takes a small ego and makes it gigantic; it takes a large ego and then steps back to see how large it can grow. Your father's is still growing even though I feel it now dwarfs a few small Alps."

"Well, ol' Ben will be out of it next year."

"Have you been thinking about college?"

"Sure. I've narrowed it down to Harvard and Yale."

"Don't be ridiculous."

"Seriously, I'd like to go to Chapel Hill."

"You can't go there for two reasons. It's too expensive for out-of-state students and your father heard that it was a training ground for Communists when we were stationed at Cherry Point."

"Dad thinks every college is a training ground for Communists."

"He heard this from an impeccable source. General Whitehead. His son went there for a year until the Communists drove him out."

"He flunked out, Mom. And you know as well as I do that General Whitehead is an idiot. Dad thinks he's an idiot too."

"Anyway, it's too expensive."

"Where can I go, Mom?"

"Well, if you don't win a scholarship for basketball, you could try to get an appointment to the Academy."

"No."

"Well, it was just a thought. I think your grades have slipped too much for that anyway."

"I make good grades in English and history," Ben said.

"You only study things that come easy to you. There's nothing character-building in doing something where there's no struggle. If you made A's in math and science, the subjects you detest, I would be certain that you were made of something tough and indestructible and that you would go far in life. I've taught you to love literature and love language but I often think I made a mistake by emphasizing it too much. A man needs to know math and science if he's going to be a pilot."

"Who said anything about being a pilot, Mom?"

229

"You don't need to say anything about it, Ben. You grew up around it. The only men you really know are pilots. I don't think you'll make the Marine Corps a career, but I think a couple of years will do you some good."

Ben lifted his left shoe up on his chair and began unlacing it. "Sometimes I think you hate the Marine Corps, Mom. Then other times I think you love it. Which is it?"

"What do you want for breakfast? I'll make you anything you want on your birthday."

"Which is it?"

"The Marine Corps has been good to us. It has provided security for us all. We've never been hungry and we've always had a nice roof over our heads. I have no quarrel with the Marine Corps. I do sometimes have a quarrel with what I think it's done to your father."

"Fix me some fried eggs once over light, bacon, toast and honey, and some yellow grits."

"Coming up," Lillian said, lighting the stove.

Mary Anne walked into the kitchen wearing her green bathrobe and slippers. On her face was a heavy residue of Clearasil left over from the bedtime toileting of the night before. Her hair was in pin curls.

"She walks in beauty, like the night," Ben quoted.

"Happy birthday, golden boy," she said. "Eighteen. That's old. That's real, real old. You're gonna be dead before you know it."

"What a terrible thing to say," Lillian said while frying bacon. "If you don't care about Ben's feelings, how do you think that makes me feel?"

"I'm sorry, Mama. I apologize. I know it must be awful being your age and having death staring into your face with every breath you draw."

"I have a lot of good years left in me, girl," Lillian said angrily.

"I imagine you have several anyway."

"Why didn't you wash your face and fix your hair before you came down to breakfast? A lady would never make her appearance until she had at least fixed her face."

"I kind of like it, Mom," Ben said. "Not many guys have a sister with a green face."

"The Clearasil needs time to work. Killing pimples requires patience. By the way, Ben, since women live seven
years longer than men on the average, I imagine I'll be
attending your funeral one day."

"Mary Anne, that'a quite enough from you," Lillian
said.

"She's just teasing, Mom," Ben said.

"No, I'm not. I'm serious. I'll even be sad, Ben. Even
though you've spent your whole life making vicious re-
marks to me, I will try not to be amused at your funeral."

"Thanks," Ben said, laughing.

"By the way, I got a great present for you, big brother."

"Dad gave me his flight jacket."

"Of course, that means that the ol' cheapo won't have
to spend any money on your birthday. I saved my tiny
little allowance to buy this present for you."

"Your allowance is certainly more than I got when I
was your age," Lillian said.

Mary Anne ignored her mother's rebuttal. Turning to
Ben she said, "Dad's flight jacket will be good to wrap fish
in or cover a body if we ever witness a murder."

"No one thinks you're funny, miss. No one in the whole
world thinks you're even mildly amusing."

The kitchen filled up with the odors of fried bacon,
eggs frying in bacon grease, toast in the oven, coffee, and
grits bubbling in the pot. When everything was ready,
Lillian took Ben's plate to a counter out of his vision. She
opened a drawer, removed a box, then struck a single
match. When she came around the stove, she had put
birthday candles into the eggs, the toast, the grits, and lit
them all. Lillian and Mary Anne both sang "Happy Birthday" as Ben blew out the candles that flickered over his
breakfast meal. Ben knew that he would find candles
in his lunch sandwiches and in his school books. Lillian
had a genius for the small rites of celebration.

Before he left the house to walk the single mile to the
high school, Lillian handed him a letter and told him to
read it when he found the time. She told him it was of no
importance but just something she wanted him to have.
The letter was passed with such palpable nonchalance

231

and unconcern that Ben knew that the letter was very important indeed.

In his second period French class, he opened the letter and placed it inside his book. He read the letter as another student in the class did irreparable damage to the French language and a short story by de Maupassant. The letter was not long but Ben felt tears coming as soon as he began to read it. "My dear son, my dear Ben, my dear friend who becomes a man today, I want to tell you something," the letter began. "You are my eldest child, the child I have known the longest, the child I have held the longest. I wanted to write you a letter about being a man and what it means to be a man in the fullest sense. I wanted to tell you that gentleness is the quality I have admired the most in men, but then I remembered how gentle you were. So I decided to write something else. I want you to always follow your noblest instincts. I want you to be a force for right and good. I want you to always defend the weak as I have taught you to do. I want you to always be brave and know that whatever you do or wherever you go, you walk with my blessings and my love. Keep your faith in God, your humility, and your sense of humor. Decide what you want from life then let nothing deter you from getting it. I have had many regrets in my life and many sadnesses but I will never regret the night you were born. I thought I knew about love and the boundaries of love until I raised you these past eighteen years. I knew nothing about love. That has been your gift to me. Happy Birthday. Mama."

When Ben walked into the Officers' Club that afternoon, he did not see his father at first. It took a long moment for his eyes to adjust to the dark. He could make out the shapes of pilots sitting around the bar, large shoulders and barbered heads silhouetted in the pale light that spilled into the bar from the dining room. The talk was loud and virile. The sound of ice against glass and crystal made a scant music as Ben tried to find the silhouette of his father.

Ben was dressed in a dark blue suit that Lillian had bought at a PX sale for ten dollars the year before. It had been a little small when she bought it and now the sleeves were high up Ben's wrists and too much ankle showed between his cuff and his shoe. His brown hair was combed into a moderately high pompadour and had the slick appearance that came with the overly ambitious application of Wild Root Cream Oil. There were white traces on the back of his hair where he had not rubbed in the hair tonic. His face had a quality of inlaid unripeness. He studied the shadows. All of them looked like his father and none of them did. Gradually, his eyes adjusted and faces materialized. In the far corner, he saw Bull and Colonel Hedgepath watching him, enjoying his uncertainty, his callowness.

"Congratulations, godson," Colonel Hedgepath said, rising to shake Ben's hand.

"Thanks, Colonel."

"Paige took our present over to your house this morning. Then she and your mother chewed the fat for about four hours. She called to tell me dinner would be late, so I decided to come over here and have a quick drink. Damn, it makes me mad that you're eighteen."

"Why, Colonel?"

"Because that means I'm eighteen years older than I was when you were baptized. It means I'm getting old."

"Sit down, boy," Bull said to Ben. "What'll you have?"

"I'll have a Coke, Dad," Ben answered.

"That's not what I mean," Bull said. "I didn't bring you over here this afternoon to drink soda pop and eat pretzels. You're eighteen and that means you're now old enough to buy a drink. You ever drank before?"

"Just when you gave me sips of your drinks or beer," Ben said.

"Well, it's my job to see that you learn to drink like a gentleman," Bull said.

"I better give you a few lessons, Bull, so you'll know something about the subject," Colonel Hedgepath said.

"Hey, Virge, why don't you go under the table and bite hard on the biggest thing you see."

"I'm tired of chewing on your big toe, Bull."

"What do you want to drink, sportsfans?" Bull said,

ignoring Colonel Hedgepath. "What would you like to drink?"

"Mom will get mad, Dad," Ben warned.

"You've probably noticed I'm shaking all over. I'm practically passing out from fear," Bull said.

"Ben's right, Bull. Lillian is not going to like it at all," said Colonel Hedgepath.

"Virge, I realize that Paige has got a ring in your nose and a handle on your ass. But some of us Marines are the masters of our households. Our word is law. I'm going to teach my eighteen-year-old son how to drink."

"It's almost basketball season, Dad. I'm in training."

"You just don't have the nads. You just got a terminal case of the yellow spine," Bull said.

"If the boy doesn't want to drink, don't make him drink, Bull."

"I don't think they serve lemonade, Ben," his father teased. "They might have a spare lollipop around."

The waiter was passing near the table where the two officers and the boy sat. Ben called him over with an inaudible snap of the fingers. He knew that the eyes of the two Marines were on him; he also knew that he was in the middle of a test that had something to do with the tortoise-slow approach of manhood. He hesitated. He thought. Then he asked, "Do you have a menu, sir?"

His father and Colonel Hedgepath howled with laughter. But most of Ben's hatred and humiliation was directed at the waiter, who shook his head with a patronizingly bemused tolerance. Without waiting for his father's laughter to die, Ben lowered his voice and said, "Then I'll have a double martini on the rocks with a twist of lemon." He had heard this drink ordered at squadron parties when his parents entertained the pilots in their home. Instead of quelling the laughter of the two men who sat with him, it merely increased it. Ben noticed that other Marines were beginning to watch their table as the word of the neophyte drinker spread around the bar.

"Do you know what a double martini is, son?" Bull asked.

"Of course. It's what I usually have when I sneak out with my friends," Ben said half-snappishly.

"What's it made of?" Bull asked.

"Leave my godson alone," Virgil said to Bull.

"It's made out of liquor," Ben said.

"That's right," Bull said seriously, "you have done a lot of drinking. I guess I'm just the old doubting Thomas. For a minute I didn't think you knew what you were talking about."

"That's a real alligator you ordered, godson," Virgil said, winking at Ben.

"If you guys think you can handle it, I might let you have a taste," Ben said.

"I'm gonna stick here and nurse my glass of root beer," Bull said.

The waiter brought the martini to the table. He looked Ben over carefully. Ben fidgeted under the scrutiny. He tried to make his face look old but had no idea which expression he possessed made him look the oldest.

"You got an I.D., kid?"

"Sure, buddy," Ben said in his toughest voice, "I got an I.D."

The waiter studied it for a moment. Then said, "Is this the eleventh?"

"All day," Ben said.

"Happy Birthday, kid," the waiter said so that the whole room could hear.

As he picked up his glass, Ben saw his father rise to his feet and begin to speak to every Marine in the bar. "Gentlemen, please excuse me. But I would like you to join me in a toast to my oldest son who is eighteen today. He has just ordered his first drink and before he begins drinking it, I would like to wish him a long life, a wife as fine as his mother, and a son as fine as he has been. To my son."

The Marines cheered loudly. Bull clinked his glass against Ben's. Ben then lifted his glass and touched it against his godfather's. For the second time that day, Ben was near tears. He looked in the face of Virgil Hedgepath and saw that Virgil too was deeply moved by Bull's toast. Always, in Virgil's face, the ache of childlessness was writ in an astonished surprise that would attack his eyes, then loosen the muscles of his face. It was what made Ben feel extraordinarily close to Virgil. Especially now, as Ben sipped his first drink. The martini went down hard, burning his tongue and throat in its passage. He tried not to wince or choke. He forced down a desire to spit the liquid across the table. He got it down, smiled, and felt a small tinge of wonder as an unfamiliar fire spread along his stomach. As he readied himself for the next sip, he thought that the flame in his stomach was the secret behind the mystery of why men wasted so much of their lives in these dark, forbidden rooms and why Lillian Meecham spent so much of her life worrying about Bull's love affair with "O" Club bars.

"How is it, big man?" Bull asked.

"I've tasted better," Ben said roughly, "but it's fit to drink." He took another swallow, thinking to himself that every line he had spoken was lifted without due credit from a half dozen different movies he had seen in his lifetime. The second swallow was easier. The third was still easier.

"I'd slow down a bit, Ben. That's a man's drink you ordered."

"That's why I ordered it, Virgil," Ben said.

"That's Colonel Hedgepath to you, mister," Bull said.

"I thought with us guys sitting around, Dad. You know, just drinking and talking. We could all relax."

"If you call me Bull, we'll be going to duke city."

Ben took a longer drink. "Hey, this is great," he said looking around the bar. "This is really great."

"Bartender," Virgil called, "another drink for my godson."

"What's in this thing anyway?" Ben said laughing.

"Liquor," Bull said, hitting Virgil with his elbow.

"This is great. This is really great," Ben said.

"How are you going to smuggle him past Lillian?"

"Hell," Bull answered, "we've got a party to go to as soon as we leave here."

"Then I wouldn't touch this next drink, Ben. You already look like you've had enough."

"Heck, Virge, I don't even have a buzz on," Ben said, giggling loudly.

236

"It's Colonel Hedgepath, son."

"That's to you, Dad. But to me he's just good ol' Virge. Right, Virge?" Ben said putting his arm around his godfather and hugging his neck.

"That's right, Ben. Ben and Virge. Drinking buddies."

"Hey, this is great, Dad," Ben said. "This is really great."

"You like it, eh?" Bull said.

"You know what I think, Dad?" Ben said, taking another drink of his second martini.

"No, what."

"I think it's great. I think it's really great! Just sitting here drinking with the Marines. I think it's great. I think it's really great. Have another drink, Dad. You too, Virge. This one's on me."

Twenty minutes later, Ben Meecham, eighteen years old, on the brink of manhood, was carried from the Officers' Club of Ravenel Air Station on the shoulders of his father. When they arrived home at nightfall, Bull bore his son past his mother, his brother, and his sisters, past a birthday cake, and presents. Bull and Lillian had a long and bitter fight that night. But Ben did not hear it. He heard nothing until he woke up to a most disagreeable noontime the next day.

18

THE ALARM woke Bull Meecham at 0300 hours on the morning of October 21. He had been cast from a restless sleep, but he rolled off the bed and onto the floor where he pumped out fifty pushups before he groped his way to the bathroom. Lillian listened to his labored exhalations as he struggled with the last ten pushups and remembered the years when Bull could do a hundred with ease. Age had thickened her husband, thinned his hair, and reduced the numerology by which Bull himself measured his fitness.

"How many did you do, sugah?" Lillian called from the bed.

"Seventy-five," Bull said.

"Do you want breakfast?"

"Negative, sportsfans."

"I always feel better when I've fixed you a good hot breakfast before you go on a long hop," Lillian said.

"How do you know I'm going on a long hop?" Bull asked.

"Darling," she answered, "the best source of information in the entire Corps is in the middle of an "O" wives meeting. The word among the girls is that 367 is going to Cuba."

"The Joint Chiefs of Staff should develop such an intelligence system," Bull grumbled.

"Then I'm right. You're going to Guantanamo. Is something going to happen?"

"That's classified."

"You mean you don't even trust your own wife?" Lillian asked coyly.

"I wouldn't trust Helen Keller. Even if you lopped her arms off."

"Do you think there might be war?"

"Lillian, I can't talk about this. It's classified."

"Do you think if we attack Cuba, Russia will intervene?"

"I hope so," Bull answered, applying shaving lather to his face as he talked to his wife.

"Aha," Lillian shouted, "then it is Cuba."

"Keep your voice down, one of the kids might hear."

"Matt says he hasn't sold secrets to the Kremlin for at least a year, Bull."

"Yeah, but what about Ben?" Bull grinned. "It would take just one Marine wife or one Marine kid to start working for the Russkies and every move the Corps made would be transmitted to Russia twenty-four hours in advance."

"Do you know if something happens, sugah, you could be in combat later today?"

"I've got to win some medals if I'm going to make bird colonel. This could make or break my career."

"I'll get breakfast. You'll need to have breakfast if we go to war."

Lillian drank a cup of black coffee as she watched Bull inelegantly consume a plate of eggs, biscuits, and country ham.

"Do you ever think of the men you've killed in combat, darling?" she said, trying to begin a conversation. Bull's mind was fixed on other things.

"What?" he answered.

"Do you think of the men you killed?"

"Negative. No sense boo-hooing over dead slants."

"Don't you ever think about their wives and mothers? Or if they had children? Or if they liked to fish or enjoyed a stiff drink?"

"After I set 'em on fire, Lillian, none of those things makes any difference."

"I wish you wouldn't say things like that, sugah. It makes me feel funny to hear you say things like that. It's so strange that I'm married to a man with so little reverence for human life."

"I've got lots of concern for human life as long as it was born between the Atlantic and the Pacific Ocean and just north of Mexico and just south of Canada. That's why I would love to drop a few bombs on Cuba. I've never killed a round eye in my whole career. I've majored strictly in slants."

"Sometimes I think you'd have made a wonderful S.S. Trooper, Bull."

"I would have," Bull said.

"You sound proud of it."

"I've always admired those bastards. They were great military men and efficient as hell. I liked the Germans a hell of a lot better than I liked the Japs. Can you imagine what it would be like if the Japs had won the war? We'd be going down to the temple each Sunday to kiss Buddha's rosy red. And I'd sure rather learn how to speak German than that bird scratch Jap talk. Naw, the Germans would have been O.K. But we had to fight the Japs for keeps because the American way of life would have been destroyed if the Japs had taken the marbles. You talk about me not having respect for human life. It's the Japs that don't have any respect for human life. It's got something to do with their being yellow and having slitty eyes."

"What about the Jews, darling?" Lillian said, her fine blue eyes set in a kind of stare.

"So the Krauts fried a couple of Jews. Big deal. It was war. We fried Germans in Berlin and Dresden. We fried Japs in Hiroshima and Nagasaki and I mean, sportsfans, we done fried 'em like eggs there, no pootin' around. In every war someone gets fried. The Jews got it from the Krauts. In war, there ain't no morals. There are just winners, losers, and those that got their asses fried sunny side up."

"They killed women and children like they were butchering hogs. They set out to eliminate Jews from the face of the earth and for no reason except that they were Jews."

"Big deal. Jews are a pain in the ass. I imagine that

240

when Hitler was a kid, he got pissed off at everyone with a big schnozzola and a fraternity beanie making more money than he ever dreamed of."

"He set out to eliminate one part of the human race, sugah. Do you hear that, sugah? Do you understand that, sugah? Is that registering in your fighter pilot brain, sugah? Doesn't that do anything to your sense of justice, sugah? To your heart, sugah? Doesn't that touch you somewhere, Bull Meecham?"

"Yeh, you're right, Lillian. It does touch me," Bull said sincerely. "I can feel it deep down inside me. It's a ticklish feeling. A powerful itch that's located somewhere on the high side of my sphincter tube."

"I don't know why I even try to have a conversation with you," Lillian said angrily. "It's hopeless to even try to make you feel things."

"A fighter pilot isn't supposed to feel things. He's supposed to kill people. You and the other split-tails can do all the feeling you want to, but I can't. I have a mission to do. Period."

"If the fighter pilot can't feel things, then how can I feel things for the fighter pilot?"

"Because that's your mission. Your mission is to love the fighter pilot, cook good meals, police up the house, and raise superior children."

"Darling, you think an inch deep on every subject. Then quit."

"O.K., Lillian. I'll play your game," Bull said. "You've been reading those books about what jerks Hitler and the Germans were for as long as I can remember. But I'm a realist. I don't believe anything I read because I know that anyone who writes about something is always picking the scabs off someone else. If Hitler had won the war you'd be reading books about what a jolly good fellow Hitler was and how jim-dandy it was that he killed every Jew that ever lived. And what if he had? What if there wasn't a single long-nosed Jew living in the world today? Do you know what would be different? Nothing. You wouldn't even notice it. I'm always hearing do-gooders bawling about the passenger pigeons and the dodo bird being extinct. I have never once in my life given a rat's fart that I never saw a passenger pigeon. If Hitler had killed off every Jew that drooled between two lips it wouldn't affect my life one way or the other. The world gets by without them."

"What about its Marines? Could the world get by without its Marines?"

"Ain't no force in the world tough enough to make Marines extinct. Marines make enemies extinct or make them wish they were."

"The thing I love about you, Bull, is your radiant love of mankind. Sometimes when you talk I wonder how two people so different could be married so long."

"Because you're wild about my bod."

"But the thing that worries me most is that my children might turn out to be exactly like you."

"Only if they're lucky."

"Sometimes I think I'd rather see them dead."

"Don't worry, Saint Lillian," Bull sneered, "you've diluted the Meecham blood with so much radiant love of mankind that I'll probably be buying the boys silk panties and hair ribbons in a few years."

"You have four fine children."

"I want the boys to become good soldiers and the girls to be fine pieces of tail for their husbands."

"There are times, sugah, when you sicken me."

"I'm just saying what's what. I can use prettier words but that's my wish for my children."

"Never talk about my daughters like that again."

"O.K. I'll talk about the boys. They aren't tough enough."

"They're too tough, darling. They've been raised by you."

"I've got to check out. Varney's giving a briefing at 0500 and I've got some stuff to do around the office," Bull said, rising from his chair and glancing at his watch.

"What time do you take off?"

"Classified."

"Can you call me from Guantanamo?"

"Negative."

"When will you be getting back?"

242

"It depends on how long the war lasts," Bull said, grinning. "I can still get you upset anytime I want to, Lillian. I think it's getting easier the older we both get."

"I'm not as resilient as I used to be, Bull. I'm feeling older and I can't take things I used to take."

Bull took Lillian in his arms and kissed her lightly, playfully.

"Sometimes I play the ogre just to make you mad," he said.

"Sometimes you play the ogre because there's nothing else there."

"See you in Havana, kiddo."

"So it is Cuba."

"It's a shame you don't smoke cigars," Bull said as he walked out the back door.

In the ready room, the pilots of 367 milled around the room or fidgeted in their seats. They were dressed for flight. An inextinguishable elation gripped the room and the voices of the young aviators were fleshed with bravado. But mostly there was a kind of reflexive professionalism and an uncommon immersion of the aviators into philosophical speculation. Bull found Captain Johnson reading a copy of "High Flight" slipped into the back page of his log book. He teased Johnson about it, but without malice.

Varney entered the ready room a few minutes before 0500 and went immediately into the clipped, faintly Oxonian accent that scraped across Bull's eardrum like a nail. Bull knew there was no real reason for Varney to address the squadron; he wanted to be a part of the grand panoply of what could be the first day of a war.

"Gentlemen," Varney addressed the pilots, "as you probably know by now, a call came from the Second Marine Air Wing yesterday placing squadron 367 on a twenty-four-hour alert. This action is culminated by the action that is forthcoming. At 0600, squadron 367 will break a day and deploy twenty planes to Gitmo. Arrive at Gitmo at 2 plus 36. On arrival Guantanamo Bay, you will be further briefed on specific missions and targets listed in op order that will be presented by the Office of Naval Intelligence. Further instructions will also emanate and be forthcoming from the C.O. of Gitmo, Captain Bruce Webster, at the time of arrival. Gentlemen, I do not have to tell you of the importance of this mission. If something breaks between Cuba and the United States or between the Soviet Union and the United States, the squadron will be expected to buy Havana. Good luck, gentlemen," he concluded.

He stopped to shake hands with Bull Meecham. "Good luck, Colonel."

"Thank you, sir," Bull replied and the two men shook hands.

Bull then walked to the same spot where Colonel Varney had stood. He did not begin to speak until he was certain that Varney had cleared the premises. "Men, this mission culminates your training in Ravenel. In reality, all our training has come to this single moment. They did not select this squadron by accident. They selected it because we were the best. As I look around, I see that each and every one of you have the capability of making this squadron the finest assembly of fighter pilots in the Corps, then by extension we are the best goddam fighter pilots in the world. Now I want you to think that this is the bell for round one and this squadron is the Sunday punch. We're going right into the teeth of the enemy. We will be expected to gain Air Superiority over the mainland of Cuba. Once we begin to clear the skies, I don't want anything larger than a sea gull still in the air over that island. But I also want to caution you on becoming overconfident. Though we are the best aviators in the world, it is fatal for any aviator to underestimate his enemy. The MIG is a goddam fine airplane and several Marine pilots who doubted that bought the farm in Korea. The MIG is capable of performing extremely well in all types of combat environment. The Russians have excellent pilots and I personally feel very bad that we're going to have to blow the asses off so many of them."

A cheer went up from the pilots, virile, primal, up from the groin, at the very source of the breed.

"Here is my hope for the younger pilots," Bull continued, eyeing the lieutenants and captains. "I hope that we go to war today. You are fighter pilots but you are virgin fighter pilots. The only way to crack the cherry is through combat experience. A cherry bleeds and you have to draw blood before you know how good you are or how brave you are. You're feeling a storm brew in the pit of your stomach and you're worried that it's fear you feel. It's not fear; it's inexperience. When we break the fly this morning then hopefully we will be flying toward experience. I'd like to be talking to this squadron in about six months and see silver stars hanging from every chest in this room. Gentlemen, let's make history today."

The pilots broke toward the flight line and the open hangars dominated by the sleek, predatory presence of the F–8's. Mechanics clambered over the planes making last-minute checks on engines and radar. The air was filled with the smell of oil. The deafening growl of engines and the sound of scraping metal made it a requirement for men to scream at each other to be heard.

"Where are you from, Corporal?" Bull screamed at an unwhiskered man who clambered off the wing of his plane. The boy smiled. He had played the game with his old man before.

"Galena, Illinois, sir."

"Second best city in Illinois, Corporal. After Chicago," Bull said.

"Galena's the best, sir. By far."

"Court-martial this man, Sergeant," Bull said to Latito. "That's heresy."

In the first light, Bull taxied his plane to the end of the runway, looking back to see the long line of F–8's following behind him. There was something coldly omnivorous in the massing of planes; it was like the gathering of sharks at a bloodspill.

Bull pushed the throttle forward and felt the plane become fire and speed beneath him. He rose into a capitulating dark and could see the glimmering lights of Ravenel on his right; in the east the sun was being born in a perishable orange that caught the fuselage of Bull's F-8 in a moment of gold.

As the squadron, in the demon pass of jets, edged offshore high above the green blaze of ocean, Lillian watched and listened from her second story veranda. She saw the night lights mount the treetops at the end of St. Catherine's Island and she heard the explosion of the afterburners and witnessed the fire that spewed from the exhaust of each plane as the squadron tightened into formation. Always, she was moved by the passage of the terrible winged squadrons. In the first plane, her husband controlled the wings and she could see his eyes set with purpose and she knew that he was at this moment a supremely happy man.

The planes formed behind him and a single vision passed through the mind of Bull Meecham, magnificent in its improbability, in its impossibility, but one that he entertained deliciously for a full minute. He imagined that a call would come to him, a voice of Command, the voice of a subaltern of God, hashmarks running down his arm for a thousand miles. It would be an avenger's voice that would turn the squadron toward the convoy of Russian ships bringing missiles to Cuba. And he, Bull Meecham, would turn his boys southeastward, interpret the exact language of latitude and longitude, then drive toward the unarmed fleet. Always, he had dreamed of the day when he could set a fleet on fire, to sink an armada to the depths. He could see it all, the fire in the water and the air filled with the nightmare of an entire squadron diving at leisure toward defenseless ships. He would cleave holes in the hulls of freighters and let continents of seawater have the missiles for the keeping. He would watch as the black waters overwhelmed the broken, foundering craft, breathing the last sunlight as they slid into the water, quenching their fires as they dropped into the easy depths and began the long journey toward the black mountains that lie in the vastest, darkest land outside the vision of God. Bull Meecham could see it; he could hear the sound of ships breaking up and the screams of Russian sailors.

During the whole flight down, Bull allowed his fantasies

to roam the country of his eyes. He needed a war. He needed it badly.

Before school began, Lillian gathered her children before the shrine beneath the stairs. She lit candles beside Our Lady of the Fighter Pilot and she dusted off the model of the F–8 that Matthew had constructed for his father one Christmas. As ordered, all the children had brought their rosaries with them.

"What are we praying for, Mama?" Karen asked.

"A special intention," Lillian answered, impatient to begin.

"What's the special intention, if I may be so bold as to ask?" Mary Anne asked.

"Peace," Lillian said, beginning the Apostles' Creed.

19

IN THE EARLY EVENING of November 10, Bull and Lillian dressed with great care for the Marine Corps birthday ball. They dressed in silence on opposite sides of their bedroom. Lillian was in a slip at her dressing table carefully applying her makeup. Bull reflected on whether dress whites that had been tailored for a one-hundred-ninety-pound man would permit the entry of the same man who now weighed two hundred and twenty pounds. They both dressed as if they did not know the other was in the room.

This was the night that always filled Bull Meecham with a deep pride in the Corps. It was a night of confirmation when he felt an almost mystical affinity with every man who had ever borne the motto of semper fidelis. All over the world, on this one night, he knew, every Marine, active or retired, in groups of thousands, in small clusters, or single sentries patrolling unfriendly borders, all of them, to the last man, turned to this night in celebration and pride. On this night, they drank to the birth of the Corps. For Bull, this night released a sad cargo of memory that held the names and faces of pilots he had seen flaming toward a violent death in Pacific waters, all the dead Marines he had known, the old faces smiling in motionless portraits frozen by recall: they came to him now, the lost squadrons of brash, cocky pilots culled from the sky by a world that thrived on the blood of young men. He remembered too giving close air support in Korea to a retreating Marine battalion, and seeing the dead Marines frozen grotesquely in the snow. At times he could close his eyes and see those dead Marines rise, see them come out of the snow, their uniforms pressed, boots shining, and their rifles gleaming; and he followed them marching, the lost battalions marching under wind-snapped flags and dancing guidons, coming at him in endless procession, calling to him in the animal roar of many men speaking as one, lifting their eyes to his plane, saluting him as he dove toward the enemy that was always there. On this night, he thought of all the dead Marines he had known and not known, and he loved all of them; the beauty and loss of this night moved him. Death in battle was the one poetry that almost released tears in Bull Meecham.

He fastened the collar of his dress blouse. In his twenty years as a Marine he had gained weight each year. At first it was a couple of pounds a year, undetectable even to him. But lately, the leanness of his youth was deserting him at an accelerated pace. More and more, he was coming to dread the yearly physical. He dieted on eggs and cottage cheese three or four times a year. Too impatient to endure a long range diet, he went on radical diets that seemed like preludes to famine. But no matter how stringent the effort, the thicknesses of middle age were encircling him and threatening to overwhelm the athlete's body, the Marine's body of which he was so proud. It was not that he looked fat; he did not. But there is a harsh message in the veracity of collars and photographs. The collar to his dress whites fit so tightly that it was an act of semi-strangulation to put it on. The Marine in the mirror was almost a caricature of the slim, youthful pilot who stood beside his Corsair in a photograph on Lillian's dresser. The Marine in the mirror unfastened his collar and would not fasten it again until it was absolutely necessary. He did not like the feeling of blood trapped in his head.

"Too tight, fatso," he heard his wife say.

"Naw, it isn't too tight," he snapped. "A uniform's supposed to be snug. It isn't supposed to fit like a nightgown."

"I can still wear the gown I wore to my first birthday ball."

"Big deal."

"There's no reason to be sensitive about being a little

overweight, Bull. A lot of people are fat," she teased. "Maybe it's your glands."

"Quit your yappin' and get dressed, Lillian, or we're gonna be late for the ball. I'm not kidding. Get a move on," Bull said, looking at his watch.

"Don't rush me, Bull. I want you to be proud of the way I look tonight. I bought a gown that could win wars."

"Just hurry it up."

"Bull, you haven't been exactly pleasant to live with since the Cuban rift," Lillian said, her voice filled with concern.

"It ain't my job to be pleasant to live with. It's my job to fly birds."

"It's your job to be civil when you get home."

Again looking into the mirror, Bull said, "Mirror, mirror on the wall. Who's the toughest leatherneck of all?" Then, in a strained falsetto, he answered his own question. "You are, Oh Great Santini." Then in his own voice, he said, "Good answer, mirror. I'd have busted your shiny butt if you had said anything else."

"Bull, darling, why don't you use some of that energy and go downstairs and talk to the children. You've been positively beastly to them since you've been home. You owe it to them to be nice on the birthday of the Marine Corps. This is supposed to be the happiest day of the year for a Marine," Lillian said.

"Not a bad idea, sportsfans. I think I'll find out how they respond to a surprise enemy attack." He went to his top dresser drawer and retrieved a bayonet he had found on a decayed Japanese soldier near an airfield in the Philippines. He also lifted out a shot putt his wife had given him for a Christmas present as a way for him to release tension built up during a day's work. From his closet, he unsheathed the Mameluke sword which he had bought the same day he was commissioned a Marine officer. He put the bayonet in his teeth, carried the shot putt in his left hand, the sword in his right.

"Put that shot putt down, Bull Meecham. The last time you used it as a grenade it broke right through a window at Cherry Point. Now you be careful with those children. You might hurt one of them."

He growled at her through the bayonet.

Silently, Colonel Meecham moved toward the den where his children were watching television and doing homework during commericals. Ben was lying on the floor with his head propped up by pillows. Mary Anne lay on the couch, her hair in pin curls. Both Matt and Karen were sitting in overstuffed chairs with unopened books in their hands. Bull calculated the distance between himself and Ben, then lobbed the shot putt in the air. It missed Ben's head by less than five feet, and tore a chunk of plaster out of the wall. Then Bull charged into the room shouting, "Tora! Tora! Tora!" Matt scrambled toward the kitchen, but his father nimbly cut off that path of retreat. Ben rolled over toward the fireplace and armed himself with a poker. He yelled at Mary Anne to arm herself with a hearth shovel while he held his father at bay. Mary Anne shouted back that she was not going to lower herself by playing in one of her father's silly war games.

"If this was a real attack, all of you would have been wiped out," Bull declared.

"Big deal," Mary Anne said, opening a book. Matt had retreated to the fireplace and armed himself with the shovel his sister had spurned. Karen had picked up the shot putt and was holding it until someone told her what to do.

When Bull realized that Mary Anne was not going to participate in the readiness exercise at all, he took his sword, and lifted her robe past her knees.

"I want to peek at those expensive silk underpants I bought for my sweet little Mary Anne," he teased. "I bought her a different color underpanty for every day of the week. Oh my, she's wearing black. She must be in mourning."

"That's a little sicko, Popsy, a little sicko-sexual weirdness, I would say," Mary Anne said, pulling her robe down.

"En garde, Colonel," Ben called. Bull wheeled toward his son. They dueled with mock ferociousness. The

251

dress sword clanked against the poker and the shovel as Matt came to the aid of his brother. In the corner near the stairs, Karen awaited her orders, still clutching the shot putt with both hands.

"Let's go for the jugular," Ben shouted to Matt.

"Simba Barracuda," Matt answered.

Colonel Meecham stepped back toward the door, unaware of Karen's presence.

"Engage the enemy," he shouted. "The good soldier will always engage the enemy and retreat only if retreat will lead to victory."

He jabbed his sword toward Ben and Matthew, driving them back toward the fireplace. One of his thrusts came uncomfortably close to Ben's right ear.

"Hey, Dad," Ben warned. "You may not have noticed, but that's a real sword you have there. I don't want to lose an ear in this battle."

"Marines have lost more than ears in their long history. But still they come, always attacking, always forging ahead, driving forward without regard to life or limb."

"That's because they're a bunch of dumb creeps," Mary Anne said from the couch.

"What'd you say, Miss Corpse?" Colonel Meecham snapped.

"Nothing."

"Nothing what?"

"Nothing, sir."

"That's better."

As Colonel Meecham looked over at Mary Anne, Karen saw her chance to join the fray. Using both hands, she made a weak underhanded lob toward her father. She intended that it hit on the other side of him so she could claim he had been killed by an incoming artillery shell.

"Oh, Jesus, Karen," Ben cried out.

With a solid thump, the shot putt landed on Bull's left shoe. The Colonel let out with a scream that was heard the length and breadth of Eliot Street, across the Lawn, and by a trout fisherman anchored in the river near the house. He fell on the couch, hopping and stumbling, almost landing on Mary Anne, who joined the frenzied stampede of siblings for the stairs. A lamp crashed to the floor throwing the room into semi-darkness. The bayonet and the Mameluke sword lay on the floor by the couch. Still howling, Bull was trying to remove his shoe to survey the damage. It enraged him as he listened to the thundering feet of his retreating children and heard Mary Anne scream, "Tora! Tora! Tora!" But his mind was not on pursuit, nor would it be until the pain diminished somewhat. He hopped on one foot to the kitchen, tore his sock off his foot, rolled up the pants leg of his dress whites, put his foot in the sink, and ran cold water over the injured toe. The toenail was already turning blue.

In the first startled moment she heard Bull scream, Lillian had started downstairs. She was nearly trampled by her children, whose flight out of the living room was a headlong sprint that left no time for explanations to anyone. "What happened? What happened?" she asked as they flew past her. They did not answer her, for that would have taken time, and very basic enzymes of survival raced through the bloodstreams of the Meecham children as they headed for their preordained hiding place. Lillian watched as they disappeared into Mary Anne's bedroom, and thought to herself that it was strange to see Karen leading the pack. So she walked into the kitchen alone and without forewarning to find out what was causing her husband's outcry.

She found him with his foot in the sink, the faucet running, and his upper torso bent forward examining his toe. He was moaning in pain.

"Athlete's foot?" she asked.

"Ahhh!" he whined in reply.

"Is it your heart?" Lillian asked, knowing that Bull feared heart attacks above all other illnesses.

"Yeah, Lillian," he said. "I'm washing my heart off in the sink. Hell no. It's my goddam big toe."

"Your big toe?" she said, trying not to giggle.

"Yeah, my big toe. If I wasn't wearing shoes, they'd be amputating this toe sure as hell."

"How did it happen?"

"Karen hit me with that goddam shot putt."

"Karen hit you with . . . the shot putt?"

"What do I got to do, Lillian? Write you a book? Yeah, she hit me with the shot putt."

"You mean that big bully Karen hit the ittle biddy Marine on the big toe during war games?"

"She pitched the son of a bitch from ten feet away. If she hit me in the head, I'd be sitting on the right hand of the Father this very moment."

"I can't wait to tell General Hurley why you're limping tonight."

"If you say one goddam word, I'll poke your eyes out."

"Oh, General, it's really nothing," Lillian teased. "My little daughter was tussling with her father and accidentally crippled him. Bull will be all right if he only learns to pick on someone his own size."

"Very funny. Notice how I'm about to die laughing."

"Why don't you go to the ball wearing just one shoe?" Lillian asked.

"Sure, Lillian, and maybe I can wear my jock strap with a couple of ribbons hanging from my butt. C'mon, help me walk. I've got to walk. I've got to give a toast tonight at the squadron table."

He put his arms around his wife, leaned on her, and tried to put his weight on the sore foot. Lillian began to laugh. It was a giggle at first that soon erupted into legitimate, unconscious laughter that spilled through the house and up the stairs like an endangered music.

The children crouched on the limbs of a water oak that grew outside Mary Anne's window, listened to their mother's laughter, and tried to interpret its meaning. "She's gone crazy," Mary Anne whispered to the others, who were in higher branches.

"He'll kill her for sure now," Matt said. "We might have to go down and save Mom."

"I'm never going to leave this tree," Karen said to no one person in particular. "I'm going to stay up here until I die."

"They've got to go to the ball in fifteen minutes, Karen. They've got to leave by then," Ben said.

"Of course, they may have to amputate Dad's foot. Colonel Hopalong Meecham," Mary Anne said.

"That's not funny, Mary Anne," Karen said angrily.

"You'll get the trophy, Karen. Just like a hunter who kills a deer, you'll be able to hang Dad's toe on your wall."

"He'll be all right, Karen," Ben said.

"Ah, the perfect one has spoken."

Matthew said from the highest branch, "I don't think he's going to be all right until he's killed Karen with his bare hands."

"Daddy's never hit me!" Karen said.

"That's because you're the apple of his eye, dear child. You're the pretty, petite little daughter he's always wanted," Mary Anne said.

"I'll bet anything that if it had been me who hit him with that shot putt, he'd be setting this tree on fire right now," Ben said.

"Is Mom still laughing?" Karen said, straining to hear.

"It's very tough to laugh when Dad's hands have cut off your windpipe," Mary Anne said.

"Karen," Ben said, looking at the branch directly above him, "Why did you throw that shot putt? I'm not saying it was a bad idea. In fact, it gave me more pure pleasure than I've had in a long time, but it surprised me a little bit that you threw it."

"I just don't know. I just threw it."

Once again, their mother's laughter spilled out of a downstairs window. The children listened in the tree, silent as fruit. Then they heard thier father laugh too. His sharp sense of the ludicrous had caught up with him, and despite himself, he became amused at the absurdity of events that had left him limping around in the full splendor of his dress uniform. His toe was now a deep and angry aqua, but the anger and much of the pain had diminished.

"My God, you're almost human again, Bull," Lillian said laughing.

"I bet the kids don't come out of hiding for three days," he replied.

"Doesn't it bother you at all that they're afraid of you?"

"Hell, no," Bull answered, gingerly inserting his foot back into his shoe. "It would bother me if they weren't afraid of me. It's my job to see that they stay afraid of me."

"That's silly, and you know it."

"Silly? It ain't so silly. They jump when I say jump. Just like you do."

"Let's go," Lillian said. "We're supposed to be meeting the squadron at the club for drinks right now. Then we're all driving over to the mess hall together for the ball."

"Don't rush me. They'll wait for the C.O."

"Have you memorized the toast?"

"Yeah, it's a great toast. Ben and Mary Anne helped me write it up. Those two are good with the words."

"Did they write the whole thing?"

"The spirit behind the whole thing was mine. They just wrote the words."

"Did they write all the words?"

"I did the polishing."

"Let's go, Bull. My God, that uniform's tight on you. You look like a package of pork sausage."

"I'm the handsomest son of a bitch ever to serve in the United States Marine Corps."

"Then, let's ride, handsome, or we'll be late for the birthday ball."

They walked out of the front door arm in arm, down the stairs, and to the driveway at the side of the house. Bull opened the door for his wife. As he walked to his door, Lillian turned to the tree where her children remained hidden, blew them a kiss, and gave them a victory sign with her gloved fingers. They heard her laugh again as the car pulled out of the driveway, and eased onto Eliot Street.

Only when the car was out of sight did the Meecham children open Mary Anne's window and clamber out of the branches into the house.

The mess hall, gracefully festooned with flowers, streamers, and brightly colored ribbons, pulsed with celebration as the pilots and their wives gathered for the 187th birthday of the Marine Corps. Arrangements of carnations and chrysanthemums sweetened the air, commingling with the perfume of the wives and the sweat of the first dancers, and made something in the vast room seem primal and libidinously manifest. Trellises wired with roses and ferns rose ten feet on the wall behind the head table; music filtered through the hall, light and airy, as the Marines gathered under the soft light to promenade their glittering wives before their peers. The hair of the wives was piled high about the room, eyelashes fluttered, and ice tinkled in full cocktail glasses. It was a night of myth and remembrance, a night of rustling gowns, long dances, and heavy drinking—a night of pride among the fiercest warriors on earth, who preened in their dress whites like birds of prey suddenly struck with the gift of bright plumage.

The women of the pilots, in long elegant dresses, clung to their husbands, guiding them around the room to make sure the proper courtesies were paid, to ensure that the fine obeisances and homages were proffered to those high ranking officers and their ladies who were in positions to make or break careers. Afterward, they returned to the long tables where each squadron sat beneath the squadron emblem, pouring drinks, laughing, the spirit of the evening inoculating them slowly.

Lillian stood at the center of a large group of 367 wives. She enjoyed her role as the confidante of young wives and the envy of the wives her own age. As she stood among them leading the conversation through small rhetorical hills, she looked around at "her girls" and could put them in categories by signs she recognized. The daily golfers had dark, unseasonal tans and the hard casualness of women who had strolled the front nine too many times to curb the restlessness they felt when exiled to the small towns where the Marines built their bases. She saw women who smiled too much or drank too much and these were the women ordered to have a good time by their husbands. There were women who clung to her and laughed at her every joke, and administered to her every whim, and she knew that these were the ambitious women who were driving their husbands forward in the ranks. There were many others who could not be shuffled into convenient categories, but it was because they were skilled at hiding the signs of their satisfaction or their discontent. Whatever their story, these wives were appendages, roses climbing on the trellises. Their roles were decorative on this night and on all others; the glory was their husbands and their sustenance came from what nourishment they could derive from his reflection. In the room, the band played slow waltzes and streamers began to sag from the roof in scarlet, gold, and forest green parabolas, and Lillian talked gaily to the wives, her friends, her comrades, her rivals.

As she went to fetch her husband she found him talking to a group of four young pilots from 367. Like pilots everywhere they had escaped from their wives to talk about flying. Bull had reached a point of inarticulateness, and he was demonstrating a maneuver by using his hands as the aircraft. Sooner or later, pilots always resorted to their hands when discussing the mysteries and secrets of flight. Lillian went up to her husband and as soon as every eye was on her, she curtsied charmingly and asked him for the next dance.

Meanwhile, the Meecham children were honoring a secret tradition among themselves. This would be the third consecutive year they had held their own private celebration of the birth of the Corps. Like most ceremonies, its origins were simple but pomp and color were added each year. The rituals, conceived by Mary Anne, were being thickened, lengthened, and enriched.

Ben was emptying a bag of dog feces onto a large plate on the dining room table. Mary Anne, using a spatula from her mother's silver service, was shaping the feces into a remote semblance of a cake. Their noses wrinkling in disgust, yet enjoying their inclusion for the first time into this forbidden bacchanal, Karen and Matt watched each detail of the operation with the keenest interest. Fearing youthful tongues, Ben and Mary Anne had not allowed the other two to participate in their bastardized version of the ball until this year.

"Do we have enough shoo-shoo?" Karen asked.

"We ought to," Ben said. "I got every piece I could find in this town."

"What if Dad catches us?" Matt asked.

"How can he catch us? He won't be home until three or four this morning," Mary Anne answered. "Anyway, we're just celebrating the birth of the Corps same as him."

"With a few variations," Ben corrected. "This is just our little way of saying thanks to the Corps for all it has done to us. You have the candles, Karen?"

"Yes, but I don't want to put them in that nasty cake."

"If Dad catches us making fun of the Marine Corps, he'll make us eat that cake."

"Quit worrying, will you?" Ben said. "If that's the worst thing he'd do to us, I'd be glad to eat a piece."

The table was immaculately set. The tablecloth was of Florentine lace used only on the most special occasions by their mother. Mary Anne laid out fine bone china and carefully placed the ornately embossed silverware beside the plates and wine crystal. Two candelabra burned with twelve new long stemmed candles. A strict adherence to form was the order of the night. The cake was the single obscenity in an atmosphere of rigorous decorum.

Dress for the night was a matter of taste. Ben wore a bathing suit, his father's flight jacket, frogman flippers, and an Indian headdress. Matt and Karen clad themselves with random selections from various summer and winter uniforms. They rolled up sleeves and pantlegs which were many sizes too large, and wore dress caps backward. Mary Anne put on pink tights, a fatigue jacket, field cap, and her father's jock strap which she stuffed with Kleenex. Then they regrouped in the dining room for the ceremony.

The children stood behind their chairs going rigid when Mary Anne said, "Ten-hup."

Ben went to the record player he had brought down from his parents' room, and put on the Marine Corps hymn. He then spoke, "Good evening, fellow officers. Fellow whores for the Corps."

"Good evening, sir."

"We are gathered here tonight to pay homage to the United States Marine Corpse. As you know, the Marine Corpse is composed of the bravest fighting men who ever lived. The Corpse cannot be killed in battle. The Corpse cannot be denied their strategic objectives by any fighting force on earth. But what is not so well known and what we have come to celebrate tonight is the fact that the Marine Corpse is also the biggest collection of farts and assholes ever to gather together under one banner."

"Hear ye, hear ye," the others shouted, reading from the scripts Mary Anne had prepared.

"We will sing our version of the Marine Corpse HYMN. This version was written by Mary Anne Meecham, the charming daughter of that modest, self-effacing, painfully shy fighter pilot, Bull Meecham, that wonderful little man who calls himself 'The Great Santini.' Mary Anne, you sweet little thing, would you wiggle up here and lead these gyrenes in your version of the hymn?"

In an exaggerated southern accent, Mary Anne replied, "Why, lawdy, I'd be pleased as sweet potato pie to lead you big strong handsome Marines in your big strong handsome hymn. All right now, all you strong handsome honey pies and you strong handsome sugar dumplings, ya'll sing along with me. Benjamin, will yo please start the record over for yo dahlin sister?"

"Why sho, sister sweet," Ben said.

"Everybody together now, you heah? Let's sing."

> "From the halls of Montezuma.
>   To the hills of Tennessee,
>   We're the biggest bunch of assholes,
>   That the world will ever see.
>
>   First to beat our wives and children,
>   Then to wipe their bodies clean,
>   May the whole damn Navy take a crap
>   On the United States Marines."

The officer in charge gave a sign and the doors to the mess hall were thrown open, as a band marched into the cleaned out center of the hall playing the "Foreign

Legion March." They passed by the officers and ladies of Squadron 367 and marched to the far end of the hall, then coming back up the hall, instruments gleaming, the band broke out into the Marine Corps hymn as Bull stood at attention, the flow of history seizing him. Lillian, standing erect, felt the tears come as they always did when she saw strong men march and heard this song that lived in the center of her. The night would go on, the Mameluke sword would cut the cake, the general would speak, and tradition would be served. But for Bull and Lillian, it was the hymn that made this night a holy night for all time.

20

IN HIS ROOM, Ben packed his gym shoes and trunks into a blue zippered bag that had the Marine Corps seal stamped in white on the outside. From his top drawer he pulled two pairs of sweat socks rounded into uneven balls, stepped back toward the door, and lofted both pairs of socks toward the open bag. He made one shot, missed the other, but retrieved the missed shot quickly, gave a head fake, pretended to dribble, went up with two defenders on him, and dunked the socks into the bag, then he adjusted the zipper.

"It's over for you today, hotshot," Mary Anne said, standing at the doorway.

"What do you mean?" Ben asked.

"First basketball practice. You become the golden boy today. Loved by all. Adored by every creep in the world. After a couple of games. I'll become known as Ben Meecham's sister. But the saddest thing of all, the really sad thing, Ben, is that there's some poor guy who's waking up this morning who thinks he's going to be first string, has planned on it for a whole year, and who doesn't even know you're alive."

"I've got to make the team first," Ben replied.

"False modesty is your worst fault, big brother. You've got to learn to enjoy bragging. I love to brag. I just don't have anything to brag about."

At school that day Ben's mind wandered far from his studies and the voices of teachers. Mary Anne was right. Ben knew that the exile was almost over, that his term of loneliness would be shortened the first time he touched the ball in practice. Since the beginning of school, his every waking hour was directed toward that moment. In new schools, redemption came from his ability to go around anyone with a basketball. But he always worried about the first essential step: the making of the team. He worried most about his shooting, that his touch would desert him, that his fingers would stiffen, and that the coach's eye would fix on him every time he missed a shot. He had nightmares that he would take ten, twenty, or thirty jump shots in the first practice and not make a single one of them. He also feared the stupidity of coaches, especially high school coaches in the Deep South who usually regarded basketball as a bastard, weak-kneed son who whined and piddled away the dark season between football and baseball. Anything could happen during a first practice. Tryouts were a time of fear for any boy.

Ben had awakened that morning, while it was still dark, with the butterflies, the old, invisible protozoa of fear that invaded the stomach on the days of contests or of testing. In the morning dark, he had thought of what might go wrong, of why he might not make the team. The thought of being cut made him physically sick and the butterflies moved within him with the burning wings of nausea. But no matter how he tried, he could not think of a reason why he should not make the team. For the past eight years on every day that it was possible, he had shot a hundred jump shots a day, made a hundred layups, and attempted a hundred foul shots. He had once dribbled a basketball lefthanded to and from school for an entire year because he had heard Bob Cousy say that a great guard must be able to dribble well with either hand. But the biggest reason he thought he would make the team was geographical. Ravenel, South Carolina, was so far removed from the proving grounds of American basketball that it seemed impossible to Ben that excellence could be found among the homegrown boys. His main concern was that some Marine kid from California or D.C. had slipped in and, like him, was biding his time until the first practice.

Ben had received his training on the outdoor courts near Washington, D.C. when his father had been stationed at the Pentagon. For three years, from sixth to eighth grade. Ben would go to the courts adjacent to the Centre Theater in Alexandria, Virginia, to learn the fundamentals from boys much older and stronger than he. For two years he was humiliated, teased, and taunted as he tried to shoot over taller boys, pass through crowds of arms, or defend against athletes who considered it a gift to let Ben guard them. But he earned respect because he returned to the courts every day no matter how severely he had been humiliated the day before. Eventually he became a kind of mascot, and the bigger boys liked him in the way they always like the smallest and the youngest member of their group. It was on this court that Ben learned he could dribble, that he was quick, and that he could beat others because he loved to hustle. He learned to fake and pass, to set pics, and to lead a fast break. In his three year apprenticeship, he learned the game. As he improved, he was called "The Weasel" by the other boys and by eighth grade he was selected to play in the full court Saturday morning games that were violent, often bloody affairs, where he was accepted by the high school boys because he could handle the ball well. No one played defense on the courts. Defense was a kind of approximation; everyone just tried to hurt the guy they were guarding once in a while to let him know they were around. Ben had seen two boys carried off the courts on Saturday morning with concussions. That was defense. Ben knew when he woke up on this morning that no one in Ravenel, South Carolina, had been spawned on such a training ground. For on the courts of Alexandria and Arlington, as on most of the courts of the D.C. area, most of the players were black and the swift passionate laws Ben had learned in those years were more valuable than the tutoring he had received from any coach, even his father. And Ben knew that south of Alexandria, Virginia, white boys didn't learn anything from black boys.

That afternoon, Coach Otis Spinks gathered all the tryouts in the center bleachers. The returnees from the previous year, already assured of a place on the team, shot layups as they glanced arrogantly toward the boys in the bleachers, sizing up the group as a whole. There was hatred in their appraisal. "Good luck, rookies," one boy called out, evoking a laugh from his teammates. Ben saw that the boy was Jim Don Cooper, the linebacker and captain of the football team, and the boy who had gone steady for three years with Ansley Matthews.

Coach Spinks stared at a clipboard while he sucked on a half empty bottle of R.C. Cola. Ben had heard the players discussing Coach Spinks's addiction to this particular soft drink. It was claimed that he consumed three sixpacks of R.C. daily, flavored with two packs of Lucky Strikes. His stomach was enormous, an incongruous attachment to an otherwise finely proportioned body. As the coach called names from his list of tryouts, Ben looked around and studied faces as lonely as his. Odd, he thought, I've never seen any of these boys, yet I must have passed them in the halls dozens of times. It gave him a feeling of camaraderie with those outcasts who had come to this gymnasium hoping to find their identity and feed on the secret bread of glory that had been denied them, who had felt isolated and banished from the main flow of student life for so long. Each boy seemed to be saying, "I have a name and a face and a laugh and a cry. Can you see me? Can you hear me?" Ben also noticed that almost every boy quivered with excitement. Hands trembled. Feet tapped out nervous tattoos. The bleachers were filled up with new basketball shoes. The shoes seemed blindingly, tragically white, as fresh as wet paint. The smell of shoes lifted straight from their boxes filled Ben's nostrils. A sadness gripped him as he realized how many pairs of new shoes were bought for nothing. The bleachers in this moment were ruled by virgin shoes and wool socks fresh from cellophane. The bleachers swarmed with youth unanchored, unpraised, and convulsed with the dreams of gangly boys and fat boys who wanted to be a part of something with a desperation that was almost palpable and alive. Then Ben listened to Coach Spinks's introductory speech.

"I'm a football coach, boys. Y'all should know that. I never have cottoned too much to basketball because, to tell you the truth, I thought it was a game invented for the boys who were too chicken to play football. It always kind of embarrasses me to see boys running around in their underwear flashing their armpits. I don't really know all that much about this game. But I've read a couple of books and talked to a couple of old ballplayers and it seems to me that this here is a simple game."

Coach Spinks pointed to a young blond boy in the the front row and said, "Do you like to put it in a hole, son?" The varsity laughed behind him as they continued to shoot layups.

"Pardon me, sir?" the boy asked, terribly flustered.

"Do you like to put it in a hole? I love to put mine in a hole," the coach said, winking at the other boys in the stands and turning toward the returnees who grinned at the old joke. "Well, that's the name of this game. The team that can put a basketball in that hole most often always wins these games. As y'all know, I got me some stud horses coming back from last year's team, so it's gonna be real tough for you boys to make the team. I don't mean to discourage you now, but with seven players back from last year's team, that means only three of you has a chance to get a uniform. Now I'll give y'all a good look over and if you can put it in the hole or pull leather off the wood, then I can always use another stud in the stable. Looking around, I don't see many tall boys in the crowd except for Mumford there," he said pointing with his R.C. bottle at a skinny blond boy who sat in the same row as Ben. The boy reddened at the mention of his name. All eyes in the gym turned on him. "And I know he can't rebound since I cut him for two years runnin' now." Laughter resounded through the gym as Mumford rested his arms on his prominent knees and stared hard at the laces of his new shoes.

"Now the first thing we're gonna do after warmups is to see how well you boys stack up against the varsity. If you can't play with them boys out there then you're gonna have a mighty rough time against some of our opponents this year. We've got ten games scheduled with teams from the Charleston area this year and that's nothin' but city basketball up there. Get out there on the other end of the court for layups. Then when I call you, line up in two lines at center court. We're gonna play two on two for a while to see if you can put the ball in the hole. Now get your butts down there for layups."

The whole crowd of boys rose and thundered off the bleachers, white shoes shining and voices raised in a high-pitched whistle as the layup line formed inexpertly. The first boy who shot missed the basket by three feet in his excitement. Ben watched Coach Spinks's face and knew that boy had been cut. Coaches were all the same: they had ineffable powers of memory when you made a horse's ass out of yourself. Ben didn't know who the boy was but was certain that his time on the team was finite and brief. Ben took his turn, receiving the pass, dribbling twice, then laying the ball softly off the backboard. He watched as it dripped in the net. He was being cautious and making sure of his moves and his shots. "That's it, son. Lay it up there soft, like it was a basket of eggs."

Then Coach Spinks turned his attention toward his returning players, letting them go one on one while he shouted instructions to the defensive players. "Get that butt down, Cooper, like you was a dog scratching for worms," the coach called out. Awaiting his turn to rebound, Ben watched the drills in progress at the other end of the court. He watched each player, looking for the unmistakable signs of the exceptional basketball player. Ben had been a ballplayer for a long time and he knew other ballplayers the way a gypsy knows other gypsies or a thief other thieves. There were things to look for, an unspoken language of movement and form to decipher, passwords to exchange, and glances to decode. First, he looked for the walk. Every good basketball player Ben had ever known walked in a certain way, insouciant, ambling, even awkward, as if to purposefully confuse boys who would guard them when they slipped into their Converse All Stars and called for a basketball. Then this creature of the strange walk turned into something ethereal, flowing. The dancer in him was loosed. Whatever poetry was in him found release as his hands rolled the ball over and over, spinning it, warming to it, touching it before he made his first move toward the basket. The walk came back to him when he did not have the ball, during time outs, when he walked to the foul line, or when he walked to the end of a line in practice. The walk was an indelible mark of identification, like a fingerprint. An unspoken joy arose in Ben as he looked for the walk and could not find it.

Then he watched for the wrist, the snap of the wrist after the shot, the hand bent at the joint of the wrist at about a 45 degree angle, the index finger pointed toward the center of the basket. His father called it the wounded duck but to Ben the hand and wrist took on the shape of a cobra prepared to strike. From this wrist snap came touch. And no good shooter was without it. Ben found approximations of it but the shooters at the other end of the court were only adequate, not gifted. None of them had the carriage and bearing that indicated they were of a royal line of shooters or rebounders; none of them had the easy arrogance of talent that was so commonplace on the courts around D.C.

Ben then concentrated on studying the individual players at the other end of the court. He was in a rhythm now, rebounding, running to the end of the opposite line, studying his enemies at the far court, moving up, cheering, then sprinting toward the basket to drop in a layup, and resuming his survey of the other court. He examined the ball-handling skills of Pinkie Taylor who had been a starting guard on the team the year before. Pinkie was Ben's size but much thinner. He had a large scarlet birthmark on his throat that made his pale skin seem almost translucent. He was in Ben's history class where he distinguished himself daily with a titanic ignorance of American history. His intellect was a sparse acreage indeed but Pinkie got along by wearing a perpetual smile on his face and having an uncanny knack for repairing the engines of his teachers' automobiles. He was uncomplicated and Ben had fantasized that if a surgeon performed brain surgery on Pinkie he would open his head to find it looking like the inside of a potato. He did have a nice set shot, though, and his small, fast hands bothered the boy he guarded.

Next, Ben inspected Jim Don Cooper, the captain of

the football team and all-conference linebacker. He looked like a linebacker, would always look like one, and if his head were mounted on a trophy wall along with cape water buffalo and sable antelopes, people would look at it and say, "That's a nice linebacker you have there." He was six feet three inches tall and weighed over two hundred and thirty pounds. An exaggerated supraorbital ridge gave him an aurignacian, sinister appearance. Ben had carried a strong antipathy for Jim Don since his one date with Ansley Matthews. Often, Ben had watched Jim Don walking the halls of school escorted by Ansley and a school of pilot fish mainly composed of third string football players. He was the most feared boy in the school, at least among the population that did not carry knives. But he was terribly clumsy in gym shoes and the court was his own private china shop. He tried to play basketball as if there were still grass beneath his cleats and pads on his shoulders. His shot, however, was surprisingly dainty and soft. He could not leap but he would gather in many rebounds because of his girth. In shorts and rubber-soled shoes he looked vulnerable and misplaced, like a Cro-Magnon man lost in the centuries.

Art "The Fart" Ballard was unquestionably the best rebounder on the team. He was squirrelly and skinny to the point of emaciation. But he could come close to dunking the ball during warmups and had the great spring that one comes to associate with tall, skinny boys. He had a poor, uninspired shot and was a terrible dribbler. But Art "The Fart" could jump higher than boys six inches taller than he. Ben had heard him called nothing but Art "The Fart" since he had arrived at Calhoun High School. It was an extension of the name that seemed natural. Sammy said Art had been called that since first grade so he had had plenty of time to grow accustomed to his nickname. Ben made a mental note never to name a son Art or Bart.

The only boy that Ben knew personally was Philip Turner. Philip was the Student Council President and had the chiseled, immaculate, Anglican features of that aristocratic breed. He sat in front of Ben in Mr. Loring's English class. They had talked several times but Ben was not important enough for them to become friends or for Philip to engage Ben in a truly serious conversation. At all times, Philip was impeccably groomed, his shock of rich brown hair combed neatly, his demeanor serious and forthright. He walked around school with a sense of urgency as if Khrushchev were calling him collect from Moscow or he, Philip Turner, had to make a decision that afternoon whether to recognize Red China or not. Teachers loved him without reservation which made it a law for students to hate and envy him. Though he laughed a lot it seemed more like good social training than the enjoyment of a good joke. He did things in earnest only if he thought it would help him later on. He played basketball because he thought it would help him win a prestigious scholarship to an Ivy League college. Always he was thinking about the future, about events that would occur two, four, or ten years hence. Teachers were always looking at him and saying to each other, "There goes the future governor of South Carolina." Philip would sometimes hear them, blush, but silently agree. Philip's father was a man of little formal education who had become a powerful social force in Ravenel. After twenty years of hard work and ruthless manipulation of small farmers, Marshall Turner had become the emperor of truck farming in one of the most fertile agricultural areas of the state. Though Mr. Turner had dirt under his fingernails and though he could never look like anybody but a man who had seen a lot of cucumbers in his life, he had trained his wife to train his sons to be gentlemen. Philip was the youngest, the most princely, and the one furthest removed from his father. As a basketball player, Ben noticed that Philip was mostly form. His jump shot looked good but he rarely made the shot. Philip would go up, his legs would come together beautifully, the arm and wrist motion was pure, but something was not there. The shot differed in small ways each time he left his feet. Several times Ben saw Philip look down at his feet when he was shooting. Philip was worried that his feet were not coming together properly; he was worried how the shot looked. He was well muscled, handsome, and proud in his uniform, but Ben saw immediately that Philip was the poorest athlete among last year's starters. He also saw that none of the other players talked to Philip at all.

The whistle blew and Coach Spinks called Ben's group to the center line where they queued up in two lines to wait for their chance to go against the returnees. Spinks called for Pinkie and Jim Don to play defense first. The seven members of the team came together in a circle, joined hands, then broke from the circle cheering and confident. Pinkie and Jim Don slapped hands and Jim Don glowered at the first two boys in the line and sneered, "C'mon, rookies."

The first two boys to face the varsity players were both overcautious, spareboned, young, and fearful of sudden error and humiliation. The boy on the right side in Ben's line received the ball from Coach Spinks, took one tentative, almost apologetic dribble toward the basket, then stopped and looked for his partner. Pinkie was on him as soon as he picked the ball off the floor. Panicked, the boy threw the ball directly into the arms of Jim Don Cooper. The whistle blew, the two boys raced quickly to the back of the line, and the next two boys moved in to challenge Pinkie and Jim Don.

Through the front door of the gym, Mr. Dacus entered silently, walked to the top of the bleachers and watched as a tall, red-headed boy, painfully clumsy, forced his way all the way under the basket where he had his shot blocked fiercely by Jim Don as soon as he made a move to shoot. The whistle blew and it was Ben's turn.

He glanced to his left and saw that his partner was the blond boy who had been cut the two previous years. Before Spinks threw him the ball, Ben called out to the boy, "My name's Ben. What's yours?"

"Lyle," the boy answered shyly.

"This ain't no social," the coach barked, hurling the ball at Ben.

Ben turned toward Pinkie who was crabbing out to challenge him. The other members of the varsity were screaming, whipping themselves up into a lather now that the season had officially started and they were strutting their skills before the newcomers. Ben watched Pinkie and made no move. "Do something, boy," the coach ordered. Ben began a slow deliberate dribble to his right. "Get under the basket, Lyle," he shouted to his partner. Lyle raced for the basket in an awkward spring. Jim Don with him every step, slowing him down with a furtive forearm shiver to Lyle's chest. "C'mon, boy, we don't have but five years to get this practice over. I didn't tell you to freeze the ball."

Ben now had a tremendous area of the court in which to maneuver Pinkie. Keeping to the right side of the court, he began to dribble rapidly, faking as if he were going to burst toward the basket, reversing hands, keeping Pinkie off balance, then slowing up, and bouncing the ball higher, close to Pinkie's reach, until Pinkie made a lunge for the ball, as Ben had waited for him to do, and Ben drove toward the basket and Jim Don. He came with speed and momentum, dazzling speed for a boy encumbered with the ball, and Jim Don moved out heavily, menacingly to stop Ben. Ben left his feet, his eyes affixed to the basket, the ball swung up in two hands, until Jim Don rose in the air to repel the attack, the two bodies of the two boys suspended, warring, in synchronization, and at the last second Ben slipped the ball toward Lyle, who waited alone under the basket, slipped the ball under the huge arms of Jim Don who crashed into Ben at the same time Lyle was making a layup with no one around him.

The players in the center of the court cheered madly. Lyle almost fell on Ben as he pulled him off the floor and slapped him on the rump, his face astonished and pleased. The varsity brooded and demanded a rematch. The whistle blew. Coach Spinks took a long pull on his R.C., then spat a huge portion of it on the cinderblock wall. Ben saw Mr. Dacus flash him the V-sign in the bleachers. "Now that was a prime example of stinkin' defense. Stinkin'. Stinkin'. Stinkin'. That was dog-doo defense. Now let's do that again. Same four. I wanna see some ass-scratching defense this time."

"Hey, Coach," Jim Don said, "let me guard the show-off rookie."

"Go ahead."

Jim Don pressed close to Ben even before Coach Spinks threw Ben the ball. "C'mon, rookie. C'mon, rookie," Jim Don growled at Ben, his breath smelling like peanut butter and onions. When the ball came Ben made a violent feint toward the basket which drove Jim Don stumbling backward. Ben smiled as Jim Don returned, the anger fanning out in his face.

"Ass down. Ass down," Spinks said and Jim Don spread his legs wide, bent his knees, spread his arms, and kept up a fierce whisper, "Come to me, rookie. I want a piece of you, rookie." In a single fluid motion, Ben bounced the ball between Jim Don's outstretched legs, broke for the basket, retrieved the ball before it bounced a second time, beat Pinkie in a foot race to the basket, and laid the ball into the basket left-handed. Going back to the line, Ben slapped Jim Don on the rump and said, "Nice try, fatso."

"That's Yankee basketball, son. We don't play Yankee basketball down here," Coach Spinks said to Ben. "I want a little less showing off next time you handle the ball, you understand?"

"Yes sir," Ben said at the end of the line.

"Hey, Coach, you tell the rookie if he calls me fatso again, he's gonna have some knuckles where his tonsils used to be," Jim Don said.

"Shut up, Jim Don, and get your butt down. I'm tired of all this dog-doo defense," Spinks said, blowing his whistle.

Three days later, on a Thursday night, the final cuts were made. On a bulletin board outside his office, Coach Spinks posted names of the players who had made the team. Singly and in pairs, boys who had tried out for the team walked up to check the list for their names. Most of them checked the list quickly, then returned to the locker room to pack their belongings, and vanish in the night to be alone with their private desolation. Ben walked to the paper and saw his name. But he felt very little cause for celebration. He had come to like the boys who were trying out much better than he liked the boys on the team. When he returned to the locker room, Philip Turner and Pinkie walked up to congratulate him. He thanked them, showered, and dressed. As he left the gymnasium, he noticed a large number of parked cars sitting beneath the street lights outside the locker room door. Within the cars the dark shadows of fathers waiting for the verdict on their sons smoked out to meet him as Ben began to walk home. He passed one car where a Drill Instructor from the training base on Biddle Island was holding his crying son in his arms. He heard the man say in a voice that shivered with pain and a stark, inchoate helplessness when faced with his son's naked hurt, "Shoot, Eddie. We won't tell Mama nothing. We'll just tell her you sprained your ankle and had to quit the team. It's O.K., Eddie. It's O.K. We'll go huntin' this weekend. Just me and you." Ben went down on one knee to tie his shoe and listened to the boy cry. It was the boy who had missed the layup on the first day of practice. All along the street, in the privacy of lightless automobiles, beneath the gaze of fathers there was a suffering that would be brief, but one that, at this moment, in this place, was all but unendurable.

Ben walked home beside the river, his gym shoes slung over his shoulder, and his thoughts going back to the one team from which he had been cut. He had tried out for the Arlington Jaycees, a Little League team with a long history of winning teams. He had been cut after the second day of practice and had gone to his room and cried for three days. Bull had come up and told him that only girls and babies cried but this had served only to increase Ben's sense of failure. Not even Lillian could soothe him and make him re-enter family life. He missed two days of school until finally Lillian ordered him to school and threatened to spank him if he did not comply with her order. Ben had blamed Bull for his getting cut. "If you hadn't been so cheap and had bought me a decent glove, I'da made the team," Ben had shouted at his father, expecting a hard slap to the face even as he said it. But the slap never came. Instead, each day after he finished work at the Pentagon, Bull went to the coach of every Little League team in Arlington, Virginia, and asked them if they were short any players. None of them were, but Bull kept looking until he finally came to the practice field below the Fairlington Apartments where he walked up to the man who would become Ben's first coach, Dave Murphy.

The next day Ben received a phone call from a Coach Murphy who said he heard from some of his players that the Arlington Jaycees had cut one hell of a baseball player and that he would consider it a personal favor if Ben would come play for his team. That was the beginning. And as Ben walked along the edge of the salt river, he realized that he wore the memory of Dave Murphy like a chain and it carried him like a prisoner to the infields of Four Mile Run Park in Arlington, Virginia, where he played for the Old Dominion Kiwanis for two of the best years of his life. In the night games, beneath the arc of lights, in his last year of Little League, Ben's new spikes gleamed like teeth as he walked toward Dave Murphy. For years Ben had walked toward him in dreams and sudden thoughts. If he could, Ben would have told him about the soft places a boy reserves for his first coach, his unruined father who enters the grassless practice fields of boyhood like a priest at the end of a life. Coach Murphy was gentle. Yes, that was it. Gentle to the clumsy, girl-voiced boys whom he trained to be average, to be adequate, as he hit the soft fungoes to the outfield green. But Dave Murphy had a gift. Any boy who came to him had moments of feeling like a king. Any boy who played for the Old Dominion Kiwanis. Any boy. Coach Murphy still haunts the old fields where his boys bunted down the line, and with graceless fever took infield in voices that cried out for fathers. Going home after practice, they waved good-bye to their coach as they slid their spikes on the sidewalk, astonished at the fire that sprang from their feet. Then they turned toward home, toward the real fathers who waited for their sons to come homeward disguised as heroes.

It was in the last game of 1957 with Ben pitching against the Arlington Jaycees before he left the Little Leagues forever that Coach Murphy rubbed his pitching shoulder with Atomic Balm and whispered for Ben to keep the ball low and throw for the knees. And he whispered, "This one's for you and me, Ben. For you and me." And Ben could remember how on a frog-choired summer night in Virginia, he pitched into a sweat as slick as birth, then hit a double in the last inning driving Ronka home with the winning run. The whole team ran to him, picked him up and pummeled him madly. Then he was lifted and hurled by Coach Murphy toward the infield lights, his spikes silvered with false light, and Ben came down laughing and jubilant to Coach Murphy. He came down like a child thrown up by a father.

Then Coach Murphy cried out, "Free Cokes!" and the Old Dominion Kiwanis sprinted toward the Coke stand. Taking Ben into the trees beyond the Park, the Coach poured two fingers of bourbon into Ben's Coke and said to Ben, "From now on, you call me Dave." Coach Murphy had this gift. He could turn a boy into a king. Ben drank the Coke and he remembered it glowing in his blood like the moon and, very deliberately, Ben looked into the softest of male eyes and said, "That's good Coke, Dave."

But we desert the coaches of Little League, Ben thought, leaving the river's edge and returning to the sidewalk beneath the huge water oaks of River Street. We leave them behind and we never think of them again until Ronka, the catcher, or maybe Schmidt at first asks me if I've heard about Coach Murphy imprisoned in the most terrible room of hospitals, benched by the hardest and most silent of coaches. "Did you hear about his face?" they asked. "It was eaten clean up. They had to cut his nose and half his face off when they probed. All he has left are holes, but he wears a mask now because his mother screamed when she saw him."

Old Coach Murphy. Thirty-one. The Coach of the Old Dominion Kiwanis has come to this hospital, to this strange outfield, to this old dominion of cancer, to this old dominion of death, coaching in the ward of the doomed. Ben went to that hospital and was sent away by nurses who said, "Family only" and Ben had said, "But Dave was my coach," and the nurses had said "Family only." But they talked to him later and Dave Murphy's wife talked to him and they told him how it was in the last days. They said that in the last month Dave tried to teach the other undermined men to bunt down the line at third and to steal signs from the opposing teams, teaching with fear-stunned eyes behind a gauze mask in the last, inarticulate fury of coaching, while the instincts were still good and before the slow-footed cancer partially stole the brain. As the cancer with its unstealable signs moved toward the eyes behind gauze.

At the end, the very end, they roped him screaming to his bed, screaming out for Ronka to take two, for Schmidt to hold fast to the bag at first, and for Meecham to call him Dave. They tied him faceless to his bed, far away from his boys who cried into their pillows, who took down the dusty photos of their coach and prayed for him from the thunderstruck source of their boyhood. At last the cancer entered his brain or maybe his soul, and far from bleachers and Coke stands, far from shoestring catches and the voices of fathers behind backstops, far from the light of spikes, and the sad, blooded moons of Four Mile Run, he screamed out his death not like a coach but a man. What kind of world is it, Ben thought, that lets its coaches die without his boys around him, buying him Cokes, calling him by his first name, and rubbing his shoulder with Atomic Balm? He died without a face in a room I never saw without my kisses in the stained gauze or without my prayers entering the center of his pain. But worst of all, O God, you let him die, let Coach Murphy die, let Dave die, without my thanks, my thanks, my thanks.

As Ben passed Hobie's Grill and the alleyway where Toomer sold his flowers, he wished that all the fathers of rejected sons could go on a quest as Bull Meecham had once done, comb the fields and gyms looking for a coach who understood a tiny bit the mystery of being a boy. But in Ravenel there was only Coach Spinks and he didn't even understand the mystery of the double post offense. He walked until he was ascending the steps of his house. He saw his mother, Mary Anne, Matthew, and Karen waiting for him in the living room. Entering the house slowly, he put on a sad, mournful expression. He paused to look at them, then as if the effort was too much, he began to walk toward the stairs, his head bent in defeat.

"What happened, sugah?" Lillian asked, her voice breaking as she prepared herself for the worst. "I heard he was a dreadful coach and a fool of a man," she continued as Ben continued to walk up the stairs. "Do tell us what happened, Ben. We're perishing."

"Nothing," Ben said softly, sadly, then looking up he said, "except that I made the team," and he ran to his mother and his family screamed out their relief.

21

IT WAS SIX in the evening on the first Friday in December. The sky was clear and dark and bright with stars. A moon of cold silver shone on the river in a brightly luminous band. When the light reached the river's edge, it betrayed the last dying green of salt marsh before dropping lightly into the forests across the river from Ravenel, losing itself as it fingered its way from branch to branch and from leaf to leaf. On this night, the moon burned like metal.

In the Meecham house, Ben descended the stairs carrying his gym bag. His hair was wet and brushed back. Outside, in the backyard, he could hear Matthew shooting set shots at the outdoor goal. His mother and two sisters were sitting before a large fire. The room smelled of oak, and flame, and December. Entering the room, Ben said to his mother. "Mama, I really do need a new gym bag to tote my stuff. You got this one up at Henderson Hall when I was in the eighth grade. That was about a million years ago."

"Your last name is Meecham, sugah," Lillian answered. "It isn't Rockefeller, Vanderbilt, or Carnegie. Your daddy didn't invent Coca-Cola and I didn't recently discover King Solomon's mines."

"It's not like I was asking you to buy me an F–8, Mama. These things only cost a few bucks."

"If I give in for one thing, then the next thing you know, I'll be giving in for everything," his mother replied.

"Why don't you put your uniform in a paper bag, Ben?" Mary Anne said. "After all, we're not Rockefellers."

"We've got a lot of expenses neither of you know

279

about. Your father and I are also trying to save a substantial amount of money each month."

"What are you saving it for?" Karen asked.

"Well," Lillian answered, "it's really none of you children's business but if you swear not to let it go any further than this room, I'll tell you. Your father and I are saving money for our dream house."

"Dream house?" Ben said.

"Yes, dream house. I've lived in over twenty houses or apartments since I married your father and I think I deserve a dream house when he retires from the Marine Corps. I want it to be an exquisite, wonderful home that will be included on garden and candlelight tours. I know exactly what it will look like and how it will be furnished. I can see it in my mind as if it were already built. I've been collecting ideas from *Better Homes and Gardens* for over ten years now. There is one thing I can tell you about my dream house: it will be like nothing you have ever seen."

"Does that mean you can't buy us socks or underwear anymore," Ben teased, "because of the dream house?"

"Don't be ridiculous," Lillian said.

"Why don't you get the dream house now so we kids can enjoy it too," Mary Anne said.

"The dream house will be for your father and me. We earned it. It will be lovely and charming and no one will be allowed to lose their temper or to be ugly or to make scenes in the dream house. It will be a place of perfect harmony and people will act sweetly toward each other at all times. There will be no pressure on Bull at all. There will be no Marines around because they tend to bring out the worst in your father. There will be no one around. Just the two of us living in the dream house."

"I've got to get to the game, Mama," Ben said.

"We've got over forty-five minutes, darling. Hold your horses. You're going to turn me into a basket case if you don't relax. Let's go pray at the shrine."

"Oh, brother," Mary Anne moaned.

"You hush, Mary Anne," Karen said. "this is the first game."

"Oh," Mary Anne said sarcastically. "Oh, a thousand

280

pardons, little brown-noser. If I'd only known that it was a prayer for the first game. There's nothing in the world as tacky as a basketball game."

"Then you can stay home, darling," Lillian said. "I'd never force you to do anything tacky."

"She wouldn't miss it for the whole world," Karen said.

"That's what you know," Mary Anne said. "I'm going to the game so I can see our golden Apollo here shoot jump shots. Of course, I have to admit that there are other reasons. I like to look at the naked legs of all the boys."

"Mary Anne!" Lillian said.

"It's true. I'm an honest person and I say what's true. But the big reason I want to go to the game is that I enjoy sitting up in the stands hating the guts out of all the cheerleaders."

"You're just jealous because they're prettier than you," Karen said. "I'm going to be a cheerleader when I get old enough, just like Mama was."

"Jealous of cheerleaders? Me?" Mary Anne sneered. "Jealous of Ansley Matthews with her perfect legs and her brain the size of a pea? Jealous of Janice Sanders with her perfect bosom and her brain the size of a bean or Carol Huger with her perfect smile and her brain the size of a BB or Sally Tomlinson with her perfect everything and her brain the size of a chigger's eyeball? I'm not jealous of them. I loathe them. I love just sitting in the stands hating them. They're so disgustingly happy and enthusiastic. They're so peppy. They bounce. I hate girls that bounce."

"Some of them are real nice girls," Ben said.

"Is that the voice of perfection?" Mary Anne said, cupping her hand to her ear. "Is that he that hath fed on honeydew? Is that my saintly, sugarcoated brother, projected hero of the first game? The patron saint of jump shots?"

"Let's pray for Ben's success in the first game," Lillian said, ignoring her older daughter.

They walked to the alcove in the front hall where the shrine was set up beneath the steps. Lillian lit two candles on either side of the statue of Mary. Then she knelt on the rug and motioned for her children to do the same. Ben and Karen knelt beside their mother while Mary Anne knelt behind them. The color in Our Lady of the Fighter Pilot's shawl was pale blue that changed hues in the flickering of the beeswax candles. Lillian prayed aloud, "Blessed Mother, thank you for my family. Thank you for their health, for their intelligence, and for their good humor." With the last words, Lillian glanced back and smiled at Mary Anne who scowled behind her. "Tonight," Lillian continued, "we ask your intercession when Ben Meecham plays West Charleston High School. Help him score a lot of points, play good, strong defense, and thread the needle with his passes. But most of all, help him to be a good sport, to hold his head high, and to make the Meecham family proud. We love you, Mary, and we love your Son."

"And let's beat the hell out of West Charleston High," Karen shouted toward the icon.

"Karen, I'm surprised at you."

"None of the girls in the sixth grade believe that Ben's on the team. They say they never heard of him."

"This is so ridiculous," Mary Anne said, removing her glasses and wiping them off with a Kleenex. Her eyes had a stunned, swollen appearance when she removed her glasses; they strained to make out shapes to translate blurs. "I bet heaven has a few more important things going on besides a silly basketball game between Ravenel and West Charleston High. Like maybe a famine or two. Or a couple of wars. I'd like to remind this family that this stupid game is not the most important thing in the world."

"You're wrong, Mary Anne," Ben said. "God appeared to me last night in the shape of a glass backboard and said, 'In this sign thou shalt conquer and you, Ben Meecham, are to cut your oldest sister's throat with a dull machete to prove your worthiness.' So Mary Anne, if you'll just step to the kitchen."

"I've raised the two most sacrilegious children I know," Lillian said sadly.

"That's nothing, Ben," Mary Anne retorted, "the Virgin Mary appeared to me in the shape of a pompom . . ."

282

"Stop it!" Lillian shouted.

"They do this all the time, Mama. I try to stop them but then they start teasing me," Karen said.

"I've never teased you once in my whole life, so help me, God," Mary Anne said.

"Where's Dad?" Ben asked.

"Your father's meeting us at the game."

"Oh, no," Ben groaned, "he's not at happy hour."

"Yes."

"That's great. That's just great. In fact, that's more than great. That's just fabulous."

"He promised to have just two drinks."

"He probably will just have the bartender fill up two washtubs and call that two drinks," Ben said.

"He promised," Lillian said, looking at her watch. "Let's go. We're on our way to beat the hell out of West Charleston."

Ten minutes later, Ben entered the overheated locker room. Odors seemed to deepen in the heat. He could smell Tuf-Skin and ankle tape, week-old perspiration, moist towels mildewing in forgotten lockers, foot powder, ammonia, and unwashed socks. It was a smell of general decomposition but one with universal dimensions, one that an athlete could identify until the day of his death. Several players were sitting on the long wooden bench beside the varsity lockers. In low whispers, they talked about the sock hop following the game that night. It was a natural law of athletics that there must be whispering before a game and nothing else. To converse in a normal tone of voice meant that an athlete was not thinking seriously about the coming game; it exposed a frivolous nature alien to victory. Coaches loved silent, frowning boys in the nervous air of locker rooms before games. Opening his locker, Ben unpacked his uniform and stared at the new Converse All Stars Bull had bought him, a purchase that had gone unreported to the iron-fisted keeper of the books, Lillian Meecham. If Lillian had her way, Ben was certain he'd be playing in Scotch tape and sweat socks. One thing about Santini, Ben thought, he always made sure my basketball shoes were the best. Carefully, Ben

283

placed his new All Stars in the locker, then entered the hushed conversation by sitting on the wooden bench and turning toward Pinkie Taylor.

"You going to the dance tonight, Meecham?" Pinkie asked.

"I'm not sure," Ben answered.

"Who have you been dating, Meecham? I've never even seen you with a girl," Pinkie said.

"I've been sort of playing the field."

"Ansley's father told me that the night you dated Ansley was the first date you ever had," Jim Don Cooper said, pulling up his uniform pants.

"A lot he knows," Ben said.

"Why are you getting dressed so early, Jim Don?" Blease Palmer, a second string forward asked.

"Because he always has to take an hour long shit before every game," Pinkie said.

"It helps me relax," Jim Don said defensively.

"They brought in a nigger band for the victory dance," Blease said. "Payin' 'em seventy-five dollars. It should be a swingin' night."

Art Bullard walked into the locker room, his long arms swinging back and forth, and a broad smile on his face. "Gentlemen. Gentlemen. Gentlemen," he said in greeting.

"What are you showing your gums about, Art the Fart?" Jim Don asked.

"You haven't heard," Pinkie said. "He's got a date with Susie Holtzclaw after the game."

"Whoopee!" his teammates shouted.

"I may just park down by the river to watch those underwater submarine races," Art said.

"We know what you're after, ya ol' stud horse," Pinkie said.

"You're gonna have a hard-on this whole game," Jim Don said, smacking his oversize lips together. "Ol' Pinkie used to date Susie until she got tired of sucking on that birthmark of his."

"Don't say nothin' about my mark," Pinkie flared.

"Yeah, let's think about the game," Philip Turner said. He had slipped up to his locker quietly. No one had noticed or acknowledged his entry.

284

"I'd rather think about the treasures of Susie Holtzclaw's body," Art said dramatically. He then broke into a low, primordial litany. "Nookie, nookie, nookie, nookie," he began to chant. He closed his eyes reverently, danced in a circle, and raised his hands, as if in supplication to the gods who decided such matters. Pinkie and Jim Don began to clap in time with Art's voice. None of the players saw Coach Spinks standing in the dooorway drinking a newly opened bottle of R.C. Ben saw him first.

"Hi, Coach," he said. Art froze on the "k" syllable.

"Good evening, Coach," Art said. "We were just discussing what kind of defense West Charleston might throw up against us."

"I told you boys I don't want this kind of talk before a game. All you boys think of is pussy. We got more important things to think about . . . like beating West Charleston High School. Now, I know all you boys got the hot pants cause I was young myself and I had to cut my horns like anyone else. But there is a time and a place for everything and this is no time to be screaming about some cheap piece of poontang." He spat some R.C. into an empty, open locker, casting an acrimonious glance at Art. He took a long swig on the R.C., then continued his harangue. "I told you boys last year what to do when you felt your peckers getting hard. You got to think about your girl friends in a certain way. You can't think about them all dolled up in lace panties and satin, skimpy nightgowns. You got to think about them differently. Think about them with their hair up in curlers, no makeup on, squattin' on the commode and takin' a shit. That'll soften your pecker. Just think of 'em squattin' on the pot with a bead of perspiration poppin' out on their forehead, with them gruntin' and fartin' tryin' to get rid of a big one. Now the girls' game's about half over so let's start gettin' dressed for war. We're waging war tonight, men. We are playing West Charleston High School and they think they're coming down here to trounce the hicks. Well we're going to surprise the big city boys by cleaning their pipes real good. Get your

285

uniforms on and get on over to the blackboard. I don't want to hear another word out of you."

When all the players had dressed, they assembled in a small alcove in the back of the locker room where the blackboard hung. Beneath the blackboard and to the left was a new whirlpool bath. The team members sat in the creaking, green folding chairs. Ben tied and untied his shoes over and over. Pinkie Taylor cracked his knuckles. Jim Don had disappeared to the toilet for his ritualistic pre-game excretion. The crowd, invisible but possessing a huge, menacing voice, roared its approval of a Calhoun girl's basket. Among the boys, tension exuded in a subtle musk, a glaze of perspiration under the arms, behind the knees, and in the hands. A whistle blew. The crowd jeered and the boys listened to the voice of the referee, faroff and muffled through the cinderblock wall, call a foul against a Calhoun player.

Then, the manager burst through the double doors that led to the court and ran breathlessly into Coach Spinks's small office. "Five minutes left in the girls' game, Coach."

"Thanks, Tommy," came the reply. "Get me another R.C.," he said, flipping the manager a dime.

A few moments later, Spinks walked to the blackboard, his eyes studying a 3 x 5 card filled with statistics. His face was businesslike, determined. A transformation had taken place. There was something noble in Spinks's face as he prepared to address his team, something military; this man Spinks, a generalissimo in the land of the jock, rising above himself and his R.C., above his coach's whistle and his small office, a speech forming on his lips, taken from storybooks and movies, and dogeared copies of *Sports Illustrated.*

But before he spoke he picked up a piece of yellow chalk and drew five X's and O's up on the board. He ran the X's through the offensive patterns the team had practiced repetitiously for two weeks. Spinks's chalkwork, with its sweeping, serpentine arrows and carefully crafted letters, was a genuine and delicate art. He had a flawless and very feminine handwriting that seemed detached from the man possessing it. But when he spoke it was in the harsh rhythms of coaches who had once been athletes who had failed in the same arenas they now presided over as adults.

"We are gonna stick to man-to-man no matter what kind of offense those sonsabitches throw at us. When I hold my arm up like this," he said, thrusting his arm straight upward, his fist clenched, "I want you to pick 'em up all over the court. I want you to scramble assholes and elbows after them. When I stand up and hold my belt, I want you to slow the ball down. And when I grab hold of my nuts, I want the manager to run over with the jock powder, cause I'm gonna have a powerful itch."

The whole team laughed, pressure released like air from a tire. The buzzer sounded for a substitution.

"I want you boys to hit that court hungry. I want you boys to be starving. I want you boys to feast on some medium rare West Charleston High School asshole. I want us to win. Win. Win. Win. I want us to win big. I want us to make our school proud," he roared out, his voice surpassing exhortation. "I want us to make our parents proud, our grandparents proud, our first and second cousins proud, our poontang proud, and ourselves proud. Do y'all hear what I'm saying?"

"Yes, sir!" came the thunderous reply.

Suddenly, Coach Spinks's face mellowed. There was a dissociation of form and substance. His eyes glistened; his gaze became beatific. "Let us pray," he said and all the heads on the team dropped floorward as though they were puppets strung to the same wire.

"O, sweet Jesus, we come again to ask your blessings and your forgiveness for our many trespasses against you and our fellow neighbor. We are playin' West Charleston High School tonight, Lord, but there's no need to tell you that since you knew about it two or three million years before I did. We ask, good Jesus, not that we beat West Charleston High but that we do our best before our God, our family, and our country. We do ask, Lord, if you see it befitting, that we score a point or two more than West Charleston, even though I know that Coach Warners is a God-fearin' man and a deacon in the Baptist Church besides. But you know as well as I, Lord, he's one of the mouthiest so and so's that ever wore socks. I'm also aware, dear Jesus, that their players are all clean cut boys and also pleasant to your sight. We don't want to ask for anything special, Lord, but help my rebounders get off their feet. Help Pinkie and Jim Don control their tempers. Give Philip and Art a little more temper. And get Ben to quit throwin' those big city behind-the-back passes. And, Lord, please help this high school if I got to make any substitutions. My scrubs is good boys but they've been havin' a devil of a time puttin' that ball into the hole. The real thing I want to ask, Lord, is that all these boys make the first team in that great game of life. If they make mistakes, Lord, blow the whistle because you're the great referee. Call time out and bring them to center court for another jump ball. Don't let them go out of bounds, Lord. If they bust a play, make 'em run windsprints and figure eights but stay with 'em, Lord. Coach 'em all the way to the championship of life. A-men."

"A-men," the team echoed in relief.

"Now you boys sit here and think about the game," Coach Spinks ordered. "I'm gonna go out and watch the girls finish getting stomped," he said, walking from the blackboard.

Then he stopped and said in an afterthought, "You know why I like to watch the girls' games so much? You probably think I'm watchin' the strategy used or something. But that's not it. Naw. I just love to watch all those titties bounce."

When he left the room and the double doors closed, Pinkie whispered, "If those prayers get any longer, I'm gonna quit believin' in God."

His teammates laughed.

The final buzzer croaked. The team formed a circle, placed their hands on top of each other, then broke in a single file for the double doors. As captain, Pinkie led the team, breaking through the papered hoop that the cheerleaders held at the entrance to the gymnasium. Three hundred voices greeted the team as they broke for the far basket, fanning out in two disciplined lines for layups. At first, Ben could see or hear nothing. He had prepared for this moment since the last basketball game he had played the season before. Fifty thousand jump shots ago he had ended his career as an Atlanta high school junior. The noise of the crowd entered his body from the air, through his skin, into his bloodstream where it burned and cooled at the same time. He shot two layups before he began picking out faces in the crowd: Mr. Loring was taking tickets by the door, Mr. Dacus sat at the scorer's table, and Ben's family sat on the front row not far from the bench where Coach Spinks watched their warmups. Matthew and Karen waved at him, frantically trying to get his attention. But Ben knew that it was uncool to visibly acknowledge one's family when going about the serious business of warming up. He winked at them when he went to the back of the layup line. He also wondered where his father was.

On the last row of bleachers the boys cut from the team sat with their backs against the cinderblock wall. In their rejection they had formed new friendships, a brotherhood of pain that they could interpret for no one, least of all themselves. But they sat together, their dreams bruised, but alive. In the faces of the boys in uniform, they could see their faces. When a jump shot split cleanly through the net, it was their hand, their phantom hand, that guided the ball. Fantasy crackled like electricity along the back wall.

West Charleston was warming up at the other end of the court. Their uniforms were bright yellow and Ben hunted for Number 5, the boy Coach Spinks had assigned to him. He found him shooting jump shots from the top of the key, hard, artless shots with almost no arch. Then, he watched the boy dribble, a teammate pretending to guard him. No left hand, Ben thought. No left hand. The boy's name was Rostelli and his father owned an Italian restaurant just off Meeting Street in Charleston. Rostelli was six-three and with a guard that tall Ben knew he would have to release his jump shots quickly if Rostelli guarded him.

From the Ravenel stands Ben heard someone ask, "Who's Number thirteen?" Ben looked down and was almost startled to find out that he was Number 13. As of that moment, he had not associated himself spiritually with the Number 13. He had asked for 22 but Philip had worn that numeral for three years.

The cheerleaders bounced, sashayed, strutted, preened, and generally acted as if they had died and gone to heaven. Whenever she could catch Jim Don's eyes, Ansley Matthews threw him long, telegraphed, slow motion kisses that stung Ben in their passage. There was a sibilance to the pompoms. Legs were golden. Desire stalked their leaps.

At the center of the court, Pinkie shook hands with the opposing co-captains. One of them was Rostelli. Ben turned when he heard a familiar voice near the door where Mr. Loring was selling tickets. "Stand by for a fighter pilot," his father said as he weaved through a crowd that had congregated near the main entrance. He was in his flight jacket and uniform. All eyes in the stands turned toward him as he swaggered down the side of the court. He shook hands with Mr. Dacus and paused to have a brief conversation with the principal. The two men laughed, Bull a bit too loudly.

"Who's that jerk?" Jim Don said, retrieving a rebound.

"That's my father, Jim Don," Ben flared, "and I don't like you calling him a jerk."

The buzzer sounded. The team ran to the bench and formed a circle around Coach Spinks, who had gone down on one knee. "I want you boys to set pics like you were Mack trucks. Work the ball around for good shots. Try to get Meecham open. Ben, I want you to drive these boys. Let's whip ass and win for ol' Calhoun."

The starting five broke to the center of the court. Ben shook hands with a huge bearlike forward, another linebacker masquerading as a basketball player. "I've got Number thirteen," he heard Rostelli say. "Let's get these country boys," their center said before he turned to jump against Art. "I got this guy with the shit on his face," a guard named Jones called to his teammates as he pointed toward Pinkie. "Don't say anything about my face, Bucky Beaver," Pinkie shot back.

Art tipped the ball to Pinkie, who snapped a quick pass to Ben. Rostelli picked him up quickly. Ben dribbled toward the center of the court, spotted Philip backdooring his man near the baseline and shuffled a pass beneath Rostelli's arms. Philip scored the first two points on a layup that breathed softly through the net.

"Take Meecham out," Ben heard his father cry out from the opposite side of the court.

Rostelli came down court, dribbling slowly with his right hand, barking out plays to his teammates. Overplaying his right hand, Ben forced Rostelli to switch hands. He faked as though he were going for the steal, then retreated as Rostelli switched hands and passed it to the other guard. "Next time, next time," Ben said to himself as he watched the forwards setting screens against Jim Don and Art. The ball came back to Rostelli who dribbled it to the right of the key, Ben overplaying the right hand again, watching, tensing, until the moment Rostelli moved the ball to his left hand. Then Ben broke for the ball, tipped it away from Rostelli, but only barely, sprinting after it with Rostelli matching him step for step, gaining control of the ball, dribbling it behind his back and breaking toward the center of the court where he heard Pinkie's shout coming into his left ear. He felt Rostelli on his right but he was moving fast now, and faster, till he felt himself rising toward the basket, the ball rolling off his fingertips, and an arm crashing over his shoulder as Rostelli came over him, lunging for the ball that was dropping through the net.

"Good move," Rostelli said, offering a hand to pull him off the floor.

"The basket is good," the referee motioned to the scorer's table. "Number thirteen will shoot one."

"Thirteen charged, ref," Bull cried out.

In the first half Ben scored eighteen points. Plays and moves, embedded in him, poured out of him. Twice more he stole the ball from the opposing guard, dribbled the length of the court, and laid the ball gently in the white square painted on the glass backboard. Three times he left Rostelli on reverse dribbles and drove the center of the lane before the forward could react and rush to prevent the intrusion, to repel the attack of the little man in the area of the court marked out for giants. Always, there was the quick, unanticipated move. It all took place in a timeless frontier, in fractional divisions of moments unrecallable, as Ben fed on the noise of the crowd, the plankton of applause as he drove and passed and shot, as the lungs strained, as the heart thundered, and as the father watched. On the court, the court he loved, the court he ruled at times, Ben felt disembodied, running to the point of exhaustion, but more alive and more human that he would ever be again. Every pore was open to the action swirling around him, every vibration, every stirring, every cheer, every carnivorous roar. The basketball was a part of him, an extension of him because of long years of dribbling around trees, through chairs, down sidewalks, past brothers, away from dogs, past store windows and before the eyes of men and women who thought his fixation was demented at best. But he had lived with a basketball, had paid his dues, and could now exult in this one small skill of boyhood. This sport in all its absurdity did a special thing for Ben Meecham: it made him happy. The court was a testing ground of purpose. There was a reason. There were goals, rewards, and instant punishments for failure. It was life reduced to a set of rules, an existential life, a life clarified by the eyes of fathers.

At half time, Calhoun led by thirteen points. In the locker room Ben drank ice water as though it were a drug. The sweat was hot on his flesh. His teammates pummeled him again and again until his back and shoulders ached. In the gym, Bull paid the director of the pep club band five dollars to play the Marine Corps hymn. Then he made every person in his section of the stands rise and sing the anthem with him. Silently, Lillian and her children left their seats and walked to the opposite side of the gym.

At the start of the second half, Ben hit two quick jump shots in a row. The night again blurred into sprints and slow walks up to the foul line. Every time he shot a foul shot, he heard the crowd stir as he made the sign of the cross. He remembered that he was in the land of the hardshell, the barren hardscrabble of the spirit where the sign of the cross conjured up rich images in lands that had been totally immersed in the waters of a hard-assed Christ. He ended the game with a drive down the right side and a behind-the-back pass to Art when Art's man moved over to challenge him. "Show-off," he heard Bull say. But then he was mobbed by his teammates and then by a perfumed, hysterical flock of cheerleaders. As Ansley Matthews kissed him and Janice Sanders hung on to his sweating arm, Ben caught a glimpse of Mary Anne watching him from her seat on the bleachers. It crossed his mind that he had never seen her so sad, but then Carol Huger kissed him on the mouth and the boys who had been cut surrounded him and walked with him to the locker room.

Rebel yells resonated through the steel lockers and scraped along the cinderblock walls. Fathers lined the dark hallway that led to the lockerroom. They were smoking cigarettes and reaching out to touch the sweating forms of the starters as they glided past them. Not a single father touched a boy from the second string even if it was his own son. The fathers whose sons had played merited a more aggrandized status in the fraternity of older men who queued along the passageway. They pounded Ben as he ran their gauntlet. Bull was not among them. He would be waiting outside in his squadron car preparing an exhaustive critique of Ben's performance.

When Ben entered the locker room, Art lifted him off his feet and danced him from one end of the locker room to the other, spinning in circles and singing the fight song of Calhoun High. The players had begun to peel the sweaty uniforms from their bodies. The scrubs who had not played removed their warmups that still smelled of detergent and their mothers' hands. Mr. Dacus moved down the long bench slapping buttocks and punching shoulders. "Jim Don, you ain't worth a tinker's damn," he shouted at the large forward. "Artie, what's wrong with you? You played well tonight."

Art put Ben down, ran over and began to shadowbox with Mr. Dacus. "Did you see me sky tonight, Mr. D.? I was jumpin' so high I felt like I was part nigger."

When Mr. Dacus reached Ben, he grabbed him in a headlock and said, "You sorry damn pissant. You're going to be sweet as potato pie if you learn to play both ends of the court. Work on your defense, Ben. Otherwise, it was a great game."

"Thanks, Mr. Dacus."

"We ain't beat West Charleston in ten years," Pinkie screamed.

"Fucking A," Mumford said.

"You've got to score more, Philip," Ben heard Mr. Dacus say. "You've got to look for the basket. You treat that ball like it's radioactive."

"I get more satisfaction out of making good passes than I do scoring, Mr. Dacus," Philip answered. "Anyway, I didn't feel very good tonight."

"You sick?" the principal asked.

"Yeah," Pinkie said, entering the conversation, "Prince Philip's got the Mongolian Zinch disease."

"What's that, Pinkie?" Ben asked.

"Everything he eats turns to shit," Pinkie said.

The locker room exploded with laughter until Jim Don said, "All right, let's hold it down in here or I'm gonna have to kick ass and take names later."

"You going to whip my ass, Jim Don?" Mr. Dacus asked.

"Naw, Mr. D., I'm gonna let you slip out the back door before I commence to doling out fist burgers."

"Meecham got thirty!" the manager cried.

"Jesus H. Christ!" someone said.

"Who's got some greasy kid stuff I can use after I clean my gorgeous body?" Art asked.

"Philip's got some," Pinkie answered. "Hey, Prince. You gonna let me use some of that English Leather jungle juice?"

"Why don't you buy your own shit," Philip snapped.

"Because my old man don't own the whole fucking state of South Carolina," Pinkie answered.

"Sure, Pinkie, I was just kidding."

"Hey Pinkie," Art called. "What do you think of the rectum as a whole?"

"I think it ought to be wiped out."

294

A transistor radio tuned to the Big APE radio in Jacksonville blared through the locker room with a song by Peter, Paul, and Mary. Then the Big Ape bellowed. The first shower burst against the tile floors of the shower room and plumes of steam inched along the ceiling and flowed down the walls. Ben rose naked from the bench and walked slowly to the shower room. The place where his uniform lay made a wet spot on the cement floor. He would be sore tomorrow, he knew, for already the stiffness was settling into trembling half-cramped leg muscles. The body always demanded and received payment for the punishment it endured in a basketball game.

Ben turned on a shower at the end of the room and stepped into water as hot as he could bear. The sweat burned off his body in an instant. He stuck his hand under the spray and felt the blood rush through his body. In a minute all ten showers were in use. The steam was so thick that the players were vague, ethereal forms in the mist. Only their voices remained clear.

"Pinkie, T. C. O'Quinn says he can take your 'fifty Ford any day of the week and twice on Sunday," Jim Don said.

"Shit, that car of mine's souped up better than Campbell's. What's O'Quinn been running?"

"He says he's got it up to one-twenty."

"Big deal."

"That's in second gear."

"Bullshit."

"Shit. Pinkie's car can stop on a dime and give you nine cents change," Art said.

"We ain't discussin' stoppin'," Jim Don said, "we's discussin' racin'."

"Pinkie's car got more horses under that hood than a John Wayne movie and you and T. C. O'Quinn both know it," Art said.

"Fucking A," Mumford said.

"Shut up, Mumford," Jim Don shouted. "Who asked you anyway. You ain't even circumcised."

"Did you hear that Pamela Wall swallowed a watermelon seed?" Art said.

"Odum Bell ain't gonna marry her either," Pinkie added. "She's going to that home in Charleston."

"If I'd known she was giving it away for free, I'd have played hide the banana with her myself," Jim Don said.

"Pamela had peanut butter legs all right," Art said, his head under the shower, "smooth and easily spread."

"I heard her old man just beat the livin' shit out of her when he found out."

"Shit, I could have told him she's only been screwed twice that I knowed of," Pinkie said. "Once by the football team and once by the band."

"Jim Don, I hear Lou Ellen Alston's got the hot uterus for you," Art said.

"I might find time to slip her a piece of my prime Grade A twelve incher."

"You gonna screw her with your foot?" Pinkie said. "That's the only thing on your body that's twelve inches long except your nose."

"Mine's a lot bigger than that little dried up piece of shit you call a pecker," Jim Don fired back.

"You're dreamin', boy," Pinkie said. "It's like comparin' an El Dorado to a Volkswagen."

Jim Don spoke: "I know my pecker's bigger than most men's cause I couldn't satisfy Ansley's biological needs for three seconds if I wasn't hung like a horse."

"You ain't never touched Ansley Matthews, Jim Don," Pinkie said.

"I touched every inch of her body," Jim Don answered angrily. "She don't even have a freckle."

"It makes me sick to think of you climbing on top of Ansley Matthews," Philip said.

"It does?" Jim Don sneered, imitating Philip's clipped, aristocratic speech.

"Don't worry, Philip," Artie said, "Ansley wouldn't let that monkey in her pants even for a little peek."

"Oh boys, I'll tell you about the first time I did the evil deed with ol' Ansley. We were parking at the old beach and I was puttin' my best moves on her. One thing led to another and before you knew it my big, hairy banana was whistlin' Dixie when it struck gold in them thar hills. I decided to make the first time a memorable occasion for her. After I cracked her cherry, I decided to write my name in her big vagina. I wrote 'Jim Don' with my big pencil."

"Why didn't you write 'James Donald'?" Philip interrupted.

"Cause my name's Jim Don," he replied, then continued his narrative. "First I wrote a capital 'J', A fancy, swirly 'J.' With all the little curls and things. Then I wrote a small 'i' and a small 'm.' I didn't want to drive her crazy by writing the whole thing in capital letters. But Lord, she was going wild. I even did the 'd' in a small letter. As a favor. Then a little 'o' and an 'n.' I was giving her too much pleasure all at once and I knew I had to slow down. But then I made a mistake. I realized I'd forgotten to dot the 'i.' So I went back and put the dot way up high. Well sir, she fainted dead away. It like to scared me to death. I thought to myself, 'Oh, God, what have I done now? I done fucked her to death!' "

"Bullshit," Pinkie said, amidst the whoops and hollers of the team.

"I've fucked over twenty women in the past two years and every one of 'em loved it and begged for more," Jim Don declared.

"That's the biggest lie I've ever heard," Pinkie said.

"How many girls you nailed, albino?" Jim Don asked.

"About ten."

"Ten, my ass," Jim Don said. "How many you had, Art the Fart?"

"Ten or eleven," Art said. "I can't remember for sure."

"Try zero. That's easy enough to remember," Philip said, walking out of the shower room.

"Excuse us, Prince Philip, for our filthy talk," Jim Don said. "We country boys like to talk about pussy every once in a while if his lordship don't mind. I bet you never even found out that thing between your legs is good for somethin' besides pissin'."

"Shit, Jim Don, Philip turns down more muff than you ever dream about. Girls love his rich little ass."

297

"How about you, Meecham, how many times you do the job?" Jim Don asked.

"Once," Ben answered in a lie that had been born out of pure adolescent instinct.

"Once!" a disbelieving chorus shouted in his direction.

"You must be queer as a three dollar bill, Meecham," Jim Don said roughly.

"You ever fucked a nigger, Meecham?" Art asked.

"No."

"Shit, I don't even count niggers on my list," Jim Don boasted.

"Me neither," Art agreed. "Only white women make the golden list. I fucked so many niggers I lost count."

Ben turned his shower off and walked half blind through the steam. He was clean and tired in a grand way. He thought for a moment about the universality of the locker room experience. Over the years, in the time before and after the playing of games, in the trembling zone of adolescence, Ben had listened to the dialogue and banter of athletes talking about girls. It had been a long, extended anatomy lesson purged of reverence or homage. It was talk that dulled the diamond-headed points of lust that cut into Ben his every waking moment. As he dressed, he realized that coming out of a shower full of boys he felt both the cleanest and the dirtiest of any other time in his life. The transistor radio played on as he dressed. Then, waving good-bye to Philip, he walked out into the cold night air to face his father.

Bull started the car when he saw Ben emerge through the locker room door. He was chainsmoking Camels as he waited for his son in the parking lot. As Ben opened the door, Bull began to criticize his play in a severe, cutting voice. It was like this after every game Ben had ever played in, so neither the tone nor the content of the speech was a surprise. With his right hand Bull hit the dashboard to emphasize his major points. As he drove, he looked at his son more frequently than the road. "I'll tell you one thing, jocko," he said, slamming his fist against the dash, "if you think you can play college basketball just because you can score thirty against that pack of pansies you got another think coming. A good college

298

guard could have cut you a new asshole out there tonight. You made so many mistakes I don't even know where to start. Your defense wouldn't have won a prize in the girls' game. Your jump shot was just sad to watch. You loafed getting back down the court after your team scored. You passed the ball off to those clowns on your team when you should have taken the good shot. If you gonna play the goddam game then you're gonna play it goddam right or I want you to turn in your uniform and try out for second flutist in the goddam pep band. Now you tell me what really pissed me off about your play tonight."

Ben was silent.

"Do you know, jocko? Do you have any idea?"

"No, sir."

"Well, I'll fill you in. The thing that really pissed me off and embarrassed me was when you knocked that West Charleston boy on his ass, then put out your hand to help him up."

"What was wrong with that?"

"I'm doing the talking. You keep your yap buttoned and just listen. I don't want to see you being a good sport the rest of the season. I want you to be a goddam animal from the time that whistle blows to start that game to the time the buzzer goes off to end it. I want to see foam coming out of your mouth. If I was your coach I'd have pulled you out of the game and kicked you all over the gymnasium when you helped pull that son of a bitch up off the court. The next time you knock someone down run up and kick him in the head. Tell him that the next time he gets in your way you're gonna break his goddam neck or rip out his pissin' kidneys. I hate a goddamed good sport on a basketball court worse than I hate a pigtailed Chinaman. You could have scored forty tonight. But you just weren't hungry enough. You got too much of your mother in you and not enough of Santini. Not enough man. You got it?"

"Yes, sir."

"You read me loud and clear?"

"Yes, sir."

"Then say it like you were a man."

299

"Yes, sir."

"I don't want to see any more of that good sportsman-ship horseshit. The next time you put a boy on the floor, you ought to make sure he stays down there awhile. Otherwise you've wasted a foul. The way I see it, the rules give you five chances to break someone's bones. When I used to deck guys, they considered it an act of God if they could get up without major surgery. I played the game like I had rabies."

They rode in silence through the streets of Ravenel. Ben looked out the window, but his eyes focused on nothing. Bull continued to speak, gesturing with his right hand, his lips moving, his eyes narrowing, as he continued the lecture in a soundless world where he was the sole audience. When they drove up to the house, Ben left the car hurriedly. As he ran up the steps, he heard his father say behind him, "But all in all, that's the best game I've ever seen you play."

The family had gathered in the kitchen to celebrate the victory while the afterglow of Ben's performance burned strongly in their memories. Mary Anne shuffled a covered pan of popcorn on the stove. Matthew dribbled a rubber basketball in the hallway that led to the dining room and shot repeatedly at an imaginary goal above the door. Karen and Mrs. Meecham poured Coca-Colas into jelly glasses of different sizes.

When Ben walked through the door, Lillian ran up to him and kissed him lightly. Ben threw his bag to the floor and picked his mother up in his arms like a child.

"A little sicko-sexual, don't you think, feces face?" Mary Anne said at the stove.

"You were marvelous, Ben," Lillian said. "Everybody around us was talking about you. I didn't let on that I even knew you. I just said, 'He isn't that good,' and every-one argued with me. Finally I told them you were my boy and they just about died."

"I sat with Mary Helen Epps, Ben," Karen said. "She couldn't believe you were my brother. Will you say 'Hi' to her if I bring her home tomorrow?"

"Naw, I'm real sorry, Karen, but I can't go around

saying 'Hi' to just anybody. A man in my position has to be pretty selective."

"Oh barf," Mary Anne said. "The birth of the golden Apollo."

"You're just jealous, freckles," Matt yelled from the hallway. "Ben's the star and you aren't nothing but a bunch of nasty freckles."

"If you ever grow to be over three feet tall, we're going to have a fist fight, midget."

"Mom, you heard her!" Matt cried.

"Put me down, darling," Lillian said to Ben.

"Hey, drop the old lady. You want to get a hernia or something?" Bull said coming through the door.

"You'd think I weighed a ton, Bull," Lillian said, then, turning toward Mary Anne, she said, "Since you're the oldest, Mary Anne, I expect you to be mature enough not to get into these fights with your younger brother."

"Are they fighting again?" Bull asked his wife. "Let me mop the floor with them. Then there won't be no more jawboning."

"That was some game Ben played tonight wasn't it, Dad?"

"He's a hot shot down here among the grits. A good Yankee guard would eat him alive."

"You can't eat me alive," Ben said.

"You'd be a piece of cake. You don't have the killer instinct."

"Yes, I do."

"Would you two killers please sit your brutal selves down at the kitchen table and eat some popcorn," Lillian said.

Taking a bottle of George Dickel from the liquor cabinet, Bull poured himself a drink. Leaning back on his chair he thought again about the game he had just witnessed. The game that night had affected him strangely and in some barely articulated way Bull had garnered some ineluctable insight into the nature of fathers and sons, a recondite lesson in the passage of blood from one generation to another. He had watched Ben's legs that night as if seeing them for the first time. They were his legs passed down to this child. The heavy thighs, the thick calves, the strange roundness of the knees, the wide feet. Those were the legs of Meecham men and a few unfortunate Meecham women. Bull took a long drink and looked at Ben who was reading the sports section of the Charleston *Evening Post*. He stared at him as if he were studying the shadows of an aerial photograph. He felt he had failed Ben badly in one critical way: he had failed to drive the natural softness of Lillian Meecham out of him, to root out and expel the gentleness that was his wife's enduring legacy to her children. Above all things, Bull wanted to pass on the gift of fury to his oldest son, a passion to inflict defeat on others, even humiliation. Deep down, he thought Ben possessed it. Bull believed that when the flesh was torn away and the bones naked, the fighter would emerge in Ben. The fighter lived in the bones. It lived in the desire to excel and win. Taking another long drink, Bull began to talk of the past.

"The first game I played for St. Mike's in high school, the other team had this kid named Rosie Roselle who was eatin' the league up with a two-hand set shot. I was only a sophomore and hadn't played much but the coach liked the way I played defense, liked the way I clawed the man I was guardin'. Liked the way I growled at him. I was a real skinny kid then, young, and it would be two or three years before I muscled out. Well we were playin' Roselle's team and no one could stop that son of a bitch from scoring."

"There are three ladies present, sugah," Lillian admonished, "and two gentlemen in waiting."

"Every time Rosie shot it seemed that the ball swished through the net. He had a fine eye. A fine eye. In the locker room at half time, Coach Kelly, Benny Kelly came up to me and said, 'Meecham, are you man enough to stop Roselle?' I looked up and said, 'Yes, sir,' and he looked down and said, 'Bullshit. Bullshit, Meecham.' "

"Is that how you got your nickname, Popsy?" Mary Anne said at the stove.

"That's enough of that, Bull Meecham."

"Then Benny Kelly screamed at me, 'You don't have the guts to stop a door from squeakin', but I'm going to give you the chance.' Well I went out of that locker room with blood in my eye. When we met for the tipoff I went up to Rosie and poked him in the belly and said, 'If you score on me, I'm gonna whip your fanny after this game.' For the rest of the game I hung on him like he was a dog in heat. I breathed in when he breathed out. I kept tellin' him that I was another jockstrap he was wearing. I even followed him to his bench during time out. I told him he would dream about me that night. He didn't score a single point in the second half. After the game Coach Benny Kelly himself came up and kissed me in the middle of the court, in front of more than three hundred people. I never sat on the bench after that. I went on to become the best that Benny Kelly ever had."

"Popcorn's ready," Mary Anne shouted. "Dad, I want you to tell me how fabulous you were just one more time. I couldn't hear the story with all the racket this popcorn was making."

"Before we eat it I think we ought to say a prayer," Lillian intoned, lowering her head.

"Thank you, Lord, for your many blessings. Thank you for letting us beat West Charleston and thank you for letting Ben do so well. But Lord, we especially want to remember in our prayers poor ol' Rosie Roselle."

"Poor Roselle," Ben said sadly, "I bet he's been a wreck of a man ever since meeting up with Meecham."

"I wonder where poor Rosie is now," Karen giggled.

"He's probably killed himself by now," Matthew said.

"Poor, poor Roselle," Ben said. "Poor Rosie Roselle."

"Cut your yappin'. I was being serious."

"The sad thing, Popsy," Mary Anne said, dispensing popcorn into bowls, "is that I'm probably the only one in this family who knows what that story means to you. But you don't care that I know. It's sad."

"It's just a story, sportsfans. It doesn't mean anything to me."

"Then why do you tell it twenty times a year, darling?"

"Because I'm a believer in history," Bull answered.

"No, you just like to brag about yourself, Dad," Mary Anne said.

"Poor Rosie," Ben cooed.

"Poor Rosie Roselle," the family chanted.

Before Ben climbed into bed, Mary Anne stole into his room. "Oh, my hero, my jump-shooter. Let me touch your feet. No, your feet smell like something dead. Let me touch your golden hair or your runny red nose. Let me touch your emerald bellybutton."

"Get out of here, Mary Anne," Ben grinned. "Great athletes need their rest."

"Of course. Otherwise you can't make jumpshots. You just lie there and go beddy-bye and little nothing sister Mary Anne will hum lullabies until the hero makes disgusting snoring noises."

"How would you like a fist where your mouth used to be, little sister?"

"How would you like a Marine where your little sister used to be, feces face?"

"You're a coward. You won't fight like a man," Ben said.

"That's right, mousketeer. I believe in prudence. Prudent people never get hurt or injured. Vishnu approves of prudence."

"Who is Vishnu?"

"Poor dumb jock of a brother. Your brain has begun to rot since basketball season started. Vishnu is the Hindu god of self-preservation. I believe in self-preservation above all other virtues. Heroes don't appeal to me. They think of others and do silly things, like die for causes. I like to think about myself. Before I do anything I ask myself, 'What good will this do my favorite person, the charming and elegant Mary Anne Meecham?' "

"You are really getting screwed up in the head, Mary Anne. You've always been a little screwed up but now it's beginning to look like you have a terminal case."

"I never thought of this, Ben, but it must be hard on you. I mean everyone in school coming up and saying to you, 'Hey, aren't you the brother of that genius and beauty queen Mary Anne Meecham?' That must be a terrible thing to live in my shadow for your whole life."

"It's been awful, Mary Anne. But I try to accept my lot."

"You're sort of like a wart on my fanny. I just got to carry you along wherever I go. Oh, by the way, golden boy, I guessed you loved it when all those tacky cheer-leaders bounced around you."

"No, I hated it, Mary Anne. I hated having those luscious, gorgeous hunks of womanflesh throwing themselves on me. I would have preferred ugly male midgets."

Mary Anne walked to the window and stared out at the river. "Do you know, Ben, if I had friends I would love this town. I love this house. I love the river, the trees, the privacy. Everything. It's the most beautiful place we've ever lived. If I had friends I'd never want to leave this town. It would be a good place to die."

"Why are you talking about dying?"

"I think about dying all the time."

"Why?"

"What else is there to think about?"

"Living."

"That shows a basic difference between you and me, Ben."

"What's that?"

"I have more depth."

305

22

ON THE MONDAY after the West Charleston game, Ogden
Loring stopped in front of Ben's desk, removed his
glasses and began cleaning them with his silk paisley tie.
Mr. Loring had a vulnerable, rubicund face with eye-
brows arched into constant and natural inquisitiveness.
He was a small-boned man with thinning red hair and
elegant clothes. In class as he lectured on poetry or the
arts, he smoked long, thin cigarettes that he pulled individually from a silver case in his coat pocket. He wrote
on the blackboard with pieces of yellow chalk. Absently
and when a subject had so consumed and excited him, he
would write with the cigarette and smoke the chalk. He
accepted the laughter and derision of his students with
an embarrassed charm and a touchingly astonished
grace. Bull Meecham had met Ogden Loring at a PTA
meeting and had come home with a single remark: "Any
man who teaches a girls' course like English is bound to
be a pansy." But Ben had been coming to a gradual and
reluctant realization that Ogden Loring was the best
teacher he had ever had.

It was difficult at first. Being educated in Catholic
schools was, in some ways, like being educated in another country. Nuns and priests were enforcers of a classroom absolutism that tolerated no opposition. Ben had
heard more noises in the basements of funeral homes
than in some math classes taught by the icy ladies who
swept down the aisles with their habits whipping up Ant-
arctic drafts in their wake. Ben was accustomed to silence
when enclosed by windows and blackboards. Learning
was an abstraction that took place beneath the stares and
approbation of the Catholic S.S. that had goose-stepped

through the classrooms of his youth. One nun, Sister Saint Ann, had been the kindest woman and the best teacher he had ever had until Ogden Loring, but even her classroom was a limbo where the children had floated in the horse latitudes of their own suppressed energy. All nuns and priests who had ever taught Ben and all Marines and their wives who had ever loved or advised him could step into Ogden Loring's senior English class and know they were in enemy territory.

His opening words to the class at the beginning of the year had been, "I am a man of strange parts," and he had then set out on an erratic odyssey and with a demonic single-mindedness to prove it. Each day when his students entered his manic kingdom, they heard music emanating from a stereo behind his desk. Sometimes the music would be classical: Brahms, Beethoven, Saint-Saëns, or Bach. Other times there would be Negro Spirituals sung by Odetta or folk songs rendered by Joan Baez, Pete Seeger, Cisco Houston, or Woody Guthrie. For one full week, Mr. Loring played rock and roll beginning with Bill Haley and continuing in a kind of inauthentic historical overview through Buddy Holly until it stopped abruptly with Roy Orbison. Ben paid little attention to the music until the first test of the semester when a quarter of the questions dealt with the identification of the music Mr. Loring had played the first two weeks of school. As Ben agonized over a blank memory, Mr. Loring busied himself by walking around the room removing scraps of paper that were wadded and thrown under each desk in the room. The class was openly hostile after the test was over. It was then that Ogden Loring had cheerfully revealed that the answers to all the test questions were printed on the wads of paper he had gathered under their desks and any of them would have been free to make use of these hidden aids if they had only taken the time to find them. "Animules," he had said, "idgits who live in the valley of the shadow of death. Be attuned to your environment. Know what is going on about you. Make yourself aware."

On other occasions, he pinned the answers to tests in obscure corners of the bulletin board. If he put up a print of a painting he had collected from the Louvre or the Prado on one of his summer journeys to Europe then it was certain that the print would appear on a future test. When Jim Don Cooper whined that he just couldn't get excited over literature, Mr. Loring brought in the varsity cheerleaders and had them lead exuberant cheers for Charles Dickens, William Faulkner, and J. D. Salinger. Instead of using textbooks, he subscribed to the *Atlantic Monthly, Harper's,* and the Sunday Edition of the *New York Times* for his seniors. "Protozoa," he would announce to his class, "I want to introduce you to some other voices in the outside world before life sinks her claws into you."

He was a starling-voiced orator who could bring his antiques to school and deliver impassioned, enraptured lectures on the exquisiteness of Waterford crystal or the fragility of the first edition books he would pass around the room. Two of his books were signed by Oscar Wilde. His *Tess of the D'Urbervilles* was a numbered edition signed by Thomas Hardy.

The class listened to one opera each month—at least made some effort to listen over the thunder of groans and barely suppressed expletives from the athletes who populated the last row of seats. But Ogden Loring seemed unconcerned whether his class applauded his material or not; he merely tested them on every single facet of classroom life. He assigned a three-hundred-word essay every Friday afternoon without fail and issued a list of twenty vocabulary words on which they would be tested the following Tuesday.

"Good morning, cracker trash," he had begun one Monday morning. "I believe in oligarchy," and thirty pencils wrote an approximation of the word "oligarchy," knowing that it would appear on some test at some future time.

On Fridays, he would often show slides of his trips to Europe, pausing lovingly over pastoral scenes in England. "Oh, lawdy, lawdy, lawdy," he would sigh. "Sweet England. Sweet, gentle England. Sweet, sad, and gentle England."

"You're bats, Loring," a voice would call in the darkness.

He showed slides of a bullfight in Spain and his voice

would choke up when the bull was felled. Then he would come close to actual weeping when he described to the class the death of Manolete which he had studied exhaustively while in Spain. On Wednesday afternoons, three of the girls in the class would go to his house where he taught them some of the mysteries of French cooking for extra credit. Extra credit was the bullion he used to bribe the indolent scholar. For every book read Mr. Loring ladled out an indeterminate amount of extra credit, making some arcane notation in his grade book that in theory counted something during those critical nights when he evaluated the performance of each student.

The truly admirable thing about Ogden Loring was that he did not care at all that the entire town of Ravenel, South Carolina, believed that he was at least half crazy.

In every class, Ogden Loring took the abuse of students, heard taunts thrown at him, and endured the bile and venom of students who could not or would not speak up in other classes. At first Ben was appalled by the lack of respect for the man and by the man's ability to disregard the stockpiled vitriol stacked on him by his students. Every day, the first minutes of class would be filled by harsh salvos of criticism aimed at Mr. Loring's round, assailable figure leaning against his lectern. It was part of the routine, like the Pledge of Allegiance. Sometimes he teased back, lashed out, or screamed in rage at his attackers, but mostly he smiled during the morning wars and listened as students who never spoke in another class joined the hunt. But the strangest thing of all to Ben was the singular realization that Ogden Loring was the most popular teacher in Calhoun High School. He had seen Jim Don Cooper almost fight Art the Fart after practice one day when Art made a disparaging remark about Mr. Loring. He knew that Sue Ellen Rodgers was enrolled in Mr. Loring's Wednesday afternoon cooking classes. It was very strange to a boy weaned on the fists and calluses of Catholic schools. But soon, through talking to Sammy and Emma Lee, he learned that Ogden Loring was a genuine property, a bona fide character, an heirloom, and for ten years his reputation had incubated throughout the town, had been passed on from brother to brother, sister to sister, and it was part of the glory and the gold of high school, the dross and the pyrite of high school, to pass through the doors of Ogden Loring's class on the way to life.

Each week a steady stream of former students returned to his class, the sad flotsam of men and women who had tasted the other side of graduation and found it wanting. Their eyes spoke of failure and they came back to Ogden Loring like ships looking for a safe harbor. It took years in the crucible of human experience to value the gentle people one meets in the eye of the storm. Almost daily they came back to Ogden Loring. A man in uniform or a woman with two or three scrubbed, shining children would appear and these old students would rush to embrace the nervous unobtrusive man who blushed deeply and was almost moved to tears so touched he was to be remembered and visited.

Ben had gone to complain to Mr. Dacus about the teaching of Ogden Loring during the first two weeks of school. Mr. Dacus had listened to Ben's complaints very patiently, then suggested that Ben wait until a month had passed before he made any final decision about the quality of Ogden Loring's teaching. If, at the end of a month, Ben still thought Loring was a poor teacher, then he, Mr. Dacus, would personally break Ben's neck and kick him out of his school.

"Pissant," Mr. Dacus had said, "it isn't very often you come across a holy man. But you have. And this one has a genius for teaching pissant. So go on back to his class and I'll accept your apology later after you decide that Og is the best teacher you've ever had."

It was weeks before Ben could gather up the crosscurrents shifting through the English class commanded by the flaccid, bird-nervous man and arrive at some theory that appeased his glandular requirements for what was and was not acceptable for the last English course he would take before college. When Ogden Loring had cast burning eyes over the students before him, shook his head sadly and said, "It is a pity. An absolute pity that some of you have not read at least ten thousand books. Then, perhaps, we could begin to have a conversation," Ben felt himself want-

310

ing more than anything in the world to sit before Ogden Loring, ten thousand books glowing in his memory like rubies, and carry on a conversation that had no boundaries, no arbitrary purlieus. Ben Meecham would dazzle this man with shimmering images and razor-cut metaphors lifted from the great works of every century. Without his knowledge, Ben had been ensnared by a single sentence, one of thousands that Loring would drop during the course of the year with the unshakable credo that the leitmotif of his class was intellectual voyage. A student could accompany him on all voyages or only a few. It was a simple matter of choice, predilection, and a passing grade.

After he polished his glasses, Mr. Loring put them back on and stared unsteadily at Ben. It had been a day of undiminished triumph for Ben so far. A single basketball game had given him a name, a face, and an identity. He had been invisible in the halls of Calhoun High for too many months not to enjoy it.

"I reckon you just think you are plain wonderful, don't you, animule?" Mr. Loring said.

"Pardon me, sir," Ben answered.

"I bet you just woke up this morning, looked at your wonderful self in the mirror, and gave yourself a standing ovation. Admit it, creeter. You think you're the cat's meow now that you're the big basketball jock."

"No, sir."

"A jock," Mr. Loring sneered. "A worshiper of muscle? A salesman of speed? I think it's absurd. Yes, absurd. Here I am, Mr. Meecham, teaching my guts out, trying to the best of my ability to make a scholar out of you and in one night's time I discover that you are a jock. A resident of those smelly, nasty locker rooms, trained by those brainless chimps called coaches. Extraordinary. I think I'll faint. I might just die. Or sing a song to the Lord. I just think it's wonderful that you think you're so wonderful."

"We're going all the way to State this year if Ben keeps up the good work," Philip Turner said, sitting directly in front of Ben.

"All the way to State!" Mr. Loring gasped. "I'll just expire if we don't get all the way to State. Yes, I must go there myself. I must go to State."

311

"You know what I mean, Mr. Loring," Philip said.

"Everybody in this town thinks you're as crazy as Crowder peas, Mr. Loring," Sue Ellen Rodgers said.

"That's right," Jim Don Cooper said from the last row. "My daddy wants to kill ol' Loring with his bare hands. Just strangle him until his eyes pop out of his bald ugly head."

"My mama says they ought to lock up ol' Loring and throw the key into the Pacific Ocean," Sue Ellen said.

Mr. Loring, unperturbed, answered Sue Ellen with calm and dignity, "It is because my students love me that I can remain in this bleak town teaching the King's English to creatures damaged geographically beyond repair the very moment of their birth. I remain here because some of you idgits will go from this class with a rather vague notion that there is a small difference between a verb and a spark plug."

"I want to learn some real English, Mr. Loring," Philip said. "We haven't diagramed a single sentence all year. I'm getting worried about the College Boards."

"Yeah, all we do is memorize these three million dollar words that I can't even pronounce," Sammy Wertzberger said.

"Quit pretending you're stupid, Samuel. Of course you can pronounce them and they'll be valuable in the future," Emma Lee Givens scolded.

"Uh oh. The daughter of God has spoken," Pinkie said. Emma Lee Givens was a stern-visaged, bespectacled daughter of an Assembly of God preacher. Her face was pretty and her sense of humor more finely developed than she revealed to most of her classmates. She sat across from Sammy and made no secret that she thought he was hilarious. Ben had found out from Philip that she was the senior class's runaway valedictorian with Philip himself an earnest but distant second.

"Yeah, why do we have to learn all these big words? Us people with normal brains. Not geniuses like Emma Lee and Philip," Sue Ellen said.

"Because you are verbal cretins," Mr. Loring shouted, "and because I have tyrannically and arbitrarily decreed it, and because you will not graduate if you don't."

312

"I'm going to incarcerate you, Loring. Then I'm going to decimate you," Jim Don cried out, utilizing the only two words from the vocabulary list he could remember.

"My mommy told me that Loring is one of those things," said Carol Huger, sitting across from Jim Don.

"I feel grievous when I ruminate about your idiosyncrasies, Loring," Pinkie called out proudly.

"Don't listen to them, Mr. Loring. They are less than thee," Emma Lee Givens said in a voice full of pronouncement.

"You sound like a letter to the Ephesians, Emma Lee. Who do you think you are?" Sue Ellen flared.

"No friend of yours, Sue Ellen," Emma Lee said quietly.

"You're always defending that thing," Carol Huger called from the rear of the room.

"I like him," Emma Lee said, "and I would appreciate it if you would let him teach me. And thee."

"Thank you, Emma Lee," Mr. Loring said, "but you do not have to defend me against the poor creeters."

"I didn't understand the assignment last night, Mr. Loring," Sammy said. "And when a brilliant scholar like me doesn't understand it you know it's got to be complex."

"Samuel," Emma Lee whispered and Ben overheard, "you know you did not read the assignment."

"Creeter," Mr. Loring said speaking to Ben again, "you think you are just wonderful this morning. You think you are the greatest thing that ever hit this high school, don't you? Admit it, so we can get on with this class. What did you think when you looked at yourself in the mirror this morning?"

"He's the star," Sue Ellen announced and Ben winced with a small pain and an exquisite, consuming pleasure.

"The star?" Mr. Loring hooted. "The star? My word. Lawdy, lawdy. The star? Here in my room. Little ol' Og Loring teaches a star. I thought stars were parts of constellations and galaxies. I didn't know they could sit in classrooms. I thought they were heavenly bodies that gave off light and heat and energy. I thought they had to be studied through telescopes. To think I'm standing up here and gazing at a star less than ten feet away. How blinding.

313

What did you think when you woke up and looked in the mirror this morning? Were you surprised to see a star?"

"I didn't think anything, Mr. Loring. I just gave myself a standing ovation."

After he had laughed, cleared his throat, and cleaned his glasses one more time, Ogden Loring began the class.

"Animules, cracker trash, and star," he began, "today I will continue to show you how teaching can be an art form."

23

FROM LONG EXPERIENCE in deciphering the arcane ways of nuns and after hearing Sister Loretta end two successive catechism classes with the admonition, "And remember, boys and girls, your bodies are the temples of the Holy Ghost," and the sudden descent into hushed reverent tones when she mentioned the last CCD meeting before the Christmas holidays, Ben and Mary Anne knew that the cloven-hoofed topic of sex waited in the wings for its sordidly concupiscent introduction.

They discussed the probability on their walks home. "There's no doubt about it," Mary Anne said, "ol' Loretta Lou is going to hit us with the ol' facts of life. That 'your bodies are the temples of the Holy Ghost' routine is a dead giveaway. Of course, it's always irritated me that my temple has freckles."

Ben said, "I bet the Holy Ghost hates living in the crummy temple you got for Him."

"It's better than living in the temple of zits."

"I bet Father Pinckney will be brought in to talk to us boys and Sister Loretta will take the girls," Ben said.

"I've seen that nasty film on menstruation four times and that disgusting film on birth at least three."

But the day before the appointed class, Ben heard an argument between Father Pinckney and Sister Loretta after 6:15 Mass. It was still dark, although the sun was beginning to shimmer and stir the rim of the eastern horizon and Ben was extinguishing the candles on the altar when he heard Father Pinckney's voice.

"I shall not do it, Sister. And all the Sisters of Mercy in all of their thunderous battalions praying nonstop, twenty-four hours a day could not make me do it. I get embarrassed, Sister. I have tried to do it before and I just get embarrassed. I am a man of keen sensibilities and a total lack of experience in the subject matter and I shall not make a fool out of myself in front of twenty boys. My God, Sister, they know more than I do."

"They don't know it from the Catholic viewpoint. They don't know what is sinful and what is not."

"Nor do I, Sister. Nor do I."

"Of course you do, Father. You hear their confessions."

"I will not do it, Sister. I will not teach sex to those loose-limbed satyrs. I'll make them memorize the Act of Hope instead."

"Then I've have to do it myself, Father, if you insist on shirking your responsibilities."

"Sister, good Sister, merciful Sister," Father Pinckney had said as Ben remained near the altar immobilized with a sense of guilt as though he were overhearing a conversation between heavenly figures, "you have prodded me in a vital spot, for I do indeed shirk too many of my responsibilities. But do believe me that I cannot do what you ask. I don't know what to say to teenage boys or girls about this tenderest of all subjects."

"I know what to say," the nun said darkly.

"Then say it, dear Sister. Say it and praise the Lord."

On the next night, Sister Loretta entered the room on the coldest night of the year and began the class with a prayer for chastity that she read from a black manual. She then announced that a registered nurse from the naval hospital was upstairs to speak privately with the girls while she herself would lecture the boys on a subject of great importance to all of them in later life. The girls rose and were herded out of the room, giggling and turning shyly back toward the boys, some of whom whispered with each other as the footsteps of the girls pattered on the staircase as they escaped the gaze of boys whose minds trembled with forbidden imagery, and a sadness seized them as they listened to the exile of their companions entrapped and made holy by the mystery of the blood flow. Ben did not understand why his mother, his sister, and his friends had to bleed, hurt, and cramp; the separateness was an abyss, a continental divide that kept them apart. When the girls had settled into the upstairs classroom, Sister Loretta began to speak to the boys.

"Tonight," she said in a lemony voice, "I would like to discuss the subject of sex with you." She mouthed the word "sex" with a visible distaste as though it were part of a most bitter and unsavory language. "Now I am going to speak to you as if you were young men. Mature young men. If anyone feels he might laugh or be embarrassed with what I have to say tonight, he is free to leave the room."

Every eye in the room focused on Sister Loretta; no one moved and not one boy tried to attract the attention of another boy.

"Now most of you probably think that nuns all have faces that can stop clocks and have no sexual urges at all. This is not true. All humans beings have sexual drives because all human beings are animals. But nuns and priests have wed themselves and consecrated themselves to the memory of Jesus Christ; they have made the supreme sacrifice of negating these urges to better serve their Master. They have purified themselves so that their prayers will be more pleasing in the sight of God. Their reward will come later and will be far greater because of their sacrifice. Their place in heaven will be higher than those who yielded to the temptations and petty cravings of the flesh."

Her voice was bloodless and her eyes seemed drawn and unlived in as though the capillaries that fed them were filled with the dust from the Catholic centuries that sustained her.

"Of course it is important for you to remember that sex is beautiful. It is God's way of perpetuating the species. But it is only beautiful if it takes place between two people duly married by a priest under the sight of God. Because of the holy act of sexual intercourse, children are brought forth on the earth. Sex in marriage is only holy if it is done for the procreation of children. If it is done for simple animal pleasure, then it is sinful and repugnant to God and his chaste Mother."

317

Two boys began to giggle uncontrollably at the front of the room. It was P. K. Hill and Gilbert Fewell. Both were in the tenth grade and both of them had turned a fine shade of scarlet during the course of Sister Loretta's presentation. They tried to muffle their laughter with their hands, but this only made it worse and they grew desperate as the nun glared at them with a glance that had known glaciers, tundras, and the bottoms of oceans.

"Children giggle at topics of utter seriousness, Mr. Hill and Mr. Fewell. If you insist on being children, I suggest you hold hands with one another like baby boys do. Go ahead. Hold hands and then I'll continue."

The two boys looked at each other, then at the nun. Painfully, they took each other's hands and blushed again as the other boys laughed.

Then Sister Loretta got to her point. "There are some boys in here who probably play with themselves at night. Abuse themselves. I am sure all of you know what I mean."

"Yes, Sister," Ben thought, hating her, "I know what you mean."

"Always remember that your bodies are temples of the Holy Ghost and when you abuse yourself sexually, you are also abusing the house of God. Scientists call this vile habit masturbation, but it is more aptly referred to as self-abuse," she said, glaring into the collective face of adolescence which suffered before her. "Self-abuse," she repeated. "Just think of these two words and you will never be tempted to engage in this again. God knows if you abuse yourself. He watches you. He sees you do it. It disgusts Him. It disgusts Him so much that He calls His mother, the Blessed Virgin, to His side to watch the hideous spectacle. Then He calls His angels to watch and all the Saints in heaven. Thousands upon thousands of Saints and Angels are watching you every hour of the day. They especially watch you when you are alone at night. They see the dirty things you do with your hands and private parts. All of heaven: God, Jesus, the Holy Ghost, the Blessed Mother, the Seraphim, and all the other Angels scream out their hatred of you, chant and sing that they despise you as they watch you flaunt yourself and weaken yourself with your filthy acts."

As Ben listened in pitched horror at Sister Loretta's portraiture of heaven's entire populace jeering at some thin lad's whacking off in the privacy of his room, not knowing he was being observed by the entire celestial civilization, Ben thought of himself, his sinfulness, and his innocence. He had received no preparation—none—for his entry into the arena of a Catholic adolescence. Sedulously, he had once avoided the clusters of boys who haunted the locker rooms with their salient, knowledgeable talk in which his finely honed sense of morality denied him participation. No one had told him that anything but urine would ever come flying up his penile tract. So on one night, one miraculous night he awoke tingling with a pleasure that turned soon into a divine madness as though God Himself had come into his center, invaded his source, as hot sperm shot into his hand and Ben ran to his bathroom amazed and afraid that he was bleeding to death. And there he had found it and, though it was still a mystery, snatches of locker room conversation came back to him, and paragraphs in forbidden books, and in an instant, he knew he was a life-giver. For the next hour he studied the sperm, analyzing it, as it cooled, thickened, and dried; the white gold mined from interior rivers, his body that tingled with mystery and the knowledge that a sweet dark angel lived in his body, lived in his body deeply.

But then the nuns and priests had gotten to him. Each year they increased their emphasis on sexual education. Most of the boys he knew laughed about what the good sisters and the good fathers had to say about sex. But not Ben. When Sister Marie Daniel stated that masturbation saps your strength, Ben felt incredibly tired, exhausted beyond imagination. When she listed warts, pimples, and madness as direct results of incessant masturbation, Ben looked at the warts on his hands, blushed though the pimples on his face, and felt madness and disorientation violate the frontiers of his psyche. And this same Sister Marie Daniel had told a class full of boys that if "thy right eye offend thee, pluck it out and cast it from

319

thee. And if thy right hand offend thee, cut it off, and cast it from thee: for it is profitable for thee that one of thy members should perish, and not that thy whole body should be cast into hell." But Ben had known that she was not talking about eyes and hands, and during the entire year that he was under her influence the image of his penis being lopped off for the glory of God haunted him always. He felt sure that if Sister Marie Daniel had had her way, she would have applied leeches to the penis of every Catholic boy who entered her domain and left them on until each penis was sucked dry of blood, a limp, desiccated sac of flesh that could be snipped off and thrown from her convent window. Nuns could pray their vespers in a penis-littered garden and the sad corpses of boy penises could be reminders that hell would not claim these lads because of sins of the flesh.

The voice of Sister Loretta smashed into his thoughts and he returned to her words.

"Satan also watches you abuse yourself. Only it pleases him and makes him happy. In his everlasting torment and damnation, this is the only thing that eases his pain or brings him any joy. He laughs and calls the other demons to his side, millions of them, screaming, howling, bat-faced men and women with their doomed, tortured faces made happy for a single instant by the sight of you abusing and desecrating the temple of the Holy Ghost—your precious body. But do keep in mind my original point. Sex is very beautiful. But only if it takes place between two people duly married by a priest under the sight of God for the purpose of procreation of children. Do you understand?"

"Yes, Sister," the class answered.

"Are there any questions?"

"No, Sister," the class answered more quickly.

"Now the Virgin Mary can help you during times of temptation. Pray to her often. Pray that she helps you become chaste. Pray to her when impure thoughts come to your mind. Have her statue in your room. Also a statue of Jesus and Joseph and other saints. Turn their eyes toward your bed. Have them watch over you and admonish you with sinless eyes. Keep your rosary beads on your bedside table so you may reach for them when the devil walks at night."

There was no movement among the fetid, dirty little masturbators who sat in an advanced state of spiritual rigor mortis before their catechist. Each boy thought that Sister Loretta was speaking directly to and about him and only him, that somehow she had learned the vile secrets of his bedroom where he waited between spotted sheets and fought with the furious dragon of his own sexuality that issued forth from a forbidden cavern unknown to him, unseen by him. And when once it had been so easy to be good, to be Christian, to refrain from having strange gods before you, to refuse to covet your neighbor's goods, to kill, to covet wives, or to commit adultery: where it had been easy to be priest-like, now there was this cataclysmic beast whose hoofs tracked across a boy's soul, flogged by a demon horseman who could ride through even the sternest gaze of Jesus or Mary, a horseman who could trample God himself if the hour was late, the sky full of stars, the boy alone, and the desire thundering through him in the thickening and enlarging that he both dreaded and loved.

If the devil caused it, if in Ravenel, South Carolina, in the year of 1962, Satan had taken possession of that vulnerable geography around Ben's loins, staked a claim in this beleaguered region; if the rise and ebb of his bright manhood was the sole armature of the Prince of Darkness, then he had developed the most potent weapon. For sometimes it came. His brain would sing with the faces and bodies of girls he passed in hallways, who sat near him in class, who walked into his life and out again in stores, theaters, or trips, and in movies. He had never touched a girl, never held a girl's hands, never made an advance to do so, and had no immediate prospects, but by night he walked like a king before a kingdom of light and flesh where breasts came to his mouth, thighs opened and legs seized him in the moonlight sacrament of entry and surrender, the blood rising, the heart in fury, and all women his lovers, his companions, his prey. Above him, the Blessed Virgin stared at him in enraged alabaster, the Christ on the crucifix

321

howled as though Ben were driving another nail into His body, and the angels in their fiery clusters and starry squadrons lamented the fall from grace in beautiful, silvery billions.

She knows about me, Ben thought to himself, she knows and this lecture is directed at me and no one else. Did Father Pinckney tell her about my confession? They probably exchange notes. Hey, Sister, by the way, did you know that Ben Meecham beats off at night quite a bit. Shocking, isn't it? I was surprised myself considering how many times he receives communion and serves Mass.

Feeling dead, Ben's mind skipped to the hills of Alabama where his mother's kin would whisper to him when Lillian paid calls alone about their private visions of Catholicism. The hill people had a warped, yet sensual, mythology invented to explain to themselves this mumbo-jumbo that Lillian had embraced when she married the pilot from the Midwest. Ben's great aunt told him the truth about priests and nuns. "They are not what you think they are. When you take a bride in the Catholic Church, one hears tell that the priest spends the first night with her while you pray tied and bound upon the altar. And I, myself, have seen, Benjamin, on motor trips to Atlanta, two or three nuns circling the walls of cemeteries praying for the bones of the murdered infants implanted in them by priests. I have heard their lamentations. When you are older we'll take you to the river by the New Zion Baptist Church and have Brother Catlett wash you in the blood of the Lamb."

Then Sister Loretta, washed in the blood of dead infants, gave out the assignment for the next meeting in January. "Memorize the Act of Hope which will be found in the index of prayers in the back of your Catechism. I think we've accomplished a lot in this meeting. P. K., you and Gilbert can quit holding hands unless you wish to walk home that way."

The class laughed except for Gilbert, P. K., and Ben. "You are dismissed. Have a happy and holy Christmas."

24

It was Christmas Eve. The tide was going out in the river. The air was cold, breezeless, and stars sparkled through moss and waited for a bright half-risen moon to climb higher in the sky. A group of carolers from the Blood of His Son Baptist Church sang from house to house, a choir of dark voices moving from one end of town to another, the collective lights of their candles winking and dancing at the end of surprised verandas. Their songs were full of renewal and their presence before the mansions set back from the Lawn brought forth the gray aristocracy of the town to wave and call to the singers whose faces, bright under stars and behind candles, smiled as they sang about the birth of God.

The Meecham family prepared for midnight Mass. Mary Anne and Ben, fully dressed, knelt before the Christmas tree rattling presents that bore their names.

"Is this all the presents?" Mary Anne asked.

"You know Mom and Dad bring down most of the presents after we go to bed," Ben answered.

"Of course I know it. I can tell you where every present in this house is hidden."

"How do you know?" Ben challenged.

"Because I've snooped around a lot. Gone on reconnaissance missions. Paid off informants. I'm real nosy when it comes to presents."

"You can say that again."

Picking up a very small present, shaking it for some telltale clue of its content, balancing it on her palm, she weighed and analyzed it with the expertise of a rapidly developing sense of human avarice.

"What's in this one?" she asked. "No sound from the little devil."

"It's a suppository. It's from me, with love," Ben said.

"Very witty, feces face," she snapped. "No, it's probably a diamond ring. Five carats or more. Probably sent by a stranger who has seen me from afar. A shy billionaire who's been inflamed to passion by the sight of my body."

"He must not only be a shy billionaire. He must be a real ugly billionaire."

"Keep it up, jump-shooter," Mary Anne said, "and I'll have to roll out the big guns."

"What could you say to me that I couldn't handle?"

"Oh, I wouldn't say it to you. I'd go up to Daddy-poo and tell him that I saw you sniffin' Mom's underwear on the clothesline."

"You wouldn't do that!" Ben cried out.

"No one messes with Big Mary Anne. It's suicide. Because there's nobody in the world that fights as dirty."

"You're just like Dad," Ben said.

"I read that in a book recently. About some poor creep who liked to stick his nose in his mama's nasty ol' panties. Of course, if I told Dad that I saw you doing it . . ."

"He'd just kill me and that would be it. No questions asked," Ben said.

"Exactly. So I would advise my golden brother to beware when he deals with his brilliant, but modest, sister."

"I got you a gift that I thought you'd like, Mary Anne. You're always complaining about your freckles, so I got you a gallon of hydrochloric acid. You just pour the whole thing over your head and it's guaranteed to remove every freckle on your body. Also your nose, your ears, and your lips."

Karen and Matthew entered the room and headed straight for the presents under the tree. Following behind them was Mrs. Meecham, radiant in a yellow dress, her red hair piled fashionably, and her finest jewelry glistening around her neck, above her left breast, and on her wrists and ears. Ben and Mary Anne sat transfixed. There

324

were times when it stunned them both how beautiful Lillian could be.

"I pay homage to the queen," Ben said with a flourish.

"Thank you, darling," Mrs. Meecham beamed, curtsying and blowing kisses to her son. "This is just an old something I had in the closet to put on. I haven't had anything new or exciting to wear in a coon's age."

"Does it ever bother you, Mama, that all your children look like toads?" Mary Anne said.

"Speak for yourself, Mary Anne," Karen said.

"I've got the most darling children in the universe. All of you are beautiful in your own way," Lillian said. "Mary Anne, you've just never realized that you'd be far prettier if you'd just take a little time to fix yourself up. It takes time and work to be pretty. Like myself, I've just got an average face, but I've learned some tricks of the trade over the years that make me seem prettier than I really am. When I was a girl I was as gawky and ungainly as they come, but I knew I had to use all the tricks of the trade available and I said to myself, 'Why Lillian, you're just as pretty as any of those northwest Atlanta girls,' and do you know what? Just saying it and thinking it made it come true. Because I saw myself as pretty, I became pretty. If you think you are ugly, you will be ugly, mark my words. I even think depression is caused by thinking about things that depress you. I feel that if you think positively, things will turn out for the better. It's also a matter of good taste to talk about only happy things."

"Have you taught me to have good taste, Mama? Is that another trick of the trade I haven't learned?" Mary Anne said.

"Good taste is not something you can be taught. It's not something you obtain in a store or go to college to learn. You either have it or you don't. It is passed down from generation to generation in a straight line, but not everybody in a family gets it. It's like high cheekbones. Your father will never have good taste and I will never be without it. You could drain every drop of blood from my body and what was left would include my innate good taste. I'm chock full of it."

"I've got it, Mama. I know I've got it. I got it from you," Karen said.

"Of course you do, sugah."

"Where's the creature from the Black Lagoon?" Ben said, changing the subject.

"Don't talk about your father like that on Christmas Eve. Shame on you," Mrs. Meecham admonished. "Your father's in the bathroom."

"That means he'll be in there about three days," Matt said.

Karen said, her face very serious, "What does that man do in there for so long?"

"He's going number two," Mary Anne said with delicacy.

"He excretes in prodigious amounts, Karen, not seen on the earth since prehistoric times when dinosaurs let fly," Ben said.

"Ben!" Lillian said.

"You don't have good taste," Karen said to her older brother.

"Y'all ever get a whiff of the bathroom when he comes out?"

"It smells like something crawled up his behind and died," said Mary Anne.

"I'm shocked to hear that coming from a young southern lady," Lillian exclaimed, but a half-smile betrayed her attempted sternness.

"That's in poor taste," Karen said, glancing toward her mother for approval.

"I bet if you lit a match right by the toilet the second he got up," Ben said, "the whole house would explode."

"Hush, Ben, he might hear you," Lillian said, again casting a quick glance to the stair and listening for his heavy walk. "I'll go upstairs and hurry him up a little."

"You better take a gas mask," Ben said.

"Poor taste, poor taste, Ben," Karen chirped.

"You will find, Karen," Mary Anne said as she watched her mother climb the last stairs, "that poor taste is a lot more fun than good taste. Good taste is real boring." Then turning to Ben she said, "Ben, do you remember

326

the time we lived in that little house with only one bathroom up in North Carolina? The one right outside of Cherry Point?"

"My bladder just screamed when you mentioned it."

"Let me tell Karen and Matt about it. They were too young to remember this famous incident. This house only had one bathroom and Dad used to stay in there poopin' and readin' the paper on Sunday morning for what seemed like weeks. The whole family used to be lined up outside the door screaming in pain and begging Dad to hurry up. He'd just sit in there grunting and threatening to kill us if we uttered another peep of complaint. When you're younger you haven't developed the muscles of steel necessary to keep from wee-weeing on cross-country trips or long Sunday mornings. Well, one Sunday morning, ol' Ben here, yes, our marvelous, hero-brother, all star, all-American golden boy that we love, couldn't stand it any longer. I mean this boy had to pee and pee bad. His very teeth were floating and his voice was a plaintive cry as he begged our father to rise from his throne and enter into family life. Finally, ol' Mom came along to save the day."

"Good ol' Mom," Karen said.

"Yes, good ol' mom, the queen of good taste, brought a quart milk carton and told him to do his business in it. Ben did so. But then he was faced with a dilemma. What should he do with the carton of foulness he now possessed? He thought for a minute, then decided to put it in the refrigerator until Dad came out. Then he would take the carton of wee-wee and dispose of it in the toilet now fully covered by Dad's behind. But Benny-boy had a short memory, and after he had relieved his swollen bladder, he went out to play with his friends. Ben was kind of dumb in those days. After Daddy-poo came out of the bathroom, he decided that he wanted a bowl of cereal . . ."

"Oh, wow," Matthew cried.

"I don't believe it, Mary Anne. You're making this up."

"Yes, my children, have respect and let your dearly beloved older sister continue. Well, Daddy goes to the refrigerator and pulls out a carton of what he thinks is nice fresh milk. Then he goes to the cupboard and gets a bowl and some Raisin Bran. The next thing the family hears is a scream that can only be described as pure disgust. Ben remembers the carton, runs into the kitchen at the exact moment our father begins puking on the kitchen table. He grabs the carton and starts to run out the door. Dad chases him. Boy with carton of pee runs for his life. Man vomits as he chases boy. Man catches boy. Carton of pee spills on the floor. Man sticks boy's face into the spilled pee until woman saves boy. It was one of the greatest family scenes in the history of families," Mary Anne said.

"Un-Jesus-Christ-believable," Matthew exhaled.

"I was close to death," Ben said, remembering.

"Shut up," Mary Anne whispered, "here they come."

Their parents walked downstairs, Lillian skipping lightly, proud of her beauty, aware of it; her husband followed, pulling at his necktie, uncomfortable in the full dress regalia of civilians. He noticed the sudden quiet of his children as he entered the room and he took this as a good sign. He liked a room to fall silent as he entered it. For him, silence was a precise instrument for gauging respect. A master sergeant had once reported to him that the rumor of his coming had silenced a mess hall.

Bull considered that report one of the highest compliments he had ever received.

It was eleven fifteen now. The eyes of the Meecham children burned with the excitement of secret gifts camouflaged beneath wrapping paper. The memories of old Christmases winged through the room like richly plumed birds and rested on the pungent branches of the tinsel-heavy tree the family as a unit had decorated. No battles were ever fought in the Meecham home on the night before Christmas. It was a time when happiness was allowed to spill over, to inundate all rooms, to rule all faces, and to reign unmolested in the turbulent kingdom of the fighter pilot. It was as though happiness was the order of the day.

Christmas Eve was also a time when the children could tease their father and know there would be no sudden explosion or descent into fury. They took advantage of the occasion.

"Hey, Dad," Ben grinned, "how long had that tree been dead when you bought it?"

"What do you mean, dead, sportsfans. That's a gorgeous tree."

"Yeah, Ben," Mary Anne said, joining in the chase. "Lots of people would be grateful for a brown tree."

"Darlings," Mrs. Meecham said, "be thankful for this tree. There are lots of children in the world who won't have a Christmas tree this Christmas. Think of the poor Communist children who won't have a tree. And the poor Jews."

"Well, having this tree is kind of like not having a tree at all," Ben said.

"Baloney, this is a perfect tree," Colonel Meecham said defensively. "It was the best tree in the lot."

"The lot was located at the edge of the Gobi Desert," Mary Anne said.

Karen said, "This tree is naked on the other side. It doesn't have but two branches."

"This tree is the most gorgeous we've ever had. The head honcho has spoken. I don't want to hear any more yappin'. We got to get to church by 2330 hours."

They walked to the church, past the great houses that rested in the shadow of the Lawn, singing fragments of Christmas carols in the atonal Meecham voices, and laughing at every joke anyone made. Ben pretended to dribble a basketball down the street while his father pretended to guard him. "Defense," Lillian cried to her husband as she broke into a strange, graceful dance that involved a series of spins and leaps with precarious high-heeled landings that halted the imaginary basketball game as every eye in the family fastened to the spinning figure wildly dancing toward the church, her yellow dress coming high above her knees. She rarely danced for her family and they in turn often forgot that she had taken ballet lessons up until the time she married Lieutenant Meecham. But when she danced, it was with a feral grace, a controlled wildness that had been preserved secretly in her body. Now, the whole family joined the dance, leaping, screaming, and racing past parked cars and the weird shadows cast by palmettos. Even Bull Meecham leaped like a fawn in imitation of his wife. This mad, violently happy dance lasted until Cobia Street met Pinckney, and then it stopped, as the small Greek Revival outline of The Infant of Prague Church came in sight and Bull growled, "At ease. At ease. We don't want God to see us crappin' around."

Father Pinckney began the high Mass at midnight. In a thick drawl, more ponderous than his low mass responses, the priest spoke the Latin phrases with a sonorous, dramatic discernment. In his more public moments, Father Pinckney tried to hide his southern accent, but even through the Latin and the incense the state of Tennessee was advertised and glorified each time he spoke a word.

The altar was adorned with thick, fragrant clusters of flowers illuminated by the slender white stemmed candles that burned from six candelabra. The priest's vestments shone with the white and gold jubilation of the church celebrating the birth of its redeemer. P. K. Hill swung the censer and plumes of incense smoked out of the chained gold globe filling the church with an odor that Ben always connected with the smell of God, just as he connected unleavened bread with the taste of God. Ben and Matthew were serving Mass in red cassocks worn only on feast days and special holidays. To Ben, the Latin responses had more gravity at night, especially when combined with a choir and a packed church. A manger scene was set up at the left side of the altar. Ben could see the Christ Child out of the corner of his eye. Above him, the Christ in agony hung above the altar. God on the borning day and the dying day brought to this single moment past midnight presided over the re-enactment of the Christian mystery by an alcoholic priest from Tennessee, a boy bent low to say the confiteor, and a churchful of people praying beside a river in Ravenel, South Carolina.

Ben believed in God on Christmas Eve above all other times, and on this night, he turned always away from the stern man on the cross, and ceased to believe in the hellmaker, the firelover, the predatory creator, the godly

330

carnivore who flung men and angels into a place of darkness and devastation, pain and endless fire. On this night, he gave himself to the child, not the gnarled carpenter who himself was nailed to the wood he once worked with until he was called to walk among the Jews. The child would not send anyone to the flames. Ben knew this; felt it; hoped it.

Ben swung his body toward the priest and the middle of the altar. He tapped his breast solemnly when he reached the words that always moved him, even though spoken in the secret tongue of a dead language: Mea Culpa, Mea Culpa, Mea Maxima Culpa. Through my fault. Through my fault. Through my most grievous fault. Somehow, Ben felt, dead languages could sway God more easily than a language soiled by everyday use.

Sister Loretta Marie prayed in the first row, her pinched face stiff with the effort of prayer. Moving her lips rapidly, she held her rosary tightly and recited each Hail Mary with a desperate gravity, as though she were flinging anvils at the gates of Heaven. There was no softness to her prayers. They welled up out of a dry unhappy place in her, the barren back-forty of a soul hurt by the savagery of the world to its ugly women. She prayed hard with her eyes fiercely closed.

Colonel Meecham stood at the back door of the church, his arms crossed, and his mind wandering. He never sat with the family in church. Instead, he stood guard in the rear to the unconcealed chagrin of the ushers. There, he half prayed, half thought. As a first prayer, he prayed for the fighter pilots in his squadron, for God to keep them safe in His high dominion. Then he would thank God for his family. He prayed in formulas that rolled out of his brain like the beat of drums. He prayed for the President, the Commandant of the Marine Corps, and other men in the top echelons of the Corps. Often, without thinking, he would go down half the chain of command before his prayers would take another form. Sometimes he would think about the relationship of Catholics and the military. Good Catholics make good soldiers, he thought. The soldier has to obey his commanding officer without questioning his orders. Same with Catholics. God's the Commanding Officer and the Pope is His first sergeant. God tells the Pope what He wants done and the Pope lays down the law. The Church is the structure wherein laws are administered. The Church and the Pentagon are alike in that respect. I am Commanding Officer of 367. God is the C.O. of the Universe. Both of us have similar responsibilities. O Lord, make me worthy of the squadron I command and please give me the chance to kill Castro.

In the middle of the service Ben was hit with the vision of Ansley Matthews naked before him. He mounted her at the gospel, drove deep inside her, her breasts soft and giving beneath him, her loins wet with wanting him, her smells the strong smells Ben imagined a woman gave off in the heat of love-making. His penis went erect under his cassock. Ansley's tongue drove into his ear; she whispered his name, then screamed his name as he bit into her phantom shoulder. "Fuck me. Fuck me," the ghost of her screamed to him in a language that was not dead nor could not die.

All during Father Pinckney's Christmas sermon, Ansley possessed his brain like a torturer, Ansley the nude, desiring him in full Technicolor. Ben only caught snatches of the sermon even though he tried hard to eliminate this forbidden yet splendid mirage by concentrating on the words of the priest. Once he saw Father Pinckney pointing to the statue of Mary and saying, "Only Mary, the mother of God, could wear both the white rose of virginity and the red carnation of motherhood." He fought against the image as he and Matt walked to the cruets for the Lavabo. As he poured the wine into the chalice, he could see Ansley's breast coming out of the chalice into his face, extinguishing all thoughts of salvation, all delusions of holiness. He sucked a nipple that was not there, slavered on the neck of a girl he had barely spoken to, foamed over a sin that took place in the uncontrolled cosmos beneath his skull.

He once had a thought. A near occasion of sin. The Pope could make a law. He could make masturbation a prayer. Make it a sacrament. He could call it self-love and give plenary indulgences for its religious performance. If he did, Ben had thought, Ben Meecham would waltz into the kingdom of God. If it became a sacrament, Ben felt that he would be a high priest, a cardinal of the upward stroke, a pope of wasted seed.

The Jesus on the cross stared at Ben's erect penis which was a stone rising out of the center of him. The Christ Child lifted himself above the manger and pointed toward Ben's belt. Then Father Pinckney lifted the holiest fingers in Tennessee, held a white host aloft, whispered the old dead prayers, believed in the deepest mystery, believed that the bread and the child and the nailed carpenter were one. The bells rang in Ben's hand, the penis withered, Ansley Matthews set his body free, and Ben turned in all the fury of a Catholic boyhood, in the dazzling cyclone of his belief, toward the moment when the bread became the light.

Father Pinckney held bread in his hands. Father Pinckney held God in his hands. Three times the bells sang. The bread trembled. Ben looked up and believed.

The host convulsed like a fetus, kicked with new blood. Arteries burst through to the strongest grain of wheat where the soul of God took root, where a new heart more ancient than time, stronger than nations, pumped god-blood to the smallest vein in the bread. Teeth formed in the grain of Christ and soft, unleavened nails scratched against the fingers of Father Pinckney. A mouth formed a cry in the voice of the bread. Eyes that came to life in the moonblaze of sacristies and witnessed the birth of the world struggled to open against the priest's grip. In the perfect circle of the host, lungs began to breathe the in-censed air, the same lungs that had breathed in the blackness of the void, the ozone of creation, and the fire of molded stars hatched by hands large enough to arrange galaxies. Softly, God grew in the hands of one priest; in the womb of his hands the Christ grew. A man and a god lives far in the bread, deep in the grain. And Ben Meecham believed.

The children were ordered to bed as soon as they returned home from Mass. Lillian came in to kiss Ben good night and whispered to him, "I wouldn't expect too much of a Christmas this year. We've had a lot of expenses that were unexpected and with you going to college and all I just wanted to warn you that this is going to be a very lean Christmas. A very lean Christmas."

"Sure, Mom," Ben said, smiling, "that's what you say every Christmas."

"Well mark my words. I just don't want you to be disappointed. I can still remember how disappointed I was when I was a little girl and Santa Claus skipped my house."

"I'm a little old to believe in Santa Claus."

"No you're not," Lillian said. "Always believe in things and people that bring you pleasure. What good does it do to throw those things out the window?"

At that moment, Bull had climbed out the attic window onto the roof. Every Christmas since Ben could remember Bull had clambered out on the roof of mobile homes, quonset huts, Capehart houses to make Santa Claus laughs and reindeer noises.

"Ho! Ho! Ho! Ho!" Bull bellowed from the roof.

"Get a gun, Mama. There's a pervert on the roof," Mary Anne called out from the next room.

"Hush, sugah, and let your daddy have his fun. Did you leave out the cookies and the milk for Santa Claus?"

"I did, Mama," Karen answered.

"Is Dad going to do his reindeer act?" Matthew asked from his bedroom.

"Moo! Mooooo! Mooo!" came the voice from the roof.

"Why does Daddy do a reindeer like a cow?" Karen asked.

"Cows and reindeer come from the same family. That's as close as he can get," Lillian explained.

"Moooo, Mooo," the reindeer lowed again.

"On Dasher and Donner and Comet and all you other guys with the weird names," Bull called out from the roof. "Now whoa, you horny sons a bitches."

"Bull!" Lillian admonished. "Don't get carried away."

"Mooooooo," he answered.

"Good night, children. Santa Claus has to get to work now. Remember what I told all of you. It's going to be a lean Christmas so don't be disappointed."

"Good night, Mama," Lillian's children called as she

went to her room and began removing hidden presents.

At five o'clock in the morning, a hand touched Ben's shoulder. He awoke slowly and unrefreshed. Stretching, he rubbed the sleep out of his eyes along with a dream he would never recover. He made out Mary Anne's outline when his eyes adjusted to the dark.

"How can you sleep?" she asked.

"Oh, I don't know," he answered, looking at the clock by his bed. "I'm kind of eccentric. I've always been one of those weird guys who likes to sleep at five o'clock in the morning."

"I'm too excited to sleep. You ought to see all the presents under the tree."

"I'll see them when I wake up," Ben yawned, putting the pillow over his head.

Mary Anne was not going to give up, however. "I'm not going to let you sleep," she answered.

"Let me remind you," Ben said, his voice muffled under the pillow, "that I can kick the hell out of you because I'm a lot stronger."

"You used to stay up all night with me waiting for morning," she said.

"I know, Mary Anne. That's true. I used to be a little kid. I used to believe in Santa Claus and leave him milk and cookies on the mantelpiece."

"Karen and Matt are down there by the tree now."

"Good," Ben sighed, "tell them I'll be down in about six hours."

"You're coming now. They sent me to wake you," she said.

"I'm tired, Mary Anne," Ben replied, "but it's been fabulous having this conversation with you. I feel much closer to you after having this talk this early in the morning. Now don't let the door hit you on the fanny on the way out."

"O.K., O.K.," she said, nodding her head sadly, "but I'm gonna tell you every present you got right now so that you won't have a single surprise when we finally open the presents."

"Don't do that, Mary Anne," Ben whined.

"Let's see," she teased, "Matt bought you a can of tennis balls and Karen bought . . ."

"All right, goddam it, I'm getting up. I'm getting up."

"That's more like it, feces face."

They padded through the hall past their parents' bedroom door and down the stairs. Matt had plugged in the lights of the tree. The sight of the presents piled beneath the tree startled Ben. It was a massive pile of silver and gold paper; ribbons streaked the pile with bands of deep color. Once again, he thought, the two children of the depression had fought the misery of past holidays by spending a modest fortune on their own children. Presents spilled off a three foot stack that surrounded the tree. Each stocking, hanging from the fireplace and swollen fat as sausages, could not have held another item. Each child, mesmerized by the assault of color, stared into the drift of presents with a seasonal greed as pure as angel hair.

"Isn't it beautiful, Ben?" Karen said.

"Beautiful," he agreed, "just beautiful."

"That's my present for you, right on top," Karen said to Ben.

"I'll open it first, Karen."

"That huge one over there is mine," Matt said. "It's the biggest present under the tree."

"I know what it is," Mary Anne said.

"What is it, Mary Anne? Tell me what it is. I'm too excited to wait," Matt said.

"It's a chemistry set," Mary Anne said.

"Why'd you tell me that," Matt half-screamed. "Now it won't be a surprise. What a crummy thing to do."

"If you don't want to know, don't ask," Mary Anne said.

"I can't wait till you see what I gave you, Matt," Karen said.

Then Mary Anne spoke, "You know what I love about Christmas? Really love? I hear people talking all the time about the spirit of giving. How it feels better to give than to receive. I don't believe that at all. I've analyzed myself very carefully and I've come to the conclusion that I love the spirit of getting. I'd much rather get things

336

than give things. I hate to give things. I hate to spend money on someone else when I could be spending it on myself. I hate to see other people ripping open presents that are not for me. Being truly honest, I wish every present under that tree were marked, 'To Mary Anne, with love.' Christmas is a time for getting things. I like things. All kinds of things. Nice things. Heavy things. Fragile things. Some people like to collect stamps, coins, or antiques. Me? I just like to collect things. I like having things very much. More than I could ever explain. I heard ol' Sister Loretta saying after catechism class that she's afraid that Christ is being taken out of Christmas. That makes me happy. I'd like to see the Christ removed altogether. Then I could get more things."

"That's the most selfish thing I've ever heard," Matt said.

"Oh it is, Matt-midget?" Mary Anne hissed. "Well why don't we just go through every present under the tree with your name on it and give it to someone else. Then you'll be giving and we all know that's the true spirit of Christmas. Anybody that says they enjoy giving more than getting is a tacky hypocrite."

"You're a big asshole sometimes, Mary Anne."

"Little brother is learning how to cuss," Mary Anne said.

"All right, let's cut the crap," Ben said with an inconsequential wave of the hand. "It's getting time to wake up Mom and Dad."

"Let's do it now," Karen squealed.

"I demand an apology," Mary Anne said.

"For what?" Ben asked.

"For Matt-creep calling me a big asshole," she said, folding her arms like a Buddha and setting her jaw.

"Apologize, Matt," Ben said. "Tell her she's not a big asshole. Tell her she's a little asshole."

"Very funny," Mary Anne said, "but I demand an apology."

"Sweet Jesus, Mary Anne. As much as you tease Matt and make his life miserable, it's stupid to expect him to apologize to you."

"Yeah, especially because you're such a big asshole," Matt said.

"I'm very sensitive. My feelings get hurt very easily. So you can tell the Lilliputian that I am not going to move until he apologizes."

"What's a Lilliputian, Ben?" Matt asked.

"It's a real cool guy, Matt. Why don't you just tell her you're sorry, Matt. Or she'll mope around for days."

"I'm sorry," Matt said without vigor.

"Your apology is certainly not accepted, creep. But it will do for now."

"I had my fingers crossed anyway," Matt retorted.

Then Mary Anne rose and ran for the stairs. "Last one up to Mom's room is part colored," she yelled.

From that moment on, they adhered to the unwritten law of Christmas past. Now, they moved in ritual.

They ran up the stairs; their bare feet drumming against the wood, their laughter announcing their arrival at their parents' door. Entering the room like resistance fighters, they vaulted the bed, pulled covers and blankets from their parents' dreaming bodies. Colonel Meecham cursed. Karen tugged at her father's arms, while Ben tried to pull his legs off the bed. Catching Ben off guard, Bull kicked him into the open closet where his uniforms hung. Matt leaped on his father's chest trying to drag him off the bed by attacking Bull close to the center. It only took a moment for Matt to fly off the bed onto the floor. Lillian had already gotten up and was putting on her robe and house shoes in preparation for the impending predawn ritual at the tree.

All four children concentrated their energies on their father. They came at him from every angle, wrestling for control of an arm or a leg, trying to get him to the floor. Each year they had to fight him to the floor before they would even consider going downstairs. Ben finally got on Bull's back at the same moment Mary Anne locked onto a piece of his ear. Mary Anne twisted the ear, Ben pushed off from the headboard, Karen grunted at the legs, and Matt had his head under his father's buttocks shouting "Simba Barracuda." Slowly, and very heavily, Colonel Meecham fell to the bedroom floor, one limb at a time.

"Who dares attack the Great Santini?" he roared from the floor.

"The children of Santini," Mary Anne yelled.

"What do the children of Santini wish?"

"They wish to open their presents, O Great Santini," Karen said.

"Then I must ask a question," Colonel Meecham said, growing serious for a moment, then exploding with an exultant cry, "Who's the greatest of them all?"

"The Great Santini!" his children yelled in unison.

"Who is the king of them all?"

"The Great Santini!"

"Who is lord of all he sees?"

"The Great Santini!"

"Who is the greatest fighter pilot that ever lived?"

"The Great Santini!"

"Who sees all, hears all, and knows all?"

"The Great Santini!"

"Then Santini commands his children to assemble by the tree," Colonel Meecham said with a flourish. "The Santini will dress, go to the tree, and give out presents at approximately 0535 hours. But Santini must have a cup of coffee before he begins."

At the bottom of the stairs, Lillian bestowed a long holiday kiss on each one of her children and wished them a Merry Christmas. Mary Anne rushed into the kitchen and poured two cups of hot coffee from a pot she had brewed three hours before. Matthew plunged into the middle of the pile around the tree and threw presents over himself until he almost disappeared from view.

"No, Matt," Lillian says. "Wait until your father hands you a present."

"I just want to feel 'em on top of me," Matt said from under the pile.

"Hurry up, Daddy," Karen pleaded from the bottom of the stairs.

"No one rushes Santini," a voice answered.

Finally, Colonel Meecham began his descent, every step a deliberate one, tortoise-slow, designed to augment the impatience of his giddily avaricious offspring. He was dressed in his fatigues which were cleaned and pressed. His brass glittered when it caught the reflection of the

Christmas lights. He was wearing his flight jacket and his inspection shoes.

Mary Anne brought him his cup of coffee as he eased into his chair near the tree. Lillian was already drinking hers. Bull thanked his daughter with an exaggerated southern accent, then took a sip of coffee.

"Too hot," he said sadly. "I'll have to wait until it cools."

"We ain't playin' the three bears, Popsy," Mary Anne said.

Matthew ran to his father's side and began blowing into the cup. "I'll cool it off, Dad." He blew wildly and coffee spilled out of the cup.

"Get outta here, jocko," Colonel Meecham ordered. "Nature will cool it off in her own good time. Ya got it? With your snotty germs, you could be givin' me a cancer or somethin'. Do you read me loud and clear, mister?"

"Yes, sir."

For a good thirty seconds, Colonel Meecham sat reflecting in his chair staring at his steaming coffee with an ineffable sadness. Finally, he took a cautious sip. He smacked his lips together, shook his head in serene affirmation, purred, and took another sip. His children applauded. He sipped his coffee as delicately as a debutante, as slowly as an octogenarian. He savored it, moaned his approval of it, praised it with clucking poultry sounds, and cries of delight. "I have drunk coffee all over the world, in two wars, before and after battles, on liberty in exotic ports and I do have to declare that this here is the finest cup of coffee I have ever put to my lips. I'd rather drink a good cup of coffee than bomb Moscow."

"I gotta open me a present," Matt blurted out.

"Not until your father hands it to you," Mrs. Meecham said.

"I'll start soon, Matt," his father yawned, relishing the drama, "right after I get me another cup of coffee."

"Boo!" his children yelled. "Boo, Santini!"

But Mary Anne grabbed his cup and sprinted for the kitchen at full speed. She returned in less than half a minute; Colonel Meecham tasted the coffee, then shook his head mournfully. "It's just too hot," he said.

Without hesitation, Mary Anne dropped an ice cube into his coffee. The other children applauded her foresight.

The second slowest cup of coffee ever consumed by man was finally empty as every eye in the Meecham living room remained fastened on the figure of Colonel Meecham. At last he set his cup down with a final, definitive click against the saucer. He picked a present at random from under the tree. He pretended to have difficulty reading the name. He squinted dramatically. He asked for a magnifying glass. Then he said, "To Karen, from Santa Claus."

His wife, sitting now under the tree, said, "I hope ya'll aren't disappointed. It's going to be a lean Christmas."

It had begun. The giving of gifts hand-delivered by Bull Meecham to his family on his finest day. In the year of our lord 1962. In the reign of Santini.

25

THE DAY AFTER CHRISTMAS Sammy Wertzberger picked
Ben up in the early evening and sped quickly out of
Ravenel toward the Charleston highway. Sammy was
wearing a new Gant shirt, an alligator belt, Weejuns, a
London Fog raincoat, cuffless pants, and Gold Cup socks.
He had applied an overdose of English Leather and Ben
rolled down the window to cut the power of the scent. Ben
had never seen Sammy dress with such an obeisance to
the totems of fashion.

"O.K., what's the big surprise Christmas present?"
Ben asked when they had broken out of Ravenel County
and in a hauntingly crepuscular light were shooting across
a causeway where the locks and sluices of an old rice
plantation were still visible.

"I don't want to tell you just yet, son. Oh, what the
hell!" Sammy said. "For my Christmas present to you,
I'm going to let you play with my pecker any time you
want to from now until graduation."

"Thanks, Sammy. Can I start right now?"

"Naw, I don't want to take it out in the car. Some
passing motorist might call the highway department and
claim he saw two men wrestling an anaconda."

"Where are we going?"

"Hold your thanks until I finish talking. I, Sammy Wertzberger, have set us up with a date in Charleston with
two good-looking college girls."

"College girls!" Ben said breathlessly.

"That's right, son. Goddam, one hundred percent, second semester freshman, college girls."

"Do you know them?"

"Naw. That's a long confusing story. My mother knows

342

this woman in Charleston she roomed with at Winthrop who knows a lady who has a daughter who brought a friend home for Christmas vacation. They haven't been out on a date once since they've been in Charleston. That's where superstuds Sammy Wertzberger and Ben Meecham come into the picture."

"I've never dated a college girl before," Ben said.

"Hell, you've never even dated high school girls. But we don't have to let 'em know that. I figure tonight we act sophisticated. Real men of the world. You can't act like high school Harry and score big with college girls."

"I guess you're kind of an expert in the field, huh, Sammy?" Ben grinned.

"Laugh now, son. But after you've buried your head in the huge bosoms of your date tonight and she's begging for more, you just remember that it was suave Sammy that put you in the driver's seat."

"What are the girls' names?"

"My date's name is Alicia West. Your date's name is Becky Bonham. Now remember, Ben, these are college girls, son. College girls. Now I shouldn't have to tell you that college girls are not like high school girls. These are grown women. They've been around. They have incredible sexual appetites just like you and me. And I mean huge appetites for the performance of the evil deed. You know what I mean."

"That's what I've heard about college girls," Ben said. "No preliminaries. They just like to get down to business fast. I've heard they actually get insulted if you don't try to make the big move on them."

"Well, some of them are pretty shy, Ben. Just like any other kind of woman. They need a firm, experienced masculine hand to guide them," Sammy said. "Others are just frigid and a man simply has to take the bull by the horns and almost be rough. That's why I developed my own personal technique. It's called the Bohemian Mountain Approach."

"What's that?"

"Well, I don't like to give away trade secrets but since you're my best friend I'll let you in on it. It can start off this way. Now this is just hypothetical, you realize."

343

"Of course," Ben answered.

"You treat the girl very kindly and softly during the whole drive-in movie. You're very considerate of her needs. You light her cigarettes, buy her Coke and popcorn, and talk about how beautiful she looks in the moonlight. Very suave, very cool. Then, when you've lulled her into a false sense of security, and just when she trusts you and knows you respect her for what she really is and that you're not just dating her for her body, you point to a scene on the movie screen and when she looks up, the very moment she looks up, you ram your hand up her dress and stick your index finger up her twat."

"That's very suave, very cool," Ben said, watching the moon light up the black waters of the Edisto River as they traveled toward Charleston going seventy-five. "By the way, Sammy," he said turning to his friend, "that's the most ridiculous thing I've ever heard of."

"It's not ridiculous. It's the Bohemian Mountain Approach. Girls can't resist it."

"Have you done that, Sammy? Honestly. Have you ever done that in your life?" Ben asked.

"No."

"Then how do you know it works?"

"I've been around, son. It's a strategy worked out over the ages. Jewboys like me have studied the ways of seduction for centuries because we know that little goy girls are saving their star-spangled banner for their blond husbands."

"Thus we have the Bohemian Mountain Approach," Ben said.

"There are variations of course."

"Of course."

"This is one of my personal favorites. You pick a girl up. Right?"

"Right," Ben said.

"You meet her parents and act like a perfect gentleman. You tell her parents how much you like classical music and poetry and going to art galleries. Then you escort your date out the door all dreamy-eyed. You speak in a gentle, well modulated, restrained voice. You open the door for her and lightly touch her on the elbow as

344

you help her in. You walk slowly around to your side of the car and remove your leather driving gloves. You get in the car, then in a flash you leap at her from across the car, pin her arms to the seat, and rip her panties off."

"A very versatile thing, this Bohemian Mountain Approach."

"It is a way of life, son. It is simply an application of firmness that utilizes the element of surprise. Once you have begun the Bohemian Mountain Approach, there is no turning back. It takes a genius in the art of love to use it properly and that's where I come in," Sammy said.

He pulled the Rambler into a country gas station, left Ben with the car still running, disappeared into the dimly lit depths of the store and returned carrying two paper sacks.

"Here's a little liquid courage," Sammy said, handing Ben a Budweiser.

"I'm in training," Ben protested.

"One beer's gonna cause you to fart out a kidney? Drink it," Sammy ordered resuming the trip up Highway 17. "We'll be there in a half hour and I still haven't prepared you properly for the night."

"What else do I need to know?"

"Plenty. There's one favor I'd like to ask of you, Ben."

"Sure, Sammy."

"You promise you won't laugh."

"I promise."

"If you laugh, can I use all the blood of your Christian children for terrible Jewish ceremonies? That's what Red thinks Jews do."

"I've heard that too."

"It's true. We pass the little fingers and toes of Christian children around on hors d'oeuvre trays. No, seriously. You promised not to laugh. But I didn't tell Alicia West my real name when I called."

"Fine. I'll go along with that. What name did you give her?"

"Rock."

"Rock!" Ben screamed.

"You promised you wouldn't laugh."

"I'm not laughing. I'm screaming."

"Rock Troy."

"Rock Troy!" Ben screamed even louder.

"Go ahead. Laugh. Get it out of your system, because when she gets in the car I don't want to hear any whooping and hollering when she asks ol' Rock Troy to unzip his britches."

"Rock Troy," Ben repeated.

Sammy took a long pull on his beer, then another one. "You can imagine a girl getting fired up to date a guy named Sammy Wertzberger. This adds a little class to it. This will only be a one-night stand anyway. Oh, and there's one other small favor."

"You told the other girl that my name is Hymie Finkelstein," Ben laughed.

"That wouldn't have been a bad idea. No. I told Alicia that I was a hotshot guard on the basketball team. Is that O.K. with you?"

"Sure. You and I are in the backcourt together. That's fine. I like it."

"Hey thanks, Ben. That's one of my great fantasies. Do me just one other favor. Please. Sometime during the night, and you can choose the time, say to your date loud enough for Alicia to hear in the front seat, 'At basketball games people are always pointing at Rock Troy and saying, "I wonder what that little fucking wizard is gonna do next." ' "

"Sure, I'll say that."

"That will be the greatest moment of my life. I'll probably just lay my head back on the seat and bask in the glory. Hey, which reminds me. Did you finish *The Sun Also Rises* for Mr. Loring's English class?"

"Yeah, I read it the first or second day over the holiday."

"I guess ol' Jake sort of reminded you of sophisticated, yet cynical, Sammy Wertzberger."

"No, he reminded me of the little fucking wizard of the backcourt, Rock Troy."

"You son of a bitch."

"No kidding, Jake did remind me a lot of you, Sammy. Especially the part about having no balls. How did you like Cohen?"

346

"Hemingway hated Jews, no doubt about it. Hell, Ben, the whole goddam world hates Jews. I was sitting there reading that book and I was hating Cohen's guts myself. I can't figure out what everybody's got against Jews."

"It's because they're stingy and have funny shaped heads and ugly looking Jew noses," Ben said, leaning across to poke Sammy in the ribs.

"It's like my father says, Ben. Thank God for the schwartze. If it wasn't for the schwartze, they'd be screwing the Jews. If it wasn't for the niggers, my father wouldn't stay in Ravenel for five minutes."

Again they crossed a river and Ben wondered how many rivers and saltwater creeks one would cross traveling along Highway 17 through the lowcountry. This river had the deep wild odor of swamp water about it. Cypress trees towered to the left of the car, an ink-black creek paralleled the highway, full of rotten winter vegetation.

"Now for the final test before we pick up our dates, Ben," Sammy said. "You pretend you're my date, Alicia, and I'm going to show you how I am going to take advantage of what I learned in *The Sun Also Rises*. Mr. Loring would be proud of me."

"What do you mean, pretend I'm Alicia? You want me to hold your hand?"

"No. Just pretend you're Alicia just getting in the car for her date with the most exciting man she's ever seen. This will be a real test. You ask me questions and really pretend you're a girl."

"Oh, Rock," Ben said in a high-pitched voice, sliding across the seat and throwing his arms around Sammy, "please take me someplace quick and screw my college brains out."

"Be serious, son," Sammy said, knocking Ben's arm off him. "Here, let me start it off," he said, reaching into the pocket of his London Fog and producing a package of cigars.

"Cigars!" Ben said retaining the girlish voice.

"El Producto Cigars, my dear. I had them imported from Spain," Sammy said suavely.

"Cigars smell nasty and poopy," Ben trilled.

"In Europe, during my many visits there, I have

347

learned that European women smoke cigars along with the men."

"My mommy would just die if she knew I was smoking El Producto Cigars," Ben said.

"You probably haven't dated too many men who were as oriented toward the European way, Alicia. I can teach you many things."

"Have you really been to Europe, Rock?"

"Ha! Have I been to Europe? Ask me how many times I've been to Europe," Sammy said, lighting a cigar from a dashboard lighter.

"How many times have you been to Europe, Rock?"

"Four or five. I can't remember precisely."

"Did you go to Gay Paree, Mr. Troy?" Ben asked breathlessly.

"Did I go to Gay Paree," Sammy said with a sneer. "Alicia, darling, I invented Gay Paree. But here, you try an El Producto, Alicia. Don't be afraid. I ordered these cigars from Barcelona, Spain. I met the man who made them when I went to the bullfights with Ernest Hemingway."

"You know Ernest Hemingway?"

"Papa?" Sammy answered imperiously with a gesture so dramatic a cigar ash flew across the car toward Ben. "He's like a father to me. He taught me everything there is to know about bullfighting and big-game hunting. And of course, women."

"Can I sit in your face, Rock?" Ben said, then screamed with laughter.

"You are breaking character. No fair breaking character," Sammy scolded.

"What was the most exciting thing you did in Europe, Rock?" Ben said in Alicia's voice.

"I think it was when Papa and I ran with the bulls at Pamplona during the El Producto festival. Racing through the streets of that ancient city, the bulls thundering behind us, young señoritas dropping their handkerchiefs to us from balconies. The excitement came from facing Death. Yes, Death in the Afternoon."

"Hey, Sammy, you are really good at that. I'm not kidding. That is really good."

"Tonight, the master leaps into action," Sammy said, puffing on his cigar.

They crossed the Ashley River bridge and headed parallel to the river until they reached Broad Street. The girls were staying in a house south of Broad Street in the muted, elegant old section of the city. The spires of St. Michael's Church shone in the half-mist slipping in from the river. The houses they passed were many-tiered, exquisitely simple, and superbly crafted remnants of a lost society. In front of a house on Tradd Street, Sammy parked the car. He and Ben slapped each other's palms and brushed back their hair with nervous fingers. Sammy knocked at the door, using a shining brass knocker that drummed nicely on the oaken door.

A black man answered wearing a dark suit. "Is one of you gentleman a Mr. Troy?" the man asked, reading from a small, white card.

"I am," Sammy said.

"Miss West offers her sincerest regrets. But Miss Bonham's fiancé arrived unexpectedly today with his roommate from Yale. She tried to contact you in Ravenel, but no one at your number had ever heard of a Mr. Rock Troy."

"Yeah, they probably got the wrong number or something. Thanks a lot, you hear. I appreciate it. Tell Alicia maybe some other time."

They returned to the car. Neither boy said anything. Finally, they both began to giggle uncontrollably. The giggling continued at several Charleston bars and had not stopped completely when Rock Troy left Ben off at his house in Ravenel.

26

EARLY FRIDAY AFTERNOON, Bull's office phone rang. He picked it up and heard Lt. Col. Cecil Causey's voice on the other end. Causey was the commanding officer of Squadron 234 which had the reputation and history of being one of the best F–8 squadrons in the Marine Corps for the past five years. The two squadrons were locked in an intense competition to win the trophy signifying supremacy among the other squadrons at Ravenel Air Base. Bull's squadron had a long uphill fight to overtake and surpass 234, and he knew it, but a strong bond and rivalry stirred the relationship, not only because the squadrons flew the same type of plane, but also because Bull and Cecil Causey were best of friends.

Bull had flown with Cecil Causey in the Korean War and had great respect for the man both as a commander and a pilot. A gifted raconteur and an indefatigable drinker, Causey was a pilot of unimpeachable courage. He had once flown a burning Corsair away from a densely populated urban area before bailing out. Three quarters of his body had been terribly burned during the ordeal, his face receiving some of the severest damage. Plastic surgeons removed half his nose, and much of the right side of his face after he was rescued at sea. Afterward they constructed a new face for him that gave him a sinister, ferocious appearance. The right side of his face did not move. Causey was a master of half expression, half smiles, and half glowers, for all nuances of expression stopped at the invisible frontier that marked the dead sector of his face. Bull thought Colonel Causey's melted, rebuilt face was a perfect one for a Marine fighter pilot. But Lillian always remarked that the doctors had taken

350

a badly burned, homely man, and with all the advances of modern medicine at their disposal, turned him into a grotesquerie.

"Meecham," Colonel Causey barked into his end of the phone, "this is Lieutenant Colonel Causey, the C.O. of the toughest fucking squadron ever to fly for the United States Marine Corps."

"No," Bull answered in a toneless voice, "there must be some mistake. This couldn't be the Colonel Causey I know because the Causey I know is the C.O. of the most limp-wristed, lily-livered, dick-sucking squadron in the history of flight. You, sir, are obviously an impostor, but you did happen to call the C.O. of the best squadron in the world. Can I help you?"

"You lowdown son of a bitch, Bull," Colonel Causey said, laughing. "No kidding, I do want to ask a favor of you. I was over at your house last week when you were on deployment to Yuma, and I left my good shoes under Lillian's bed. I wonder if you'd be kind enough to return them as soon as possible?"

"Yeah, Lillian told me you were over, come to think of it. She said she screwed a guy with the smallest dick in the Marine Corps, and I instantly thought of you. How are you doing, No Nose?"

"Pretty good, Bull. Here's why I'm calling. I thought it would be just outstanding if your squadron and mine could meet tonight at the club for happy hour. Let the boys let off a little steam. Let 'em drink together. Insult each other a bit. Maybe have a few fist fights. You know, Old Corps stuff, like when we were young Marines."

"What do you mean when *we* were young Marines. I'm a youngster compared to you, No Nose. By the way, I've always meant to ask you, what was it really like in the Halls of Montezuma?"

"We could start off by having a beer chugging contest," Causey answered.

"You sure your boys could handle beer, No Nose? We could chug mother's milk or something so your boys won't get nauseous or anything."

"Beer's fine, Bull. Tell your boys not to wear nylon

stockings and lipstick this time 'cause there's gonna be some real Marines at the bar come 1700."

"This is a damn good idea, Cecil. I'll call a meeting of my troops to get 'em fired up for happy hour. By the way, should you and me start the fisticuffs?"

"Hell, yes. That's great. The last time you and me fought was down at Rosey Roads in 'fifty-eight. Didn't I end up sitting on your face?" Causey asked.

"No, that was the time I punched you in the nose and nearly broke my hand. No one told me those quacks who built you a new nose made it out of cement. Sure, Cece, let's you and me start if off to show the young lieutenants how it's done. By the way, is Varney going to be there at happy hour?"

"Negative, I've already had my scouts turn in intelligence reports. He and most of the other brass punched out this morning for a high level meeting with the Great Kahuna at Cherry Point. They'll probably discuss the implementation of a vital campaign for good dental hygiene among pilots. You know how they do. They'll make it a court-martial offense for pilots not to use dental floss twice a day."

"Ha! Ha!" Bull laughed. "I've missed you, Cecil. Where've you been keeping yourself?"

"I've been flying my L.M.D. ever since the Cuban rift. Everett thinks if you can fly your large mahogany desk as well as you fly an F-8, then you shouldn't command a squadron. I'm lucky to get ten hours of flying time in a week, Bull, and that's no shit. And you remember the days when I'd get in sixty or seventy hours a week with no sweat."

"That was the Old Corps, No Nose, the Old Corps."

"Yeah, Bull. You and I are the last of a great breed."

"I'm the last of a great breed. You are the last of the scum and dross."

"How's Lillian and the kids?"

"Fine. The troops are shaping up, I think."

"I've been reading about Ben. It looks like a chip off the old block as far as basketball is concerned."

"He ain't as good as the block."

"I can vouch for that. I still remember that game

against West Point when you were playing for Quantico."

"I scored thirty-two that night," Bull said, "and ate their forward Saleesi alive."

"Naw, you scored two and Saleesi ate you alive."

"You son of a bitch."

"Bull, you still got an ego the size of a battleship. Anyway, get them lace panty pilots over to the club at happy hour and I'll let 'em drink with some men with real hair on their peckers. And one more thing, Bull. I want you to do me a favor."

"Anything, Cecil. You know I'll do anything for you," Bull said, growing serious.

"I've got a real turkey of a lieutenant that I want taught a lesson by one of your studs. Maybe put him out of commission for a little while. Perhaps ten years."

"What's his name, and what does he look like?"

"His name is Beasley. You'll recognize him right away. He'll be wearing an ascot, a Sam Brown cartridge belt, and a Bowie knife. I'm making him leave his pearl-handled revolver at home."

"You're kidding, Cecil," Bull groaned. "Anyone that wears that kind of crap to happy hour either has to be the best pilot in the world, or he's got the biggest set of nads in the southeast."

"You'd think so, wouldn't you? We got a pool goin' at the squadron about when ol' Beasley's gonna kill himself in a plane or kill one of us. This guy already is well on his way to becoming a black ace."

"How many planes has he lost?"

"He's lost three and he's only been in the Marine Corps four years. One of his crashes happened when he punched out on takeoff."

"Is this the same guy flamed out near Jacksonville in December?" Bull asked.

"That's my man Beasley."

"I've heard about him, No Nose. I hear he punches out if he feels a sudden blast of moonlight on his wing."

"I want one of your studs to let him know he is not the most beloved of all pilots. I'd get one of mine to do it, but you know the kind of problems that can cause. Anyway, I'm afraid of something."

353

"What's that, No Nose?"

"Everytime I see ol' Beasley, it pisses me off royally. It pisses me off when I see him breathing. He's using up oxygen that I could be breathing. Or my kids. Or egg-sucking dogs. Or even you. I'm tired of seeing him breathing, Bull. I even hate it when he blinks. You ever met anybody like that?"

"Yeah," Bull said, "I'm trying to think of who it is though. Oh, I know. I felt that way when I first met you."

"Good talking to you, Bull. I'll see you and your squadron at 1700 hours. By the way, I heard Everett say the other day that it's unbelievable what you've done with 367."

"If only it was Varney and not Everett."

"He was saying it to Varney, Big Fella. Now get Beasley for me and for God's sakes, get those shoes under Lillian's bed."

"See you at 1700 hours, No Nose. And do me one favor in return for Beasley."

"Name it."

"Wear a bag over your head. I don't want that shitty looking face of yours scaring any of my young pilots."

"I can't wait to beat on your head tonight. Over and out, turd."

"Outstanding," Bull answered.

Bull replaced the phone on the hook, smiled at himself with anticipation of the coming fracas, then bellowed for Sergeant Latito. "Hebe, get in here for a second, on the double. Your skipper needs you."

"Yes, sir, skipper," Sergeant Latito answered, hurrying through the door with a clipboard in his hand.

"Get Captain Brannon to my office pronto. He's out on the flight line. And pass the word that there'll be a meeting of all officers in the ready room at 1500 hours."

"Yes, sir."

"And Latito, one very important thing," Bull said, the hint of a suppressed smile stealing through the hard lines on his face. "Did you know that the clitoris on a female dinosaur was three feet, four inches long?"

"Yes, sir. Fascinating, sir," Latito answered. "I just

talked to Gillespie, and he told me that the radar malfunction of your bird was more serious than first reported."

"Just tell Gillespie that his C.O. is going up first thing Monday morning."

"He's got his best man on it, sir."

"Is it Harter?"

"Yes, sir. He's one of the best radar men in the Corps."

"Then how come Harter's only a PFC?"

"Bad attitude, Colonel. Besides, he gets drunk and picks fights with NCO's all the time."

"Sounds like a good Marine to me. Let's try to get Harter a few stripes. I like a happy man to work on my bird."

"Yes, sir. I'll send Captain Brannon to your office as soon as possible."

"Before you go, Sarge, I want to tell you one thing. You prove the old saw that a good top sergeant runs the squadron for the old man. You're the best I've run across, even if you are just a goddam Jew."

"Thank you very much, sir."

Ten minutes later Captain Brannon stood in front of Bull's desk. Though not as tall or physically commanding as Bull's, Captain Brannon's body was stacked together with the knotted muscles of a stevedore, and an implied menace shadowed his whole appearance. His eyes were dark, coffee-hued, and his jaw was an aggressive promontory. His expression had the insouciance and arrogance of the carnivore for there was nothing in his demeanor where one could not detect a glimmer of civilized ripeness. His entire body had a violent definition, a primal joy in aggression that caused men of equal size to afford him caution, and especially distance.

When Bull had spoken to Captain Brannon after taking over the command of 367, he had asked Brannon why he had chosen the Marine Corps for a career.

"I joined the Corps, sir, so I could help defend white America from all foreign aggression."

Bull had promptly nicknamed him "White America," an appellation that Brannon bristled at to the undiluted joy of his commanding officer.

Each day Brannon ran three miles, worked out on the punching bag in the gym, and boxed a few rounds with anyone he could insult or entice into the ring with him. At lunch, he walked outside the squadron headquarters and pounded a huge iron stake in the ground with a sledge hammer he kept in the trunk of his Jaguar XKE. When he had almost buried the stake, he pulled it from the ground with his massive hands, and repeated the ritual until he felt he had punished his body enough. The enlisted men quaked whenever he was in view. Officers feared his temper. Even Bull had no desire to match his strength with Butch Brannon. As Captain Brannon stood in front of Bull's desk awaiting instructions, Bull thought that it was one of God's minor vices that such an admirable physical specimen was such a mediocre pilot.

Twice Bull had hassled with Brannon in their F–8's, and twice he had come away believing that Brannon was either an imcompetent fighter pilot or a coward. There were thresholds of flight that Brannon could not or would not pass.

"At ease, Captain," Bull said, stretching back in his chair. "Does my nickname for you still ruffle your feathers?"

"I've never liked nicknames, sir."

"Well, what's Butch?"

"It's my real name, sir. It's on my birth certificate."

"Well, since I'm the C.O., and I like nicknames for my troops, you'll just have to put up with my nickname for you, White America. Do you read me loud and clear?"

"Yes, sir."

"Outstanding. Now I have a job for you, Butch. A little mop-up job that should just take a couple of seconds. The target will be wearing an ascot, a Bowie knife, and a Sam Brown cartridge belt. He will be a pilot from 234, Colonel Causey's outfit. Beasley's been going around bragging that he can whip your ass, Butch. Some of his fellow pilots have been laying money on the line," Bull said, eyeing Brannon, "and the betting has been going pretty heavy against you."

"I could break every bone in his body, sir."

"So you say, Butch. So you say. I've seen you out there hammering in that stake every day like you're practicing up for a job if crucifixion ever comes back in style, but I've never seen you fight anyone. A lot of folks think you're musclebound, Butch. They don't believe you could handle yourself in the real McCoy."

"I could kill Beasley, sir. Or any of those other guys running their mouths."

"Well, if anything starts up at happy hour today when we get together for a little fun with 234, I want you to remember Beasley."

"Yes, sir."

"And one more thing, Captain, my X.O. and I have been talking, and he and I agree you'd get a lot more done if you'd wipe that silly grin off your face that you wear all the time."

"Yes, sir," the man answered darkly.

"I mean it, Butch, you're always fucking around, raising hell, and playing practical jokes. You've got to be serious, man. We're in the business of war, and we can't have a Harpo Marx like you flying an airplane."

"You're joking with me, aren't you, sir?" Brannon asked, as a smile began to build on the spartan isthmus around his mouth.

"No, that's not all," Bull shouted, enjoying himself as he always did when facing a man totally without humor. "I've been looking at that fat-assed sloppy body of yours, and I am going to order you to stay in shape. You're a Marine, Brannon, and you may think all that baby fat is cute, but we've got an image to uphold."

"I keep in shape, sir. I'm in better shape than any man in this outfit, and I'll prove it if you like."

"I want you to take me more seriously, Captain. You've got to try to be more literal. I never, and this is an order, I never want you to think I'm being sarcastic or that I'm shittin' around with you. Because, White America, I mean what I say."

"Yes, sir. Will that be all, sir?"

"See you at happy hour, Captain. And I'll buy every drink that touches your lips if I see Beasley carried out of the club."

Before leaving for happy hour, Bull placed a call to his home. Mary Anne answered the phone.

"This is Rock Hudson," Bull said. "I'm calling from Hollywood to see if Mary Anne Meecham will accept my hand in marriage."

"What do you want, Poopsie?"

"Don't call me 'Poopsie,' " Bull ordered. "Where's your mother?"

"She's shopping downtown."

"When she gonna get back?"

"She didn't say, Daddy dear."

"What's Ben doing?"

"Oh, superhero is resting up for his starring role tonight."

"Well, don't make any noise. We want him fresh tonight."

"Oh, of course, we do, Poopsie. I'd just die if precious allstar went out on the floor not fresh. I think I'd feel personally responsible."

"You're a real wiseass sometimes, Mary Anne. Tell your mother I'm going to happy hour with the boys, and will meet you at the game."

"If Mom calls you up at happy hour, you'll have to buy a round of drinks for everybody at the club, won't you, Poopsie, dear? I'll leave her a note to call you as soon as possible."

"Tell her if she does, I'll have to get morose with her," Bull growled. "By the way, how are your studies coming?"

"Fine, Poopsie, fine. I'm failing algebra, American History, and French," she said, knowing that her father's thoughts had drifted to other matters.

"That's good," he answered. "Keep it up. Good grades are the only things that count for a girl. Tell your mother I'll meet her at the game. That's an order I expect to be carried out."

"Oh tremble, tremble. Yes, sir. Bye-bye, Rock Hudson."

When her father put the receiver down, Mary Anne, whispering a tuneless half-remembered melody, thumbed through the telephone directory, and with her pen, marked the number of the Ravenel Air Station's Officers' Club.

At five o'clock across the eastern seaboard, in the darkening skies of January, with the week's mission accomplished, the nation safe, the enemy quiet, the wings of aircraft folded, the rifles oiled, the radar screen unthreatening, and the tanks parked, it is then, at that sun-ruled moment that the armed services of America in general, and Marine pilots in particular, pay homage to the laws of happy hour and settle down into the serious business of drinking. All across this soldier-filled nation, gathering around dark mahogany bars, the fighting men gather, druids of the cold war, who in the communion of men bound by the same violent destiny, assemble each Friday for the lifting of glasses and eloquent toasts to their branch of the service, and their mother country.

Bull Meecham required his pilots to go to happy hour every Friday. Not only was it a ritual that stimulated esprit and fraternity in his squadron, it also helped relax his pilots and provided them an outlet to cut loose from the tensions of flight, from the unspoken knowledge that every time a pilot took a plane up, he was riding with death on his wings. Bull himself was obsessed by a carefully concealed fear that he would die in a plane, and he knew that death in flight could assume many shapes, a light on a control panel, a subtle change in an engine's pitch, a frozen control, a migratory bird. To Bull, death could be a matter of inches and could be read as clearly as an alphabet in the lidless eyes of gauges. Though he could not explain this to Lillian or his children because he thought it would frighten them, he wanted to tell them this someday: that pilots are killed in the blink of an eye. He had seen injured jets fall from the sky as inexorably as arrows pulled from strong bows. Death itself had assumed human shape for Bull, and there were times, like landing on an aircraft carrier at night, that he felt its presence, a dark, slouching rider on the wing, a cold stranger who lived on the wing, and in the pit of the stomach. But fear and death were laughed at and another round ordered. Happy hour was a good place to bray, to regenerate courage, and to be infected with the enthusiasm of other men who lived to fly. So as Bull pulled up to the parking lot of the Officers' Club, he saw groups of pilots arriving wearing their flight jackets. They have come back to earth for another Friday, he thought, they have come down to celebrate the brotherhood of men who fly, an inviolate brotherhood closed to other men, to lesser men, to unwinged men. Bull walked into the club as Friday grew darker and the sun moved toward El Toro.

In a large room adjacent to the main bar, the pilots of 367 and the pilots of 234 faced each other from opposite sides of the room. Two tables were set up in the middle of the room with twenty-four bottles of cold Coors beer on each one. The pilots had bought drinks from the bar and were beginning to warm up to the festivities. They began to taunt each other across the room.

"Hey, 367, I heard one of your pilots had to get a hysterectomy last week," a voice rang out.

"That's right. It turned out to be your wife dressed in your flight suit. We recognized her by her mustache," Major Reynolds, Bull's executive officer, shot back.

"Why don't you pussies from 367 go buy yourself some Kotex and leave this room to some real fighter pilots?"

"We're afraid if we leave ol' 234 might have a circle jerk here."

Finally Cecil Causey stepped to the center of the room, slapped a twenty dollar bill on the table and announced, "I'll bet drinks on the house that Captain Clifford Strait of 234 has the hairiest ass of any pilot in this room."

"Bullshit," Bull growled.

"He's right, Colonel," Captain Johnson said. "Strait's got an ass on him like an ape."

"I know that, Johnson," Bull answered in a loud voice. "The only reason Strait ain't classified as an ape is 'cause he has an opposable thumb. The same goes for all those ape bastards in 234."

"Shit," Captain Brannon said, "I know a lot of apes who have too much fucking pride to join 234."

"I know one that didn't, sure enough," someone from the 234 crowd said.

"Where's Strait?" Brannon said. "I'll match my ass with any man's. Get him out here."

Captain Strait swaggered out from the ranks of 234 as though he had a long and distinguished history of victory in contests of this ilk. He was swarthy, dark haired, and one of those men who always look as if they need a shave no matter what the time of day. Slowly, he unbuckled his pants and dropped his trousers to the floor. Brannon removed his trousers at the same time. Then, dropping their skivvies, both men bent over to allow their asses to endure the careful scholarship and unoccluded scrutiny of the two squadrons. Soon there was heavy laughter coming from 234.

"Brannon ain't got a hair on his ass compared to Strait," Causey said to Bull. "You buy the first round."

"Well," Bull replied, conscious that every pilot from both squadrons was listening for his reply, "it's good to know that 234 is first in something. They can't fly, they can't fuck, and they can't drink. But they are the goddam champs when it comes to hairy assholes. Now let's get serious, and get to the beer chugging contest. Of course, after looking at Strait's ass, I think we ought to have a banana eating contest, and let Strait start it off."

A bartender brought a phone into the room with a long extension cord. He walked through the Marines and handed the phone to Bull. "It's your wife calling, Colonel."

An explosive cheer went through the room as all the pilots headed for the bar to order their free round of drinks. "I'll have Wild Turkey on the rocks," shouted Cecil Causey, leading the charge to the bar. Bull was blushing as he took the phone, and spat savagely, "What in the hell are you calling me for at happy hour, Lillian. Have you gone out of your goddam bush?"

"Poopsie," Mary Anne's voice said, "I just wanted to call you, and tell you how much I appreciate your love and affection for me, and how I will dedicate my whole life to being worthy of your blind worship of me."

"Mary Anne, this little prank has cost me over fifty dollars," Bull said, controlling himself with effort. "I would advise you to start running now. I would suggest you go south toward the swamps because when I find you, I'm going to break every bone in your body."

"I think I'm in love, Poopsie," Mary Anne continued. "I think I'm going to marry a Ubangi."

"You ain't gonna be in any position to marry a Ubangi or anyone else when I get finished with you."

Some of the pilots were drifting back from the bar, still laughing at the rare faux pas of a colonel's wife calling her husband at happy hour. Normally, this heinous breach of decorum was the pitfall of young lieutenants' wives. Bull grabbed Cecil and put him on the phone. "This is my daughter, not my wife. Here, talk to Mary Anne, Cecil."

"Oh sure," the pilots laughed.

"Hello," said Colonel Causey.

"Hi, Colonel Causey, this is Mary Anne. Please pretend that you're talking to my mama. My brother and I have been planning this for a long time."

"That's right, Colonel. This is Ben. I'm on the upstairs phone."

"Hello, Lillian. How are ya doing, honey? Why sure I'll tell him," Colonel Causey said in an extravagant, generous voice. His eyes were dancing from pilot to pilot. "You want him to bring home paper towels and a bottle of Ivory Liquid. Bobby pins, cigarettes, and what? Oh Lillian, I can't tell him that. No, he's my friend. And so are you. Oh, if you insist. Bye-bye, honey," Cecil said, putting the phone down, his forehead wrinkled as though something of great urgency was weighing upon him.

In a sepulchral voice filled with concern, Cecil said, "Lillian said she wanted me to send a pilot from 234 home with Colonel Meecham tonight. It seems as though Lillian ain't had none in a year or two. She did say that she didn't want to do nothing immoral with one of my pilots. She just wanted to lay her hand down there be-

362

side it, and dream of those days when Bull could get it up."

For thirty seconds, both squadrons whooped and hollered in an obstreperous rally that was becoming more paleolithic in nature in direct proportion to the number of drinks consumed. Some pilots had drinks in both hands. Others were making discreet but frequent runs back to the bar to replenish empty glasses. Bull and Cecil sparred with each other, both landing pulled punches to the body, then backing off to begin the beer chugging contest.

"Are your four pilots ready, Colonel?" Colonel Causey asked.

"That is affirmative, Colonel," Bull replied.

A neutral lieutenant from an A–4 squadron quickly and efficiently snapped the caps off each bottle of beer. The two C.O.'s would begin the contest, followed by the squadron executive officers, then followed by the youngest lieutenant in each squadron. The real warhorse among the contestants drank last; this position of honor was reserved for the best chugger in the squadron.

The rules were simple. When a pilot had finished a beer, he would slam it down on the table, step quickly aside, and let the next pilot continue the chugging. Each pilot would chug six beers. The squadron that emptied their twenty-four bottles first would be declared the victors, provided that when the judge poured the residue of beer and foam from the twenty-four bottles into a shot glass, the glass did not overflow.

"If anyone pukes, the other squadron wins," Bull shouted above the din.

"If one of my boys pukes, he's gonna lick it up himself," Cecil said.

"My boys ain't gonna puke unless one of them accidentally looks at that fucked up looking face of yours," Bull teased.

Captain Brannon, lining up in his position as premiere chugger, shouted to Captain Strait, who was nursing a drink in the crowd, "Hey, Monkey Ass, you ain't drinking with the men?"

"Leave him alone, White America," Bull growled. "Strait's a specialist. He only enters hairy ass contests."

Major Reynolds, the exec, was giving last-minute instructions to Lieutenant Snell, the youngest man in 367, and fresh from flight school. He had been in the squadron less than a month and was noticeably unnerved by being thrust into competition so early in his tenure with the squadron.

"Throw your head back, close off your wind pipe, and just let the beer flow down your throat. Don't gulp, and goddammit, don't try to breathe."

"I was in a fraternity, sir," Snell said.

"Who gives a shit?" Captain Brannon observed.

"Give the kid support, Butch," Reynolds said.

"If we don't win, kid," Butch said, "I'm going to be awfully pissed."

"Colonel," Bull said to Cecil, "if any of your pilots need to go potty during this contest, some of my boys will take them to the men's room and hold their hands."

"You sure that's all they'll hold?"

"Stand by, fighter pilots," the A–4 pilot barked, as Bull and Cecil grasped their first bottle. Out of the corner of his eye, Bull saw Beasley for the first time, and the only mystery to him was how he had gone so long without at least capturing a glimpse of the man. Beasley had pulled up another table and was standing on it, shouting encouragement to the gladiators who drank for him. His face was unlined and innocent to the point of being virtuous, a Botticelli in a flight jacket. His voice carried above the general disharmony and virile hum of the squadrons. But the voice was not what had attracted Bull's attention to Beasley. It was his dress. He spied the ascot beneath the flight jacket, the cartridge belt crisscrossing his torso, the Bowie knife, and the crowning touch, a World War I Von Richthofen flying cap. Bull turned to Brannon and received a thumbs down signal.

"Start your engines," the A–4 pilot's voice resounded through the room. "Taxi down the runway, and take the fuck off."

Bull finished his first beer a full second faster than Colonel Causey, stepped quickly aside for Reynolds, who had sucked down three large swallows before his opponent's hand had touched glass. The din created by the two squadrons was deafening, and it rose in volume as each bottle was emptied and the new man stepped in to attack a full bottle of beer, his neck muscles straining as the liquid horizon in the bottle plunged downward like a thermometer thrust in cold water. Soon, foam flecked upper lips of all eight men and thin lines of beer and saliva ran like threads of light from mouths to flight jackets. The lieutenants received the loudest hosannas, for the veterans knew these contests were won and lost through the lips of these lieutenants. But 367's most puissant weapon in this frothy olympiad was the prodigious guzzling powers of Butch Brannon. An audible hiss of disbelief arose from the pilots of 234 every time he assaulted a beer.

Beasley grew more animated as it became apparent that 367 was pulling into a tenuous lead. He pointed his arms behind him like the wings of a plane and made staccato sounds like a jet on a strafing run, shooting imaginary bullets at the pilots outdrinking his comrades.

Three-sixty-seven won by a single beer. The A–4 judge poured the contents of the twenty-four bottles into a shot glass, and it did not overflow. The winning squadron broke into a chant of victory. Whistles stung the air. Hand clapping and rebel yells filled the room. With a stiff sense of formality, but with a flair for ceremony, his carriage soldierly, his demeanor proud, Cecil Causey walked up to Bull Meecham and poured the last beer over Bull's head.

On cue, Bull punched Cecil in the stomach, and drove his shoulder into his chest, knocked him over a table, and onto the floor. In that instant, lieutenants dove for lieutenants, and captains clawed their way toward captains. In the first tumult of bodies, the first instinct was to punch someone of your own rank. But soon fists were swinging without making discreet distinctions of rank, and a simple desire to throw a memorable punch and to survive the melee became the common standard. Fists flew at any visible jaw. Every unpinned arm flailed away at every visible assailant. Beer bottles broke at intervals around the room. Two captains fell across a chair, and splintered it. A man screamed in the center of the fray and tried to free his arms to pound the man biting his thigh.

In the first seconds of the brawl, Captain Brannon had pulled Beasley from the table where he was making his strafing runs and tried to strangle him with his ascot. Pilots from the other squadron were pulled into the center of their fight simply by their proximity to the maelstrom. The X.O. of 234 found himself punching the genitalia of his own wingman. A body flew over an unused bar at the back of the room, and disappeared from view. Bull and Cecil had rolled under the heaviest table in the room and watched the fight without being devoured by the fury in the storm's center. They took turns getting on top of each other, trading ineffectual blows with inharmonious sound effects that made it seem as though they were fighting to the death. Once Bull was kicked in the side of the head by a free-swinging captain from 234 who had gone berserk and was teeing off on anything that moved. Bull excused himself from Cecil's embrace long enough to send the captain directly over an indistinguishable pile of flight jackets with a backhand across the mouth. Then he dove at Cecil again, both of them giggling like schoolboys.

The fight lasted less than a minute and a half. The sirens of M.P trucks heading for the club ended the brawl. Bull barked orders at 367 to straighten up quickly. Cecil shouted for the lieutenants to get brooms and for every officer to clean the blood off himself or fellow officer.

"Get rid of the broken glass, the broken chairs, and all the dead men killed by the studs of 367," Bull shouted.

"I want this room in inspection order when those M.P.'s barge through that door," Cecil snapped to his men. "And I want everyone to be at the bar enjoying a drink."

Bleeding pilots disappeared into the head. Others handled brooms and sent shards of glass leaping across the room. Two pilots were carrying a dazed pilot out the back door.

"Who's that?" Cecil asked one of the lieutenants.

"It's Captain Beasley, sir. He got cold cocked pretty good."

"He must have slipped on this waxed floor, don't you think, Colonel?" Bull asked.

"No doubt about it, Colonel, this floor is slippery as hell," Cecil replied.

When the M.P.'s arrived, they discovered the classic scene of pilots hovering around a bar, drinks in hand, enjoying the fellowship and camaraderie of their fellow officers. The M.P.'s looked for the senior officers in charge. They found them sitting at the bar smoking cigars and seemingly deep in conversation with a well built captain who was wearing an ascot, a Bowie knife, a cartridge belt, and World War I flying cap.

"Typical flyboys," the M.P.'s thought. "They're not really Marines at all. No discipline."

A group of pilots had gotten together around the piano of the bar and were singing their squadron song. Soon every member of the squadron was singing, turning toward each other with lifted glasses, their voices rising powerfully on the last four lines:

> "Stand by your glasses ready,
> Let not a tear fill your eye,
> Here's to the dead already,
> And hurrah for the next man to die."

27

BULL MEECHAM had grown fond of being in Hobie's restaurant in those early morning hours before the sun had
time to penetrate the deep winter shadows that hung between the buildings of River Street. Only in its external
serenity was life abnormal there, but Bull felt comfortable as he claimed the middle stool each weekday morning and entered into the matrix of warm wood colors,
breakfast odors, and a glass window where the history of
Ravenel could be unobtrusively charted on any given
day by the voluble fauna who formed its early morning
cadre. He had been a regular for over six months now
and as he drove toward Hobie's at 0710 hours, he knew
the ceremonies that had taken place only minutes before.
Ritual had a tang of divine law and was strictly adhered
to by the boys of Hobie's.

At seven A.M., Ed Mills entered the restaurant the
moment Hobie Rawls turned the lock. The two men
nodded to each other ceremoniously, a wordless saluta-
tion that had not changed in twenty years. Ed walked to
the first stool nearest the window and sat down. Even
though he was not carrying his mailbag, he listed to his
right as though he were. It was unwritten protocol that
neither of the men would speak until Ed had consumed
his first cup of coffee.

At five after seven Zell Posey, the one-legged lawyer,
walked through the door, the bells announcing his entry.
He walked slowly with a constrained dignity, hoping to
conceal the presence of his artificial limb. He was followed by Johnnie Voight, Cleve Goins, and Doc Ratteree
but the order of their entry was subject to caprice and
alteration. A man could set his watch by the arrival of

Ed and Zell; he could sort of set his watch by the arrival of the next three.

Bull was dressed in his dark green winter uniform when he parked his squadron car in front of the bank and walked the six storefronts to Hobie's. It was the first Tuesday in February and his breath was visible as he tightened the belt around his blouse.

"Good morning, grits," Bull roared as he entered the restaurant and proceeded to the middle stool.

"Oh, Jesus. Here comes Douglas MacArthur," Ed Mills said.

"Smiley, how you doing? Ed, your face is sunshine itself, but that's because you're just a slaphappy southern boy."

"A man used to be able to enjoy a cup of coffee in here, Hobie. Before the General came to town, that is," Ed lamented.

"Good morning, Colonel," a couple of men said.

"Hey, Doc," Johnnie Voight said, "I been having a bad cough for about a week. What expert advice do you recommend?"

"For you, a frontal lobotomy, you god-blessed dimwit."

"Doc's just sore because Willis Taylor strangled to death in Doc's office the other day. The Doc killed him by checking his throat with a tongue depressor," Hobie said pouring Bull a cup of coffee.

"By the way, you guys going to the big game tonight?" Bull asked.

"What game?" Ed Mills asked.

"Is there a game tonight?" Doc Ratteree said, smiling.

"I don't know about no game," said Hobie.

"O.K., sportsfans, don't give me a hard time. But you better get there early if I'm gonna be able to save any seats around my family. A couple of pilots from my squadron will be at the game, too."

"Does Ben think Calhoun's got a chance?" Cleve asked.

"Chance? Calhoun's gonna eat 'em alive tonight."

"Peninsula's got some tall boys coming down here tonight. Built like Marsh birds," Johnnie added.

"Zell, you ain't seen the general's boy play yet, have you?" Hobie asked.

"I've never liked spectator sports."

"He prefers opry and ballerine shows," Cleve teased. "Zell's a man of culture."

"Zell, it'd do you good to come to that game tonight," Bull said. "You're starting to get the smell of stacks about you. You've been hanging around that law office too long."

"General, you know ol' Poyster at the hardware store?" Ed Mills asked.

"He comes in here some mornings, doesn't he?" Bull said.

"Yeah, the tow-headed so-and-so with two busted A-holes for eyes. Well, he was in here the other day running his mouth about how good Peninsula was and how they were gonna beat the stuffing out of Calhoun."

"What'd you say to him, Ed?"

"I just walked up to Poyster and gave him a chance to shine his butt in front of everybody. I said, 'Poyster, I'd like to make you a little bet about that Peninsula-Calhoun game.' He looked at me kind of funny and said, 'How much you willing to bet, Mills?' I looked back at him and without blinking an eye I said, 'One hunnert damn dollars' and you can ask anyone in here if that ain't the New Testament Truth."

"It's true, O.K.," voices said.

"What'd he say then?" Bull asked.

"He put the emergency brake on that motor mouth of his."

"What would you have done if he'd taken the bet?" Bull asked.

"They'd had to clean that stool Ed was sitting on," Cleve Goins laughed.

"See you boys at the game tonight. I've got to go and keep the world safe for democracy."

"Hey, Colonel," Slinkey yelled at Bull. "Why don't we just go ahead and nuke the hell out of Moscow, Havana, and Peking? We're gonna have to do it someday anyhow, so why don't we just get on with it so we won't have to worry about it?"

370

"Sure thing, Slinkey. I'll send you three lieutenants this afternoon to get the job done. There's no sense in procrastinating any longer."

That afternoon Bull returned home early, too excited about the game with Peninsula to concentrate on the niggling administrative details that caused him more annoyance than any other element in his role as squadron commander. When he walked in the back door at four in the afternoon, he found his family sitting in the kitchen listening to Arrabelle reel off stories of her late husband. "Now Moultrie was a hardworkin' man. You go ask anyone about Moultrie Smalls and they tell you that he wouldn't run from no work. My man work many jobs during the Hoover years. Lord, we hate them Hoover years. If it wasn't for the river and the shrimp and fishes we could catch, Arrabelle wouldn't be talkin' this trash to you folks right now."

"This kitchen is filthy," Bull said sternly as he walked in the door.

"What you mean, Captain?" Arrabelle snapped from behind the stove. "The whole kitchen clean as a collection plate. What you talkin' about?"

Bull did not answer. Rather he continued into the dining room inspecting corners and wiping his index finger across furniture. When he returned to the kitchen, he sighed heavily then sat down on a chair next to the stove. "The whole house is one big garbage dump."

"Cap'n, you just talkin' stuff. You just pleasurin' yourself by runnin' your mouth about nothin'."

"Don't listen to him, Arrabelle," Mary Anne said. "Dad is so juvenile sometimes."

"It's gettin' gone time anyhow. I'll see you folks with the sun."

"Bye-bye, Arrabelle," Lillian said.

"Say hi to Toomer for me," Ben called as the maid walked out the back door. He then began to take imaginary jump shots against the kitchen wall.

"Get off your feet, jocko," Bull said to Ben, "you don't want to wear yourself out before the game. Go on upstairs and take a nap. I'll give you a yell before we have to leave for the game."

"It so happens, sugah, the whole family was having a very pleasant conversation before you barged in and insulted Arrabelle."

"That's great," Bull answered, "but you're going to continue it without Ben. I want his mind to be on the game and nothing else. I hear there are going to be college scouts all over the stands tonight."

"This helps me relax, Dad," Ben said. "Just sitting and talking."

"Who asked you? Get upstairs and into the sack on the double. I didn't ask you for a speech."

"I think you're more nervous than Ben," Lillian said after her son had left the kitchen.

"This is the big game, Lillian. The big game. If he screws up in this game, Calhoun doesn't go to the tournament and he blows his chance for a scholarship. So I want everybody in this family to cut the yappin' and start thinking about the big game."

"It's so pleasant to have you home early, darling," Lillian said lightly.

"I couldn't sleep last night I was so worried about the big game," Mary Anne said. "I woke up with a cold sweat. And fever. And three different types of cancer. And a touch of rabies."

"Where's the paper?" Bull said, ignoring his daughter. "The afternoon paper's supposed to have a big spread about the game."

"It's in the living room," his wife said. "Would you like me to make you a drink and send it in?"

"Affirmative. Now let's break up this little pow-wow and think about the big game."

"Daddy, I got an A in an English theme," Karen said. "Would you like to read it?"

"Naw, let your mother read it," he said, leaving the kitchen.

"All right children. Why don't all of you go do your homework so you'll have it done by the time we leave for the game," Lillian said, ushering Matthew and Karen toward their bedrooms. "Take this drink to your father, darling," she added, handing a silver glass to Karen.

"I finished all mine in study hall," Mary Anne said. "I think I'll go into the living room and read a book."

"I wouldn't if I were you," Lillian warned. "You've got to learn how to interpret the signals your father gives off."

"I can. He always gives off the signals of a psychopathic killer so it doesn't really make any difference how you interpret them."

"Shame on you. You're so disrespectful sometimes."

"You're always telling me I should try to get to understand my father better, that I never try to penetrate beneath his gruff exterior."

"I would choose my time with caution. Sometimes beneath that gruff exterior is a far gruffer one."

"Do you know that Dad and I have never had a single conversation in my whole life."

"That's just as much your fault as it is his, Mary Anne."

"He doesn't know me at all and I don't know him."

"Your father loves you very much, Mary Anne. He brags about how smart you are to everyone he knows."

"Does he really?" Mary Anne said with obvious delight.

"Of course he does."

"He never tells me that he thinks I'm smart."

"He probably never thinks about it," Lillian said, turning toward her daughter and appraising her with arctically critical eyes. Even the temperature of her voice plunged when she said, "Why don't you go upstairs and find something real pretty and lacy to wear to the game tonight?"

"I don't want to wear anything real pretty and lacy to the game. I prefer to wear something real ugly and frumpy instead."

"I didn't want to tell you this, Mary Anne. But you've backed me against a wall," Lillian said, her voice becoming a whisper trembling with the promise of conspiracy. Lillian loved conspiracy, whether real or imagined. "Your brother, Ben, came to me yesterday and asked me if I'd talk to you about how you're dressing."

"Ben did?" Mary Anne asked. Lines of doubt radiated from her narrowed eyes as she watched her mother.

"Yes."

"Why didn't he talk to me?"

"He didn't want to hurt your feelings. But he did tell me that it embarrassed him to see you going to school and to basketball games so sloppy looking. He thinks you ought to have a little more pride than that. He says—and this is strictly between us boys, Mary Anne, because he made me swear not to tell you—he says that he is humiliated beyond words to see you walk into the gymnasium dressed in those baggy, wrinkled clothes you seem so fond of."

"Ben didn't say that, Mama. That's you talking."

"Ben mentioned it to me yesterday."

"No, he didn't. Ben wouldn't care if I went stark naked. You see, I know Ben a lot better than you do. I even know you better than you do. And Ben wouldn't say that. But you would and just did."

"Well, he's thinking it, Miss Smarty Pants. You had better believe he's thinking it. If you have so little self-pride that you can't put on a little makeup and wear clothes that fit properly, then it's no wonder that your brothers and sister are growing ashamed of you. When I was growing up a young girl wouldn't be caught dead walking out her front door looking the way you do. Now, you've got a fairly nice figure, Mary Anne, and instead of wearing clothes to show your figure off, you wear clothes to hide it. And that's unnatural. That's why I'm so afraid you'll never catch a man worth a salt."

"I hope I never catch a man like you caught."

"You have to be so smart and so superior and so cute. Remember that it was me who gave you your love of reading and literature. But I never taught you to flaunt the fact that you are smart and can use words to hurt people. Men find that very unattractive."

"Creep Marines find that very unattractive."

"Sugah, I know men. A man's a man and any man who isn't should go out with the morning trash. A woman has one job. To be adorable. Everything else is just icing. Dressing nice to catch a man's eye is part of the game."

"I don't like creep boys looking at me."

"That's what every woman wants," Lillian said harshly, "or should want."

"Not me. It's too sicko-sexual for me."

"Well, if I were you, and I'm certainly not, I'd dress nice for Ben's sake if for nothing else. He's very upset."

"I thought we decided Ben never said anything, Mama."

"Get out of this kitchen this instant!" Lillian ordered. "I don't even know why I waste my time trying to teach you how to be a woman. Karen wants to put her best foot forward. She takes advice."

Mary Anne began to move toward the living room. She stopped, adjusted her glasses, and turned back to face her mother once again. She took a deep, sad breath and said, "You like Karen better than you like me, Mama."

"That's not true," Lillian countered. "I love all of my children equally. I love you for different things but I love all of you exactly the same."

"You know why you don't like me, Mama?" Mary Anne said.

"Maybe everybody would like you better if you weren't so know-it-all. It's best for a woman not to know so much," Lillian snapped.

"The reason you don't like me is because I'm not pretty."

"That's the silliest, most asinine, most hateful thing I've heard in my whole life."

"It's true. You don't know how to relate to an ugly daughter. Ugliness disgusts you."

"Hush up, Mary Anne. Hush up before I slap you across this room. What you're saying is not true. I am not that shallow. I am not that shallow and I refuse to sit here and let you tell these terrible, vicious lies about me. It hasn't been easy. It hasn't been easy living the life I've lived. Nothing worked out like I expected it would. Nothing. I thought everything would be lovely and everyone would be sweet and charming. There is so much poison in the world. You must learn to see the beautiful in things. I have. I can look at the ugliest man in the world and see a prince. I swear I can. It's the product of good breeding."

"I look at the face of the ugliest man in the world and

feel sorry for the man," Mary Anne said, "because I know what it's like to feel ugly."

"Beauty is only skin deep."

"That's not true. It's a lot deeper than that. It's the deepest thing in the world. It's the most important thing in the world."

"You're just like your father!" Lillian spit. "You are exactly like your father. Sometimes I can't even believe you're my child. If I ever leave your father, I'm going to take the other children with me and leave you with him."

"You used to tell me that when I was little, Mama. And it scared me to death. But it doesn't bother me at all now."

"Why not?"

"Because you're not going to leave him."

"You're the most hateful child I've ever met."

"You've never liked me."

"Don't say that. Don't ever say that again. You make me feel like I'm something vile. That's the way you've always made me feel," Lillian said, beginning to cry. "Go! Go on now! Get out of my sight! I don't want to look at you or think about you! Everywhere you go you make people feel unhappy. I want to think about something happy."

"Think about the big game."

"Go in and talk to your father. Try and drive him crazy like you do me."

Mary Anne left the kitchen, her head arched proudly, yet somehow her departure had the look of retreat, of irredeemable loss. Lillian leaned against the stove and began to cry soundlessly. Then she stopped and resumed cooking the dinner with an unnatural smile on her face as she stirred the greens, and forced herself to think about happy things.

Mary Anne selected a chair directly opposite from where her father sat reading the paper. Choosing a magazine from a rack beneath her chair, she began to thumb through an old edition of *The Saturday Evening Post*. Then she began to steal glances at her father. In her heart, she was his silent ally, a fifth columnist, in Bull's inveterate assaults on the trellised escutcheons of the Old South that Lillian shoved in front of him. Lillian spoke of the Old South when Bull was in earshot as though it were a private garden deeded to her in a last heroic proclamation by the Confederate Congress. Mary Anne looked up from the magazine and made a conscious decision to have her first real conversation with her father.

"Hey, Dad, why do you love me more than any of your other children?" she began, hoping to loosen him up with humor.

"Beat it, Mary Anne. I'm reading the sports section," he said, not unkindly. The paper did not quiver as he answered her.

"You know, Dad, you love me so much. It's about like incest. Do you know in literature that some fathers have been physically attracted to their daughters? That's pretty interesting, isn't it?"

"Hey, Lillian," Bull yelled to the kitchen, lowering the paper to nose level, "your daughter's going ape crap out here. How 'bout dragging her back to the kitchen and giving her a couple of dishes to wash."

"Let's have a conversation, Dad," Mary Anne continued. "Just you and me. Father and daughter. Let's bare our souls and get to know one another."

"I don't want you to get to know me. I like being an enigma. Like a Chink."

"Let me ask you a few questions, Dad. Just a couple."

"Shoot," Bull answered, his head still hidden behind the newspaper.

"What's the saddest thing that's happened in your whole life?" she asked.

"When DiMaggio retired."

"What's your favorite book?"

"*The Baltimore Catechism.*"

"What's your favorite poem?"

"By the shores of Gitchee Gumee, by the shining big sea water."

"Who is your favorite person in history?"

"The Virgin Mary."

"Who is your second favorite?"

"That Greatest and Bravest of all fighter pilots—Bull

Meecham," Bull said; then he made a sweeping gesture of dismissal with his arm. "O.K., the game is over, Mary Anne. Go knit bootees for your first kid or something. You're starting to bother me."

"Hey, Dad?" Mary Anne asked.

"Vamoose, Sayonara, Adios, Au Revoir, and beat feet it out of here," Bull snapped.

"Am I a Meecham, Dad? Can girls be real Meechams? Girls without jump shots. Or am I a simple form of Meecham? Like in biology. Mary Anne, the one-celled Meecham. Or maybe I'm higher than that. Maybe I'm a coelenterate Meecham."

"Yeah, Mary Anne, you're a simple form of Meecham. You're a girl. Now scram. I'm starting to lose my temper. I'm gonna give you a break and just pretend you're not here. I'm not gonna listen to you or answer when you speak," Bull said, hiding himself behind newsprint once more.

Mary Anne began a slow, arduously clumsy dance that began to accelerate as she circumnavigated her father's easy chair. What began as a dramatically delusory ploy to recapture her father's attention turned into a sad tarantella of girlish desperation. She began to sing as she danced around him. "Hello, Dad," she sang, tickling beneath his chin as she circled him. "Hello, Dad, it's me, your invisible daughter. You can't see me, but I'm always here. I'm always here, Daddy-poo. I can't shoot a hook shot. Or a jump shot. I can't drive down the lane or score the winning bucket. But I'm here anyway. Yoo hoo. Dad. It's me. It's the Phantom. Yes, it's Mary Anne the phantom girl, the real ghost of the old Huger Mansion. I'm always here hovering about, unseen, unheard, and unspoken to. Dad? Dad?"

"Beat it, Mary Anne, you caught a bad case of the weird somewhere today," the face behind the newspaper ordered.

Mary Anne knelt down and hugged her father around the knees. He made no response to her gesture at all.

"Dad, I have something very important to tell you," she said, in a voice that could not stop singing. "I'm pregnant, Dad. Yes, it's true. I'm pregnant."

She stopped and waited for the newspaper to drop beneath eye level. Bull was reading an account of a Celtic-Knickerbocker game that had gone into overtime.

"You didn't hear me, Dad. I'm pregnant. I'm going to have a baby."

Rising again, Mary Anne resumed her dance around the chair. This time she pulled at her father's earlobes and tousled his hair. "I'm pregnant with your grandchild, Dad."

"Get off my back, Mary Anne. Go to the kitchen and help your mother fix dinner. All I want to do is read the goddam paper."

"I'm pregnant by a Negro, Daddy. A huge, fat-lipped, kinky-haired Negro named Rufus. Did you hear me, Daddy? Your son-in-law is a Neeeegrooow. And your little high yellow grandchild is going to come up to you and say 'Pappy.' I didn't want to tell you this, Dad, but since we're baring our souls to each other, I feel I ought to tell you he's also a pacifist. A pacifist homosexual. But you'll get to like him after a while. Dwarfs are easy to like. Especially when they're crippled. And retarded."

"Cut your yappin', Mary Anne. Go do your homework," her father said.

"I'm leaving, Dad. But I want you to know I can see through your gruffness," she said, reaching the first stair. She had stopped her song. "I can see right through it. And I want you to know that I understand. Just me. Just me."

As Ben awaited his father's call to dinner, he lay on his back, shooting a basketball toward the ceiling of his room over and over again. It was the wrist snap he worried about most before a game. If the wrist failed him, then the touch had fled and he would be forced to challenge the tall men who dwelled beneath the basket with swift drives that they would quickly move to intercept. Karen opened his door softly and asked, "Can I come in, Ben?"

"Sure, Karen," Ben answered, although he was somewhat puzzled by her visit. When he saw her entering the room, Ben realized how very few times he and Karen had ever spoken to each other without another member of the family being present. "How's school going?"

"Fine. I'm the third smartest girl in the seventh grade."

"That's nice, Karen," Ben said.

"Guess what, Ben."

"I give up."

"I had my first period this week. That means I'm a woman now. That's what Mom said anyhow."

Ben resumed shooting the basketball toward the ceiling. Three times he shot, making sure his hand was parallel to the ceiling when he had followed through.

"What kind of grades did you get on your last report card, Karen? Mama told me you did real well."

"Mama says I can have babies now. You can't have a baby until you've started having your period."

"Have you talked to Mary Anne about this . . . thing?" Ben asked.

"Yes. She told me you'd want to hear all about it."

"Yeah, that's great, Karen. I'm sure glad you told me. Are you all keyed up for the big game tonight?"

"I was one of the last girls in my P.E. class to have a period. I was beginning to think I was never going to have one."

"Yeah, that must have been a big worry."

"I tried to tell Matt, but he didn't even know what I was talking about. He ran away. Matt is such a child sometimes."

"Yeah. Poor ol' Matt," Ben said, twirling the basketball on his middle finger. "Hey look, Karen, it's been a lot of fun talking to you, but I've really got to get my mind on the game."

"I'm going to be sitting with some girl friends from my school. We'll be right under the scoreboard. Will you wave to us during warmups?"

"Sure, but you'll have to watch close because I can't let Dad or Coach Spinks see me."

"These friends want to meet you after the game. Is that all right too?"

"Meet seventh grade peasants! Me? Of course, Karen. This is all so silly."

"They want me to get your autograph too."

"C'mon," Ben said, grinning.

"No, they want it."

"You're kidding. You're kidding. You've got to be kidding."

"I'm not either. They made me promise to get it before the game."

"Why do they want it? I mean, it seems ridiculous to me."

"You're the star. Here's some paper."

"This must be a great group of friends you've met here, Karen. They sound like real nice girls. What are their names?"

"Cynthia Waters and Mary Helen Epps."

"O.K.," Ben said as he wrote, speaking the words aloud. "To Cynthia, the most beautiful woman I have ever laid my eyes on, Passionately yours, Ben Meecham. And to Mary Helen, the most gorgeous creature on earth, Adoringly yours, Ben Meecham."

"Thanks, Ben. They'll love that. I'll see you at dinner."

"Before you go, Karen," Ben said rising and walking to his window, "do you know about . . . well, let me put it this way. You know. Very simply. You were talking about how you could have a baby now. Do you know about how you have babies and all that kind of stuff?"

Ben could feel a blush moving the length of his body, one that in a matter of seconds would be a full five feet, ten inches tall. It was the first time that he ever thought a blush could have a measurable, quantitative dimension.

"Sure, Ben," Karen said simply. "You have sexual intercourse with a man."

"Yep. Well, it's been great talking to you, Karen, and I'll see you later on. It really has been great talking to you."

"Bye, Ben."

"Oh, Karen," Ben called.

"Yes."

"Congratulations on being a woman."

"Isn't it great?" Karen said and left the room.

The late afternoon consisted of a series of chance meet-

ings, quiet conversations, and controlled showdowns all
dedicated to the belief that Ben required a matrix of
silence for his fury to build against the invaders from
Peninsula High School. When Lillian announced dinner,
she did so in a barely audible whisper to Karen who bore
the news to her father in a hushed voice, then carried it
to the other children upstairs as though she were a nun
carrying news of a friar's death. She mounted the stairs
with estimable lightness.

"Is this all I get?" Ben asked when he joined the
others at the dinner table.

"Your father makes out your menu before the game,
sugah," Lillian said.

"Toast and tea isn't enough," he argued.

"You got to have a light meal, otherwise you'll blow
your cookies all over the place," Bull explained.

"Hey, Dad, you know what I can do?" Matthew asked.

"Wait a minute, Matt, I'm talking to Ben. I think you
can drive on this team son. They play man-to-man and
that ought to be a piece of cake for you. At the beginning
of the game, drive down the middle to see what they
got. If somebody tries to stop you, lay the ball off."

"You know what I can do, Dad?" Matt repeated.

"Hold your horses, Matt. If you can get their big
man, Sanders, in foul trouble early in the game, then it
ought to be a piece of cake for the whole team. Now
that little pimp of a guard they got, Peanut Abbott," Bull
said; opening the newspaper and checking the name,
"Yeah, that's the pogue's name. Well he says in the paper
and I quote, 'Meecham will be lucky to score a point.
We're going to cut his water off good.' How do you like
them apples? Huh? I guess that gets your blood boiling. Huh? How about it?"

"Yes, sir," Ben said.

"Hey, Dad," Matt said.

"What in the hell do you want, Matt? For crying out
loud."

"If you'd just listen to him, Bull," Lillian said.

The family stared at Matt, waiting for him to speak.
Instead he rose from the kitchen table, went to the
cupboard where the canned goods were kept, and re-

sweet potato pie and bring it down to you sometime this week."

"No, ma'am. No n-need," the man answered, smiling.

"I didn't ask if I could. I told you I was going to bring you a pie and I'm going to do it. May the Lord stick pins in my eyes if I don't."

She ran into the house to put the flowers into water before the family left for the game. Ben walked up to the mule and looked up at Toomer, who watched him with eyes that were dark and kind. It embarrassed Ben when he realized he had not seen Toomer at all since basketball season had begun.

"Hey, white boy," Toomer said.

"That's a nice looking donkey you got there," Ben said.

"That isn't no d-donkey, white boy. This here is Man o' War, the f-f-fastest mule in Ravenel County."

Well that's about the ugliest mule I ever did see."

"That so. Well, I r-r-reckon you about the ugliest white b-b-boy I've ever seen too."

"How you been doin,' Toomer. I've missed seeing you," Ben said, jumping up on the wagon seat beside the black man and punching him affectionately in the arm.

"Not so b-b-bad. Been readin' in the paper you some kinda shiny s-s-stuff now. You too much stuff to go h-h-hunt up Mr. Oyster this weekend?"

"We got an away game on Friday," Ben answered.

"Weekend only last one d-day for you?"

"I'm riding around with Sammy Wertzberger on Saturday. There's church on Sunday. How about Sunday afternoon?"

"That's good."

"I wish you could come see me play tonight, Toomer."

"I ain't no fool, white b-boy. Only a crazy nigger would go struttin' in the middle of them shabby d-dressin' white folk. But show 'em some strut tonight, white boy. Wiggle when they want to see some w-w-waddle."

"I will, Toomer. Thanks for coming by."

"Now don't play too good so you think you got too much s-s-stuff to come see Toomer."

"You know better than that, Toomer."

"Get off this wagon, white boy."

"Get this damn donkey out of this yard 'fore I call the police, flower boy."

On this night, the locker room had exposed nerves. Philip Turner vomited into a janitor's sink surrounded by mops and pails. Coach Spinks put out a cigarette by dropping it into a newly opened bottle of R.C. Art the Fart combed his hair for fifteen minutes straight, sat down to await the pre-game talk, then excused himself explaining that he had forgotten to comb his hair. Ben tied and untied his shoes without a single recollection of having done so. Finally, the whole team was dressed, had listened to Coach Spinks's pre-game harangue, and now waited on that trough of suspended time when each second seems weighed down by the glistening bullion of tension.

"We got to take the challenge to them," Jim Don shouted.

"Yeah," everyone agreed.

"They're ass is grass and we're the lawnmowers," Art added.

There was a commotion at the locker room door and the manager's voice was raised in a shrill, feckless protest. "Ben, Ben, where are you, Ben?" a voice boomed.

Mortified and more than slightly irritated, Ben answered, "Back here, Dad."

Colonel Meecham walked into the alcove red-faced, expansive, and massive. It was the first time that Ben had noticed that his father had not changed into his civilian clothes since he had gotten home. Bull walked past several players to get to his son.

"There are college scouts from four different colleges in the stands tonight. Four colleges! You gotta gun it up tonight, boy. Those guys are looking for a scorer."

"Dad would you go back and sit with Mom for god's sakes. We're trying to get ready for a game."

"I'm trying to get you fired up, Ben. There's people come to watch you, son. You ought to go for about forty big ones tonight," Colonel Meecham said, unable to contain his ecstasy.

"We'll help Ben get it tonight, Colonel," Pinkie said.

"Attaboy, Pinkie. I want all you boys to shine tonight. The largest crowd in the history of the school is out there screaming their lungs out. The cheerleaders are so happy they're . . . they're . . . they're jumping through their own assholes."

Ben could smell the heavy presence of bourbon on his father's breath. Beneath the flight jacket he could detect the slim outline of his father's silver flask. Since it was not a Friday and there was no happy hour, he had forgotten to keep track of how much liquor his father had consumed. But all the signs were there. Bull Meecham was approaching that prime meridian of inebriation that his wife, his sons, and his daughters, based on a grievously embattled history, had come to fear.

"I'll see you later, Dad," Ben said.

"These boys think they're tough," Bull said, slurring the last two words. "Bust 'em in the chops the first play of the game, sportsfans, and they'll know you mean business. You've got to draw first blood against a bunch of hogs like this. If you show weakness or fear, they'll chew you a new bellybutton."

"Thanks, Dad. See you later," Ben said, leading his father by the arm toward the door.

Bull whispered to Ben when they reached the door, "I want you to look like a goddam gatling gun, you're shooting so much."

"O.K., Dad. O.K. Go sit with Mama."

"A great ballplayer always has his best games against the best teams."

"I will, Dad. I promise."

When Ben returned the other players grinned at his obvious discomfiture at his father's intrusion into the forbidden realm of the pre-game locker room. Coach Spinks would not have been amused.

"I'm sorry, gang. Dad gets excited at times like this."

"You think your dad's excited," Art said. "Mine ain't taken a shit in three days."

"Neither have I," said Pinkie.

"Boy, your dad's really tanked up," Jim Don said.

"No, he isn't, Jim Don. He's just excited."

"You don't think I know a drunk when I see one," Jim Don countered.

"Shut up, Jim Don," Pinkie said fiercely. "Don't talk like that about someone's old man."

There was a period of silence. Two of the players went to wash their mouths out. Ben leaned over to Pinkie and asked, "Where's your daddy, Pinkie? I haven't seen him at any of the games. Is he here tonight?"

The silence deepened. Ben felt immediately that the question was lanced with pain.

"He was cut in half by a skier's boat two summers ago," Pinkie said.

"God, I'm sorry, Pinkie."

"You didn't know," Pinkie said.

In the moments that followed Ben forgot about the game and concentrated instead on his uncanny instinct, his intuitive genius for asking the wrong question. This ability normally asserted itself when he was nervous or did not know what to say or felt it was a social obligation to say something. Throughout Ben's life, he could walk up to a complete stranger, ask him a single question, and hit with remarkable accuracy the raw nerve. "Did you sprain your ankle?" Ben would ask. "No, I limp because I had polio as a child," the stranger would reply. "Where is your mother?" Ben would ask. "She died of cancer last night," would come the reply. The nadir of his distinguished career in asking the wrong question had come when he was playing second base in pony league and a boy walked up to bat who clearly had not been trained with an eye for style or classicism. Ben yelled out in one of those rare yet complete moments of silence, a doldrum among the spectators, "Hey, why doesn't someone teach that kid how to bat!" Ben heard the gasp from the crowd and in one of those desperate moments of prescience before the trial by fire begins, he knew that the dragon of hurt was hissing out of an empty, grief-ruled place from the boy at home plate. "Why don't you come here and teach me how to bat, wise guy?" the boy said, holding up the stump of his left hand, the bone encased in skin and tapering to a thin, vulnerable cone. The moment had become a metaphor and Ben had found something pure

388

and universal in that moment of exposure, and he carried the image of that stump in his mind as though it were a talisman that could ward off future errors of judgment. But it had not worked that way. If there was an affliction, if there were a secret that caused great pain, if there was something hidden behind a smile or protected by a grimace, then Ben could bring it to the surface with an innocent, ill-conceived question. And he had an instinct for preciseness. He could ask the absolutely worst question at the most inopportune moment. "Why didn't you and Mr. Smith ever have any children?" Ben would ask. "We did," would come the answer from a voice of immeasurable cold, "they all died in a fire." There was never a proper or adequate response to these answers. One merely withered.

The buzzer went off ending the girls' game and the voice of the manager squealed out for the team to take the court. Then there was movement and the borning once more of the transcendent fraternity that comes between athletes in the unseen moments when they move together toward the lights of an arena and the waiting crowd. Suddenly bursting into light and the vision of eight hundred eyes that had gathered to see them prevail, they spread out thoughtlessly, the layup lines forming without conscience, animals of habit. And each boy according to his own capacity drank in the applause that poured over his entrance. Ben bathed in the unction of his shouted name.

Bull and Lillian occupied the fourth row above the scorer's table. They sat with Paige and Virgil Hedgepath and several other pilots from the squadron. Behind them sat Ed Mills, Cleve Goins, Hobie Rawls, Johnnie Voight, Dr. Ratteree, and Zell Posey. Sighting Karen with her two friends to the right and beneath the scoreboard, Ben waved to them and winked as he retrieved a loose ball. He could not find Matt and Mary Anne in the crowd.

At the jump center in the middle of the court, a short, stocky, fat-faced boy came up to Ben, grabbed him by the belt, and growled at him, "You aren't going to score a single goddam point tonight, Meecham, 'cause I'm gonna be on you like stink on shit."

"I ain't Roselle, Peanut," Ben answered.

"What?"

Peninsula was the tallest team that Ravenel had encountered all year. Their center, Sanders, was six feet five inches tall and both their forwards were over six three. Art looked undernourished and lost as he stepped into the circle to jump ball with Sanders.

Sanders tipped the ball to Peanut Abbott as he had done to begin every game in the whole season. Only this time Ben anticipated where Sanders would tip it, left his position as soon as the centers were airborne, reached the spot where the ball landed at precisely the same moment as Abbott, gained control of the ball, and broke for the bucket. Abbott crabbed along beside him until Ben whirled with a reverse dribble, sprinted for the basket, and laid up the first two points of the game. The crowd erupted in a deep, sinewy exaltation of triumph.

Peanut took the ball out in confusion, angry at himself, and anxious to repair the damage and erase the embarrassment. Bull saw Ben set up a trick that Bull had taught his son. Ben pretended to start back to the other end of the court for defense, but his eye was on the rattled guard, Abbott, who stepped out of bounds quickly and looked for the other guard who motioned for the ball near the foul line. The flow of every man on the court was heading for the opposite end of the court until the ball left Abbott's fingers and Ben cut back between the two guards, intercepted the ball cleanly, and in a single dribble scored his second layup in less than twelve seconds.

Then the game assumed a dimension of reality. Sanders began to work the pivot with a grace and instinct that was a pleasure to watch. There was an artistry to his shots and a lordliness to his moves. He scored on three straight turn around jump shots as the pace of the game quickened. Jim Don scored on a tap in. Abbott scored on a layup when Ben failed to get back on defense. "Defense, Meecham. You bum," he heard his father scream. Philip scored on a long jump shot from the side. Sanders faked Art, wheeled around him, and soared up high for a dunk shot. Coming down court, Ben got by Abbott and drove straight at Sanders, who moved up to stuff the layup. Ben slid the ball off to Art, who scored an unmolested layup.

Toward the end of the quarter, Ben stole two passes from the same forward and drove the length of the court to score. On both shots he was fouled by Peanut Abbott. Both shots were answered immediately by two arching, swooping hook shots by Sanders.

In the middle of the second quarter, Ben had a spurt where he played the game better than he had ever played it in his life, played it better than he was capable of playing it. He scored on three savage drives to the basket and on two of the drives he was fouled by Sanders. Then he hit on two jump shots and led two successive fast breaks where he shuffled bounce passes to Philip and Art filling the lanes. To end the half, he took the ball away from Abbott on the dribble and scored on an ostentatious reverse layup after a behind-the-back dribble that had more relationship to the big top than it did to basketball.

But no matter what Ben did, his efforts were matched by the unmeretricious competence of Wyatt Sanders. He was simply as good as he had to be.

Several times he slapped Ben on the fanny as Ben passed him going to the bench between quarters or during time outs. It was a meaningful slap and Ben understood the message it conveyed. There were times during athletic contests when two of the athletes became aware that the true contest was between them and that their team would win or lose according to the quality of their performance. When Ben's eyes met Sanders' eyes, something of worth was transferred between them. The relationship grew stronger as the game wore on and the sense of competition between them intensified. By the fury with which they strove to win, they were honoring each other and celebrating each other's gifts. It was a feeling, a tenderness in the sweetly savage brotherhood of athletics that came very seldom.

By half time Ben had scored twenty-one points and

was in the middle of the best game of his life. Sanders had scored sixteen points and was in the middle of one of his best. Calhoun trailed Peninsula by six points. But Sanders had picked up his third foul while trying to intercept a drive by Ben at the end of the half.

The strategy derived by Coach Spinks during intermission was sound and surprisingly so. He wanted Ben to get the ball and drive straight toward Sanders, trying to draw the fourth and fifth fouls. Without Sanders, Spinks felt that the Peninsula team would be demoralized beyond redemption. The key was to eliminate Sanders as soon as possible in the third quarter.

At center court for the second half tip-off, Abbott once more seized Ben's belt and said, "You aren't gonna score a goddam point this second half, Meecham."

"C'mon, get off it, Abbott. I told you I wasn't Rosie Roselle."

"You wait and see if you score."

Sanders easily controlled the jump ball, tapping it to the red-headed guard who played opposite Abbott. The guard dribbled it into his own back court as he watched for Sanders who was maneuvering to get free underneath. When Sanders broke for the foul line, the guard lofted a lazy pass in the middle. Jim Don anticipated the pass and intercepted it on the run. Ben broke for the far basket. Jim Don's pass was long and Ben had to sprint for it. As he caught the ball, he had to shoot at the exact same instant. He threw the ball up softly, off balance as he headed out of bounds. The ball rolled around the rim and dropped out. Ben tried to regain his balance before he slammed into the folding chairs and spectators sitting at his end of the court. He gained control of himself by falling against a man and a woman, bracing his fall against their shoulders. At the split second he was turning around Peanut Abbott cracked into the back of Ben's head, his forearm shivering against the base of the brain. Ben flew over two rows of folding chairs and fell on top of a small girl who screamed until a host of arms lifted Ben out of the wreckage and off the girl.

Ben's vision had blurred and he had difficulty fixing his eye on a single point in the mayhem that had unleashed itself. One of the referees was keeping Jim Don from swinging at Peanut Abbott. The noise was deafening. As Ben tried to clear his head he had one crystal clear vision: his father coming out of the stands, massive, enraged, and shouting words that Ben could not hear. Then Bull was over him screaming, screaming, screaming, "You better get that little bastard or you don't come home tonight! I'll beat your ass if you don't get that little bastard! You hear me, boy?"

And Ben nodded yes. Yes. And the referee signaled that Ben was to shoot two foul shots for an intentional foul. He heard a warning being issued to Peanut Abbott and he felt the hands of his teammates grasping his shoulders and asking him if he was all right. Yes. Yes. He answered through a haze that was alternately too much light and too much darkness. Coach Spinks called time out to let tempers cool and let Ben collect himself. Bull followed Ben to the huddle, "You get him. I'm gonna stay down here on this floor till you put him on the deck." Then, Ben tasted the water that the manager held in a ladle. He poured it over his head. He splashed it against his face, closed his eyes, and jerked his head back when the ammonia capsule was placed by his nostril. "You all right, poot?" Coach Spinks said. "Yes. I'm all right." "Get that little pimp," he heard his father cry out near the huddle of players, "or I'm gonna get you."

He went to the foul line, his head clearing slowly. He missed the first shot. He missed the second one. Looking to the sidelines, he saw his father keeping step with him, following him down the court in front of the first row of spectators. His face was savagely contorted. "Get him. Get him," his father chanted. Ben intercepted a pass intended for Abbott, beat him down court, and laid the ball in. Bull had run with him, sprinted along the sidelines along with him, stalking him, stalking his son. "You'd better get him, goddammit, or don't come home." His father's voice entered Ben's ear like an icepick. There was not another voice he could hear in the crowd of four hundred. It was the voice of his besieged youth. The voice that had screamed out the death of enemy pilots in the Pacific. The voice that had swept down on retreating battalions crossing the Naktong River in Korea. The voice that could order a squadron from the heavens to set fire to Havana or to decimate a Russian fleet or to start a world war. But most of all, as Ben watched the violent figure of his father pacing the sidelines, it was a voice that Ben knew he would obey, that he was programed to obey, a voice that he dared not disobey. Sanders scored. Pinkie took the ball out of bounds and passed it to Ben. "Get him, son." "Yes, sir," Ben said in reflex as he brought the ball up the court, eyes pinned on that rodent face of his enemy. As he neared Peanut, Ben suddenly flipped the ball directly in Peanut's hands, stepped aside, and with a flourish of his arm offered Peanut Abbott the whole court and an easy layup. Surprised, Peanut hesitated, then broke for his basket, not noticing that Ben trailed him and not noticing that a flight jacketed figure trailed Ben on the sidelines. As he reached the foul line, Peanut slowed up, wanting to make sure he did not blow the sure layup. When he left his feet, Ben Meecham was there. Timing Abbott's leap perfectly, Ben's shoulder cut the boy's feet from under him when Abbott was at the apex of his jump. Abbott somersaulted, wildly, dangerously out of control. He came down hard, his arm hitting the wooden floor first, then his head. The crack of a broken bone shot through the gymnasium. Ben was tackled by one of the forwards who flailed at him with both his fists and his feet. Whistles blew, both benches emptied, coaches sprinted to the floor, Mr. Dacus wrestled Jim Don Cooper to the court, and the man on the P.A. system pleaded for the fans to remain in their seats. Pinkie and Philip had mounted the back of the forward who had tackled Ben.

When order was restored somewhat, the referees called time out while Dr. Ratteree examined the injuries sustained by Peanut Abbott. One of the referees came to the Calhoun huddle, pointed to Ben, and said, "Number thirteen, you're out of the game. Go to the shower room. Coach Spinks, there will be a report made to the high school commission about this boy." Ben trotted down the sidelines toward the locker room. Before he could enter the doorway, his father caught him and clapped him on the back again and again. "That's my boy. That's playing like you were a Chicago boy. That's how a Chicago boy would do it. And don't think those scouts weren't impressed. They're looking for a guy with a killer instinct. That's showing guts, Ben. I'm proud of you, son." And then desperately, Ben plunged through the double doors, away from the voice of the crowd, into the anonymity of the dressing room where he sat on the wooden bench before his locker and cried out of shame.

For two minutes he wept, his arms folded on his thighs, his head buried in his arms. He did not hear Mr. Dacus enter the locker room nor see him sit down against the cinderblock wall. Finally, Mr. Dacus spoke to Ben. "How's the little pissant?"

"I've never felt worse in my whole life," Ben choked out between sobs.

"Abbott's got a broken arm. I bet he feels worse than you do."

"I'm sorry, Mr. D. Oh God, I am so sorry."

"He looked like he was hurting pretty bad. The bone was sticking through the flesh when we put him in the police car with Doc Ratteree to go down to the hospital. You messed up bad, pissant."

"Yes, sir. I know."

"What do you think I ought to do about it?"

"I don't know, sir."

"Well help me think about it, Ben. Calhoun is my high school. I'm damn proud of it and damn proud of the kids that attend it. It's well thought of all over the state because of the accomplishments of these kids. They've worked hard to make the image of Calhoun High respectable and worthy of that respect. Then along comes some sorry damn pissant who doesn't have the guts to tell his father to go take a flying jump when that father is just about as wrong as a father can possibly be. So because he has no guts, he breaks a boy's arm in the most unsportsmanlike display I have ever witnessed in my whole life. What you did, Ben, was low, base, cowardly, and unforgivable."

"Yes, sir. I know," Ben said.

"What do you think I ought to do about it?"

"Take me outside and kill me," Ben answered.

"No, pissant. I'm not going to do that. But you are never going to participate in another varsity sport at Calhoun High School. You have four games left in the basketball season. You will not be playing in any of them, nor will you be allowed to play baseball this spring. Do you think that's fair?"

"Yes, sir."

"I don't. I don't think that's a fair exchange for a broken arm. I think you're getting the best end of the deal."

"Yes, sir."

"I want to extract as much bad feeling as I can from you, Ben. Most of all, I wanted you to know how disappointed I am in you personally and how what you did tonight disgusts me as badly as anything one of my students has ever done. Take the uniform off. I don't want to see a Calhoun uniform even near you," Mr. Dacus said, walking slowly toward the door. Before he went back to watch the final quarter he turned to Ben and said, "See you in school, pissant. It isn't the end of the world."

That night in bed, Ben heard his mother tiptoe in the room and sit down on his bed. He braced himself for one of Lillian's cold, puissant lectures to enfilade the dispirited citadel of his self-respect. He waited for her anger to come in fusillades of outraged motherhood, smothering southern platitudes, and Catholic theology. Her stare impaled him through the dark. But she said nothing. She merely groped until she found his hand. Then she just held it. Nothing more.

28

On the Saturday after the Peninsula game, Sammy Wertzberger drove up in front of the Meecham house driving a 1959 Fleetwood Cadillac. He honked his horn twice and waited until Ben rushed through the front door, bounded down the stairs, and entered the passenger side of the car. The Big APE radio from Jacksonville was turned to such a high volume that Ben did not hear the first three sentences Sammy spoke to him after he was in the car. Finally, Ben leaned over and turned the volume knob.

"I said Dad let me have the big Jew canoe tonight," Sammy said, cackling his high-pitched laugh.

"Why do you call it that, Sammy?"

"So I can beat the Christians to the punch. They also call this car 'Sammy's Jewish Submarine.' "

"It must be tough being a child of Israel."

"No tougher than being a child of Rome. Everyone in this town thinks you're weirder than hell for that shit you do at the foul line," Sammy said, turning down River Street and cruising past the storefronts, the image of the Cadillac sliding dream-like past the illuminated plate glass windows.

"That's not shit. That's the sign of the cross."

"Yeah. Shit. Why do you do that stuff anyway?"

"If I make the shot, Sammy, then there's a God. If I miss it, then there's not."

"That makes sense to me. Hey, what do you want to do tonight, Ben? Go to the Shack?"

"Naw. The whole team will be there. I feel like Cain when I'm around those guys now," Ben said as the car turned a corner on Rutledge Street and passed the

397

small white framed grocery store that Sammy's father owned. "What does your daddy do anyway, Sammy? Does he make a living off that store?"

"No, Ben, that's just a front. I was going to tell you sooner or later, but you've forced my hand. That store's just a front. He makes his real cash dough screwing Saint Bernards for stag movies. I wish he would screw Red Pettus in a stag movie."

"Red giving you some more trouble?"

"Not real trouble. He just says things every time I see him."

"Why don't you just punch him once or twice?"

"There's one thing you seem to have forgotten about Sammy Wertzberger, Marine brat, and it's very important in understanding the nature of that great and noble man. Sammy Wertzberger is one of the greatest cowards that ever lived. Sammy Wertzberger doesn't fight unless he's fighting blind or crippled people. Or real small women."

"Red's just a bully. You've got to stand up to him sometime."

"Oh no. That's where you're wrong. I can sit and whimper and fall to my knees and beg for mercy for my whole lifetime. That's the nature of a true coward. I've made a very careful study of myself and from every conceivable angle, I'm a total chicken shit. Oh, I forgot to tell you, Ben," Sammy said, slowing the car down and looking over the back seat. "Look on the floor and bring it up here with us."

Ben pulled a 12-gauge double barreled shotgun off the floorboards of the back seat. "Is it loaded?" Ben said, handling the weapon with caution. "What did you bring this thing for?"

"It's not loaded. I brought it because the next time I run with the bulls at Pamplona I'm gonna take this baby with me. If one of those big bastards gets near me I'm gonna make about ten thousand cheeseburgers out of him," Sammy shouted, gripped by one of the Hemingway fantasies which came to him, Ben had noticed, with more and more frequency. "Now, I thought since neither of us have dates tonight . . ."

"Yeah, it's very rare when you and I don't have dates."

"But since this does happen to be one of those rare occasions when we are not seducing fair young maidens, I think we ought to head for the beach and have a little fun with those young lovers parked in the moonlight. You know, sneak up on couples making out and shoot the shotgun off right beside their car."

"What if the guy jumps out and beats hell out of us?"

"Who's gonna jump out and beat the hell out of a guy holding a shotgun, man? Besides, we'll just shoot it and run our nuts off."

"O.K., but you do the shooting and I'll do the running."

They were on the beach highway now, passing long stretches of tomato and cucumber fields that quilted both sides of the road, passing the lights of the blue-shuttered shacks of the barrier-island blacks, passing over the small bridges that spanned the salt creeks that fingered deep into the marsh, passing black men walking the shoulder of the highway, black churches, and a hundred other reminders that once you left the town of Ravenel and crossed the waters toward the barrier islands, you had entered the land of the freed slave, the gullah black, and it was a very different land from the one you had just left. Ben had asked Arrabelle where the voodoo people lived in Ravenel County and she had replied, "Every time you white folk go to the beach to color yourself up, you pass by some haint-fearin' people. And I'll tell you this, a bad spirit ain't gonna enter no house which done got the shutters painted blue. Now I just know that be a fact." The Cadillac passed small, smoke-filled clubs with loud music and black people spilling out of open doors and sometimes overflowing into the highway.

"Hey, Ben," Sammy said after they had passed several minutes in silence.

"Yeah, Sammy?"

"Do you realize that there are guys out there gettin' it right now. I mean gettin' it while we're just riding around talking about it."

"We're not talking about it."

"Well, I want to start talking about it. Here's what I would like to be doing right now instead of being with you. No offense, Ben, buddy-roo. No, I'd like to be biting Mary Lou Scoggins on her left thigh. And then I'd like to take my whole head and put it between Olive Tatum's boobs and bounce them back and forth between my nose. But mostly, I'd like to walk up to Cindy White in in the hall at school, bite her on her delicious little fanny and hang on for dear life as she raced around the hall trying to shake me off. By the way, Ben, you know who wants to date me?"

"Frankenstein's daughter."

"Very funny. But Emma Lee Givens has put out the word that she's hot for Sammy's bod."

"That's really nice, Sammy," Ben said. "She's just about the nicest girl at Calhoun High. And you know she's one of the smartest."

"Yeah, I heard she liked me from Mr. Loring. He just hinted around a bit and I got the message. Teachers love to be matchmakers. I guess Emma Lee just drooled over my gorgeous body in silence all these years and finally could bear it no longer. She knew she had to make a move fast because she was just one of ten thousand girls who were making plans to sample the bodily wares of that stud, Sammy Wertzberger. Sammy Wertzberger," he repeated. "Do you think my name sounds funny, Ben?" he asked.

"What?"

"Tell me the truth. Do you think my name, Sammy Wertzberger, sounds funny?"

"No, it sounds O.K."

"You're lying."

"No, I'm not. I don't think it sounds funny."

"All right. We'll conduct a test. You pretend that you're me and you're meeting someone for the first time. Now walk up to this imaginary person and introduce yourself without laughing."

"Hello," Ben said seriously, "my name is Sammy Wertzberger." Then he giggled.

"See, it's impossible. It's impossible to say my name

without laughing. I can't even do it. That's why I always wanted to change my name to something like Rock Troy," Sammy said. "That sounds good."

They heard breakers crashing against the beach and the air was heavy with salt and spray. There were several cars parked along the beach road with couples welded together in clenched silhouettes.

"I want to find someone who's parking alone. Someone who really means business. I know the best spot in Ravenel County. Not many people know about it. Only the real lady-killers like myself."

Sammy drove along the road that paralleled the beach for more than a mile. Then the road took a slight turn inland at the point where private homes and private property began and the state beach ended. Turning out the lights of his car, Sammy grabbed the shotgun, loaded two shells in the barrels, and motioned for Ben to follow him quietly. Soon, they were creeping down an infrequently traveled dirt road lined with palmettos and mossy live oaks. It was a cold, soundless night, black as obsidian, and Ben could only follow the sound of Sammy's insistent plunge toward the ocean. He had lost sight of Sammy as soon as they left the main road.

There was a long curve in the road that led them to an arch of trees that covered the dirt road before it died in a series of low sand dunes near the beach. Parked beneath the trees was a car. Sammy grabbed Ben by the wrist and pulled him behind a tree thirty yards away from the automobile. A radio was playing loudly from the car. But as the two boys watched from their covert looking post, the thing that held their fascination the longest was the fact that they had advanced to within striking distance of a police car.

"I'm getting out of here, Sammy," Ben whispered. "See you back at the Jew canoe."

"Wait a minute. That's Junior Palmer's prowl car. He's a deputy sheriff."

"I'm leaving, Sammy. You could end up dead shooting that shotgun off near a sheriff."

"I'm not going to shoot this shotgun. I'm going to do something far more exciting and far more dangerous."

"Let me know how it turns out when you see me Monday, you hear?"

"You don't understand, Ben," Sammy whispered, "I'm gonna sneak up there and find out who Palmer's with. He's married and has two kids."

"Sammy. You are nuts, man. Weren't you the guy who was telling me what a big coward he was just a little while ago? Anyway, that might be his wife in the car."

"Oh, c'mon, Ben, nobody goes out and parks with his wife. He's messing around with somebody. Now I'm gonna sneak behind that tree where the car is parked and see if I can't see in the window who Palmer's with. I've always wanted to get something on that son of a bitch. You hold the gun," Sammy said, slipping off commando style toward the police car. He paused after he had gone a few feet and said, "Cover me."

Keeping to the shadows and taking his time, Sammy advanced to the strategic oak and remained concealed in the shadows for over five minutes. Then Ben saw Sammy's shadow, quiet as a ferret, retreating along the same route he had advanced, but stopping behind each tree to ensure that he had not been seen.

"It's a nigger, Ben! It's a goddam nigger!"

"Jesus Christ! Let's get out of here!"

They sprinted down the dirt road, Ben taking a commanding lead with every stride, until he heard Sammy trip over a stump and somersault into an oleander bush. He went back and pulled Sammy up, holding his elbow, and they resumed their headlong flight away from the parked car.

Entering the Cadillac with equal desperation from two sides, they were soon accelerating down the beach road and back on the highway that headed from town.

"Whoopee!" Sammy said. "We just got hold of a real important piece of information. We have just seen Deputy Sheriff Palmer putting it to a colored woman, also known locally as a nigger, in the back seat of his patrol car out here in Dumfuck, Egypt. That is what I call a real important piece of information."

"I don't think it's so important. I'm just glad as hell to be getting out of there alive."

402

"Man, we got a lot of planning to do."

"Planning for what?"

"I figure Jehovah put us out there tonight for a reason, Ben. He wants us to punish Junior Palmer for his transgressions against the God of Abraham. Now while we are figuring out how to punish Deputy Palmer we must also figure out how we can profit by this little piece of good fortune. We are probably the only people in the world that know about Deputy Palmer and his weakness for dark meat."

"So what? Best we forget it right away, too."

"Forget it! Are you crazy, Ben? The way I see it, we accidentally stepped into high cotton back there. This is a real chance to pick up a little cash dough."

"You don't mean blackmail?"

"No, mercy me," Sammy said, shrinking back in mock horror. "Wash my mouth out with horse piss if I mean blackmail. We are just going to have Deputy Palmer invest in a little occupational insurance. If he wants us to keep our loud yaps closed, then he can grease the palm with a few measly little greenbacks. That way he can protect that silver badge he's so proud of."

"I don't like one word that you've been using pretty freely, Sammy. It's a pronoun that you keep throwing in. It's plural. It's the word 'we.' I want you to change this pronoun to the first person singular. Then I can enjoy this plot much more."

"Man, we're in this together, Ben. We're partners because we saw this together. I wouldn't think of making money off this without splitting it with you."

"Oh, no, I insist that you take it all for yourself. I wouldn't think of cutting you out of any earnings you make off this, especially since I don't want to end up dead or in prison."

"This is foolproof, Ben, and we can have a little fun making that jerk-off sweat for a couple of days. I was thinking of asking for twenty-five dollars, but I think I might just up the ante to a cool fifty."

"That's a lot of money, Sammy."

"We are just agents of God picked out of all humanity

to perform this unpleasant task. Do you think I like the fact that I have to do this, Ben?"

"I think you love it."

"I eat it up," Sammy cackled. "Now help me compose the letter. 'Dear Deputy Palmer, comma.' Or should I put a colon, do you think, Ben? You're the English star."

"A comma's O.K."

" 'If you want it to remain a secret that you were seen copulating with a woman of color,' Hey, how do you like that phrase? 'A woman of color,' eh, Ben?"

"You're a poet, Sammy."

" 'Bring fifty dollars and place it,' Goddam, where will we have him leave it?"

"Why don't you have him drop it off in your mailbox?"

"Oh, sure, Ben, you ever thought of getting a job as a guidance counselor?" Sammy said, driving in silence for several minutes as he considered a suitable drop-off point. "There," he finally said, pointing at the water tower that served the residents of St. Catherine's Island, the first and the largest of the sea islands separating Ravenel from the mainland. "I'll have him tape the money on the catwalk at the top of that water tower. Hell, yes, then there won't be any monkey business."

"Let me know how it turns out," Ben said.

"Hey, you'll go with me, won't you, Ben? Shoot, we won't keep the money or anything. We'll give it to charity. I know one charitable organization that plans to keep Sammy Wertzberger drunk from now until graduation night."

"I'll come along and watch, Sammy. But this whole thing is your idea."

"You'll drool when I'm folding the fifty loaves of bread into my wallet too. And then for the rest of the evening you'll probably just sit there in awe of me and my master criminal mind."

"Maybe I should get at least half of what you get, Sammy. After all, you're going to have to bribe me to keep me from telling Junior Palmer that you blackmailed him."

"Then we are partners in crime?" Sammy said.

"Partners," Ben answered.

29

THREE TIMES Sammy drove past the water tower on St. Catherine's Island to make sure that no one was lying in wait to apprehend the author of the blackmail note. Satisfied, he extinguished his headlights and hid the car in a natural cul-de-sac on the edge of the forest. Then, both he and Ben scouted the terrain beneath the water tower half expecting the tubercular, sallow face of Junior Palmer to appear as an apparition before the long climb to the catwalk could begin. But they found nothing to either arouse their suspicions or allay their fears. Sammy hauled himself up on the ladder first and began climbing slowly. Ben followed him, staying four or five rungs behind his friend. At first they ascended in a dead silence.

"I wish there was a moon tonight," Ben said.

"Are you crazy?" Sammy whispered in reply. "Then some dope would see us climbing up this thing and every cop for a hundred miles would be there when we were climbing down."

"You sure that fifty dollars is going to be up here?" Ben asked.

"It better be," Sammy answered, "or Junior Palmer's name is going to be spelled S-H-I-T by tomorrow morning. Of course it'll be here. You know he must have had a cow when he got that note."

"Where'd you leave it?"

"Under his windshield wiper. I hid and watched when he came out of the jail and read the note. There's nothing but gold at the end of this rainbow."

"God, I feel like I'm high enough already to be climbing a rainbow. This thing is a lot higher than it looks from the ground."

Both Ben and Sammy were breathing hard now. Ben felt a slight quivering in his thighs as though sinew had turned to gelatin; his knees felt vulnerable, even collapsible, the higher up the ladder he went. His wrists began to ache from grasping each rung too tightly. His hands were slick and untrustworthy. Looking down and to his left, he saw Ravenel shimmering across the river, the white yachts gleaming under marina lights, and shrimp boats ghostly below their nets. The higher he climbed, the more subject to delusion Ben became. He was teased only slightly by the phantoms of vertigo, but slightly nevertheless. All was delusory. The steel ladder was made of paper, of silk, of quicksilver, of air. Sammy would disappear. The ladder would climb toward infinitude. Ben would feel himself falling. Then he would stop climbing and look up at Sammy. He would set his bearings on Sammy's behind like a pilot would fix his eyes on the horizon. Then he could resume climbing.

"Why couldn't you have had him tape the money to the bottom of the railroad trestle or leave it beneath the bridge, Sammy?" Ben said, anxious to begin a dialogue again.

"No challenge in that. This was the most romantic place I could think of."

"If you wanted a challenge, you could have had him tape it on Coach Spinks's left testicle," Ben said.

"Now there's a challenge," Sammy agreed.

"How was your date with Emma Lee last night?" Ben asked. "You haven't told me a thing about it."

"I think it's love, son. I think she's absolutely out of her mind in love with that suave, latin Romeo, Sammy Wertzberger."

"Well, she's only human. Even if she is a preacher's daughter."

"She talked about books the whole night. I felt like I was out with you and Mary Anne. But later on the old mover sprang into action. She was inexperienced, but Casanova was very gentle."

"Did you kiss her good night?"

"Kiss her good night! Are you kidding? Sometimes you are such an innocent, Ben. No I didn't kiss her good night.

But it will all come in good time. You don't use the Bohemian Mountain Approach on a girl like Emma Lee."

"God, it's high up here. I can see the runway at the goddam air station."

"We're almost to the top," Sammy's voice said above him. "Almost to the end of the rain . . ." Then Sammy's voice stopped abruptly. And Sammy stopped.

"What's wrong, Sammy?" Ben asked. "Is something wrong?"

A boy with a shotgun stuck against Sammy's throat said, "Yeah, boy. Something's bad wrong." Ben recognized the voice. It belonged to Red Pettus.

Far below him, Ben saw the revolving light of a police car spinning in a slow, malevolent circle.

The county jail was a windowless, antiquated structure that had served as an armory in the decade before the Civil War. It was located on the edge of Paradise, backing up against Joe Louis Lane, a dirt path that snaked through the back alleys of the black community. Inside the jail, Ben and Sammy could hear the semi-sweet, candently primitive rhythms of jukebox blues diffusing out of unseen nightclubs. The music, the anthem of Saturday night debauch, filtered to them through the jail stones that now enveloped them, isolated them with Junior Palmer.

They stood in a bare room, handcuffed together, as Palmer unloaded shells from his automatic shotgun. He had paid Red Pettus ten dollars and sent him home as soon as the patrol car had pulled within sight of the jail. The only thing Sammy had been able to say to Ben since their capture was that "Red and Junior are third cousins." Ben had said, "How many million cousins does Red have?" but the opportunity for speech had died a swift death.

Now Junior Palmer stared at the two boys, a reptilian coldness in his eyes that reminded Ben of his mother's warnings. She had always told him to beware the law behind closed doors, the yellow-toothed men behind silver badges who had been betrayed by their chromosomes and their birth. She would talk of power as a yeast that could activate a malevolence that no force on earth could overcome once it had begun. Beware the feral, washed-out, hare-lipped genes that sculpted the occasional unfathomable barbarisms of the poor white South. Beware of the men I have protected you from knowing, she had said. And would say again, Ben knew, after this night.

"You boys got me between a stone and a hard place," Palmer said, his voice a whine.

"It was just a joke, Junior," Sammy said. "Honest, it was just a joke."

"Then how come I don't see nothin' funny in it, Sammy? How come I ain't fuckin' laughin' one tiny little bit."

"O.K., it was a lousy joke," Sammy said.

"Now, Sammy, I got me a big problem. Your daddy's been in this town too long and knows too many people and might just run his mouth in too many of the wrong places. You understand me? I can't afford nobody asking no questions about tonight because even though you boys falsely accused me of doin' somethin' I would never do, just the mention of this kind of trash can kill a man in this town. This town's all mouth sometime. You boys see what I mean?"

"Yes, sir," they both said.

"Now, what did you boys see out there at the beach?"

"Nothing; we didn't see a thing, Junior," Sammy said.

"Nothing, sir," Ben answered.

"Now what makes you think I was spending time with some blue-gummed nigger girl?"

"It must have been my imagination, Junior," Sammy said.

Walking slowly around the table, Junior lit himself a cigarette, inhaled deeply, blew smoke into Sammy's face, then drove a fist into the boy's solar plexus. Sammy went to his knees, emitting desperate sounds of strangulation as he tried to catch his breath.

"Don't you ever call me 'Junior,' Jew. You call me 'Mr. Deputy.' Or you call me 'sir' but don't you ever call me by my name again," he hissed, walking back toward the desk where he sat down and threw a leg over the arm of his chair. "Now my big problem, the way I figure it, is this. I can only keep one of you boys because I'll have to answer too many questions if I keep both of you in here. Now Red don't know nothin' because I didn't tell him nothin'. The only people in the world that knows about this alleged incident is us three. Or have you told anybody else?"

"We haven't told anybody, sir," Ben said.

"Well that's mighty kind of you, Mr. ——. What's your name again, boy?"

"Meecham, sir. Ben Meecham."

"That's mighty thoughty of you, Mr. Meecham," he grinned, showing his yellow teeth. He gazed down at Sammy who had just begun breathing with some degree of regularity again.

"Sammy, I been shoppin' at your father's Jewstore for a long time, now haven't I?"

"Yes, Mr. Deputy."

"And me and Suzie still go to the Jewstore for a lot of stuff even though it's a lot cheaper at the Piggly-Wiggly, ain't that right?"

"Yes, Mr. Deputy."

"Now I don't want to hear no talk around the Jewstore of you ever being here. I don't want your daddy to know or your mama or nobody else. I don't want your daddy calling up no councilman or no sheriff asking no questions. You understand?"

"Yes, Mr. Deputy."

"Fine. That's nice. Now you get your Jew ass out this door and if I ever hear about you talking about me and a nigger at the beach, I'm gonna circumcise you just one more time for good measure. You understand?"

"Yes, Mr. Deputy."

"I mean do you understand?" Palmer screamed, coming across the table and pulling Sammy by the collar until they were nose to nose.

"Yes, Mr. Deputy. But you got to know this was all my fault. Ben just came along for the ride."

"That's too fuckin' bad. He came. Now you get out of this jail."

Unlocking the handcuffs, Palmer began pushing Sammy toward the front door of the jail. When he reached the outer office beyond the interrogation room where Ben now stood in a despairing paralysis, the deputy kicked Sammy in the buttocks and sent him sprawling down the front steps. "Not a word to anyone, Jew."

Ben was placed in a dark cell on the white man's side of the jailhouse. Black offenders resided in the east wing with the offices of the sheriff and his deputies in between. As Palmer locked the cell, Ben asked, his voice so tremulous as to make speech nearly impossible, "Why am I here, sir? Don't you have to charge me with something?"

"Red told me some bad shit about you, Marine brat. I don't know what I'm holding you for right now, but when I think about it you're gonna go along with it or I'm gonna double the number of your bellybuttons. I'll be back a little later to tell you what crime you committed."

Sitting on a small, rancid cot at the side of the cell, Ben moved his hand along the wool blanket waiting for his eyes to grow accustomed to the dark. His hand grabbed something involuntarily. Wings flared and rabidly desperate insect legs dug into Ben's palm for leverage. He threw the roach across the cell to the opposite wall where its back clicked against the cement. Other roaches scratched along the floor in wild countless battalions as Ben lifted his feet off the floor and prayed that his pilgrimage and exile among the roaches would be brief. He lay still and the smell of mildew and decay overpowered him, contributing an odor to his despair and his fear. Lying on his back, staring at a ceiling he could not see, Ben felt discarnate, a voiceless body buried accidentally, smelling the top of the coffin for the first time. For an hour he lay without moving, listening to the sprint of roaches beneath him.

Then a light went on in the anteroom leading to the cell block. There were voices, unidentifiable whispers. A key worked into lock and a huge silhouette came through the door followed by Deputy Palmer. The figure was wearing a flight jacket.

"Dad," Ben called, rushing to the front of the cell nearly crying with relief, with the single joy that he had a family and a father who would always be a buffer between Ben and the malignant men of the world. "Dad, over here."

Bull charged at Ben's cell, his hands reaching through the bars clutching at Ben's sweater. Before Ben could protest or pull back, Bull had hit him beneath the eye with a closed fist. Ben's head snapped back, but not far enough to avoid the backhand that sent him staggering backward out of control with his head cracked against the far wall. Ben slowly slid down the length of the wall. Stunned, he sat there vaguely aware that roaches were fleeing across his hand and over his body.

"If you ever hit an officer of the law again, I'll beat you so goddam bad even your mother won't want you," Bull roared.

"You better lock him up good, Sheriff, because if he gets out of here too soon I'm liable to kill him."

"I'm sorry to have to disturb you like this, Colonel," Palmer said. "But I thought a father ought to know right away. The boy didn't mean no harm. He'd just been drinking a little too much."

"If he gives you any lip while he's here, you just let me know about it," Bull said, his voice fading now. The light went out in the anteroom. Ben was alone again, his eye swelling in the dark.

The light went on again and Palmer came to Ben's cell laughing. Fear engulfed Ben, its talons sliding down the tissues of his belly. Palmer clicked on a flashlight and pointed it at Ben's eyes. The light tortured him and Ben turned his head toward the lit-up back wall where he saw the grotesque silhouette of his head. The light, his head, and the wall, he thought, as though he were an initiate or some perverted eclipse created without the consent of nature.

"I like your daddy real fine," Palmer said. "I liked the way he just slapped you down and didn't ask no embarrassing questions."

"If you think my father was rough on me tonight," Ben said, "just wait till he finds out you were lying to him. You'll be wearing that badge in your asshole."

"Now watch your mouth, sonny. I know you're mad now, but you still ain't in no position to be mouthin' off to Daddy Junior here. You're in bad trouble, boy, and you just made it worse by runnin' off at the mouth. Now, here's what happened tonight and you listen good, Marine brat. You was driving Sammy's daddy's big ol'

411

Cadillac and I pulled you over because I saw you weaving down the highway. You were liquored up pretty bad and when I told you I was gonna have to take you in, you started throwing punches at me. Does that sound good to you, boy?"

"No, sir."

Palmer tapped a large, ugly-mouthed hunting knife against the bars of the cell. Ben turned and saw the blade glint with a pale, slim hunger as Palmer twisted it back and forth in the light.

"You're getting smart with me, boy, and that's not smart. Let me tell you what I've done with this knife. I've slaughtered me a couple of hogs. Skinned a few rattlers. A few deer. But that ain't the true beauty of this here knife. When I was a young stud, before I took up with the law, I cut the nuts off a few niggers who been fuckin' with the wrong white folks. Now you ain't never heard a man scream until you hear one with a knife ripping into his balls. Them niggers would a died of bleeding to death or pain if we hadn't taken human pity on 'em and lynched 'em."

"You're gonna wish you were lynched when my father gets back to you," Ben shouted.

"Now, boy, you started making me uneasy. You can get out of this mess without no one really gettin' too riled up and no one asking too many questions. But I'm gonna have to convince you one way or the other that I picked you up for drunk driving and you took a swing at me. Now, I don't want to have to come in that cell and rubber hose you until you're so broke up inside that blood's pourin' out of every openin' you got, but if I have to . . ."

"Good evening, Junior," a voice said from the doorway.

The deputy pivoted in the direction of the doorway and shouted at a featureless face broken up in equidistant penumbras by four bars, "Who's there?"

"It's me, Junior, your old football coach."

"Mr. Dacus," Ben said.

"You come back tomorrow, Mr. Dacus. You have no business here tonight. The trusty will show you how to get out."

"I know how to get out," Mr. Dacus said in a soothing yet ironic tone. "I want to get in where you are."

"I said you ain't got no business at this jail, Dacus."

"Yes, Junior. I reckon you're right. I guess the only place I got any business at all is over at Wolf Bowditch's house. It's probably too late for this week's paper. No, what am I saying? I still got two days to get it in. You'd think I'd know that since I've been calling in school news for so many years. But Wolf might be interested to know that a married man like yourself, with a wife and two sweet kids, an usher at the Baptist Church and a deputy sheriff to boot, was out copulating with a colored woman on taxpayer's time in the taxpayer's squad car. Yep, that's what I call headline news. But you're right, Junior, I don't have any business bothering you at this time of night. I'll be seeing you around. Good night, Ben."

"Wait a goddam minute, Dacus," Palmer ordered, unlocking the outer door, then he said in a voice that had lost its power to intimidate, to bully, in a voice that was nearing hysteria, "That fuckin' lyin'-ass Jew."

Mr. Dacus walked into the cell block and faced Junior Palmer nose to nose. They stared at each other in a long, hostile silence. Finally Mr. Dacus spoke.

"Junior, did I ever tell you that you were a pussy football player?"

"I don't want no trouble with you, Dacus. But if you want trouble, I can give it to you in spades, clubs, hearts, and diamonds. Any way you want it," Palmer said, still holding the knife in his right hand.

"This town sure has a thing about knives, Junior. My suggestion to you, and it's only a suggestion and should not be interpreted as a threat, is for you to put that knife away right now."

"And what if I don't take the suggestion. What'll happen then, Dacus?"

"Oh, nothing serious, I don't think," Mr. Dacus answered. "I think the only thing that could happen of any concern to you is that I am thinking about breaking both your arms. And the funny thing about it is that I'm really getting a lot of pleasure from the thought."

"You are?" Palmer hissed.

"I am," Dacus said in a voice bled of emotion.

"You know who you're talking to, Dacus? You, sir, are talking to the law."

"And I happen to know for a fact that the law was the biggest pussy football player I ever coached. The law was afraid of human contact. The law was afraid to block, to tackle, to run, or to bump heads. I also know that the law was afraid of his football coach and still is."

"I ain't afraid of nothin', Dacus."

"I know of two things you're afraid of, Junior," Dacus said, rolling up the sleeves of his sweater, slowly, deliberately. The muscles on his forearm were defined in brutal knots. "You are afraid of these two hands, Junior. I want you to look at these two hands and study them. These are mean hands, Junior. They're much larger than yours. Much faster. These are boxer's hands. Boxer's hands are also called killer hands because they can break up a face. You've never seen me use these hands, Junior. But you've heard. You've heard about how I can use them."

"You get out of here, Dacus."

"Sure, Junior. Unlock the boy. He's not going to say anything about what he saw. You aren't going to say anything about his being here tonight. No one's going to get hurt by all this. I'll talk to Ben's father and tell him it was all a case of mistaken identity. I'm not going to say a word. Nothing happened. This affair is over. Just unlock the door, Junior."

As Palmer was releasing Ben, Mr. Dacus said, "If I ever hear you talking to a kid from my high school like I heard you talking to Ben, I am going to leave my size eleven footprints on your scrotum. Do you understand me, Junior?"

"Don't you ever come back to this jail, Dacus. Don't you ever come near me," Palmer spat in the half light of the anteroom, a wantonness twisting his face.

"I hope I never have to, Junior."

"Move, boy!" Palmer screamed at Ben. "Don't you open your fucking mouth! This could hurt me bad if it gets out, Dacus."

"Then why are you still talking about it, Junior?"

The cold night air outside the jail entered Ben's lungs like the fires of resurrection. He screamed out his freedom. Then he got in step with Mr. Dacus as the principal walked toward River Street. "Anything," Ben said. "Anything at all I can do for you, Mr. Dacus. You just let me know. If you want you can use my body as a doormat and wipe your feet on my back when you go in and out of your house. You can hang me by my feet from your ceiling, put candles in my nose, ears, and mouth, and use me as a chandelier. What I'm trying to say, Mr. Dacus, is thanks for coming to get me."

The principal was walking with long, rapid strides. His blond hair was brushed straight back and his face shone with a ruddy health in the February air. "It's a funny thing, Ben. The power old coaches have over their former ballplayers. Once you've played for someone, sweated blood for them, won and lost games for them, then that person is transformed forever in your eyes. He simply isn't human anymore. He's something better than human, something stern and demanding. He tries to extract performances from your body that exceed your talent. He makes you more than you really are. He gives you a uniform, an identity, a feeling of brotherhood like you have never known before and most likely will never know again. He includes you. Because he chooses you, selects you from the scrawny bunch of boys who come out for the first day's practice, you owe him something. All you can do for the rest of your life is feel gratitude that he let you taste the small dose of glory, a dose that really means nothing, but means absolutely everything to a boy growing up. What I'm saying, Ben, is that the reason I could get you tonight was because I used to coach Junior in football."

"Was he as bad as you said he was?" Ben asked.

"Hell, no," Mr. Dacus chuckled, "he wasn't bad. God knows there were some poor pissants a hell of a lot worse off than he was. He was a little afraid, that's all. Just like a lot of kids are. Just like I was the first time I put on a uniform in high school. A lot of times fear is a good healthy thing. Fear made me get out of boxing."

"You went to the Olympics. You couldn't have been too afraid."

"I didn't go to the Olympics, Ben. I went to the Olympic trials. Before I die this town will have it that I beat hell out of Joe Louis at Madison Square Garden. The boy who beat me in the trials nearly killed me, Ben. He beat me all over the ring for three rounds. I was blinded by my own blood when the referee stopped the fight. I had come to the limits of my skill as a boxer. The boy that beat me was knocked out cold thirty seconds after the first round began by the best boxer I ever laid my eyes on. That boxer went on to win the Olympic bronze medal, then lose his first five fights as a pro. Athletics is a strange world. You climb to your peak, but often that is not very impressive unless there are very small peaks around you."

"Then why play sports at all?"

"It's very important, Ben. Sports show you your limits. Sports teach humility. Sooner or later the athlete becomes humble no matter how good he is. But he plays until he has reached as high as he can."

"I play basketball because I have to win a scholarship," Ben announced.

"No, that's not true," Mr. Dacus disagreed, turning down River Street and walking down the sidewalk beneath the massive wind-sculpted water oaks that paralleled the river. "That's not even close to the truth. You play basketball because you love your father."

"I hate my father," Ben said darkly.

"No, you love him and he loves you. I've seen a lot of Marine fathers since I've been at the high school, Ben. Hundreds upon hundreds of them, year after year. They're a tight-assed lot and your father is as tight-assed as any of them. They love their families with their hearts and souls and they wage war against them to prove it. All your dad is doing is loving you by trying to live his life over again through you. He makes bad mistakes, but he makes them because he is part of an organization that does not tolerate substandard performance. He just sometimes forgets there's a difference between a Marine and a son. Did he give you that shiner?"

416

"Yes, sir. Palmer called him down to the jail and told him I resisted an arrest for drunken driving. He hit me when I came up to the bars to talk to him."

"Your father is the dream of a high school principal or a deputy sheriff. He believes in the institution over the individual even when the individual is his own child. That's why he's such a good Marine."

"And such a lousy father."

"You'll come to understand him better when you grow up."

"I'll never love him, though."

"Sure you will. I told you that you love him right now and I meant it. There's something profound about boys and their fathers. There's bad blood, it seems, almost always, and yet there's this inevitable tenderness that neither of them recognizes when it's present. But over a lifetime it's hard to hate the seed that fathered you."

"How did you know to come down to the jail tonight? Was it Sammy?"

"He called me and told me the whole story. He's really upset. We better call him when we get to my house."

"Your house?"

"Yeah, I want you to spend the night with my wife and me tonight. We can put some ice on your eye, give you a little dinner, and let you get some rest. I'll go over and talk to your father tomorrow morning. We got to be good friends during basketball season and if he isn't mad at me for kicking you off the team, I think I can smooth the whole thing over."

"He thinks you were right to kick me off the team."

"I was," Mr. Dacus said simply.

"But he still loved it that I hurt that boy."

"In both cases, he is the perfect Marine."

"I'm cold," Ben said, looking out toward the river.

"Why didn't you tell me, pissant," Mr. Dacus said. He put his arm around Ben and pulled him close to his body. It was not the hardness of the principal's body that amazed Ben; it had something to do with the realization that he had never been held this closely and this lovingly by a man. Slowly Ben put his arm around the man's waist as they turned toward the Dacus home.

30

BEN AND MARY ANNE waited for Sammy and Emma Lee Givens. They drank huge glasses of ice tea, sugared and garnished with mint leaves. Mary Anne was lying on the Pawley's Island rope hammock that Lillian had bought for Bull's birthday in early February. Ben was sitting on the bannister looking out toward the houses that lined the lawn.

A screendoor slammed shut and a lawnmower started up somewhere down the street. The fires of spring had come to Ravenel in a rush, in a blaze of color and odor, and spring could be tasted everywhere in the bee-emblazoned gardens and the seed-gifted winds. The old part of the town, fiercely antebellum, rested in the stillest slackwater celebration of itself, in the habiliment of azaleas cutting into shadows with a soft-winged blue, or a deepening ruby. This spring was a fire without thrift in the grand literature of the seasons the Meecham family had watched from their verandas. Ben breathed deeply, catching the scent of gardenias, and the river, half honey, half wine.

"God, this town is beautiful at this time of the year," Ben said.

"What a deep and profound thought, Ben. I bet no one else has ever said that before," Mary Anne said. "You really should try to train yourself to think in original phrases."

"How would you like to digest thirty-two teeth that once were fastened to your gums?"

"That's better. You ought to thank me for making you more aware of the language."

"I'm so lucky. Other guys have sisters that set them up

with dates with gorgeous girls. Me. I got a sister who makes me more aware of the language."

"Do you realize that next year, Ben, you and I will be separated for the first time in our whole lives."

"I hadn't thought of that," Ben said. "I hadn't looked at the bright side of leaving home yet."

"You'll appreciate me one day. After my suicide and the entire literary world is in mourning and after kings and princes hurl their bodies on my casket so intense is their grief, then you'll appreciate me. Then you'll regret the vicious way you've treated me all your life. But you're a Philistine, Ben, and I'm an artist. It's been perfectly obvious to me for years that I must suffer at my family's hands until I blossom into the greatest writer of the twentieth century."

"You'll be lucky to blossom into a horse turd."

"Your bathroom humor does not amuse me. But no kidding, Ben, I've wondered in how many thousands of different ways you'll miss me next year. My wit, you'll miss. There's no question about that. Being raised with the wittiest, most charming woman in America has probably ruined you with other women. Next, you'll probably miss my genius. A mind like mine only comes along once every couple of generations and I know you'll look back and think, 'I never really appreciated that brilliant sister of mine.'"

"Hey, brilliant sister," Ben said, "you going to write me when I'm in college?"

"No, not unless you promise to save every letter I write."

"Why do I have to save them?"

"Because they'll be collected someday after my death. Then they'll be published in a small, elegant volume."

"This is after your suicide."

"Precisely. There will be many letters from great poets, novelists, scholars, barons, dukes, and captains of industry. Your letters will be placed at the very end of the book where they will not be obtrusive. Your letters will be of absolutely no literary importance, but they will show that Mary Anne Meecham did love the barbarian members of her family even though they treated her viciously. Mary Anne Meecham's vast and compassionate spirit will shine through these letters."

"How shall I act at your funeral?" Ben asked. "Subdued? Ashamed of having treated you viciously? Or should I just be the ol' barbarian I always was?"

"I want there to be no holding back at my funeral. I don't want there to be any stiff upper lips when it comes to my death. I want there to be real grief. I want blubbering and wailing and loud gnashing of teeth. I want people to kill themselves rather than face a world that does not include Mary Anne Meecham. I want people to wonder aloud about whether it is really worth it to continue without the friendship of this magnificent human being, this goddess, this genius, this radiant beauty. And I will want an open casket, Ben. Remember that, because I imagine you'll have the honor of being in charge of the petty details that will go along with my funeral. I want to be buried in a black dress with a strand of pearls around my snow-white neck. I will have no freckles then, since freckles tend to fade as a woman gets older. But the important thing, Ben, is that I want there to be no one in the audience who is not absolutely heartbroken that I have departed this life. If you spot anyone who seems only saddened, throw him out. If you spot anyone who is not wracked by sobbing, then get him the hell out of my sight. Can you imagine what an empty, desolate place the world is going to be without Mary Anne Meecham?"

"I don't know. It sounds kind of nice to me."

Sammy pulled his car into the driveway along the side of the house. Sammy and Emma Lee walked up the front stairs holding hands.

"Hi, Ben and Mary Anne," Emma Lee said.

"I wouldn't let him hold your hand like that, Emma Lee," Ben said. "I know the boy well and he's a sexual maniac."

"Don't listen to my sicko brother, Emma Lee," Mary Anne said. "How are y'all doing tonight?"

"You look nice tonight, Emma Lee," Ben said.

"I'm doing fine tonight, Mary Anne. I guess you're eaten up with jealousy seeing another woman out with the man you love."

"It's killing me, Sammy."

"Try not to be a total fool, Samuel," Emma Lee said. "And thank you, Ben."

"Would you and Mary Anne like to go to the movie with us?"

"No, thanks," Mary Anne said.

"C'mon, Mary Anne, let's go," Ben said.

"No, I have some reading to do."

"She's almost finished one of the Dead Sea Scrolls and she hates to put it down now that she's at the good part," Ben explained.

"Why don't you come, Ben?" Sammy said.

"Naw, I'm going to stay here and torment my sister. I just have a couple of more months to do that."

"You are both more than welcome to accompany Samuel and me to the theater," Emma Lee said in her strangely formal manner. It was incongruous to hear her starched Puritan voice and see her holding hands with Sammy at the same time.

"Not tonight, Emma Lee. Maybe some other time. But before you go, come up to my room and I'll get you that book I promised you," Mary Anne said, rising from the hammock and walking toward the front door.

When the girls had disappeared from sight, Sammy pointed to his car parked in the driveway.

"See that automobile right there."

"No, where?" Ben joked.

"Right there, Bucky beaver," Sammy said.

"The Jew canoe."

"Yeah. Well in about two hours that car is going to turn into a passion pit. I didn't get a chance to tell you that last night we made out for at least five minutes in her driveway."

"No kidding."

"When you have the right moves and the cool tools, women just melt in your arms. I'm going to try to talk her into parking out at the beach."

"I know a good spot if Junior Palmer isn't using it tonight."

"You read my mind, son. As soon as the movie is over

421

at the Sea Oat, Mr. Suave is hauling ass out to the beach for a little lock lip."

"It's supposed to rain tonight."

"The darker, the better."

Emma Lee and Mary Anne came out the front door. Emma Lee walked over to Sammy and shyly took his hand again. Sammy winked at Ben, then turning and saying good-bye, they got into the car and drove to the movie.

After the movie, Sammy turned his car down the dirt road that led to the spot where he and Ben had discovered Junior Palmer and the black woman. The rain had almost stopped now but water dripped in torrents from overhanging trees and he kept his windshield wipers on as he pulled up to a small rise and heard the breakers on the other side of a group of small sand dunes. He switched off the ignition and turned with what he hoped would be taken for a gesture of surety, of casual mastery toward Emma Lee.

"Samuel, I am frightened out here. You did not tell me that you were bringing me out to the jungle."

"There's nothing to fear. Sammy Wertzberger is here," Sammy said, putting his arm around her shoulder. "Anyway, I'm the only one in this whole county who knows where this spot is. It's the most romantic place in Ravenel County."

Emma Lee took off her glasses, laid them on the dashboard, and slid across the seat. Sammy kissed her inexpertly. Their mouths opened and their tongues met. Emma kissed Sammy on the neck, then snuggled against him tightly. Sammy could feel her small breasts pressing against his body. He shifted his weight and pulled her chin up until her eyes were looking into his.

"Do you know I can hardly see without my glasses, Samuel?" she said.

"Good, that means you don't have to look at my ugly mug," Sammy answered.

"I think you are very nice looking, Samuel. I was proud to introduce you to my parents the first night we dated."

"You were?"

"Yes. They thought you were a well-behaved gentleman. I had only dated boys at the church to Sunday school affairs."

"Then I knocked you off your feet," Sammy giggled, kissing Emma Lee again.

This time the kisses were softer, more relaxed, less hurried and strained. They were learning how to kiss now, taking their time in the darkness, savoring the taste of another mouth, the shape of other lips. Sammy was amazed how small and diminutively boned Emma Lee was and how clean her brown hair smelled. She made a small moaning sound as Sammy kissed her on the neck. They hugged each other again. Sammy, through his range of vision, could see her white blouse, the opposite door, and her John Romaine purse which lay on the seat almost within his reach. Her cheek against his, Emma Lee kept her eyes closed feeling the soft and hard contours of Sammy's face. When she opened her eyes, she was staring out the window. A face was staring back at her and she screamed.

The door was opened and a huge hand reached in and dragged Sammy out by the shirt. Sammy's head hit the side of the car on the way out. A cut opened up above his left eye. When he hit the ground a knee crashed down on his chest and Sammy's eye focused on the point of a butcher knife a half inch away from his eyeball. The voice of a black man whispered violently, maniacally above him. The voice came hissing out of the butcher knife.

"Run away from here, boy, or I'm gonna cut our your fuckin' eyes."

The knife came down to a spot on Sammy's cheek and opened a slight cut that ran down to Sammy's chin.

"Please, mister, don't hurt us," Sammy pleaded.

The man jerked Sammy up and ran the dull side of the blade along Sammy's throat. Then he shoved him away from the car and screamed, "Run, boy, or I'll cut this girl into small pieces! Run! Run!"

Sammy sprinted down the dirt road calling back to Emma Lee, "I'll get help, Emma Lee. Do what the bastard wants. I'll get help in less than a minute. Do what the bastard wants!" He was crying and screaming as he ran. An animal whine of unequivocal desperation and absolute hopelessness rose in his throat as he ran and ran and ran.

The black man made Emma Lee get out of the car. She leaned against the hood of the car, her legs buckling from fear.

"I can't tell my father I was out here," she said to the man.

The man grabbed her by her hair, jerked her head backwards and stuck the point of the butcher knife just below her eye.

"Take your fuckin' clothes off or I'm gonna put your fuckin' eye out."

"Please, no. Please. I can't tell my father."

"I'll put your fuckin' eye out now!" the man screamed.

Slowly, Emma Lee undressed. She unbuttoned her blouse with a strange, incongruent dignity. The eyes of the stranger watched as the skirt dropped to the wet ground. She could smell his hunger, feel it in her blood, in her fear. Then she removed her slip. She was crying the whole time. She was crying and undressing and looking at the butcher knife. She could smell his evil.

When she removed her brassiere and panties, the black man who had no face, just a voice and an appetite, hit her across the mouth, threw her to the ground and forced himself into her.

"Please. Please. Please," she said, almost a prayer. Then she began to scream. Every time she screamed, he slapped her and then began to punch her in the face. He came inside her driving himself as deeply into her as he could. She began to vomit and he began to hit her again and again, stopping only when Emma Lee Givens lay unconscious in the blood-darkened sand. She never saw him leave down the same road Sammy had run minutes before.

At first Sammy had searched for another couple parking along the beach, but this failing, he began the long run toward town, hoping to intercept a car on the highway. He stopped twice and started back toward Emma Lee, but knew that there was nothing he could do against a grown man and a knife. It was four miles before he could flag a car down. Two had seen him and avoided him, thinking he was drunk or crazy or both. Finally, he was picked up by a black foreman who worked on one of the large tomato farms owned by Philip Turner's father and driven to the nearest house with a phone. Two police cars were dispatched immediately to pick Sammy up. Every patrol car in the county raced to the beach. A highway patrolman found Emma Lee walking down the beach road with half of her clothes on, hysterical, her face beaten past all recognition.

31

BY MORNING news of the rape glowed like a wound in the consciousness of the town. Along River Street a harsh silence prevailed as white men clustered in doorways and nodded their heads ruefully, then looked toward the street. The id of the town was bared, gathering into something terrible, fed by the slow accretions that came with a blazing hunger for retribution. In his alley, Toomer unpacked his flowers for the day and began his song to the few shoppers who had come downtown. His voice brought a kind of normality back to the street, but it could not cut through the smell of blood that came off the town like a musk.

In Hobie's restaurant Bull heard a stunned and angry group trade disgusted accounts of the rape. Cleve Goins thought Sammy Wertzberger should be tarred and feathered for leaving Emma Lee to the mercy of a crazy nigger. Half the restaurant agreed with him. A manhunt was in progress at the beach and an army of men scoured the whole island, including the black-gum swamp at the northern end. SLED agents from Columbia were bringing carloads of bloodhounds down to Ravenel. Reporters from the Charleston *News and Courier*, the Columbia *State,* and the Savannah *Morning News* drove into town and were refused interviews by both Sammy's parents and Emma Lee's father. Ford's Hardware Store on the corner of River and Granville streets ran out of ammunition and shotguns an hour after the store was opened. The Ku Klux Klan planned a rally and a march down River Street. Women, black and white, cried in the street when they heard what happened. From the principal's office at Calhoun High, Ben tried three times to call

Sammy and each time the phone was busy. The ladies' auxiliary of the Rotary Club canceled the azalea contest which was to be held in the gymnasium of the high school. Sammy Wertzberger received two death threats before eight o'clock in the morning and before his parents took the phone off the hook.

Paradise became a magnetic field for the possibility of violence. Carloads of white men rode up and down the streets of Paradise, three in the front and three in the back seat, slowing down and staring at every black man outside of his house. But there were not many black people visible on this day and Paradise had the look of a town desolated by plague or the rumor of plague.

In the Meecham kitchen, Arrabelle Smalls washed dishes and looked out the sun-filled window and said, "It's a bad day to be colored, Miss Meecham. I seen it like this before. The white mens gone nigger-hungry today. The snake is in 'em and he ain't leavin' till they catch up with that man who runnin' around here now not knowin' he as good as dead."

After school, Ben walked over to Sammy's house. Rachel Wertzberger answered the door. Her eyes were bloodshot, raw, and it was easy to interpret the suffering the previous night had brought to her house.

"Where's Sammy, Mrs. Wertzberger?" Ben asked.

"He's gone. We sent him away," she answered. "We had to, Ben. He's so upset."

"How long will he be gone? Where did he go, Mrs. Wertzberger?" Ben asked.

"New York. Where else? Where else do we have relatives besides Charleston and that's too close. All day, Ben, we received phone calls saying that they want to kill Sammy. And for what? For running from certain death for both him and that girl. That poor girl."

"New York! But he won't be here to graduate."

"Just as well. To graduate in New York means that he won't graduate? We put him on the train at one o'clock in Charleston. He left you this note," she said, handing him a sealed envelope. Then she began crying again and Ben made an awkward gesture to comfort her.

"Go now, Ben. Come back soon so we can talk and we can call Sammy on the telephone."

Ben walked toward town forgetting a moment that he was holding Sammy's note in his right hand. The reality of Sammy's absence came to him slowly, but there was no form or substance to the reality. He had talked to Sammy the night before, had joked with him, had heard the high-pitched laughter and watched his car pull out of sight. It was as though his father had received orders in the night and the Meecham family had broken camp, relying on their old swiftness, the old canniness of flight, and had abandoned their house and all their friends yet another time. But this was different and strange to Ben. In his whole life, no friend had ever left him. Sammy had stolen his role, his birthright.

Then, remembering the note, he tore the envelope open and read, "It was awful, Ben. I hope I never see this town again. You'll always be my best friend. If you still want to be. Remember the Bohemian Mountain Approach. Mom and Dad are sending me to New York to live with my Uncle Sidney. They say northern girls just do it and don't ask any questions. If they catch this guy I'll have to come back for the trial. Maybe I'll see you around then. Send me the graduation program. Your friend, Rock Troy."

For the next hour, Ben sat with Toomer in the alley helping Toomer clean crabs when no customers were in sight. Cars filled with unfamiliar white men passed them again and again, turned right at the bridge and crossed toward St. Catherine's Island and the beach beyond.

"Do you think they'll catch him, Toomer?"

"Catch 'em be the nicest thing they d-d-d-do. Ain't no p-p-place to go much unless he long g-g-gone from these islands. That's gonna be a sad colored b-b-boy when they get up with him."

"Where'd you get the honey, Toomer? You harvested already?"

"No, white b-b-boy. I hold this out from last year. This my last f-f-four jars. I sell 'em to ol' man Fogle at the store

428

by the bridge. He buy this bushel of Mr. Oyster I got in the back of the wagon, too."

"I thought it was too late to gather oysters."

"It ain't May yet. This month still got an 'r' in it. You go shrimpin' with me next F-f-friday?"

"Sure."

"We can c-c-catch us a freezerful of shrimp in just one night. Those creeks are fillin' up with Mr. Shrimp right n-n-now. Then maybe we can gig some f-f-flounder on the way home."

"Great, Toomer. I'll come here Friday after school and just go on to your place with you," Ben said, leaving for home, the ends of his fingers abraded from the crab shells.

At five o'clock, Toomer drove his mule and wagon up in front of Fogle's General Store at the base of the bridge. He removed the burlap sacks from the bushels of oysters and began carrying one of them into the store. He had not seen Red Pettus watching him from the interior of the store. Red was sitting on a counter drinking a beer. Both he and the men in the store had spent the entire day hunting for Emma Lee's assailant in the brush and swamplands of the beach. None of the other men paid Toomer any mind as he limped in with the oysters.

"Hey, Toomer," Red said, "did you hear that the nigger who raped Emma Lee Givens had a gimp foot and a bad stutter?"

Toomer did not answer but continued toward the back of the store where Mr. Fogle was putting up cans of vegetables.

"Got any singles, Toomer?" Mr. Fogle asked.

"Not too m-m-many," Toomer answered.

"Yeah, she said the n-n-nigger had the worst stutter she ever heard," Red said loudly. "They said that Emma Lee could hardly understand a word that nigger said he was stutterin' so bad."

"Ignore that bastard," Mr. Fogle whispered, eyeing Red nervously.

"I got one more b-b-bushel," Toomer said.

"What's a b-b-b-b-b-bushel?" Red asked. "I ain't never heard of a b-b-b-b-bushel. Is that a new word?"

Toomer went outside, brushing by Red with caution and with an understated obeisance, a dropping of the eyes and an expression of half-humility and half-fear that he hoped would defuse the violence in the boy that had not played itself out during the manhunt. As he lifted the second bushel of oysters from the wagon, Red grabbed two of the honey jars and said, "Let me help you, Toomer. I always like to be of some help to a good neighbor." He was playing for the edification of the men who gathered at the window to watch the drama.

"N-n-no. I don't need help f-f-from you."

"You don't, Toomer?" Red said with mock hurt and winking at the men who watched from the store. "In that case, then I just won't help you."

He dropped the two jars of honey on the cement and waited for Toomer to respond. Toomer did not even look back, but continued into the store where he heard the laughter of these white men whom he had known all of his life. He looked around the store and memorized their faces in a glance, feeling something dangerous gnawing in him, boiling over, and he could sense that the trifurcated vein in his forehead was protruding now, and his bottom lip trembled uncontrollably. He waited until Mr. Fogle paid him for the oysters before he said, "I got two more jars of h-h-honey in the w-w-wagon." But then he heard the sound of two jars breaking against the brick walls of the deserted cotton warehouse beside the general store.

"That was mighty clumsy of me," Red said to the other men. "I broke four jars of honey tryin' to help my good buddy-roo, ol' Toomer over there. Toomer, no kiddin', I'm sorry about my butter fingers." A few of the men were chuckling loudly, but the laughter had a closer kinship to obscenity than to joy.

As Toomer turned to leave the store, Red began following him, imitating his broken walk and his agonized, wavering speech. "T-t-t-t-toomer, I h-h-hope y-y-you n-n-not m-m-m-mad a-a-at m-m-me."

The black man had whirled snake quick and grabbed Red's throat in one hand and Red's testicles in his other. He pulled Red screaming and gagging toward the wagon, then tripped him with his bad leg. Before Red could recover, Toomer was on him again, the black hand coming around the throat with such fury that Red could feel the blood flow cut off from the brain. Toomer twisted Red's neck until the boy's head was square up against the inside of the rubber truck tire of the wagon.

"You move, Red, and I'm gonna tell M-m-man-O-War to get gone and she'll take your h-h-head with her."

The place filled up with white men who had sprinted from both the general store and from Ford's Hardware Store across the street as soon as Toomer had grabbed Red. But Red was screaming for no one to touch Toomer. Red's face was obscured by the shadow of the tire. Finally, Ed Mills came up to the wagon and told Toomer to release Red.

"Just do it, Toomer. None of these boys are going to hurt you. Every one of 'em like you better than they do Red Pettus." And the crowd erupted in laughter.

So Toomer rose, limped to the other side of the wagon, mounted, shook the reins, and climbed the causeway leading to the bridge.

"I'll see you later tonight, you fuckin' gimp nigger," Red screamed at him.

"You make me sick, Pettus," Ed Mills said, walking down toward Hobie's, pausing once to watch Toomer's wagon as it crossed the bridge.

They came for him as the sun was falling behind a red-fringed line of clouds that had banked against the horizon. They came as the river had its moment of deepest gold. Two Pettus brothers and two Pettus cousins walked boldly down the dirt road that led to Toomer's bus. A bottle of Rebel Yell was passed back and forth between the four men until Red drained the last swallow and flung the empty bottle into the bushes along the road.

"I hear ol' Toomer whipped you good, baby brother," Mac Pettus giggled.

"He fought dirty, Mac. So how 'bout shuttin' up," Red said.

"Where them fuckin' dogs?" one of the cousins said.

"I thought they'd be all over us by now," Red said.

431

"You just remember that Daddy said just to put a good scare into Toomer," Mac said to Red.

"I'm gonna scare the black shit out of him," Red said.

Toomer had gathered all the dogs, the largest to the smallest, and secured them inside the bus. The barking became deafening as the four men neared the clearing. Toomer saw the big Gray standing on his hind legs at the rear of the bus wailing at the invisible strangers in a half-human bark that hung in the air, a lower octave that endured through its particular quality of menace. But all of the dogs, the great and the small, the powerful and the weak, locked in the bus with their nostrils filling with the presence of malevolence on their urine-anointed land, bayed together as Toomer sat holding the end of a long rope on the bottom step of the bus. The door of the bus was opened just enough to give the rope free play. He knew if he released the dogs the Pettus brothers would slaughter them with salvos from their repeating shotguns. But he also knew that he was seeing something instinctual and primal taking hold of his penned dogs. The twenty-six dogs were throwing themselves at the windows of the bus and their barking became like a single feral note, except for the whine of the big Gray whose voice was taking on a new dimension of wildness with each step the Pettuses took. Toomer's dogs in the deepening decline of the sun were becoming a pack.

Red was holding a .38 revolver in his hand as he emerged from the shadows of the huge oaks that masked the beginning of the clearing. The light was poor but Toomer interpreted the gaits of the other three men and could tell the gauge of each shotgun as they passed between the hives.

The men were laughing as they caught sight of the dogs in the bus. Toomer heard their laughter, thick with the bravura of men deep into the bottle, and though he was crouched on that bottom step, his eyes dark and appraising, his eyes steady through their fear, he saw that Red was not laughing. His two hands tightened on the rope.

When the light caught the Pettus boys between the eight deep humming boxes of bees, when they walked across a predetermined point, a zone of violation and trespass from which he knew there would be no turning back, Toomer yanked the rope. Two of the hives crashed off their bases and fell into the road, one of them striking Mac Pettus on the leg. In an instant, the bees were on them. Red sprinted toward the river slapping at the first wave of bees that stung his arms and face. Then, as he ran, there was a single moment when he felt as though his whole body was on fire and he protected his eyes with his free hand and fled toward water, dropping his revolver on the edge of the bank just before he plunged into the creek and clawed his way to its soft mud bottom where he felt the saltwater ignite each sting like a match in his flesh. For as long as his breath allowed, he stayed submerged in the kind and beeless creek, his eyes exploding with light whose source came from the fiercely honed and polished stingers that moved and contracted deeper into his body. When he surfaced, one of his eyes was closed and the other filled with the delicate silver of a moon small as a nail clipping. He began pulling stingers out of his face, working down, and taking his time looking back up the bluff at Toomer's bus.

The other three men had run in a panic down the dirt road they had come in on. Toomer chuckled, hearing their screams grow dimmer as they headed back toward the highway.

"I ain't gonna let no white boys hurt my chillun," he said to his dogs as he limped among his pets trying to calm them. They had shifted to the other side of the bus now, still in a frenzy, still bound in a strangely ineluctable bondage of something rooted deep in all of them, in the subliminal frontiers of the species. Toomer rubbed his hands along the shoulders of the big dogs who had commandeered positions by the windows facing the river side of the bus. He felt the stiff, arched withers of two German police dogs who ran together and often teamed to fight and get licked by the Gray. Staring out into the night, he saw nothing, but he knew the bees had assured his safety that night. He lit a kerosene lamp.

Red Pettus, his face and body swollen, came dripping out of the creek, nauseated and feverish after the attack.

He saw the light go on in the bus. Searching on his hands and knees along the bank, he retrieved his .38. Then, he began to walk toward Toomer.

The phone rang at the Meecham house. Ben and Mary Anne were talking at the kitchen table. Lillian was making a novena at the Catholic Church and Bull had duty at the air station. Ben answered the phone and heard the voice of Arrabelle Smalls frayed with hysteria and almost unintelligible as she wept and tried to speak at the same time. Her dialect deepened as she spoke, abandoning the smooth lyrics she had been trained to use when she worked in the houses of white men. Here on the phone, she screamed at Ben in the voice of the sea islands. The Gullah-fleshed cry of her girlhood.

"Go get Toomer, Ben, and make that boy come on over to my house tonight. Make him come on over. He got a stiffy side to him, Ben, but I be so scared about the Pettus boys. I hear just now that he grab hold to Red today and make that boy holler and it just not a good time to be colored in this town. So you got to fly and take hold to Toomer and make him come to my house tonight. I just hear the Pettus boys been runnin' their mouths about scarin' Toomer for what he done to Red. He's a stiffy boy, so you just go drag him out of that bus and tell him his mama say for you to do it. Go on, now. Get on gone, Ben. Please. Please."

"I will, Arrabelle," Ben said. "I'll have to call Dad. Then I'll go get Toomer. I promise."

"What did Arrabelle want?" Mary Anne asked.

"Where's Dad's number?"

"How do I know? He's on duty."

"He leaves it near the phone in case Mama wants to get in touch with him."

"Yeah, he also threatens her with death if she calls him for anything besides a death in the family."

Ben found the number scribbled on the cover of the small thin Ravenel telephone book. He dialed the number quickly.

"Why are you shaking, Ben?" he heard Mary Anne ask strangely.

"I'm not shaking," Ben answered.

"Yes, you are. You're shaking all over. Your hands are trembling."

"Hello. Hello. May I speak to Colonel Meecham, please."

"What's wrong? What did Arrabelle say?"

"Hello, Dad," Ben said.

"What do you want, sportsfans. I can't just shoot the shit. I've got the duty."

"Yes, sir. I know. Arrabelle just called and thinks that Toomer might be in trouble. Red and his brothers are going over there to get him. I'm going to take Mama's car and go pick him up and take him over to Arrabelle's. Is that all right?"

"Negative," Bull answered. "You stay right in that house. You hear me? Keep out of that nigger shit. You don't want to get between the niggers and the grits when they go for each other's throats. Consider yourself locked up in your quarters."

"But it's Toomer, Dad. He might be in trouble."

"I don't care if Toomer is being attacked by the whole Mediterranean fleet. You are not leaving that house. You got it? You read me?"

"Yes, sir."

"Toomer can take care of himself, hog. Over and out. And don't leave that goddam house."

Hanging up the phone, Ben walked to the kitchen table and sat down. His hands were trembling out of control and adrenaline flowed through his body in giant, unseen torrents. He tried to hide his hands from his sister.

"Why did you call Dad? Why didn't you just take the station wagon and go get Toomer?"

"I don't know."

"Were you afraid to go to Toomer's?"

"No."

"Were you hoping Dad would tell you not to go?" Mary Anne said.

Ben looked up at his sister, looked into her eyes, felt the fear in his stomach, half sea, half fire and said, "Yes."

"Then I'll go get Toomer," Mary Anne said, rising and going toward the back door.

"Stop, Mary Anne!" Ben shouted. "You can't go out there!"

"Why not?" she asked.

"Because Dad ordered us to stay in the house. We're confined to quarters."

"You're confined to quarters. He wouldn't dream in a thousand years that I would go get Toomer. So you just sit there and shoot jump shots until I get back. I won't be long, brave brother. Brave golden boy."

"You can't go, Mary Anne. Goddam it! You can't go! I can't let you."

"You can't stop me," she said.

"What about Vishnu, Mary Anne? What about your goddam Vishnu? What about your goddam Hindu god of self-preservation?"

Mary Anne turned and walked for the door again. Then she stopped and faced Ben, the kitchen light reflecting off one lens of her glasses, and said, "What about Toomer, Ben?"

"All right, all right you sickening little bitch," Ben screamed. "You know I can't let you go because if something happened to you Dad would never quit punching me. But if he calls, you'd better cover for me. Sometimes you don't know when to stop, Mary Anne. You don't know when to quit running your mouth and just let things alone. I know what you're doing. I know what you're doing and it really pisses me off."

"I can't help it, Ben," Mary Anne smiled with a grotesque sweetness. "We sickening little bitches just do these things sometimes. Now you better hurry. Mom keeps her extra key in the ashtray."

"I wish she had taken the goddam car," Ben said putting on the flight jacket his father had given him for his birthday.

"Just go get Toomer."

Moments after Ben pulled out of the driveway and Mary Anne heard the station wagon squealing down the street, the phone rang again. She knew it would be her father and she let it ring ten times before she answered it.

436

"Colonel Meecham's residence. Mary Anne speaking," she answered pleasantly.

"The phone's been ringing for three days, sportsfans. I'm glad you found time to answer it. Let me talk to Ben, on the double."

"Don't you want to talk to your sweet, adorable oldest daughter first?"

"Hey, I don't have time to crap around with you. Put Ben on the line."

"I decided just tonight that I was going to name my first son after you, Dad. Isn't that a tremendous honor. Aren't you pleased beyond words. I'm going to call him Taurus or El Toro."

"I'm gonna give you five seconds to get Ben on the phone and if you don't I'm coming right home to put a dozen hashmarks on your butt."

"But you can't come home, Daddy-poo. You've got the duty. They shoot Marines if they desert their posts. Before I get Ben I just want to tell you one thing I've been thinking about that I think you'll find mildly humorous."

"You need a working over bad, hog. You're getting rock happy in this burg. Get Ben on the phone."

"Just this one observation, Daddy-poo. You told us that you got your nickname because of your large neck and the fact that you were stationed at El Toro. Well, it occurred to me how funny it would have been if you had been stationed at a base named La Cucaracha. You'd be Colonel Cockroach Meecham right now. Pretty witty, huh?"

"Get me Ben," Bull said in a suddenly subdued tone.

"Uh oh, the voice of the killer. He's in the bathroom, Dad. He can't come to the phone."

"Get him on the goddam phone."

"He says he has stomach cramps. I think he has diarrhea."

"I don't care if he's passing bowling balls, I want him on this phone."

"I'll go see if he can come to the phone," she said, laying the receiver down and not returning to the phone for a full minute. When she finally picked up the phone she said, "He's passed out on the bathroom floor, Popsy.

He's screaming for me to run out and buy him some Preparation H."

"Mary Anne, I'm going to ask you one question and you better answer me straight. Has Ben gone to Toomer's house?"

"I cannot tell a lie, Dad. That always has been one of my greatest virtues. I can joke and tease and mess around, but I just can't lie. No. Ben has not gone to Toomer's house. He's upstairs screaming for Preparation H."

"Did he go to Toomer's place, Mary Anne?"

"Mary Anne?" she said. "Who is that strange creature? I know who sportsfans is. I know who jocko is. I know who hog is. But who is this person, Mary Anne? I do not know such a person."

"Is your mother's car out in the driveway? This is important, Mary Anne because Ben may be in bad trouble if he goes out there. I just called Arrabelle and she said the Pettus boys have more guns than I have short hairs. Now, you've got to tell me if Ben went to Toomer's."

"Do you remember what you always tell us, Dad? Meechams always help out the little guy. When someone's in trouble you'll find a Meecham right there lending a helping hand."

"I ordered him not to go. He disobeyed a direct order," Bull said.

"Are you afraid, Dad?" Mary Anne asked.

"Hell, no," Bull growled. "Afraid of a few skinny grits? I've fought in two wars, sportsfans. I'm not afraid of nothing."

"Ben's real afraid, Dad. He was too afraid to let me go with him. If he gets hurt it's going to be your fault because you didn't have the guts to help him."

"I'm on duty for Chrissakes. I can't just waltz out of here, Mary Anne."

"Just admit it. You're afraid. Big Bull Meecham is afraid. It's not a sin to be afraid."

"I've fought in two goddam wars, you little broad," Bull screamed.

"Ben's never fought in one," she answered.

"When I get home tomorrow, Mary Anne, there better

be miles and sunshine between us because, so help me, God, I'm going to rearrange your face."

"Nighty-night, Daddy-poo, and one last thing."

"What?"

"Stand by for a fighter pilot." And Mary Anne hung up the phone.

Bull immediately called Virgil Hedgepath. When the colonel answered, Bull said, "Virge, this is Bull. Ben's in some kind of trouble. Can you get dressed on the double and come over here for an hour as O.D.? I'm leaving now so there's gonna be a time when I am just a plain fucking deserter."

Unhooking the Mameluke sword, Bull threw it on the desk in front of Captain Bledsoe who was the junior officer on duty with Bull.

"Cover my ass, Captain. Colonel Hedgepath is on his way."

"Aye, aye, sir. I don't think there should be any problems at all."

"You're not bad for a gravel cruncher, Captain. Carry on. I'll be back as fast as my little ass will carry me."

Bull ran to his squadron car and headed it quickly toward the main gate. As he returned the salute of the guard and headed toward Ravenel, he realized that he, Bull Meecham, for the first time in his life, for the first time in his history as an officer and a Marine, had deserted his post.

Red returned to the bus slowly but without caution. His face was swollen, obsessed, and pale with a need for vengeance. He came from the water and the marsh possessed by a stern angel that burned in the blood around his eyes.

In the bus a fresh resurrection of the warning cries arose as the dogs caught the scent of returning peril. Toomer could not control them, could not silence one of them, though he screamed and lashed out at all of them within reach of his voice or his hand. In the kerosene glow he stared out toward the river, seeing nothing but his own reflection, unable to see the danger whose approach was published in the nostrils of the orphan pack who surged protectively around him. It was an aboriginal darkness now that Toomer studied, waiting for a face or a voice to materialize. He needed something to confront. He needed to see or hear Red. All he could see were the distant lights of Ravenel strung like a bracelet down the river shore. All he could hear were the dogs and the rush of blood through his ears.

Then Red screamed at him and entered a perimeter near the bus where the light gave him a surreal visibility. "I got to hurt you, Toomer. I got to hurt you bad."

"Get on n-n-now, Red. Get on home now 'f-f-fore somethin' else happen," Toomer said.

"We were just gonna scare your black ass, Toomer. For what you did to me today at Fogle's. A nigger's got to learn not to go touchin' a white man."

"You got what y-y-you ax for, Red," Toomer shouted over the noise of the dogs.

"It wouldn't-a hurt nothin' if you'd just let me have my fun. You made everyone laugh at me, Toomer. The whole town's laughin' at me. And now they'll laugh some more because of you and your fuckin' bees. I got to teach you, Toomer. I got to teach you that I'm a white man. I got to be treated with some respect. You ain't never respected me in your whole life, but you'll goddam respect me from now on. That's what I came back to teach you."

"G-g-get on, boy, before I get y-y-your m-m-mama on you."

One of the police dogs had mounted the small kitchen table and was barking in a blind rage, snapping his fangs at Red through the window. Red fired at him through the window and knocked the dog off the table and onto the small wood-burning stove that stood at the back end of the bus. The dog was dead when Toomer reached him.

When Toomer rose again to face Red his expression had changed and his eyes seemed akin to those of the pack for the first time.

Spittle flecked his lips as he screamed, "I'm gonna get you, Red. I'm gonna hurt you for that, boy."

"You ain't never gonna do nothing to me again,

440

nigger," Red said, squinting through his one blue eye that was still open and functional. He aimed the gun for the big Gray, but did not see Toomer coming over to pull the Gray from the window. The bullet caught the black man full in the stomach and for a moment the two men looked at each other in a suspended moment of horror, of incredulity.

"Did I get you, Toomer?" Red cried out. "I didn't mean to get you. Oh, God, I didn't mean to get you." But he could hear nothing and Toomer could hear nothing but the scream of the dogs. Toomer stumbled toward the front of the bus, trying to keep his balance as he weaved his way through the dogs, trying to keep the blood in his body with his two hands. Unsteadily he fell against the front window of the bus and his right hand grasped for the handle to the front door. At first he could not find it, believed it was not there, that it was betraying him at this final moment, until finally he had it, cold, in his hand, and he slammed it back hard toward the window, opening the door, and freeing the dogs.

The dogs poured through the door with the Gray in the lead. Red had waited too long to interpret Toomer's harrowing walk down the center of the bus. When he saw that Toomer meant to set the dogs on him, he sprinted thoughtlessly toward the dirt road and the highway, passing the hives in a blur of recognition, and making it almost to the first line of trees before he heard the sound of a pack in a full cry, and in one voice, pursuing him.

One hundred yards from the bus, the Gray pulled Red Pettus to the ground. The Gray, eyes yellow, man-hating eyes, went for Red's groin. The other dogs followed closely, going for the face, the throat, the arms, the stomach, anything that was flesh, anything that belonged to the man who had hurt Toomer. Red twisted and fought but every time he moved meat was torn from his body. He reached up to knock a dog from his ear and found he had no ear. The forest filled up with screams of Red and the growling of the pack until gradually only the noise of the dogs was heard.

Ben turned down the dirt road that led to Toomer's,

braking the car hard when he hit some holes that sent the car airborne. He passed the tomato field on his left, then entered the dark overhang of oak that would take him to Toomer's bus. His hands still trembled violently and he squeezed the steering wheel as tightly as he could. Then he heard the dogs, and the headlights caught a body lying to the side of the road.

It was only because of the hair that Ben recognized Red Pettus. The face was torn in a dozen places. The entire corpse was covered with blood. Ben rolled down the window to get a closer look, fascinated by the first dead man he had ever seen. He did not see the Gray appraising him in silence and coming up from behind him, stalking him.

The Gray sprang and came halfway through the window, catching Ben's arm and tearing at the flight jacket. Ben punched at the dog with his right fist, punched at the throat, feeling the dog's teeth go through the jacket and sink into the sinew of his forearm. Then, he remembered the car was running and he stomped the accelerator and the dog slid off him but not before the teeth had torn up the sleeve of the flight jacket and raked through muscles and veins as the dog was jerked from the arm by the sudden acceleration of the car.

Ben drove to the bus, past the fallen hives and parked his car flush against the side of the bus, making sure that there was no way for a dog to challenge his presence again. He rolled down the window on the passenger side and climbed into the bus. He saw Toomer lying on his back, his two large hands clamped over a stomach wound.

"Toomer, Toomer, Toomer!" Ben cried, rushing over to the man.

"Hey, white boy," Toomer said. "L-l-l-looks like we can't go shrimpin' on F-f-friday."

"Sure we can, Toomer. You promised," Ben said.

"Dead men don't make too good a fishermen."

"We're going to the hospital. Doc Ratteree's gonna make you well, Toomer," Ben said, grasping Toomer under his arms and pulling him toward the door. Toomer

442

screamed with pain and the dogs began to gather as a pack outside the school bus.

"I'm sorry, Toomer, but I got to get you to the hospital," Ben said. "Jesus Christ, you've lost a lot of blood!"

"I hurt," Toomer moaned. "Gawd, I hurt."

Ben backed into the car window, then struggled to pull Toomer down the steps of the bus and through the window without hurting him. He was sweating from the effort and grunting from bearing the weight of the injured man. But he was glad that Toomer was no longer moaning.

Finally he pulled Toomer into the front seat and propped him against the front door. Toomer's eyes were wide open but there was a strange depth to his stare. In a moment of measureless agony, Ben Meecham knew he was staring into the face of a dead man. He fumbled for a pulse, felt for a heart beat, prayed for a stutter, or a limp, or a song of flowers. He placed his hand against Toomer's stomach and covered it with Toomer's blood. There was nothing to do now, nothing to hurry for. He rolled up the window of the car, Toomer's side of the car, he thought. He removed the flight jacket and covered Toomer's wound with it. Then, very slowly, he drove back down the dirt road, the pack hurling themselves at the car, appearing before the headlights, snapping at the wheels, demonic and carnivorous once again.

He drove down that road he had come down so many times before and would never come down again. His brain flooded with images and memories. But the images broke up of their own accord, weightless chimeras routed by a numbness that ran through him unchallenged. It took several moments for it to register that there were headlights blocking off access to the highway. He slowed down and stopped in front of the car.

All fear had left him now and the numbness identified itself as a beleaguered, voiceless resignation. There was a disenfranchisement from both the present and the past, from the body beside him and the headlights in front of him; he was enclosed in a timeless realm without margins, outlines, or tense. And he saw a large man with a pistol walk between both cars.

Ben opened the car door, put his feet on the ground, and stood up.

"Dad," he said.

Bull rushed forward and stood before his son for a full five seconds before he slapped him with the back of his hand. The blow caught Ben on the mouth and small capillaries exploded against the teeth and Ben could taste almost instantly the salt liquor of blood, a marsh taste, like the aftertaste of oysters when Toomer would open them fresh.

"Hey, jocko," Bull screamed, "when I tell you to stay in one goddam place you better let grass grow out of your asshole before you move without my permission! You got it?"

"Yes, sir."

"You disobeyed a direct order, hog. A direct order issued by the head honcho."

"Yes, sir."

"You knew you were in deep trouble if you were caught, didn't you, hog?"

"Yes, sir."

"Therefore you expected to be punished if you were caught."

"Yes, sir."

"Why'd you do it?"

"I didn't think I was going to get caught, sir."

"I want the real reason, sweet pea. Because you've never had the guts to go against me before and I goddam want to know why the fuck you came out here tonight in defiance of Santini."

"Because I promised Arrabelle and I thought Toomer might be in trouble. And . . ."

"And what, sweet pea?"

"And because I was your son," Ben said, almost bitterly.

"What's that got to do with it?"

"Because you'd have done it. Santini would have done it."

"Santini doesn't go around disobeying direct orders."

"You just did, Dad. Remember that you made me memorize the guard orders? I've always had trouble re-

444

membering them. But I never had trouble remembering the most important one. You deserted your post."

"I didn't desert my post. I was worried you would step into some deep shit coming out here. You made me come out here."

"No, sir, I didn't."

"I thought you might be in trouble, Ben. Can you get that through your thick goddam little southern boy skull?"

"I thought Toomer might be in trouble."

"I told you Toomer could take care of himself."

"Yes, sir. That's what you told me."

"Is that Toomer in the car?" Bull said, looking for the first time into the interior of the car but looking through the front window at the silhouette propped against the door.

"Yes, sir."

"Hey, Toomer. How you doin', sportsfans?" Bull said, walking to the other side of the car and peering into the window.

"Jesus Christ! Jesus H. Christ! Is he dead?" Bull asked his son.

"Yes, sir."

"Well, that's a good way to ruin a flight jacket, sweet pea. Jesus Christ. Jesus Christ. You better take him to the hospital, sportsfans. You got it? Jesus Christ. I'll go get the sheriff and tell Arrabelle. Jesus Christ. Why didn't you tell me? Why didn't you say something?"

"It wouldn't have made any difference, Dad," Ben said, getting back into the car. "It just wouldn't have made any difference."

32

MESS NIGHT was a formal dinner, a rigidly proper gen-uflection toward the stiffest and most chivalrous origins of the Marine Corps and one that Bull Meecham be-lieved to be the single most efficacious ceremony for stimulating esprit de corps that a commanding officer had at his disposal. It was a night when Marines could celebrate their identity and their origins as Marines; it was a night to sustain and honor the transcendence of their history by a return to the essences, to the lattice-work of ritual that tied them to the brotherhood of war-riors that had gone before them and the men who would bear the scarlet and gold in their wake. Mess Night was a testament of linkage, an evening that allowed for the lyrics of both form and ferocity. Mess Night for the thirty-eight pilots of 367 began at 1920 on the first Friday in March.

The aviators were resplendent in full dress as they drank cocktails in the anteroom before the call to dinner. Part of the Marine Band from Biddle Island played light classical music as the pilots mingled and took their first drinks. Several of the pilots had made a Coors run to the West Coast the previous week and many of the Ma-rines were beginning the long evening of institutionalized drinking slowly sipping on a Coors beer. In the Marine Corps a passionately articulate school of thought had arisen that Coors was the finest American beer; its unavailability on the East Coast made it de rigueur for any Marine aviator who made it to the Coast to return laden down with all the Coors an F-8 could carry. It was an unwritten law in Bull Meecham's squadron that anyone who neglected to bring back a shipment of Coors from the West Coast would be court-martialed upon his return and probably shot.

There was a caution to the early evening drinking, almost an abstemiousness, for the Mess Night that began with the dignity of a coronation often ended with the survival of the species as a major concern. Many of the younger lieutenants and several of the captains had never attended a Mess Night; they had only heard.

But in the beginning hour, there was only a glittering retinue of officers and gentlemen, a low and decent murmur of conversation, an uncommon restraint among the slim, muscular, seemingly invulnerable men who, slightly titillated by the light that could dazzle off cordovan and the understated correctness of the full dress uniform, seemed to Bull Meecham to represent everything that was right with the United States.

The wives of the 367 braced themselves for the uncertain homecoming of their spouses. They were neither invited nor welcome at Mess Night. Since its origins in the deckrooms of British warships, the Mess Night had evolved as a gathering of men. At the Meecham house, Lillian told Ben that if necessary he might have to ride out to the air station to drive his father home. Bull had promised Lillian that he would not get drunk, but she was not a young wife and she had heard such promises before.

At 2000 a drummer and fifer began to play "The Roast Beef of Old England" and pilots began filing into the dining room where gleaming candelabra reflected off both the silver service and the finely polished mahogany tables. But before any pilot entered the dining room, he made a last strategic run to the head, for the Mess Night dinners sometimes lasted over two hours during which time wine was consumed in a limitless flow. But one of the most entrenched traditions of Mess Night was that a man could not exit to relieve himself until the dinner was completed unless the president of the Mess granted permission. As President of this Mess Night, Bull Meecham had spread the word that he would grant permission for no head runs during the course of the evening, knowing full well that this one arbitrary rule would become a serious test of manhood before the ceremony was done.

Bull had gone over the menu with the chef of the Officers' Club weeks in advance. He wanted the finest roast beef possible; he wanted the wines to be superb. He wanted to throw a Mess Night that would worm its way into the oral history of the Marine Corps. His normal intolerance of affectation did not extend to the elegant symmetry of Mess Night. The ceremony itself was one which began in refinement, in a spirit of proper felicity.

He had issued a call to the most legendary aviators he had known in the Marine Corps, the ones who had combined uncanny abilities as pilots with the personalities of carnival barkers and exhibitionists. On the invitations he had sent out he wrote personal notes to the six Marines who were stationed as far away from Ravenel as El Toro and as near as Cherry Point. He had written that he wanted to show the sweet peas in his squadron what the Old Corps was like. He wanted to dredge up some of the old dinosaurs that Bull Meecham came up with in the late days of World War II. Three out of the six officers he had invited had flown in for the occasion and now occupied the head table with him. He had not told a single person in the squadron who he was inviting. Instinct told him that if Colonel Varney had discovered who the men Bull had invited were, then Varney would have done his best to cancel the whole event. But Bull felt an obligation to his men that they be exposed to some of the true wild men who still inhabited the ranks of the Corps.

The meal proceeded with a stateliness and underplayed grandeur. Bull had sent Ben out the day before to gather enough fresh oysters for the oyster cocktails. The French Onion Soup was hot when it arrived, a rarity, all noted, at the Officers' Club. The head waiter marched into the room flanked by the drummers and fifers, rolling a huge roast before him. Stopping behind the Mess President, he cut a small piece of the beef and laid it on Bull's plate. Bull ate it slowly with all eyes on him. Finally he announced as Mess Presidents before him had done as long

448

as there had been Mess Nights, "This beef is tasty and fit for human consumption."

When the dinner was over, the waiters cleared the tables quickly and bottles of port were brought out for the traditional toasts. After the glasses had been filled, Bull rapped a gavel on the head table for silence. He then rose and, lifting his glass, he said with feeling, "Gentlemen, the President of the United States."

All Marines in the room rose as one and lifting their glasses they said in unison, "The President," as the band played the national anthem. When the band had finished playing the officers took their seats. After a minute had passed Bull rose again and, lifting his glass of port, this time he stared at Lieutenant Snell who was serving as Vice President of the Mess at the far end of the table.

"Mr. Vice," Bull said in a voice that rang through the dining room, "Corps and Country."

Lieutenant Snell stood and with his glass at eye level returned the toast by saying, "Long live the United States, and success to the Marines."

The other Marines, lifting their glasses, thundered, "The Corps!" and the band struck up the Marine Corps hymn.

The old hymn, Bull thought, as the band played "Semper Fidelis." In it were continued all the old poetry and stern cadences of what the Marine Corps embodied and embraced. It was a song that offered more goosebumps per square inch than any song he had ever heard. He mouthed the words to the song. Montezuma. Tripoli. And felt himself nourished by the plasma of letters and syllables that had come to denote a commitment to gallantry among the men with whom he had chosen to spend his life. In the room were close to fifty men who would die for this flag, this country, this service, and this song. It was a worthy song and it could stir the embrasures and battlements of a strong man's soul.

When the hymn was over, the waiters brought coffee and Bull rapped with his gavel once again and announced, "The smoking lamp is lighted." Cigars were passed around the tables, contraband from Cuba that had been commandeered while the squadron was at

Guantanamo. Bull grinned and motioned for his guests to watch as he spotted Captain Brannon urinating into a water glass beneath the table as he carried on a conversation with the officers who sat across from him.

Then Bull rose to introduce the guests.

"Gentlemen," he said, "before we begin the fun and games portion of the evening, I'd like to introduce our honored guests and give a brief biography of each of them. I think the biography will explain why I invited these particular men to our Mess Night.

"First on my right is Colonel John 'Blue Balls' Conners," Bull said, motioning his hand toward a thin, rangy man who had worn a constant smile the whole evening. "Blue Balls is one of the best dogfighters in this man's Marine Corps. He is also one of the sloppiest, grossest Marine aviators ever to make the rank of bird colonel. I would like to explain his nickname. For some reason which I will never be able to explain a flight of four of us Marine types got snowbound in South Dakota one winter and, sportsfans, you ain't never been snowbound till you been snowbound in South Dakota. The blizzard lasted for five days and being men not afraid to take a drop of liquor we proceeded to get as drunk as humanly possible. One of our companions lapsed into a state that resembled rigor mortis, but the rest of us just kept drinking. The snow kept falling and piling up in huge drifts around the BOQ where we traded war stories with some pussy Air Force types," Bull said, pausing for the derisive roar he knew would come at the mention of the Air Force.

"Tempers were growing short because Blue Balls had started punching out promising young Air Force pilots because he didn't like the fact that they claimed to have legitimate fathers. Well, one of the Air Force pilots bet John over there that he couldn't run naked around that BOQ through all that snow. John, a man not known for his moderation, started tearing his clothes off his body and before we could stop him, he raced out the front door and was in the snow. Now it was ten below zero outside and the snow had piled up in drifts of seven and eight feet in some places. We ran to the windows on the

450

second floor and began a reconnaissance mission of following Conners around the building, 'cause we thought sure the boy was gonna die before he got ten feet. All we could see was the top of Conner's head charging through the snow like a plow, busting his ass for the pride and honor of the Marine Corps. The boys in the Air Force started making bets about how long it would take for Conners to die out there in the snow, but we knew he had been drinking for three days and that the alcohol was acting as an antifreeze in his body. We also knew Conners wouldn't dare die and leave us humiliated in that Air Force BOQ. Well, on he charged around that building, disappearing from sight in a ten-foot drift on one occasion, freezing his skinny little ass off, and kept on charging until he collapsed in our arms at the front door. His whole naked ugly body was as red as a strawberry, except for his two balls which were the brightest blue you have ever seen. It was also on this occasion that we discovered that Blue Balls had the smallest pecker in the Marine Corps. Gentlemen, I present to you Colonel Blue Balls Conners."

Colonel Conners arose to a tumultuous ovation which he finally calmed by raising a muscular arm in the air to signal for quiet.

"Gentlemen," he said in a mellifluous voice, "Your C.O. is the most notorious liar in the Marine Corps. It has also been proven beyond the shadow of a doubt that he is a homosexual. He goes down on generals and statues in parks. The story he just told you is pure fabrication. There was only a touch of frost on the ground and what slowed me up on that particular occasion was the prodigious size of my member. As I raced around the BOQ, my member dragged a full three feet behind me as I ran. I finally just had to pick the thing up, hurl it over my shoulder, and continue to run. My nickname is not Blue Balls, as your lying C.O. asserts. Gentlemen, my nickname is Python Penis."

Bull stood again, joining in the applause for Colonel Conners's retort, then, when the noise subsided, began to introduce his second guest of the evening. He gestured toward a swarthy, hatchet-nosed man whose face betrayed not the smallest nuance of emotion. "The next guest I would like to tell you about is Lieutenant Colonel William Blitcher, better known as Apache Bill to us oldtimers. Apache Bill is a full-blooded Pawnee Indian and the reason we named him Apache is because it pissed him off so damn bad every time we called him anything besides a Pawnee. Apache Bill joined the Corps so he could screw white women and fly airplanes. He's a quiet man with a powerful temper. I'd like to tell a story to illustrate why it's bad news to piss off Apache Bill. When I was a new captain, long before I rose to the meteoric heights of light colonel, my squadron at Cherry Point, of which Apache Bill was a member, was simulating carrier landings on the runway and a senior captain was acting as the Landing Signal Officer, giving us cuts or wave-offs as we came in to land. Well, Apache Bill had a hot date that night with one of those monstrous things that passed for a female in his eyes and he was anxious to land his bird and go spooning. Well, he came in for his landing, made a perfect approach, and much to his surprise was waved off by the L.S.O. Now, Apache Bill was not getting along too well with the L.S.O. anyway and being a man with a legendary short fuse, he circled around and, instead of making another pass at the carrier landing, decided to cut the L.S.O. in half with his Corsair. He came in low on a strafing run and would have chopped the pogue in half had the L.S.O. not prudently flattened himself in the runway. Well, to make a' long story short Apache Bill chased that poor son of a bitch all over that runway for an hour with most of the base watching and laughing like hell. And yes, gentlemen, there was a court-martial and yes, gentlemen, Apache Bill was found guilty. He was moved back two hundred numbers on the seniority sheet. One of the court-martial board said later that the board found him guilty for not catching the L.S.O. Gentlemen, I present to you with great pride and admiration Apache Bill Blitcher."

"Gentlemen," Apache Bill said when the tumult of his introduction had subsided. "I knew Bull Meecham long before he had his sex change operation."

Even in the midst of the whooping and hollering

following his opening line, Apache Bill did not change expression, did not give even a hint that his face was not a mold or the image on a coin. When the shouting stopped, he continued, "I love flying with a passion, purple. I love flying with good pilots, period. I love flying with Bull Meecham because he flies a bird the way it ought to be flown. He disproves the old saying that there are old pilots and there are bold pilots, but there are no old, bold pilots. Bull Meecham is an old bold pilot and so am I. Since he always tells that story about me and the L.S.O., I will tell the story about how he got his nickname. Do you know that story?" Apache Bill asked the pilots of the squadron.

"No," they screamed.

"He was a first lieutenant and he was taking a little R and R with a real young innocent kid. They went to a beach in Hawaii and upon seeing all those broads down on the beach sunning their gorgeous, willing bodies the young boy said, 'There's a field of cows down there, man. Let's make like young bulls, run down there real fast, and fuck one of them.'

" 'No,' Meecham said after pausing for a moment, 'let's make like old bulls. Let's walk down there real slow and fuck 'em all.' "

Once again the full-throated hurrahs arose as the Marines began to cut through the membrane that enclosed the first half of the Mess Night and began to cross the threshold to where an institutional wildness became the final confirmation of brotherhood. The Mess Night was bridled by stiffness and form only in the first hours; now the evening was moving quickly toward a more visceral, more wanton kind of tradition. In the voices of thick-necked men was heard a rising quality of debauch, the baying of a collective id.

"Before I sit down, I would like to tell you who the Landing Signal Officer on that field was that I chased for an hour," Apache Bill said.

"You're gonna get me in trouble, Apache," Bull said.

"It was Colonel Joseph Varney, U.S.M.C., and I regret to this day I didn't cut his legs off."

When Bull arose to introduce the last guest, he winked

at Butch Brannon, then pointed to a massively constructed lieutenant colonel who was pouring himself glasses of bourbon on the rocks from a bottle he had brought with him from the bar. The man was the largest and most physically imposing man in the room. He had soft places and was girdled with a ponderous stomach and huge buttocks, but the weight did not diminish his formidability.

"The final guest here on my right is this puny, frail-boned creature who goes by the name of Rabies Odum. Now I want you folks to be very careful of Rabies because he has a few peculiarities which will get you in trouble if he takes a keen dislike to you. He is known to hate grunts more than any aviator in the Marine Air Wing. Every time he sees a grunt, he acts like a mad dog, foams at the mouth, and if not restrained, eventually bites the grunt on the leg causing gangrene and death. He was an All-American football player at Alabama the year before they started taking boys on the team. He shot down two enemy planes in Korea and is one of the best air support pilots I have ever seen. He's proud of his fat body and he considers himself to be the strongest, toughest, meanest son of a bitch ever to don the uniform of a U.S. Marine. The only way I got him down here tonight was to tell him we got someone in this squadron who can chew him a new asshole."

"Brannon," someone yelled.

"Where's this Brannon," Odum growled.

"Here, sir," Brannon said, rising out of his seat, egged on by the cheers of his squadron.

For ten seconds Odum stared at Brannon, silently measuring the man against old opponents. Finally he began to laugh and shake his head sadly, "Ha ha. This is the best you got, Bull? This muscle-bound abortion got me to Ravenel from the West Coast?"

Brannon straightened himself up, took a long drink from the bottle of port, set it down and said to Odum, "Sir."

"Yes, son, what is it?" Odum said, almost yawning.

"Sir," Brannon said, "you are fat."

Odum rose from his seat, walked around the table,

grabbing a fresh cigar as he went, and pulled up a chair in front of Brannon. He straddled the chair backward and stared into Brannon's eyes as though he were a carnivore studying food. Brannon stared back and the two men hung suspended in a moment of unanimated hostility until Odum began to roar like a lion at Brannon. Again and again, louder and louder, Odum would unleash a thunderous feline howl, a cat sound, unbridled, fulminating from deep within the man until Brannon, a servant to the wishes and moods of his fellow pilots, began to roar back, and the waiters who were clearing silver and china from the table witnessed two Marines in full dress snarling and hissing at each other like animals.

Until Odum suddenly stopped and offered Brannon the cigar. Hesitantly, Brannon accepted and offered Odum a cigar from his section of the mess. Odum struck a match, lit Brannon's cigar, then threw the burning match into Brannon's lap. As Brannon extinguished the match, Odum began eating his cigar, taking large bites and swallowing the tobacco with the relish of a gourmand. Brannon, now bound to play out whatever mad charade that Odum wished, dutifully and with utmost gravity began to consume his cigar after he had carefully extinguished it in his water glass.

At this moment the gavel of the Mess President resounded through the room and Bull Meecham released all pilots from the strictures and controls of the formal Mess with these words: "Gentlemen, will you join me at the bar."

Now was the time of hard drinking, rising volubility, and the games of pilots. Bull was drinking martinis out of either hand. A projector started up and a stag movie flickered grainily on a wall opposite the bar. A naked woman smiling concupiscently at the camera fornicated with a donkey, a German shepherd, a Negro, and her own finger. Sitting at the bar, Odum and Brannon arm-wrestled while members of the squadron slapped down money on the bar betting on their favorites. Veins stood out in bas-relief on the necks of both men but neither arm moved more than two or three degrees to the right or left of the fulcrum point. Four bartenders moved in an unrehearsed dance as they tried to provide drinks to the impatient Marines who screamed at them above the broadening dimensions of pandemonium loose in the Officers' Club. A line of young pilots were trying their skill at throwing down flaming hookers. They each ordered a glass of Courvoisier brandy, lit the fumes that rose invisibly above the lip of the glass, watched the blue flame until it was burning brightly, then, picking up the glass, they tossed the liquid down their throats. If they were good, a small blue flame would still be burning at the bottom of the glass when they slammed it down on the bar.

At midnight Apache Bill and Blue Balls Conners began wetting down a long slick black table with Coors beer and issued a call to all pilots with hair on their asses to prepare for carrier landings. A line of pilots began to form at the opposite end of the room, many of them removing their shoes and socks. Bull Meecham was the first in line, chugging what was left of his two martinis, then throwing the glasses the length of the room into the brick fireplace. Two dozen glasses followed his in a bright shower of crystal.

Several lieutenants rolled up tablecloths to act as landing cables and stood on either side of the far end of the beer-slick table. There were three landing cables that could stop a plane from rolling off the carrier deck into the ocean. Apache Bill found a huge summer fan which he placed at the very end of the carrier deck with the blades of the fan an added inducement for pilots to make sure they hooked onto one of the three landing cables.

"There's a bad fucking wind you have to land into, you bunch of Bull's pussies," Apache Bill yelled. "If you don't hook onto the last cable, then you get a bad case of the chicken shits."

Captain Johnson stood on the chair with two napkins in his outstretched arms. Blue Balls had designated him as the Landing Signal Officer. Blue Balls himself stood near the middle of the table with a bucket in his hands; opposite him stood Apache Bill with another bucket.

Bull straightened his arms out behind him in the angle of an F-8, then ran as fast as he could toward the table keeping his eye affixed on the arms of Captain Johnson.

The noise was deafening as he neared the point where he would leave his feet and slide the entire length of table, hooking his feet into one of the landing cables before being chopped up by the fan. Right before he jumped, Johnson gave him a cut. He catapulted to the center of the table, his arms behind him, and shot down the table with extraordinary speed, his eyes filling up with the vision of silver blades waiting for him like a mouth.

As he passed Apache Bill, a bucket of water was thrown on him. "Rain squall," the men screamed.

As he passed Blue Balls in a blur, he felt the sting of ice cubes flung into his face and the voice of Colonel Conners warning, "Hailstorm," and still he watched the blades and felt himself pass over the first cable, and the second, and lowering his feet quickly, his toes dug into the table and his feet hooked into the third cable right before he slid into the teeth of the fan. The third cable stopped him dead. He rose, blowing kisses to his squadron, then hopped down to watch the next pilot racing at full speed toward the landing deck.

At three in the morning, Bull ordered his entire squadron to line up single file behind him. Three of the men had passed out and could not obey this direct if slurringly articulated order. When he looked behind him and saw a wobbling, pixilated mass of men doing their best to imitate a line, he barked, "Follow me, hogs. Follow your C.O. and that is an order."

Bull marched them through the bar, past the dining room, out past the barbecue pits, the tennis courts, and toward the swimming pool. He led them to the deep end of the pool, mounted the diving board, and, still marching, shouting the cadences of Quantico, Bull marched off the end of the board followed by every pilot in 367 and the three guests who had flown to Ravenel for the celebration.

At four in the morning, Bull Meecham arrived home. Lillian awaited him in the kitchen.

Ben awoke and heard the unsteady voice of his father raised in a song that in the history of late-night homecomings was a traditional chant of warning. Over the house, the song hung from the ceiling, each word roach-faced and menacingly out of season.

"Silent Night, Holy Night,

"All is Calm, All is Bright."

And then he lay there as the danse macabre of the demons of fear that lived in his body began in earnest. And he heard his mother's voice, the voice of Lillian, the voice of the prettiest girl in Atlanta, Georgia, toughened, forged into a blade, a voice of a lady-in-waiting who had sallied forth to duel with the mailed knight crossing a moat that separated them. He heard the voice of the woman created by a marriage that had its own surprises and labyrinths, its own shadows and secret minotaurs. The song rose in volume, strangely bled of Christmas or of celebration. Now, at this moment, Ben thought, this song is a summons to battle, and as his senses sharpened in the dark, he could hear the forces of wrath gathering around the house and he knew that this would be one of the bad times. He girded himself and knew this would be a conflict that would extend the thresholds of his fear of his father and his cowardice before the plowman who had granted him life. He would act bravely; he would force himself to act bravely. But he knew. Even brave acts could not allay the fear: the consuming fear that ruled him whenever he had to face Bull Meecham boy to man. As he lay in his bed, he heard Karen's door opening and the sound of small, frantic feet on the stairs. Karen is first down, Ben thought. Good for Karen. And then Matthew's door and Mary Anne's door opened simultaneously and he could imagine Mary Anne straightening her glasses and Matthew's fury contained in that small body as they ran to help their mother, as they ran toward the song that always meant the same thing. But Ben knew that the only child who could influence the battle at all was lying in bed awaiting the gift of courage. Then he heard his mother begin to scream at his father and Ben thought, "Don't Mom. Don't fight him now. Let it go."

Then he heard Karen scream out, "Quit hurting Mama," and Ben was out of bed, borne down the stairs by the old Irish version of the divine wind, by the blood of the kamikaze, and he was running now as he heard

Mary Anne cry out his name, and he entered the kitchen in time to see his father hideously drunk and laughing. He had Lillian pinned against one wall holding her by the throat as she tried to scratch out his eyes. Matt was holding on to one leg, trying to lift it off the floor. Mary Anne was biting his wrist, trying to pull one arm away from her mother's throat and Karen was hitting his back with fists that could inflict no pain. Of the noises loose in the room, of the screams, of the words, Bull's laughter was the most ominous. And his eyes were wild with the drink. The dragon was loose in his eyes. And Ben came with momentum, driven by fear as he entered the kitchen as a footsoldier bound by the rites of a perverted chivalry written into the family's history. Each time he came to fight his father only one thing had changed: each time Ben was larger and stronger than he had been the time before. With his head down he drove one hundred and sixty pounds of sonflesh into his father's stomach. He pumped his legs hard and felt his father's weight shift and the man stumble. Bull's grip was wrenched loose from Lillian's throat and Ben saw Mary Anne and Matt fly off and away as he drove his father into the refrigerator. But then he realized that the moment of surprise had slipped away forever and that he could not take his father to the ground. And a new dimension entered the combat: a father's awareness of a growing son, the son as challenger, the son as threat, the son as successor, the son as man. But before Bull could turn to the business of Ben, Lillian came at him again, came for his eyes with a five-bladed hand, but he backhanded her and she slumped against the counter, blood spilling from her bottom lip, blood and tears commingling as in a sacrament. Then Bull turned on Ben and his hands went around Ben's throat, both hands tightened, gained control, and Ben was lifted off the floor by his throat. Then Mary Anne sank her teeth into her father's right arm, but Bull lashed out with his right arm, holding Ben suspended by one hand. Mary Anne crashed off the kitchen table, her glasses shattering on the floor, but she came back across the room, running blindly, going into battle against a blurred enemy. Matt received a slap to the face that spun him to the floor where he lay for a moment crying because he was small and because he did not matter and because he could not hurt the man who was hurting him. Then, for a second, there were Ben and his father, eye to eye, as intimate as lovers, and the fingers tightened on the throat and Ben gagged. Slowly, Bull took Ben's head and began slamming it into the wall. Once. Twice. Three times. Then the family was on him again, resurrected by the sound of Ben's skull meeting the wall. They came at him from four sides and they came at him with teeth and nails and tears and the fury of four small nations who have nothing left to lose. Bull dropped Ben and stood there, his hands down beside him. He no longer tried to fight, but acted stunned as if for the first time there was some illumination, some comprehension of the enormity of the resistance in a once placid kingdom. Bull stood there accepting the small hurts of the border skirmishes waged on four frontiers of his body. Ben saw the dragon melt out of Bull's eyes and there came a moment when Ben could have hit his father in the face with a fist that was a lifetime in coming. There was nothing to stop him and he could feel the fist tighten and the punch being telegraphed for eighteen years and he almost sang for joy and through the membrane of his hatred he kicked like a fetus and he prepared to hit the face and make it bleed. But he could not. He would have if he could, but he could not. Though he wanted to hurt this man like he had been hurt, like he had known hurt, he could not hit him. He could not hit the father; he could not hit the face of the father that would be the face of his father for all time.

In a wilderness of screaming and weeping, in a wasteland of his own creation, Bull shook off the inconsequential warriors that swarmed around him and stumbled out of the kitchen, down the back stairs, and into the night.

They listened to the screen door slam. They lay on the floor and wept. Mary Anne was holding a hand over one eye while Karen leaned against her shoulder and cried. Matthew's face was buried in his hands and sobs burst out of him without a sound. The weeping had an accidentally contrapuntal harmony, a symphony of grief in the blood-stained kitchen. For ten minutes they sat in their appointed places where they had been flung in the last moments before the furious exit.

It was Mary Anne who broke the silence when she called out to the blurs on the floor around her.

"Who's the biggest jerk of all?!" she shouted. But no one answered or knew how to answer.

The family did not recognize immediately the nature of the game.

"I said, 'Who's the biggest jerk of all?' " she cried out again.

This time the family was ready, primed for the question and they screamed out, "The Great Santini!"

And Mary Anne continued in a voice that broke into fragments as she spoke, "Who stinks the worst? Who is a big dope? And who is made out of puke and fish feces?"

"The Great Santini!"

"Who wears a brassiere and women's panties all the time?"

"The Great Santini!"

"Who's a Communist and a homosexual and probably passing for white?"

"The Great Santini!"

Then they were laughing, the species of laughter that often comes as a bridesmaid of violence. It comes for no reason or from a geography of the spirit that is an untracked and foreign land. It was Lillian who began to laugh and it spread to her children and possessed them, a laughter one part hysteria and one part relief. It was an affirmation that the fight was over and that they had banded together, fought for each other, bled for each other, and that they would fight anything that moved, anything that lived, anything that entered the house of Meecham to wage war against a Meecham. Even if that thing was the source and originator of that house.

As Ben was getting back in bed, Lillian appeared at the door of his bedroom and said, "Your father's not back yet. I'm getting worried about him."

"I hope he died of pain out in the marsh," Ben said.

"He didn't take the car, sugah. That means he's afoot.

461

I'm worried that he passed out somewhere in the neighborhood."

"Too bad. A real shame, Mama."

"I want you to go look for him."

"Give me a loaded gun and I might give it a try."

"I want you to go bring your father home, Ben. And I want you to bring him home now."

"I'm not going to do it, Mama."

"Yes you are, Ben," she said patiently. "*I* am asking you to bring your father home. Now hurry before the sun goes up."

So Ben dressed and left the house in the dark not knowing where to search or even to begin. First, he skirted the edge of the marsh near the house. He walked the length of Eliot Street until he reached the Catholic church, then came back down Rowland Street. He began to call out, "Dad! Dad!" but heard no response.

It was after five in the morning when he found him lying almost in the dead center of the Lawn. There was blood on his dress whites and his uniform was still damp from the plunge into the swimming pool at the Club. He had retrieved a bottle of Tanqueray from his squadron car and had come to the middle of this acre of grass, this common land flanked by mansions, to drink alone far from the dissonance of his children's eyes. He was moaning when Ben reached him and was lying in his own vomit.

Ben stood over his father, astride of him. For a moment it did not register to Ben what he was seeing. For the first time in his life he was studying a helpless Bull Meecham and thoughts began to gather in storm clouds as his father's face turned toward him. Ben had a notion to stomp the face until it was indistinguishable from the grass, to kick the belly until his foot broke through to the spinal cord, to bring the blood flow from every orifice in the body, to thumb the fighter pilot's eyes into permanent darkness, to smash the testes until the life-giving power was extinguished forever. But, as in the kitchen, Ben did nothing. Atrocities occurred only in his brain.

"Dad," he said, and the figure moaned in the grass. "I got to get you back to the house, Dad."

"I'm sick, mama's boy," Bull answered.

"I know, Dad. I got to get you back to the house. You've got to help me because I can't carry you by myself."

Ben's rage had fled and it angered Ben that he had no camel hump of spirit where rage could be stored, preserved, and called upon whenever it was needed. Twenty minutes before he would have spit on this obscenity in the grass or he thought he would have done it. Now he was trying to resuscitate the hatred he had felt in the kitchen. But it would not come. Rage blazed up in him often, but its atoms were too active for preservation and its life span was brief like the kick and the flame of an afterburner in his father's F-8.

He tried to get under his father and lift him up, but could not. He went down again and managed to coax Bull up on his hands and knees. Then he hooked Bull's arm around his neck and together they rose, and began staggering toward home. And as they walked a feeling came over Ben that he tried to control but could not. He felt himself about to say something and he fought against it. He warred against it, but his tongue was a transient orator who, in moments of madness or in the dazzling half-nelson of a father's arm, assumed a life and career of its own. He heard himself saying, unbelieving, unwilling:

"I love you, Dad."

Bull Meecham increased the tempo of his slouch homeward and acted as though he didn't hear.

And the voice came again and Ben listened to it with the same sense of wonder as his father.

"I love you, Dad."

Ben saw his father looking over at him as though he was witnessing the birth of something wild and schizophrenic in the psyche of his oldest son. Bull pulled away from Ben, then wheeled back toward the middle of the lawn and began running into the darkness. But the liquor still had his legs. He ran in an agonizingly circuitous pattern, weaving and stumbling, falling once, but

463

immediately on his feet again, running slowly, unable to escape anything.

Running behind his father, Ben began to feel a disproportionate joy rise in him. He began to catch his father, sprint past him, slap him on the rump in passage, and turn him like a steer. And he started chanting joyously, teasingly, the master of his tongue again, "I love you, Dad. I love you, Dad. I love you. I love you. I love you." And each time Bull would turn away from the phrase and hunt the part of the night that would enclose or hide him. Then he fell a last time and began vomiting again.

Ben stopped. He was smiling, exhilarated, liberated and meanly enjoying a weapon he did not know lay in his arsenal. When Bull had finished throwing up, Ben thought about resuming the chant, but did not. He hooked his father's arm around his neck again, got him to his feet, and walked him toward the house in silence.

33

By the end of April the air was full of summer and the small wind that lifted off the river was heavy and uninvigorating. Lillian Meecham sat on the lower veranda with her children rocking in a chair and waiting for the sun to go down. Even the sun seemed to be affected by the air.

"Is Dad going to be transferred anywhere this summer, Mama?" Karen asked.

"No. He'll be at Ravenel at least one more year."

"This will be the first time we've been in one place for two years in a long time," Matthew noted.

"I wouldn't leave my new friends for anything," Karen said passionately. "I'd kill myself before I'd move somewhere else."

"You won't have to, sugah. We're staying in Ravenel next year," Lillian consoled.

"Hey, Mary Anne," Ben said from his perch on the green railing where he leaned against the white doric column.

"Yeah, fish feces," she answered, not lifting her eyes from the book she was studying in the diminishing light.

"The Junior-Senior Prom is in two weeks. Anybody ask you yet?"

"Very funny. What a joke," Matthew cackled.

Mary Anne raised her eyes imperiously and cast a withering glance at her younger brother who returned it in full.

"As a matter of fact, I have had hundreds of phone calls from some of the smartest and best looking boys at Calhoun High. But none of them are mature enough to converse with such a chic and worldly woman."

465

"That's a laugh," Matt said. "No one's ever called you for a date in your whole life."

"That will be quite enough, mister," Lillian said to Matthew.

"Why'd you ask, golden boy?" Mary Anne said.

"Because, I, Benjamin Meecham, being of sound mind and body, do hereby announce that I intend to take my sister, Mary Anne Meecham, to the Junior-Senior Spring Formal, if she but permits it."

"Oh, puke," Matt said, leaning over the railing and pretending to vomit in the side yard.

"Have you lost your gourd?" Mary Anne said, her eyes returning to her book.

"I think that's a very sweet gesture, Ben," Lillian said.

"I ain't no charity case, big brother. No thanks."

"Wait a minute, Mary Anne. I know you're not a charity case. But look at it this way. I don't have a date. I'm too chicken to get one. I tried to call up a few girls, but as soon as I did my face broke out in pimples and my nose hair grew to a length of three feet . . ."

"You don't have to sink into vulgarity, darling," Lillian interrupted.

"Earwax poured out of the side of my head and sweat rained down from my underarms," he continued. "So I don't have a date. Since Sammy isn't here, he can't ask a girl for me. So we ought to go together. It's your Junior-Senior too and it looks like no hunchback or blind man is going to call you."

"I don't think that's funny," Mary Anne said.

"Nor do I, Ben," Lillian agreed. "But I do think it was adorable of you to ask Mary Anne, sugah."

"C'mon, Mama, don't say that kind of stuff or I'll never get her to go with me."

"You'll never get me to go with you anyway," Mary Anne said to her book. "It sounds a little sicko-sexual to me."

"Why, for God's sake?" Ben demanded. "Why don't you want to go?"

"Because I honestly don't want to. Besides, you ought to get a date. It will look perverted and I can't dance."

"I don't want to get a date," Ben answered. "I am perverted and I can't dance either."

"Your father and I can teach you how to dance," Lillian stated. "He and I are the two best jitterbuggers in the Marine Corps. We can teach you in one or two nights."

"They don't do the minuet much anymore, Mama," Ben grinned.

"I didn't even know Godzilla could dance," Mary Anne said.

"You ought to go, Coke bottle eyes," Matt said. "This'll probably be the last chance in your whole life to go to a dance."

"You do wonders for my ego, paramecium," Mary Anne reported.

"I'll go with you, Ben," Karen said, "if Mary Anne won't go. I'd love to go with you."

"You're right up there among the top two candidates, Karen. But this is Mary Anne's first Junior-Senior and my last. She's going to be my date. First we'll have a candle-light dinner down at the Officers' Club. Perchance, a little wine or a bit of champagne from the land of the Frog. Then we will dance the night away beneath the streamers decorating the high school gymnasium."

"What do you think Jim Don and Pinkie and all those other imbecile jocks will say?" Mary Anne asked.

"The hell with them," Ben said, pulling both of his feet up on the railing, encircling his bent legs with his arms. "We'll have a ball."

"Those people will laugh at us."

"If they laugh, I'll punch them on the cheek," Ben said.

"You ought to go, pig nose," Matt said.

"You've got a pig nose, too, Midget," Mary Anne said. "It's just that you're so small I never notice it. I'm always looking at the top of your head."

"If you two don't stop being nasty to each other, I'm going to take a broom to both of you," Lillian said furiously.

"She's too ugly to get asked to the prom by anyone else," Matt said.

"You're going to get slapped, mister," Lillian said, drawing her hand back.

"Matt didn't mean that, Mary Anne," Karen said. "He really didn't mean that."

"Mama," Mary Anne said, her eyes once again fastened to an unseen, unfocused word in the book on her lap, "aren't you happy that you're beautiful?"

"I am not beautiful. I've told you that a thousand times."

"Don't be pious, Mama. You're beautiful and beautiful women get everything they want."

They heard the back door slam and the heavy footsteps of Colonel Meecham coming through the house. Before he reached the front door on the way to join them, Lillian leaned over toward Mary Anne and whispered fiercely, "I didn't get everything I wanted."

Bull Meecham strode down the length of the veranda holding a Budweiser in one hand.

"It looks like the troops are goldbricking again and the C.O. needs to revamp the work detail. Let's cut the idle chitchat and police up the area."

"You should have called me if you weren't coming home for dinner, sugah," Lillian said, rising from her chair and kissing her husband on the cheek.

"I got into a little wrestling match with Jack Daniel over at the club and forgot to call," Bull said, winking at his children.

"Ben's taking Mary Anne to the Junior-Senior Prom," Karen said.

"Hey, that's great, sportsfans."

"You and Mom are going to teach them how to dance," Matt added.

Taking Lillian's hand and bowing dramatically, Bull pulled his wife to her feet, held her close to his body, and they began to waltz around the veranda. For a large man, he danced with surprising grace. They seemed to flow into each other and move as one body, a coupling of flesh that came so easily that it embarrassed Ben.

"You've got to be loose. You hogs must have inherited some of Santini's rhythm," Bull said.

468

"I inherited Santini's legs," Mary Anne answered.

"I've always been able to dance like a nigger," Bull shouted.

"Negro! Bull. Negro," Lillian corrected.

"What's that book you're reading, Mary Anne?" Ben asked, directing his attention away from his parents who were beginning to lose themselves in the spirit of their impromptu and somehow nakedly sensual dance.

"It's really none of your business but it's Halliwell's *Dictionary of Archaic and Provincial Words,*" Mary Anne said. She was not watching her parents dance either.

"You mean it was you who stole my copy of Halliwell's?" Ben laughed.

"Why on earth are you reading that? That's just a book of dead words."

"I relate very well to dead words. They interest me and they help me. I can insult people without their knowing it. For instance, Matt is a cuglion."

"Did you hear what she called me, Mom? I bet it's dirty," Matt cried.

"It is simply a stupid, cattle-headed fellow. Mom is a dangwallet, which means a spendthrift, someone who just loves throwing away money. Dad is a slubberdegullion, which is a paltry dirty wretch. Karen is a grizzle-demundy, which is a stupid person always grinning."

"That's not very nice, Mary Anne," Karen said.

"It's all a joke, Karen. I bought this book for a quarter at the Catholic Bazaar and I've got to use it or Mom will say it's a waste of money."

"Speaking of money," Lillian said, "what are you going to wear if you go with Ben to the Junior-Senior?"

"I haven't said I was going yet," Mary Anne said.

"She'll wear the prettiest dress at the dance," Bull said.

"I don't have anything to wear to a formal dance," Mary Anne said.

"We'll buy you a goddam dress," Bull bellowed.

"I'll try to borrow one from one of the young 'O' Club wives. We can't afford to go out and buy a formal dress that Mary Anne will only wear once in her life."

"The hell we can't," Bull disagreed.

"Times are lean, Bull," Lillian said, pulling away from her husband and breaking step. "I'm sure one of the girls has a spare formal that will do just fine for Mary Anne."

"She's going to have her own dress. The Great Santini has spoken."

"The Great Santini doesn't handle the books," Lillian answered fiercely. "The Mrs. Great Santini does."

"You see," Mary Anne said to Ben, "she is a dang-wallet."

"Hey, sportsfans," Bull called to Mary Anne, "are the other girls in your class buying dresses or borrowing them?"

"They'll say they're buying them. But they'll be borrowing dresses, mark my words," Lillian insisted.

"They're buying dresses," Ben said.

The following day, after a furious argument with his wife, Bull Meecham drove Mary Anne to Sarah Poston's dress shop on River Street and bought a full length formal gown for the Calhoun High School Junior-Senior Prom of 1963.

Dressed in his tuxedo and feeling conspicuously elegant, Ben came downstairs on the night of the prom. His father was reclining on the sofa reading the evening paper. Ben walked over to his father and came to attention by clicking his heels together and pulling his shoulders back.

"You look good, sportsfans. Your hair's sticking up in the back but otherwise you win the Commandant's Cup. Where's Mary Anne?" Bull said.

"She's upstairs still getting dressed."

"She's been getting dressed for about three days."

"She really likes that gown you bought her, Dad."

"She ought to, sweet pea. Your mother's been jawbon-ing about that dress for two goddam weeks. I told her that I only want the best for my hogs."

"Do you think this coat's too loose?"

"Naw, it looks fine. You'll probably be raped by a broad or two before the night's over. Go on out to the porch so your mother can complete the inspection."

Lillian was sitting on the steps, smoking a cigarette and

looking out at a barge coming through the opened bridge.

"How do I look, Mama?" Ben asked.

"Like a prince," she said. "Turn around."

Ben spun around in a circle pretending to dance. Lillian rose and went to him. "Let's practice those steps once more," she said, taking his left hand and putting her arm around his neck. They danced in silence for a moment or two with Ben watching his feet and Lillian smiling at his adolescent discomfiture in formal dress.

"Any girl would be proud to go to the prom with you," Lillian said.

"Mary Anne acts like she's mad that I asked her," Ben replied.

"She gets that from your father's side of the family. Let's sit down and breathe in the river. There's nothing more beautiful than a southern night in late spring," she said, sitting on the top step again and taking out a cigarette. Ben fumbled to take her matches away from her, then lit a match, the glow of the flame catching her for a moment, framing her in the nimbus of its brief life. "Thank you, darling. At least I've taught you to be a gentleman. That's something no one will ever be able to take away from you."

"Mama?" Ben asked, his eyes staring into the darkness. "Am I southern?"

"What a silly question. Why do you ask, sugah?"

"Because I want to know."

"Of course you are, darling. You were born in Georgia and you've always lived below the Mason-Dixon Line."

"There are times when I don't feel southern, Mama, when I don't feel much of anything. Philip Turner knows everything about this town, knows every person in it, knows a story about every house we pass and the history of every person we see. I don't know anyone's history, not even my own. I do know that Dad is midwestern and Irish. And I know that you're southern. Sammy Wertzberger is southern and so is Mr. Loring and Mr. Dacus. But I'm not. I don't talk like a southerner and most of the time I don't think like a southerner. I'm really not anything. Do you know what I mean?"

"I have worried about it some, sugah. All the boys I

471

grew up with could hunt and fish, knew what to wear, had a strong feeling about the land, and about the traditions of their homeland. You've got to stay put to have this. You can't move every other year and be anything but a transient. I've worried that my children would grow up and be neither southern nor Yankee but something far worse—that my children would be nothing but geographical mulattos with no roots. That's why I take you back to Atlanta every time your father goes overseas. I want you to get to feel that Mamaw's house is your real home, the place you go back to when you think about where you belong. I've always hoped you would build up a storehouse of rich memories from that house. It's also why I encouraged your nights out with Toomer. He was all the South used to be and all it should still be and all it's never going to be again. So is Arrabelle. You can look into her face and see a most glorious and noble history of pain and even of victory. I knew when Arrabelle walked in my back door that I would hire her and we would become friends. Some of the strongest and most admirable people I have ever known came to me through kitchen doors. But to answer your question, Ben, and I think it's a most important question, indeed—you are not completely southern but you are more southern than anything else and I'd rather be almost southern than almost Queen of England."

"Can you be southern if you want to be?" Ben asked.

"No," Lillian said. "It doesn't work like that. A southerner is. And a southerner knows he is."

They heard Bull give a piercing wolf whistle from his vantage point on the sofa and they knew Mary Anne was coming down the stairs. Together they rose and entered the house.

The dress was blue with white ruffles at the shoulder and Mary Anne made her way down the stairs cautiously, afraid of tripping. She had borrowed a string of pearls from Lillian and a pair of long white gloves from Paige Hedgepath. She was not wearing her glasses and she held tightly to the bannister during her descent.

"You look absolutely stunning, sugah," Lillian said.

472

"I didn't know you were so stacked, sportsfans," Bull crowed.

"Hush, Bull," Lillian admonished, "before God or somebody hears you."

"How sicko can you get?" Mary Anne said, but she blushed with a forbidden pleasure at the compliment. When she reached the bottom of the stairs, Ben pinned an orchid corsage on her, bowed deeply, offered his arm, and they promenaded across the living room to the sofa where Bull lay, pivoted, then walked to the stairs again. Karen and Matt had come from the kitchen to watch.

"Wait here while I get my Kodak," Lillian said, going toward the kitchen.

"You look beautiful, Mary Anne," Karen said.

"Thank you, Karen. But I'm tired of all these honors befalling me because of my beauty. I've been homecoming queen for two years in a row now and it just isn't fair to the other girls. But this year when the captain of the football team begs me for a date, I'll just politely refuse and let the honor fall to some other fair maiden."

"Boy, what a joke that is," Matt said. "You a homecoming queen."

"Go twit out the window and find Peter Pan, Tinkerbell," Mary Anne snapped.

"O.K., Dad," Matt said turning to his father, "belt her one for that or it's gonna be Simba Barracuda for ol' four eyes."

"Shut your yap, Matt," Bull said.

"Hold still for a picture," Lillian said, returning with a small camera with a flash attachment.

"Where are your glasses, Mary Anne?" Karen asked.

"They detract from my heavenly beauty, so I'm not going to wear them. Of course, I'm blind as a stone without them. Ben's not only going to be my date tonight. He's going to be my Seeing Eye dog."

"You hogs better hurry," Bull said, glancing at his watch. "Your reservations at the Club are at 1900 on the button."

"Let's see you walk across the room just one more time, sugah," Lillian said to Mary Anne, "only this time

473

remember what I told you. Lift your legs high beneath the dress. Prance like a pony."

Once again Mary Anne crossed the room under the careful scrutiny of her mother's gaze.

"You got that walk from your father's side of the family. But that's much better. Now give me a kiss, both of you, and be off to the Club."

As Lillian kissed Ben, she looked into his eyes and said, "Your eyes come from my side of the family, Ben. They are a brilliant blue."

"Dad has blue eyes, too, Mama," Karen said.

"Yes, but his blue eyes are washed out, almost colorless. Ben has Barrett eyes. All of you do. Eyes with character and depth."

"Yeah," Bull said. "My eyes ain't nothin'."

"We've got to hurry," Ben said.

As Ben opened the car door for Mary Anne, Matthew appeared on the porch and shouted, "You look nice, Mary Anne," then ran back inside the house.

"What do you think we got from Dad's side of the family?" Mary Anne asked Ben as they drove to the air station. "Mom doesn't give the beast too much credit for passing on good genes."

"Let's figure it out," Ben answered. "What would Mom attribute to Dad's side? The dread Chicago side."

"Freckles, pimples, a vile temper, a funny walk, wide feet, stubby fingers, a tendency to be alcoholics, and madness," Mary Anne suggested.

"True," Ben agreed. "All that comes from Dad's side of the family. Also things like boogers. Our boogers come from his side of the family."

"Very inferior boogers," Mary Anne said. "Her side of the family produces Grade-A, government-inspected boogers, or so she thinks."

"Also we inherited the turds of the Meecham family," Ben said. "Mom's side of the family poops vanilla ice cream."

"That's not true," Mary Anne said. "They poop moonbeams, dimes and quarters, and sanctifying grace."

"You realize, of course, how guilty I feel talking behind Mom's back. You realize that our mother is a saint," Ben said.

"Of course she's a saint."

"God likes her a lot."

"She's also a dangwallet. But her being a dangwallet fits in perfectly with her conception of what a saint should be. Lillian is perfect. Absolutely perfect. She is beautiful. She is good. She is holy. She prays all the time. And she is married to The Creep. Her sainthood is assured and God has no choice but to like her."

Ben said, "I only wish she would take herself a bit less seriously. I mean just the other day I heard Mrs. Grantham tell her that she was a saint on this earth. And do you know what Mom did?"

"I'm afraid to ask. Truly afraid."

"Mom just nodded her head as though she agreed one hundred percent with Mrs. Grantham and was pleased as punch that Mrs. Grantham was so, so . . . you know, so perceptive."

"Mom has only one fault. She has no faults. That's why a lot of people hate her guts. I've known some women who have pretended to like her who really hate her and will always hate her. I've seen them look at her when she wasn't looking back."

"I'll take her over Dad any day."

"Not me, brother man," Mary Anne said with conviction. "Dad's not so bad. I remember when I was a kid and Dad used to have fun by punching me in the fontanel and I thought he was a wee bit wanting as a father. But not now. That was just Dad preparing me for life as he knows it. Dad is Bull Meecham and he's never pretended to be anything else. Sometimes he is the beast, I admit, but he is a consistent beast."

The car pulled up to the main gate and Ben pulled down the sun visor and tried to age his face five years by assuming a stern, no-nonsense expression. When the sentry snapped a salute at the car, Ben nodded his approval and said, "Good evening, son."

"You got that from Dad's side of the family," Mary Anne said as Ben drove toward the Club.

The maitre d' of the Officers' Club seated them at a candlelit table in the center of the room. There were very few couples dining in the main room, but the bar was crammed with young Marine officers, their wives, and their dates. Ben ordered for both himself and Mary Anne since Mary Anne could not decipher a single letter from the menu without her glasses. She blamed the dim light.

Before the first course arrived, the headwaiter brought a dozen red roses and presented them to Mary Anne.

"Who sent them?" Mary Anne asked, frowning as though she were the victim of a joke or a conspiracy to embarrass her.

"Read the card," Ben said.

"I can't read it and you know I can't read it," she said. "The El Cheapo Marines use this candlelight because they hate spending a dollar or two on electric lights."

Ben took the card and, holding it close to the candle, read aloud: " 'Here's twelve roses for the prettiest girl at the hop. Don't tell the dangwallet or she'll jawbone about the cost of the flowers. Have a good time. The Great Santini.' "

"Dad is so childishly sentimental," Mary Anne said. "Isn't this ridiculous?"

"I thought you were going to come up with a dead word," Ben said.

"Dad is an assinego," Mary Anne said promptly.

"What does that mean?"

"It means that he's a young, silly ass sometimes."

"What are you?"

"I am a damirep. A very flighty woman, too free in her manners."

"Did you look up butthole?" Ben asked.

"You're just jealous, Ben. You don't know any big words you haven't learned from Mr. Loring's vocabulary lists. It makes you mad that I'm discovering things about words that you'll never know because you're a jump-shooter."

"Well, you're just showing off learning words that aren't even used anymore. And it doesn't do any good to

476

insult someone when they don't even know they're being insulted."

"I feel sorry for dead words," Mary Anne said. "Have you ever wondered how a perfectly good word dies and a useful word at that? If I use a dead word then I think it's possible it can come alive again."

"God, that's weird," Ben said. "Do you know what I worry about, Mary Anne? I'm worried that someday I'm going to be visiting you in some nut house where you'll have turned into a rutabaga or something. I can see me bringing you toothpaste and deodorant and you'll be sitting there with your brain burned out, drooling in your shoes. And some nurse will say to you, 'Rutabaga, do you remember your brother Ben?' "

"And I'll say, 'Yes, I remember the sin-eater.' That's my dead word for you, Ben. It was an ancient custom at funerals to hire poor people to take upon themselves the sins of the deceased. You know, to eat the sins of the rich. But you, Ben, would be much too pious to eat sins for money. You'd do it just to be good."

"This is why you never have any friends, Mary Anne. You're always trying to be so goddam smart and know-it-all."

"When I die, Ben, I want you to eat all my sins just like you're eating that salad there. I want to shoot like a rocket up to heaven. For all eternity, I want to float like a Sputnik around God's head. All because you chowed down on my acts of commission and omission."

"You don't always have to show off what you know," Ben said.

"If you don't show it off, feces face, then who's going to know it?"

"You'll know," Ben answered. "That's what's important. I've always admired quiet people who have achieved a lot much more than I have loud, obnoxious people who brag about their achievements."

"You have?" Mary Anne said sarcastically.

"Keep your voice down," Ben whispered. "People are beginning to notice us."

"I wish they gave a Congressional Medal of Honor for piety. Saint Lillian is the Patron Saint of piety, but you ought to receive some kind of recognition for your efforts. When Saint Lillian is assumed into heaven, then you're going to be a shoo-in for the title of Patron Saint. You're so sweet, Ben, so innocent, so God Damn Christlike. God missed a good bet not having you born in Bethlehem."

"Why are you attacking me? I'm the one who's taking you to the Junior-Senior."

"I'm attacking you, Ben, because you are the one who is taking me to the Junior-Senior. There are two things about you I can't stand, golden boy. One is your sickening fake modesty. The other is your goodness. Just like Dad can't stop drinking, you can't stop being good. You can't be satisfied with being an average nice guy, you've got to be the nicest guy that anyone will ever meet. But I've noticed that you're always good in ways where people can see it and compliment you on it. And by far the best thing you've ever done, the grandest act of all, the crowning glory is taking your fat, freckled sister to the Junior-Senior. Long Live Saint Benjamin! Who asked you to take me? Mom or Dad?"

"No one," Ben said, cutting the steak just brought by the waiter.

"How noble."

"No one, I said," Ben flared.

"It was just natural sugar-coated goodness. Pure saintliness."

"That's right. I'm beloved of the Lord."

"Let me say one last thing, jock brother, and then I'll become sweet Mary Anne again."

"Sweet Mary Anne? You'll have to introduce me," Ben said, attacking his steak and talking with his mouth full.

"You and Mom can hurt people more with your piety than Dad can ever hurt with his temper. You always know where Dad stands and he knows where he stands, but no one will ever know where Golden Ben and Darling Lillian stand, not even Golden Ben and Darling Lillian," Mary Anne said, ignoring her food. "You know why Dad hits you—not all the time, but sometimes. He sees her piety in a male face and sometimes he can't help but hit it. If he can beat it out of you, he thinks maybe that some of it will be drained out of her."

"If you don't eat, Mary Anne, I'm going to throw you in the swimming pool or pour A–1 Sauce on your orchid."

"You wouldn't do that. You're the Perfect One."

"Eat," Ben ordered.

For several minutes they ate in absolute silence. Ben was acutely aware that the couples at the other tables were staring at them with a mixture of curiosity and chagrin. Struggling with her steak, Mary Anne looked hunched and bruised beneath the pale blue dress that covered her delicately, as though the dust had been scraped from a butterfly wing. She had to bring her face close to the plate to see what she was eating. Ben wanted to say something to hurt her, but could not force himself to do it. She would attribute it to measureless wellsprings of piety or stewardship of the phantom herds that bled out the milk of human kindness. But it was something different and far deeper, he thought. Though they had grown up in the same household and were shaped by the same two parents, Mary Anne had been damaged more severely in the passage. He had grown up to be afraid, but he had not grown up to suffer. He was not a member of that forsaken elect. But his date across the table was.

Finally, he said, "Here's what I figured, Mary Anne. Next year, I'll be in college and this will be the last time we ever go out together like this and anyway I'm going to miss you and you've been my best friend and who cares anyway."

"I think I'll kill myself," Mary Anne answered.

"Good."

"No, I mean really."

"I mean really, too. I mean really good," Ben said. "Anyway, you're too chicken to do it."

"You'll be sorry, Ben. When the doctor pulls the blanket over my head, you'll become hysterical, because you had a chance to stop me and did nothing. They say that a suicide always gives off warning signals and that's what I'm doing right now. This is a warning signal."

"Why are you going to kill yourself?"

"Because I'm real depressed," Mary Anne answered.

"You're always depressed."

"Yeah, but this time I'm real depressed. Suicidally depressed and, buddy-roo, you can't get more depressed than that."

"How you going to do it?" Ben asked.

"Painlessly. That's the most important thing. I want there to be no pain. None whatsoever. And no blood. I will not tolerate a bloody corpse. I want to be lovely in death."

"Why don't you die on the operating table while you're having a nose job."

"That's one thing that always bothered me about you, Ben. You get serious when the world's screaming with laughter around you. Then you get witty when you're trying to talk a very valuable human being out of killing herself."

"I just wanted you to be lovely in death. C'mon," Ben said looking at his watch, "we've got a rendezvous in Paris."

The theme of the dance was Gaieté Parisienne and the gymnasium where Ben had once thrown up jump shots and broken a boy's arm was decorated in one corner with La Tour Eiffel and in another with a cardboard frontispiece of Notre Dame. Beside the home bleachers, Ben and Mary Anne walked past les boutiques de Paris as "Moon River" was played by the band hired for the evening. The band was dressed as Apache dancers and three of the female teachers came modestly attired in can-can outfits.

Ben danced the first slow dance with Mary Anne, both of them counting steps and laughing as they counted. Philip Turner cut in before the dance was over. Mr. Dacus danced the first fast dance with Mary Anne and Ogden Loring took the second slow dance. Ansley Matthews, forsaken by Jim Don who had slipped out to the parking lot to drink, asked Ben to dance twice. Memory books were passed back and forth. A flower cart pushed by a sophomore distributed flowers as souvenirs.

Streamers hung from the steel rafters almost to the head level of the tallest boys. The water fountain had a sign that read "Le vin Beaujolais." Pinkie danced twice with Mary Anne, Art the Fart once. The evening passed quickly, even magically at times. Parisian times in the marshes of Ravenel. No one laughed.

34

It was a night flight and Bull Meecham had flown from Ravenel to Key West, an out and in flight that would satisfy the requirement of four hours night flying a month.

At 0330 in the morning he departed from Key West estimating his arrival in Ravenel at 0520. He would fly at 32,000 feet. As the F–8 took off, Bull thought about how lucky he was that flight was still a glorious experience for him; he had not grown bored over the years; rather, he still got a small boy's pleasure out of flying a jet plane.

The jet rose in darkness, humming with energy and God-strength beneath Bull Meecham as he climbed toward his pale, his frontier, as the earth grew puny around him. It was here in an aircraft that he had strange gods before him and his religion was a theology of wind and current, a worship of stars blinking in the intransient dark. Stars, to him, were fixed mariners, old friends, fine compasses, light pure, and druids in the silvery separateness of the night flight. When he left the earth, Bull knew that he had every chance of passing through a square foot of sky unviolated by man before. He could dance as no man had ever danced before; he could spin, dive, or whirl, and his antics in a cloud kingdom thirty thousand feet above the earth would be pure flirtations with absolute limits, with thresholds. His dance in the sky was a ballet of power and menace and there were times when his love of flying possessed him and he would want to heel and toe across the length of one wing, then leap the fuselage and soft-shoe with hat and cane across the other wing, dropping to one knee, and extending his arm to all who would understand this fixation at last; this addiction that certain men develop for flying.

He had begun his career as a night fighter and still practiced the skills of that subphylum of aviator. To him the most feared soldier ever created was the pilot who came at night, hiding from the cast-eyed light of half moons, coming winged and unannounced out of the black, out of the void.

At ten thousand feet, the jet emerged from a cloud bank and the moon filled the cockpit with a light that seemed more than light; it was something distilled through air, something with a smell and a taste and Bull drank in the moon through his eyes and nose and the pores of his skin, a soft Chablis of light suspended between earth and sky. The song of stars tonguelessly entertained him. Bull Meecham was silver, winged, and timeless.

Ben and Mary Anne slept in hammocks on the upper veranda porch. A dog barked somewhere in the dark. A barge, laden with Georgia timber, its lights sliding toward the bridge, sounded its horn, and the bridge swung open. Ben awoke fully awake. He slipped downstairs, out the back door, and made his way to the end of the dock where he watched the barge pass by the house. It was turning colder and the air was heavy with the threat of rain, but the kind of rain that on cool mornings is bled out of the unsubstantial flesh of the fog. The tide had turned and as always when he went to the river's edge and studied the movement of the water, he thought of Toomer and those long nights when stuttering, fishing, and singing, the black man had made a textbook of the river and told Ben things he would never have known, the calculus of approach and recall that ruled every living thing in the tight, contained beauty of returning river. Toomer had taught that all fish, the greatest and smallest, listened to the testimony of the tide in their every nerve ending, in every bone, and in every cell. The smallest fish must play the tide to the last possible moment, hugging the marsh while there is still water, hanging back, and not rushing headlong into the creeks where larger fish were also gambling against the land trapping them. But eventually, the tides forced all creatures to the open waters. For the marsh itself was both a sanctuary and a tomb, its slender grasses rich in both food and safety, in both food and danger. Spines and fins were severed in the morning before the awakening of the town; claws and pincers worked in mute terror at the soundless approach of serrated teeth. Muscles snapped and veins broke as Ben studied the waters with sleep-hungry eyes. He looked across the river to Youman's docks where a shrimper with a Coleman lantern lighting his deck prepared to cast off for the deep waters of St. Catherine's Sound.

The town awoke in ritual, ten thousand different ways. In Ravenel, the shrimpers rose first. Their coffee was always the earliest coffee fixed by the men with the calloused, fin-cut hands as their puffed, ascetic boats moved into the stream of tide returning, cutting through the dark artery of the marsh, through the green empire heaving in the tumult of retreat, alive with the instinct of billions obeying the unbenign law of the tide. Their coffee tasted slightly of shrimp and the sea.

The river seemed to quicken as Ben began to walk back to his house. A trout flared like a match in the light where the lights of the bridge and the river met. Coins of fire ignited the mullet's back as two shrimp boats slid past ringing buoys, tethered yachts, and storefronts. The shrimp boat captains watched for the channels and markers, somehow feeling that they were the lords of all this, of all they saw and felt. For a time, the early riser ruled the world. It was the grand illusion of the darkness.

Ben returned to his hammock with a heavy blanket for himself and one for Mary Anne. The temperature was dropping faster now and there was surprise in the May chill. In her sleep, Mary Anne was moving her lips and gesturing with her hands and for several moments he studied his sister dreaming and felt sad that dreams were not objects that could be catalogued, put away, and studied at leisure. This dream of Mary Anne's

484

would die by morning like all the other dreams of the town. In the town of Ravenel, ten thousand dreams hovered over the town each night and ten thousand died each morning, their washed-out corpses borne away for burial at sea by the first breeze. Somewhere, the billion dreams of the town since its origin stirred in a maelstrom far from the reach of the shrimpers' nets. Old dreams still burned with the power of their one night on earth, but burned deep and forbidden in regions denied to men.

Flying high over Brunswick, Georgia, and closing fast on Savannah, Bull contacted Atlanta radio.

"Atlanta Center," Bull said, "Marine 657 over Brunswick at flight level three-two-zero. Requesting a Tacon approach to Ravenel. Over."

"Roger. 657 is cleared to Sand Dollar intersection. Contact Ravenel approach control on 325-0 at this time."

Bull switched frequencies and called the Ravenel tower. "Ravenel Approach, Marine 657 inbound. Sand Dollar intersection for Tacon approach. Flight level three-two-zero."

"Roger, 657. You are cleared to approach altitude. Report leaving three-two-zero."

Bull loved the simplicity inherent in the language of pilots. In these highways of flying men, their tongue forbidden the people of the earth, all fat had been trimmed, all excess removed. Mankind, by its nature, produced infantrymen and Bull approved that the grunts of the world could not enter into the language of aviators.

He went to the radio again. "Six-five-seven out of three-two-zero. Request weather."

"Ravenel 0515 observation. One thousand feet ceiling with one half mile in light rain with fog. Surface wind light and variable. Ground Approach is standing by. Roger and out."

To Bull it was always extraordinary how the two strangers would speak to each other in disembodied voices, passing vital information back and forth that could mean the difference between life and death and yet Bull had never met one of these unnamed men who coaxed him homeward toward earth. He was a number and the voice that answered him was a tower. In the jet now, time never moved. Time was motionless, even nonexistent. When Bull Meecham vaulted continents and oceans Time did not move a single inch, nor did it change, grow, or diminish. Man on earth had a shotglass of time allotted to him, but the pilot approaching the speed of sound was a conqueror of time measured and time lost. He could gain hours, lose hours, or in a single day fly from winter to summer, to spring or fall. A flower was always in his grasp, as was a glacier, or a glimpse of the southern cross.

As Bull turned his plane slightly out toward the sea, sliding down now, dropping in altitude, and preparing to land, his eye suddenly filled with another eye watching him. Mutely appraising him was the red warning light that sat high on the cockpit panel to his left. Like all the instruments on the panel, it relayed a specific message. This warning light meant fire.

"Ravenel Approach, this is Marine 657. I have a fire warning light. Request penetration and vector for expedited landing. Over."

Bull slid his finger between his cheek and his oxygen mask and sniffed for smoke. The smoke he hunted was not visible but he knew the nose could tell of presences in the cockpit of which the eye was unaware.

"Roger. Turn right to 330, begin descent to 2000 feet."

At 20,000 feet Bull began his turn toward the air station, his eye affixed to the warning light as to the face of a new lover, and every sense he possessed tuned to changes in pitch, vibration, and the handling of the plane. His flesh could sense the steel that enveloped it was in a kind of trouble, an augmented desperation. His ear focused on the howl of the aircraft and an unformed prayer arose in him that this engine retain its demon whine, its savage articulation.

He called the tower again and said, "Approach Control, Marine 657 out of penetration at 17 miles. Request Ground Control Approach pickup. No indications of fire other than warning light. Request the tops of overcast. Over."

"Marine 657," the voice replied immediately, "tops of overcast at 12,000 feet. Out."

Bull had started down the slope now, his boards out, and he was descending, alive, alive, adrenaline reinforcing every platelet, every blood cell, and his mind radiating with its response to danger. Then the plane, already in the overcast, entered into the sightless suspended world that had enveloped Ravenel. But he was close now and coming fast toward the safety of runways and the smell of hangars. The red light controlled his eye like a mucilage. Then, in his bones, Bull felt the nature of the emergency change; even before he had proof or corroboration of what his viscera told him, he felt a change in his aircraft, and a change in himself as he went to the radio once more and called out words he had never used before:

"Mayday. Mayday. Six-five-seven. I'm in the soup at 2000. Have severe engine vibration and over-temp. Am going to guard channel and squawking emergency. Out."

Bull switched the button to 243.0 and he went immediately to guard channel. Now, all along the east coast, on every radar screen, the eyes of radarmen that Bull Meecham would never see or never know sighted in on a large, abnormal blip that exploded suddenly on their screens. The eyes watched and those many-towered men knew that a plane was in agony and a pilot was trying to bring that plane home at his own peril.

In the control at Ravenel, Staff Sergeant Alexander Brown began to sweat and fidget as he awaited the next communication from Marine 657, from the voice of the aviator whose panel was screaming "Fire" in a theater of one. He waited, tense, water bleeding out from his forehead and underarms. Then the voice came again.

"Six-five-seven is out of 5000 feet at ten miles. Unable to contact GCA. Request a straight-in approach. Give me full lights. Losing power and engine vibration severe. Will try to bring it in due to proximity of populated areas. Out."

Populated areas. The phrase meant something to Bull.

487

That was where people lived and slept, where families slept. Families like my family, wives like my wife, sons like my sons, and daughters like my daughters. He was now bulldogging a fatally stricken F-8 that was beginning to break up inside itself, beginning to destroy its own vitals. He needed sight and he needed it badly. His every resource as a pilot now came into play as he held the stick that fought the convulsions of a maimed craft shuddering downward like a kind of ruin. Then he heard something that made him reach for the radio in a panic.

Sergeant Brown tensed as the voice came again. "Tower. Engine explosion! Cockpit lights out. Am commencing starboard turn to avoid populated area. Will attempt to punch out when wings are level. Wish me luck. Over."

"Marine 657. Good luck. Crash crew alerted and ready."

But even as Sergeant Brown spoke the radar screen no longer bore witness to the presence or the existence of Bull Meecham. The FAA controller in the radar room called up frantically to Brown. "I've lost your boy, Sarge. I've lost him. I've lost your boy."

"Any fires near the runway?" Sergeant Brown called into a phone.

"Negative," replied the Ground Control Vehicles.

Sergeant Brown grabbed for the emergency phone. "Angel 5! Angel 5!" he said, "plane down in area approximately ten miles east of runway in the Combahee Island area!"

In less than two minutes, the rescue helicopter was airborne toward the area where Bull Meecham had disappeared from the screen.

It was growing colder, unseasonably cold for the middle of May, and the fog, though not heavy, was rising off the water, thickening imperceptibly, and obscuring the lowcountry in its passage across the land.

But a rumor was born in that instant and began to assault those hangars and duty shacks where Marines who kept the base alive and functional at night congregated: Bull Meecham, lieutenant colonel, commanding officer of 367, war hero, fighter pilot, Bull Meecham was down.

Ravenel began to wake in earnest at six in the morning. Hobie made his way through the gloom of River Street to open his restaurant. Ed Mills woke to arthritic cramps that made each morning a matins of pain for him. The sun was not up yet, but the town braced for its arrival. The earliest birdsong whispered through the streets. The time was marked down and all eyes turned eastward toward the waters and breakers along the barrier islands. Doc Ratteree delivered a stillborn black child at this time and washed his hands slowly, dreading the moment he would have to walk out and talk to the father who at this moment thought this would be the happiest day of his life. It was the time when night trembled before the coming resurrection, when the air sighed like a lover, when the first fingers of light came stealing out of the abyss to find the secret, soft places. Light and dark groped for each other in the birthing of dawn. Dawn spilled, mist-filtered, into each window, into each leaf, into the river, into each creek, and into the eyes of Ben and Mary Anne. Light danced quick in the river and the marshland, as quick as death or the snap of a claw.

Ben heard a car door slam at a quarter of seven. He woke slowly, looked through the banisters and saw Colonel Joe Varney coming up the front walk accompanied by the chaplain. If a lifetime as the son of the fighter pilot had taught him one thing, it was that he knew instinctively the meaning of this ill-timed visitation: This was a promenade of ruin. The message was irrefutable, for Ben was fluent in the rituals of disaster. He had known too many Marine wives and children who had come to their front door and found dour messengers, their faces carved from the ices of duty, standing with tragic news welting their tongues. But they really need to say nothing. They could stand there and the family would know, would scream at the sight of them, and would wish that their shadows had never desecrated their homes. They could roost like

489

vultures in the trees, birds that bring the famine of grief into unprepared homes. They could come wordless into the house of any Marine family, but no matter how they came or what shape or appearance they assumed, their very presence was the equivalent of some form of apocalypse.

Ben slid out of his hammock and made his way quickly to his mother's room. He knocked on the door, then opened it. Lillian rolled over on her back, rubbed her eyes, and said, "Good morning, sugah. Why are you up so early?"

"I think something's happened to Daddy," Ben said.

"Why, darling? What makes you think that?"

"Colonel Varney and Chaplain Poindexter are at the front door."

Lillian threw on a robe and hurried downstairs. She was there at the very moment Colonel Varney knocked at the front door. She looked into the eyes of Joe Varney and saw the embarrassed look she had seen in the eyes of strong men who had to convey news of disaster. She screamed once, raising her knuckles to her mouth, then threw her head against Joe Varney's shoulder.

"He may be all right, Lillian. We might be laughing about this over a drink tonight. He went down about ten miles east of here. We don't know if he punched out or what. He was trying to fly his bird away from the town. He could be hitchhiking back to town for all we know. But we don't know anything and the fog is hindering the rescue operation. I wanted to get the word to you before someone called."

"Thank you, Joe," Lillian said. "You think there's a chance Bull might be all right?"

"There's a chance," Colonel Varney answered, walking Lillian into the house with his arm around her protectively, "there's always a chance. Let's hope for the best until we have a reason to think otherwise."

"All we can do is pray," Chaplain Poindexter said.

"Beth is on her way over here. She's contacting the wives of 367," Varney said.

Ben was standing on the bottom step listening to this

news, trying to absorb it, but feeling it rejected like a transplanted organ. His body fevered and froze in alternating currents of temperature. Lillian saw him, straightened herself, dried her eyes, and gathered herself into a woman in control of events. During her whole existence as a Marine wife she had prepared her psyche for the possibility of a crash. There was a strength derived from living with the possibility of disaster and it was a source of energy that could be used when it had to be. Like her husband she had her duties.

"Ben, sugah. Go wake the children and have them gather in my room. I want to tell them about their daddy."

"Yes, ma'am," Ben said.

"I'm going to make these gentlemen some coffee."

At seven o'clock Ed Mills walked into Hobie's restaurant and in some mysteriously official way, the town was awake. He was followed by Zell Posey and Cleve Goins. The men who inhabited the first light at Hobie's, who drank coffee and exchanged tales until the stores were opened and the call to labor was sounded, began to fill up the restaurant. But when Doc Ratteree reached Hobie's at a quarter of eight, there was not a single man in the restaurant. Cups of freshly poured coffee still smoked on the counter and a cigarette, half-smoked, was dying in the ashtray where Ed Mills sat every morning. Hobie's wife, Helen, was cleaning off the table tops at the back of the restaurant when the doctor entered.

"God bless them all!" the doctor exclaimed. "Where's the fire, Helen?"

"The colonel went down over near Combahee, Doc. They can't find his plane in the fog and the Marine Corps has asked civilians to help in the search. All the boys are in the river."

Lillian had often shared the agony of other wives whose husbands had vanished from the protective embrace of radar. Of one thing she was certain, when Joe Varney's message had settled in, once the word was out among the wives, they would be coming; they would be on the way to her house; they would gather and sustain her in whatever anguish or grief there would be in this time of waiting. They would be there while the search parties scoured the swamplands and marshes, the rivers, the beaches, the forests, and the surface of the sea. They would let her weep, let her laugh, let her posture, be silly, or fall apart, but they would be there; these women of the Corps would gather around her in assent of their humanity and the shared terrors of their species. They would gather in the knowledge that they were different and distinct from any other women in the world and that the wives of pilots lived with a cobra in their entrails and that in their most undermined dreams they saw their husbands, their lovers, plummet like stones of fire from the extremities of the earth. At the end of these recurrent dreams, they watched the grim-lipped officer and the chaplain move toward the unhinging annunciation at the front door. Paige Hedgepath was the first wife to arrive. She and Lillian held each other in a long embrace and they rocked back and forth without saying a word to each other. There was nothing to say now; it was the hour of waiting, the hour of prayer.

The wives began coming as soon as the word was passed. They swarmed into the house, furiously cleaning the kitchen, preparing meals, and taking phone calls with the efficiency born of experience and instinct. The children hung back, not knowing what to say to any of the ladies except Paige, but they wanted to get Paige away from the others where she could tell them how to act and how to feel. The children wanted to take Paige upstairs, isolate her, and have her speak to them with the directness and the concealed softness about the chances of their father being alive. She would not mention prayer or God. She would tell them whether she thought Bull Meecham was alive or dead. But Paige knew where her duty lay; she monitored the energies of the women who walked through the door to be with Lillian. She assumed the position of commander as more and more cars pulled into the Meecham yard and began to park on the edge of the Lawn. Ben and Mary Anne found themselves in an upstairs room alone and free from the stares and sympathies of the wives. They looked at each other but had nothing to say. At this moment, they were strangers.

At nine o'clock, Ben saw Mr. Dacus pulling up on Eliot Street with a boat and trailer being pulled behind his car. Ben ran down to meet him.

"Let's go look for your daddy, pissant. You'll go crazy sitting around here with all these women."

"You're supposed to be in school, Mr. Dacus," Ben said.

"So are you, pissant. But I'm the boss and I decided to take a day off. Let's hit the river."

They drove to the Old Jones Landing at the end of St. Catherine's Island where they were met by a man with a map and a radio who was organizing the searchers who pushed off from this landing. The landing was clogged with the cars of men who were already on the water looking for Bull Meecham.

"Hey, there, Mr. Dacus," the man called.

"Vardis. How are you, boy?"

"You looking for the pilot?"

"Sure am. Where you want us to head for?" Mr. Dacus asked.

"Do you know where Ashley Creek is?"

"About seven miles from here, isn't it? Isn't that the one that cuts into St. Catherine's Sound near Garbade's place?"

"That's the one. Check that one out."

When they were in the river, Mr. Dacus said to Ben, "That's the best duck hunter in the state. With boys like that in the search, they'll find your daddy."

They pressed close to the riverbank, avoiding the middle channel for fear they would lose all orientation in the fog. It was not a thick fog, but it had a deceptive quality about it. It was not a fog that one would normally take with any great seriousness but a clear-eyed man could not penetrate it any deeper than fifty yards. In the back of the boat, Mr. Dacus studied a compass as he guided the boat toward Ashley Creek.

Coming out of a small tributary that emptied into the sound, they spotted Jim Don and Pinkie searching a shoreline on foot. Their boat was beached on an indentation in the marsh which provided a natural landing. Pinkie spotted them before they disappeared in the fog and shouted,

"Don't you worry, Ben. We'll find your daddy. Philip and Art are up by Goat Island looking. Even Mr. Loring's in a boat looking."

"We'll probably have to send a rescue party out looking for Ogden after this, Ben. He doesn't know how to work a pencil sharpener, much less a motor."

They were two miles into the sound when they heard a helicopter pass them overhead flying in the direction of the naval hospital.

"You think they might have found Dad, Mr. Dacus?" Ben said, his eyes following the sound.

"I don't know, pissant."

Before they went another mile, they passed a boat bearing two men dressed in work clothes. One of the men was Ed Mills. The boats pulled alongside each other, the motors idling.

"Good morning, Dacus."

"Good morning, Ed," Mr. Dacus replied.

"Good morning, Ben," Ed Mills said.

"Good morning, Mr. Mills," Ben said.

"You became a man this morning, Ben. They found your papa."

"Yes, sir."

"He's dead, son."

Then there was the business of death, the complexity of how to deposit a badly burned corpse into the ground of a National Cemetery as quickly and with as much dignity as possible. Lillian spent a full, enervating day on the telephone notifying a staggering number of relatives on both sides of the family. She spent two hours with the legal officer from the air station straightening her affairs. An endless stream of friends, well-wishers, townsmen, Marines, the regulars at Hobie's, and teachers of her four children came to the house to offer their condolences. There was no time to dwell on the death; there was too much to do and so little time to do it. Lillian was graceful, courageous, and indefatigable. She attributed Bull's death to God's will, the inexorable will, the unrecallable will and she had no quarrel with that. They had lived together nineteen years and had produced four lovely children. There had been

494

good times and bad times. She hoped he had not suffered in the end. The pilots assured her he did not. At times, she would break into tears at moments she seemed most in control. There was a dignity to her grief and an acceptance of the fait accompli—the fatalism that the pilot's wife must beget whenever her mate forsakes her for his aircraft. The chaplain kept referring to "the remains." Bull Meecham had become remains.

The night before the funeral they brought the body of Bull Meecham home, a reflex from Lillian's early days in rural Alabama when the coffin was always brought home, maybe not opened, but brought home to be with the family one last time. Lillian lined her children by the front door and friends cleared a path as the funeral director and his assistants bore the casket in through the front door to rest in his house the night before he would be buried.

"I want your father home with us," Lillian explained to the children. "That is how it is done in my family. Now I also want to tell y'all something very important and I want you to listen to me very carefully. Tomorrow is going to be very hard on us all, but I want you to remember that the Meecham family will conduct itself honorably at the funeral. We will not cry in public. Bull would not have liked it. He would not have allowed it. He would want us to be strong. He would be proud of our strength and we are going to make him proud tomorrow. Our grief will be a private one. If you wish to cry, cry now. Cry here at the house. Cry with each other or with our friends, but tomorrow at the funeral, there will be no tears. You will remember at all times that you are the children of a fighter pilot. You are the children of Bull Meecham and you will act accordingly. You know how to act. You have been reared to know."

"Can I sniffle a time or two?" Mary Anne had said.

"Don't you dare start this now, young lady. This is no time for your ugliness," and Mary Anne had wept in her room for an hour.

At the same time the relatives were coming from Chicago and Georgia, the Marine pilots from around America began to land in Ravenel, began to arrive in transports and jets, and private planes. The airways filled up with men who had heard about the death of Bull Meecham and they were coming to pay homage to one that had fallen. The brotherhood of aviators was coming to bury Bull Meecham. And on the night before his funeral, the Ravenel Officers' Club filled to capacity as old pilots told stories to young pilots of Bull Meecham in the Pacific and Bull Meecham in Korea. They drank to the life of Bull Meecham. They celebrated his estimable gifts as a fighter pilot and in those first days of his death the stories began to enlarge and a mythology was born that had the capacity to grow into something larger and more universal than his life was or could have been. He should have punched out sooner and the hell with the civilians some said. But acts of small heroism are admired, not understood in all their vague complexities, but at least admired. They drank to the death of Bull Meecham and they sang. The song started in a far corner of the bar but was quickly picked up and relayed from table to table, from glass to glass, from Marine to Marine. By the last four lines of the stanza, most of the Marines were on their feet. Others had mounted the tables and two of them screamed out their song from the top of the bar. It ended not as a song but as an anthem in defiance of death and in praise of the men who wore the wings of gold. It ended as a challenge flung into the face of the rider on the wings who rode with all pilots in all lands. The song was of affirmation and of witness.

"As we stand near the ringing rafters
 The walls around us are bare.
 As we echo our peals of laughter
 It seems as though the dead are still there.
 So stand by your glasses ready.
 Let not tear fill your eye.
 Here's to the dead already
 And Hurrah for the next man to die!"

Lillian kept a solitary vigil beside Bull's coffin, staying the night with him as she prayed the rosary.

At two in the morning, Ben slipped downstairs to sit with his mother awhile. Images of his father danced in the havoc of a brain overstimulated by events. He had no belief in his father's death. He wished to open up the coffin, to smell the burned flesh, to put his hands in the hurt places, to feel the tongue that had once invoked the name of Santini for the world to hear. He came and sat down beside Lillian. For a moment, neither of them spoke.

"How did you meet Dad, Mom?" Ben said, for no other reason than to begin a conversation.

"At a dance."

"Did you like him right away?" Ben asked.

"Heavens no, sugah. I thought he was a barbarian. He had no idea how to conduct himself at an affair with ladies and gentlemen present. He was pushy and boorish and kept cutting in every time some poor boy wanted to dance with me. Then he would refuse to let the other boys cut in on him. He was a scandal at that first dance, an embarrassment at the second, and was thrown out at the third."

"Why did you like him, Mama?"

"Because he was a charmer. Because he was persistent. Because he was romantic and sent me flowers every day for two weeks after he met me."

"He really liked you, huh?"

"Like me! Sugah, at that time in my life I thought any boy who didn't ask me to marry them was both physically and emotionally sick."

"How many boys asked you to marry them before you said 'yes' to Dad?"

"Eleven or twelve. Maybe more. Most of them went away to the war. Some of them were killed. There was a quarterback from Georgia Tech who was killed that was a charming boy. Of course, back then I thought all quarterbacks from Tech were charming. Some of the boys were just in love with love. Some were just too young."

"Did you date any Marines besides Dad?"

"Certainly, sugah. Two Marines asked me to marry them before your father. Those were good days for me. I was looking and feeling good. Your mama was a dancing, finger-snapping, riding-in-fast-cars girl, you better believe."

"Why didn't you marry the other two Marines?"

"Because that would have been bigamy, sweetheart."

"You know what I mean, Mama."

"One of them was killed at Okinawa. The other one was transferred thinking I was going to wait for him until the war was over."

"Then ol' Dad came along."

"Then ol' Dad came along," she said.

"Do you know what I came downstairs to tell you, Mama?"

"No, darling."

"Do you know that for most of my life I hated his guts?"

"No you didn't, sugah."

"Yes, I did, Mama. I really did. And I'm scared saying it now because I've always been so afraid of him. So afraid of his hurting me. I don't know how to feel about Dad being dead. I used to pray for his plane to crash. I used to pray for it all the time. I'm scared that one of those prayers was up there floating around lost and he accidentally ran into it on the way back from Key West."

"It doesn't work that way, Ben. God wanted your father with him."

"Do you know what I wanted to do for a long time, Mama? Without you or Dad knowing about it, I wanted to graduate from college and go into the Marine Corps. I wanted to sneak into OCS and not call home or tell anyone where I was. Then I would suddenly call up and ask him to come to Quantico, to ask him to pin on my second lieutenant's bars. Then I wanted to go to flight school in Pensacola. I'd become a fighter pilot, a hotshot, graduating at the top of my class. I'd try to join Dad's squadron and we would fly together, go on hops together, and dogfight at thirty thousand feet with each other. We'd try to beat the hell out of each other like we used to do on the basketball court. But I'd get better and better and one day I'd end up on his tail, coming in on his tail at six o'clock. I'd have beaten him in his airplane.

498

Then I would quit the Marine Corps as soon as I could. Then I'd have been free of him. Do you understand, Mama?"

"I understand perfectly, sugah. And in his own way, I think your father would have understood."

"Now I'll never be free of him," Ben said.

"Now, sugah," Lillian said, looking toward the coffin, "you don't have to be."

Ben turned and walked toward the stairs, pausing on the landing. "Mama, who was the Marine who thought you were going to wait for him?"

"That's been a secret for a long time, Ben. But you're old enough to keep a secret too. It was Joe Varney."

"Jesus Christ!" Ben said. "That explains a lot. Good night, Mama. If you need me, let me know."

As Ben got in bed his door opened and Mary Anne stood in the opening.

"I thought of something, Ben," Mary Anne said.

"What is it, Mary Anne?"

"It makes me sad. Sad."

"What is it?"

"I was in bed thinking and it suddenly came to me," she said.

"What?"

"Santini is a dead word," Mary Anne said.

The children of Bull Meecham did not cry. They made the long walk up the aisle with every eye in the church on them. The church was overflowing with people, with friends, relatives, and men in uniform. Lillian was stunning in a black dress and even managed to smile as she acknowledged some friends whose faces she picked out from the crowd. They sat in the front row as Father Pinckney began the Mass for the Dead. The National Colors were draped over the coffin. Over the remains. In the middle of the service, Virgil Hedgepath rose to deliver the eulogy. At times, Ben forgot how handsome his godfather was, how quietly distinguished and impressively put together. His voice was strong and it rang through the church with a power that brought every head erect.

Every head but Ben's. He did not hear the first part of the eulogy. He heard the voice and admired its power. But he was remembering a walk with Toomer in the black-gum swamp of St. Catherine's Island when Toomer had come across the track of a large Eastern Diamondback rattler. Toomer had stopped, hunted for a stick, and with great deliberation had marked a large "X" across the track of the snake.

"That snake gonna die by next sunrise, white boy," Toomer had said and Ben knew that Toomer was sharing with him one of those secrets of the lowcountry whose origins came from the myths of lost tribes; the black men of Ravenel had remedies for their daily fears. Somehow Ben felt that the snake too shared the belief of its extinction and could feel the "X" cut into the long, beautiful spine, severing the diamond at an intersection between the rattlers and the fangs the moment Toomer planted the "X." And as he tried to catch hold of Virgil's voice and focus on the praise of his father, Ben thought that maybe some angel of death had beheld Toomer's act, liked its mystery and style, and had been watching as Bull Meecham flew back from Key West, and had seen the jetstream cut across the state of Florida in a keen and perishable track. Maybe this diamondbacked angel had picked up a stick and marked an "X" across the track of Bull Meecham. Maybe that is how death worked with all things: someone would come upon your trail, your markings, and violate them with an "X." Some friend or enemy or angel would kill you by defiling the marks you left in your passage.

Then, fighting to return to Virgil, Ben heard the words, "Bull Meecham was a lover of flight, a pilot who took joy in the immense pleasures, the supreme and indescribable pleasure in flying an F-8 faster than the speed of sound. No one besides a fighter pilot will ever know this feeling. There is no way to explain it or to tell how it feels or how wonderful it is. Bull Meecham loved it and because he loved it, he became one of the best fighter pilots that ever stood up for Semper Fi.

"I like the fact that if Bull Meecham had to die, he died like a fighter pilot. He was lucky enough to die in his plane. If the truth were known, that is the way all of us would choose to leave this earth. Bull Meecham died as a pilot, as a Marine, as a Marine fighter pilot. I like the fact that Bull did that stupid, reckless act of turning away from the town before he punched out, an action that cost him his life. But I can see him thinking in that stubborn, mule-like way of his, 'If I punch out of this bird down there, I got kids down there. Other hogs got kids down there. I got friends down there.'

"I want to tell his kids that their father was a strange man, but all the pilots in this church are strange men and we cultivate this strangeness, this separateness that makes us a breed apart, hard to understand, hard to explain, even to ourselves. All fighter pilots are enigmas, but Marine fighter pilots are not of this world.

"I honor Bull Meecham. I honor his courage, his career, his achievement, his sense of duty, his love of flight, and his love of the Corps. I honor Lieutenant Colonel W. P. Meecham. I honor the Marine. I honor the Hero. I honor his family. I honor his death and I promise that I shall remember him. I also want to tell Ben, Mary Anne, Matthew, Karen, and Lillian that I will like the world less without Bull. It will be a duller, more colorless place. I want to cry but cannot. That is one of the things wrong with fighter pilots. I cannot cry. But I shall remember him and I shall honor that memory.

"Even now I honor it. For I can hear Bull saying now even as I speak his eulogy, 'Hey, Virge, cut your yappin'.' And that would be the voice of the real Bull Meecham. That would be the voice of the fighter pilot."

At the graveyard as the priest said the final prayers and the riflemen prepared their farewell volleys, and the bugler stood erect until the moment for taps, Ben heard the planes coming for the fly-over that was traditional for the death of a pilot. He looked up as he had looked up as a child when his father would bring the black-winged Corsair over their house in New Bern, North Carolina. Ben was seven years old and he would run outside and watch his father dip his wings, wheel like a hawk, then climb high above the Neuse River and plummet like a falling angel as Ben looked up.

The jets flew over the burial cortège in a tight formation that had an odd imbalance to it. It took Ben a moment to realize what the misalignment was, but he had forgotten about the military's allegiance to symbolism. There was one plane missing in the formation. Bull Meecham's plane. The fallen aviator was represented by his absence. As he watched, Ben wished he could be watching the man in the Corsair once again, young again, showing off in the black cold wings once more, performing for his son a last time before he had to turn from Ben, to wave once and turn away from his son, point his craft straight up and climb toward stars and suns, toward galaxies and night.

Ben appeared on the veranda of the empty house. It was three o'clock in the morning and the station wagon was packed for the night journey to Atlanta. He was wearing his father's nylon flight jacket and he was carrying the last two sleeping bags to the car. He walked down to the car and tightened the straps on the baggage carrier on top of the car. He heard his mother behind him.

"The movers left this broom, Ben."

"I can strap it on top of the car, Mama."

"Are you sure you're not too tired to drive?"

"No, I feel good. We high school graduates are often called upon to drive at night and we rise to the occasion. Is Okra in the car?"

"Ask Matthew."

"Hey, Matt!" Ben said, leaning in one of the windows. "We got Okra?"

"There he is on the front seat."

"He's got to go in the back. Did he go to the bathroom?"

"How would I know, Ben?"

"Did all of you go to the bathroom?" Ben asked.

"Do you want a written affidavit, feces face?" Mary Anne said from the back seat.

"It's just so we don't have to stop every fifteen seconds."

"Why are we leaving at three in the morning, Ben?"

"We always leave early in the morning," he answered.

502

"There's no traffic. You make better time. Dad was right about that. Anyway, Mom has an interview for a job in Atlanta tomorrow afternoon."

Lillian Meecham got in the car. Ben started the engine and they moved out of the driveway slowly, each of them looking at the grand and elegant house for a last time.

"I don't want to leave Ravenel, Mom. I'll never see Mary Helen and Alice and Cynthia ever again."

"We'll be back to Ravenel, sugah. We'll come back to visit."

"That's what you said about Cherry Point and New River."

"We'll get back to Cherry Point and New River someday."

"No we won't, Mama. We never do."

"That's right, Karen. You'll never see any of them again," Mary Anne said. "They're all dead."

"Please don't," Lillian said to Mary Anne.

"It's time, Mama. As far as Karen is concerned, Mary Helen and Alice and Cynthia are as good as dead."

"Well it's good-bye, Ravenel," Matt said. "I'm ready to move. I like moving. I wish we weren't going back to Atlanta. I'd like to go somewhere completely new."

Ben eased the car down Eliot Street and onto Granville. Every point they passed was a landmark; every block contained memories. They passed the cemetery where their father was buried and none of them looked in that direction. Lillian began the rosary for a safe trip. The family did not feel like singing.

They were out of town and heading down the Atlanta road when Ben felt something warm and wet on the back of his neck. With his left hand he wiped away a warm inconsequential water from his neck. He looked into the rearview mirror as he slowed for a crossroads and saw Mary Anne with a silver spoon catching tears as they fell from her eyes and flicking the spoon at her brother.

"Hey, cut it out, Mary Anne," Ben said angrily. "I'm not Santini." That he had invoked his father's nom de guerre surprised him. He thought about the words he had just said and felt more tears splash against his neck. He pressed the accelerator and they were traveling again, moving down a dark southern highway, moving, rolling again as they had done so many times before. The tears hit again in the purest form of grief and protest.

His anger subsided, for it was Mary Anne and at that moment he knew she would always fling tears at men who sat in front seats and at all the men in her life. Her weapons would always come from her eyes and her tongue, from her face. For his whole life, Ben had thought that he was her most significant ally, but lately, he had come to look at himself differently. He was beginning to suspect and recognize his own venomously subtle enmity to his own sister. Because he had been afraid, he had said "yes" to everything his parents wanted, had let himself be sculpted by his parents' wishes, had danced to the music of his parents' every dream, and had betrayed his sister by not preparing them for a girl who would not dance. But Ben knew that there was a girl named Mary Anne in the back seat who could teach Lillian and all the other lovely women in the world things about beauty they would never know. He had always thought that Mary Anne had been harmed by the coldness of her father and the beauty of her mother. It was only lately that he was having small moments of clarity, of illumination, and seeing himself for the first time as the closest of Mary Anne's enemies, the kindest of her assassins.

Then he said the words again. "I am not Santini," but this time he said them where only he could hear.

And he realized that he lived in a Santiniless world now and he trembled when he thought that he was, in many ways, relieved that his father was dead. It made him angry that a burden was lifted from him at his father's funeral and it made him suffer. He wanted to wake his mother and ask her questions but he knew that Lillian could not help him now. Twenty-five miles of highway passed without his knowledge, twenty-five miles vanished because Ben had retreated to the land behind the eye again. The children of violent men develop vivid powers of fantasy. Ben Meecham wanted to pray but he was afraid he was not worthy of prayer. But he was even more afraid that he had no belief in prayer. Yet he had belief in wonder and in the next twenty-five miles of black Carolina highway, he thought:

Can a boy begin a prayer with the hatred of his father in his heart? Can that boy walk up to the altar of God and can he lay that hatred out? Can he spew his hate and tell his story? Can he tell about beatings and humiliations? Can he tell of the Marine who stormed the beaches of his childhood? Can he look into the eye of God and spit into that purest source of light for engendering his soul in the seed of a father who did not know the secret of tenderness, a father who loved in strange, undecipherable ways, a father who did not know how to love, a father who did not know how to try?

And what would this God be like, this God of Ben Meecham, this God that Ben was losing fast and barely believed in? In the privacy of the next hundred miles, Ben thought about the kind of God he would approach, that the God would have to look a certain way, and in his mind Ben began to assemble the God he would speak to about his father. This would be the God of Ben Meecham:

Ben would give Him the sweetness of Lillian, the dark, honest eyes of Arrabelle, the soft virility of Mr. Dacus, the birthmark of Pinkie on his throat, and Ogden Loring's upcountry drawl. Ben would give Him the shoulders of Virgil Hedgepath, the innocence of Karen, the spoon and tears of Mary Anne, the high-pitched laugh of Sammy, Matt's intensity, and the loyalty of the Gray. And Ben would put this God on a street like River Street and he would have this God lift his voice in the holy song of Toomer. The hands of this God would be bright with flowers that would never die and this God would sing and stutter and limp along an alleyway and pass judgment in the land beside the river. He would hold mercy in a bouquet of azaleas and he would listen to Ben.

On the sixtieth mile, Ben could see this God as he crossed the Savannah River into Georgia. He could see him in the canvas of his eye, in the brilliant kingdom of his eye. This God was leaning back against the wall of Hobie's restaurant dazzling the universe with the beauty of Toomer's song. Ben would interrupt this God and this God would not mind.

And can one boy who has said ten thousand times in secret monologues, "I hate you. I hate you," as his father passed him, can this boy approach this singing God and can he look into the eye of God and confess this sin and have that God say to him in the thunder that is perfect truth that the boy has not come to talk to him about the hatred of his father, but has come to talk about mysteries that only gods can interpret, that only gods can translate? Can there be a translation by this God all strong and embarrassed, all awkward and kind? Can He smile as He says it? How wonderful the smile of God as he talks to a boy. And the translation of a boy screaming "I hate you. I hate you" to his father who cannot hear him would be simple for such a God. Simple, direct, and transferable to all men, all women, all people of all nations of the earth.

But Ben knew the translation and he let the God off with a smile, let him go back to his song, and back to his flowers on River Street. In the secret eye behind his eyes, in Ben's true empire, he heard and saw and knew.

And for the flight-jacketed boy on the road to Atlanta, he filled up for the first time, he filled up even though he knew the hatred would return, but for now, he filled up as if he would burst. Ben Meecham filled up on the road to Atlanta with the love of his father, with the love of Santini.